EXPLOSIONS

Stories of Our Landmined World

Edited by Scott Bradley

A Charity Anthology for Mines Advisory Group

saves lives builds futures

EJP

New York

Also by Scott Bradley

NON-FICTION

The Book of Lists Horror
(edited with Amy Wallace and Del Howison)

FICTION

The Dark

For Amy and For My Dad

"Landmines are blind weapons that cannot distinguish between the footfall of a soldier and that of an old woman gathering firewood. They recognize no ceasefire and, long after the fighting has stopped, they can maim or kill the children and the grandchildren of the soldiers who laid them."

—Nelson Mandela

ACKNOWLEDGMENTS

No book is created in a vacuum, and that's exponentially true for an anthology.

First and foremost thanks goes to Mines Advisory Group (MAG) for the work they do. In a better world, they wouldn't need to exist, and this book wouldn't either. That said, it is a privilege to have undertaken this project in order to help the cause of ridding the world of the scourge of unexploded mines and ordnance.

Secondly, I thank each and every one of the contributors to this volume for their imagination, richness of vision, and generosity. I often felt merely like ballast, with the amazing work of these artists guiding the way.

Special added thanks to the magnificent work of Matt Wuerker and Sarah Lauren Bell on the—literally—EXPLOSIVE cover.

Deepest gratitude to the memory of Diana, Princess of Wales, for her tireless work on behalf of the anti-landmine cause during her all too brief lifetime. And thanks to her sons, Harry and William, for continuing that work.

This book is for Amy Wallace (July 3, 1955 - August 10, 2013)— the love of my life, who guided me through the minefields—I only wish I could have done the same; and for my father, Scott G. Bradley—my best friend and travelling companion, with whom I saw first-hand the vital work of MAG in Southeast Asia.

Thank you to my cat Hank, who tethered me to life when all I could think about was Amy's death.

James Grady is essentially my un-credited co-editor. Not only a brilliant writer and thinker, but also an amazing human being, Jim picked me up when I fell, facilitated vital connections, and helped me get my head straight when I was ready to eject. It has been a life-changing experience to be mentored by him on this project.

Charles Day of Evil Jester Press provided the absolute dream of what one would want from a publisher. He was there when I needed him, but never pushed or became impatient.

Travel Indochina is the agency through which my Dad and I were able to visit Southeast Asia. Their guiding philosophy—to show travelers all aspects of the country, not just the "beauty spots"—was hugely influential on the conception of this book. Special added thanks to Travel Indochina's real-life Lara Croft, the beauteous Nikki Zimbler.

I love my family so much, even though I don't always let them know. Thank you to my grandmother Shirley Brake; my sisters Tammy Walker and Sherri Cervantes, as well as her husband Ray and their extraordinary children: Joshua, Jonathan, Aaron, and Danielle. My mother Linda Bradley (1942-2006) would be so very, very proud of them. I certainly am.

This book was in progress when Amy passed away, and I would be remiss not to mention those who loved her as well, and helped me survive: Amy's brother David Wallechinsky; Emily Bradley; Russell Sakamoto; Sophie Duriez; William Dailey & Shana Nys Dambrot; Danny Biederman; Jeff Scott; Richard Jennings; Jeremy Graham & Melissa St. Hillaire; Scarlett Amaris.

In addition, I must mention several friends who showed kindness and endless patience through the very worst time of my life: Charles Pinion, Randy Focazio, Will Huston, John Skipp, Collin Green, Darwin Green, Richard Heft, Eric Press, Courtney Joyner, Weston Ochse, Lee Lankford, Joey O'Bryan, Tom Gauer, Ken Bussanmas, Eric John, and Bryce Abood.

Arthur Tiersky for tech skills, endless wit, and making my job about 1000% easier.

Eric, Rhoda, and Benjamin Shapiro.

Liz Matney, Joe Straughan III, and Suzanne Straughan.

Everyone at the House of Pies in Los Feliz.

Facebook friends, near and far: Lael Gold, Trent Zelazny, Peter Briggs, Kevin Jackson, Bobby Morgan, Gigi Blum Peterkin, Mark Protosevich, Tim Lucas, Judith Rascoe, Ian Cooper, Paul Rowlands, Lloyd Fonvielle, and Eric Red. Plus two of my favorite grown-ups: John Bertram & Ann Magnuson.

Joe Lansdale, his Ownself, for letting me keep going forward on *The Night They Missed the Horror Show* adaptation. That has little relevance to the topic at hand, but it means the world to me.

For existential assistance during the process of assembling this volume: The film *Only God Forgives* and the TV series *The Big Bang Theory*.

Table of Contents

Introduction

In December of 2010 I visited the Lao People's Democratic Republic, which, upon arrival in the former capital of Luang Prabang late one rainy night, instantly became one of my very favorite places on Earth.

Laos is a beautiful and gentle landlocked country in Southeast Asia that has the nightmarish distinction of being the most bombed nation per capita on the planet. During the Vietnam War (which is called the "American War" in Southeast Asia), Laos—while technically neutral—was (and is) a Communist country, and the "Ho Chi Minh Trail" of supplies and support ran from North Vietnam to the Viet Cong in the South via Laos and Cambodia. The effect of bombing on Cambodia resulted in the destruction of an entire society, and genocide under Pol Pot and the Khmer Rouge. Laos, thankfully, did not devolve into the extremes of mass murder but, like Cambodia and Vietnam, is haunted to this day by unexploded munitions.

It's impossible to travel in any of these nations without seeing the effects of war, forty years on. Just as other regions—Africa and the Middle East for starters—will be haunted by similar legacies far beyond our lifetimes.

My moment of mind-boggling realization of this problem came when I went to the Plain of Jars. The Plain—located in central Laos—is a megalithic site made up of large stone jars. Legends and theories abound as to just who created these and for what purpose. My favorite posits a king who used the jars to store vast amounts of *lau hai*—rice alcohol. Whatever is true, the Plain is in its own way every bit as extraordinary as better-known sites like Angkor Wat in Cambodia. Whatever your spiritual beliefs, the Plain makes you feel you're glimpsing something transcendent, what my friend John Skipp calls "the Face of God."

Yet if you step off the well-marked paths, you are in jeopardy of being injured or killed by unexploded ordnance.

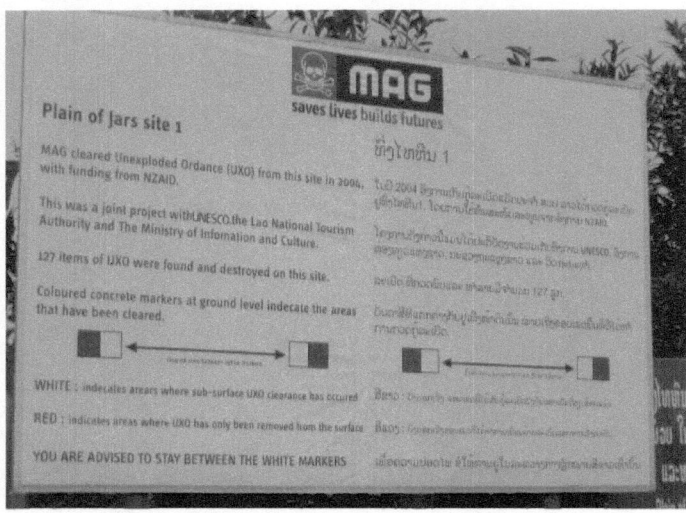

That's right. Follow the red-&-white brick road. You're not in Oz anymore.

It is thanks to the work of Mines Advisory Group (MAG), in conjunction with UNESCO and the government of New Zealand, that the Plain of Jars—at least parts of it—are now safe and accessible for visitors from around the world.

I found this supremely haunting, and began researching MAG. I discovered that they not only do the nuts-and-bolts of ordnance removal and disposal, but also—with affiliated charities—help people begin new lives on land that was formerly deadly to human life. Villages expanded, crops planted, and opportunities for tourism and travel have been created.

In a world of so many gray areas and moral conundrums, the work of MAG represents, to my mind, an example of the highest and purest good. No politics and no agenda beyond the humanitarian. These are true heroes in a world where the word "hero" has trivialized and degraded into virtual meaninglessness

From that point on, I made sure to donate to MAG whenever my finances permitted. But I felt compelled, for existential reasons too complex to elaborate here, to do more. I knew I wouldn't make a very good volunteer. I am, to say the least, psychologically and physically unfit for the rigorous work MAG undertakes on a daily basis.

But I am a writer and editor of some experience, and—on my second trip to Laos in December, 2012—it became clear I did have a way to join the cause, using my skillsets. I even have a coaster from one of my favorite restaurants in the world, the Blue Lagoon Café in Luang Prabang, on which I jotted the fateful words "MAG charity anthology."

Now that coaster is the book you hold in your hands.

Everyone involved in this project has given of themselves—their time, their creativity, and their humanity—to produce a volume that I think (though I'm admittedly biased) holds its own with any anthology out there. It was fascinating to see this book evolve, as well as to see how different writers took different approaches to the theme of "our landmined world." Some of these stories are directly about that subject; some don't even mention the word landmine. But every single one of them—stories that were commissioned specifically for this book and reprints of works previously published—has a powerful sense of humanity and understanding.

One early thought was to incorporate the concept of *Noir* into the title of this book, but I feared readers being misled by the term's connotations of private eyes and spies (though you'll both in these pages). All the same, these are dark stories that I hope fulfill filmmaker Paul Schrader's definition of *Noir* as being "not a genre" but rather a complex intersection of "cultural and stylistic elements." You'll find moments of horror balanced by humanity; tragedy in tandem with humor; life among too much death. My commercial goal was to deliver a collection of stories well told, worth any reader's money, 100% of whose profits going to MAG and its work.

You've done the hard part.

Now, sit back and enjoy the work of these extraordinary storytellers. And, should you wish to learn more about MAG and how you can help further, please visit their website at www.maginternational.org.

—Scott Bradley,
14 February 2014,
Los Angeles, California, USA

Scott Bradley on the Plain of Jars, Laos, December, 2010

Scott Bradley co-edited *The Book of Lists Horror* (HarperCollins, 2008) with Amy Wallace and Del Howison, and co-authored the metaphysical thriller *The Dark* (Ravenous Shadows, 2012) with Peter Giglio. His short fiction, solo and in collaboration, has appeared in the anthologies *Werewolves & Shapeshifters; Help! Wanted; Psychos; Mirages;* and *Evil Jester Digest Volume 2;* his criticism and journalism have been featured in *The Kansas City Star, Film Quarterly, Creative Screenwriting,* and the book *Butcher Knives & Body Counts.* He again collaborated with Peter Giglio on a currently unproduced feature adaptation of Joe R. Lansdale's classic short story "The Night They Missed the Horror

Show," and is at work on an original screenplay called *Topanga Canyon* with writer/director Charles Pinion. In addition to writing, he worked in development at RKO Pictures, at a Hollywood talent agency, and as a video store clerk; he also appeared fully clothed as a nightclub emcee in the porn extravaganza *Misty Beethoven: The Musical!* (2004), and was an assistant to legendary director Michael Cimino on the short film *No Translation Necessary* (2007). Highlights of his adventures in Southeast Asia include eating a beating cobra heart in Vietnam (2010) and being detained by customs in Myanmar (2012). Scott lives with his cat Hank in the Los Feliz neighborhood of Los Angeles, California.

God of Pestilence
Ryan Gattis

One bullet had made two holes in the kid's head.

Nobody was arguing that.

Each opening was visible in the eight-by-ten autopsy photo that First Sergeant Johnny Ban of the Japanese Ground Self-Defense Forces held in his tingling left hand. The entry wound looked like a black beetle on the right eyebrow, and the exit had turned the neck's left side into a kind of question mark, open beneath the ear where it met the base of the skull. It was a straight-on photographic headshot, and its contents kicked Johnny's stomach for one reason: he *knew* this kid.

Granted, twenty was too old to be called a kid in just about anything but boxing, but Johnny Ban couldn't think of him any other way, and now his first official mission briefing in Iraq had turned into a lesson.

"*This* is what snipers do," Major Ross paused so Johnny could translate it into Japanese for his superior officer, Lieutenant Takanori, who was seated immediately to Johnny's left at the only table in a canvas tent. Takanori took the photo before letting out a long breath. He recognized the kid too.

Outside, an engine turned over and tires churned sand before catching and driving off. Johnny had imagined the Japanese military's role in Advise and Assist—the transition from combat force to community and security builder—would be greeted with better facilities. But as he shaded his face from a shaft of Iraqi sunlight that had been creeping through the tent flap for twenty minutes, over the sand-beaten floor, up table legs and into both his and Takanori's eyes, he realized he'd been naïve. Much of this job would be no better than camping with heavy weaponry.

This, of course, had its downside.

"Insurgents," Major Ross let the word hang before continuing, "are smarter than you think. This casualty came from a trap set at two different points in a village outside Halabja, where unexploded ordinance was purposely placed inside the community's lone aqueduct. What our removal teams didn't know is that one of these sites contained real landmines, while the other contained non-functional canisters packed with scrap. Snipers took up positions of intent not far from where the decoys were buried, and when our specialist here set to work—well, you see the effects."

After translating this, Johnny made certain to add that he didn't know why the kid was so far north after being at the Contingency Operating Base only two days previous. It didn't matter, really. Orders were orders. Still, Johnny felt responsible.

"If you will forgive me for speculating as well as speaking freely, Lieutenant," Johnny added in Japanese, "are you about to tell me that this is not my fault?"

The Lieutenant furrowed his brow.

"No punch of yours put a bullet in him, First Sergeant." Years of smoking had worn Takanori's voice raw. He sounded like a samurai movie hero filtered through a carburetor. "So, shall we let him finish, *Ban no Yoshio*?"

Ban no Yoshio. That was the name of a Japanese god of pestilence. Takanori had teased him with that wordplay on his last name before Johnny had fought the kid. His lieutenant hadn't known then how uneasy it made him.

It took effort for Johnny to bow and turn his attention back to Major Ross. This briefing was the first since their observation detail. The U.S. Armed Forces deemed it imperative that its allies knew the risks of engineering work before shipping them out to fix grids and water systems destroyed during Operation Iraqi Freedom. The Japanese contribution to the Coalition of the Willing was this: they cleaned up, and when they were done doing that, they fixed what needed fixing. In a post-9/11 world, Johnny and his countrymen were nothing more than highly skilled handymen, plain and simple.

Except the world wasn't plain, and it wasn't simple. Not when a twenty-year-old specialist Johnny had beaten to a pulp two days ago caught a bullet with his face while trying to save a whole village from losing its water supply.

"*That* is what terror means." Ross angled his chin at the picture. "Remember it. When you're posted in Samawah, you cannot let the area's comparative safety make you complacent. You must proceed as if each situation has been engineered with a specific purpose in mind, that being loss of human life on our side."

Takanori swiped his fingers over the kid's picture.

"You cannot be responsible for everything," he whispered.

It was supposed to make Johnny feel better. It didn't. All Johnny could think about was the half-healed cut over the kid's right eye, the one he put there with a series of brutal left hooks. He thought of how he'd done it on purpose, again and again, and he thought of something else too: how it'd never heal now. Not ever.

***

On Fight Night in Iraq, guitar rock rippled the ceiling of the C.O.B.'s massive congregation tent, amping up an already overloaded crowd of a thousand soldiers who swigged, toasted, or held their non-alcoholic beer aloft to salute an emcee doing his best Michael Buffer impression in a boxing ring at the center of the maelstrom. Drumbeats thudded in Johnny's chest as he moved down a central aisle to the red-white-and-blue-roped ring lit by floodlights. The closer he got to the canvas, the more Johnny was certain that fighting was a bad idea. He'd had no training time, no preparation. Of course, it didn't help that he was just following orders.

"Do not, under *any* circumstances"—Takanori was behind him, shouting into Johnny's ear—"tell them you used to fight professionally."

Johnny shook it off. He had to tell them. It'd be criminal to go into that ring without letting his opponent know. Still, it was strange. Johnny 'Be Good' Ban had joined the Japanese Ground Self-Defense Forces as a translator to get away from a life in the ring, so it was safe to say the last thing he expected when setting boots in Iraq was to put the gloves back on. It'd been four years and twelve days since the last time he'd punched anybody for profit. That much time off wasn't rust, it was ruination.

Be Good's Won-Loss record as a prizefighter was a glittering 1-1-0 with one technical knockout and one almost-knockout in which his bloodied opponent had to be propped up by his cornerman to earn a tainted win. After that, Johnny couldn't get a fight. The long of it was that Johnny Ban refused to be managed by anyone other than a retired U.S. Navy ex-pat living in Osaka unlicensed by the Japanese Boxing Association, but the truth was a darker thing: since Johnny Ban was *hafu*—born of a Japanese mother and a white American father—no trainer would put a 100% Japanese boy in the ring with him and risk losing a career, not after what he did to the first two comers, and this was how Johnny learned the deepest secret of prizefighting: it wasn't so much a sport as a platform for tribalism. Nationalism too, for that matter.

Partway to the ring's glowing square, Johnny felt sweat drip down his spine. His hands had been wrapped and taped by a blonde medic with her hair pulled back in a bun, he'd put on borrowed black gloves in his size and borrowed blue shorts and a robe still wet from its last user, he'd gotten a new mouthguard and he'd worked himself warm in a storage closet doubling as a locker-room, but what greeted him on his ring-walk was another level of heat, as if someone had installed a sauna under his soles. Leave it to Johnny to still have his old boxing shoes, the lone personal items he'd allowed himself in his operational packing. Lucky him.

Pats on the back came from everywhere, and for each one Johnny got, two shouts of disappointment rang out. Apparently, the crowd had been promised Mixed Martial Arts for their Friday night fights, and here came Johnny, ruining the fun.

Negotiations had been fast. The Japanese contingent was invited to put a fighter forward, in the spirit of goodwill and community. Invited was a funny way of putting it. The tone made it obvious that to refuse was cowardice. Without even asking if he could, Takanori nominated Johnny on one condition: the fight had to be a boxing match. When the organizers agreed, they made it clear that weight class was out the window.

At ringside were three squads of Johnny's comrades, fresh off the plane from Japan. They were all clapping, sure, and they were screaming *ganbatte* as loudly as they could, but Johnny saw their excitement hid boatloads of nerves.   He didn't blame them. Collectively, they were the first Japanese soldiers to set foot on foreign soil since World War II. The very first. This was a yoke they wore daily. In fact, they'd only been in-country thirty hours and everywhere they went they got asked about Nagasaki or Hiroshima, Manchuria or Burma. It turned out military people the world over had long memories and they knew war. These questions weren't calculated to hurt, but each one was a needle in their collective skin.

Takanori's gleeful shout broke through to Johnny: "Win this for the honor of the Japanese people!"

Johnny stopped at the apron. He couldn't let it pass. "Did I ever tell you why I quit boxing, sir?"

"Your trainer died."

"That was part of it. The other part was matching a full Japanese boxer against a *hafu* was bad business." Johnny's words hit Takanori and drove the man's eyebrows up. "So being here, a fighter who was never Japanese enough, actually fighting for the pride of Japan and its armed forces? You will have to forgive me, sir, if I find it complicated."

Takanori nodded under the heat of the ringside floodlights. Behind him, the crowd told Johnny to get the hell into the ring and fight.

"Just like Ban no Yoshio," his lieutenant said, "he owed his country for favoring him while he was in its service, and when he became a god of pestilence after his death, he always petitioned the older gods to reduce the severity of earthly epidemics."

Johnny smirked. Even in its folktales, Japan was hierarchical and bureaucratic. He was nothing like Ban no Yoshio, the former major counselor who turned arsonist and died in exile, only to show up as a minor god years later in Edo, appearing to a lowly cook and proclaiming he had persuaded the gods to spare the city.

"Like it or not, First Sergeant," Takanori said as he drew close, "you owe your country everything. Japan shaped you into who you are. So I suggest you go out there and petition the other gods with your fists, because if you lose tonight, we all do."

Johnny didn't need to scan the ringside faces full of equal parts hope and dread to know Takanori was right, but he did it anyway.

"Absolutely, Lieutenant," was Johnny's only reply as he scaled the ring's steps, ducked the rope, swiveled lightly into his corner, and sat down on a chair with its back hacked off to look like a stool.

Across the ring, his opponent angled an upward nod in his direction. The kid looked five-ten with a shaved head, tattoos from waist to wrists, and a pasted-on sneer. Skinny legs, big arms, and bigger shoulders, he was built wrong for a fighter. Still, the kid had three inches of height on him and twenty pounds. But with those proportions, it was puppy weight. The kind that could be thrown around. Though whether Johnny could throw it was another matter. He had the lungs for a fight, he knew that, but his punch muscles weren't what they used to be. He had to be careful.

To the blonde medic smearing Vaseline over his brow, Johnny said, "You should tell him I've fought before."

"Oh? This one was Golden Gloves." She hiked a thumb behind her at the kid. "I think he'll be just fine."

She finished up and offered him water but he declined as the ref beckoned the fighters to the center of the ring, so Johnny went. The ref was a big man with broad shoulders and he went through the rules slow—protecting one's self at all times, not hitting low, not hitting behind the head, and ranks being disregarded in the ring—so Johnny talked over them.

He told the kid, "I used to fight pro circuit."

"Shit." The kid cracked a smile that was anything but nervous. "Only reason I got dragged up here is cuz nobody else would fight you Queensberry-style."

Up close, Johnny noted the kid carried scar tissue above his right eye from old fights. With a few punches, it might split. Johnny knew where to aim now.

The ref told them to touch up so they tapped leather, but before they broke, Johnny leaned close and said, "Where you from, soldier?"

The answer came quick as the kid pushed off. "Riverside, motherfucker."

"California? That's not far from where I was born," Johnny replied.

The kid looked at him funny, like he knew he was being screwed with, but the ref shooed them back to their corners before more could be said. This was fine by Johnny. Letting the kid chew on the great mystery of an American-born Japanese in the Japanese military wasn't a bad thing.

Johnny didn't sit again. He hopped in place until the bell rang and he went in hunched and ready.

***

Round 1

Years after his mother had moved them from Los Angeles, back when Osaka was as unwelcoming as any place could be, being inside the ropes was the only thing that made Johnny feel safe. The ring had rules, and rules always mattered to a child who grew up getting ambushed by bullies. Johnny smiled as he read the kid coming in fast and straight with his right hand low and his left hand coiled and cocked, protecting his chin. It was like old times.

As the kid came into range, Johnny angled out. He stepped right and beat the kid for hand-speed, and as a sloppy jab zipped by his ear, he shot a left hook at the kid's right eye, chasing it with a straight right to the body—bang, bang—and on the other end, the kid grimaced as awareness bloomed in his eyes: Johnny had power.

This was useful for Johnny too. Knowing it banished any thought of Ban no Yoshio. What was left was muscle memory, instinct.

The kid ate two more jabs before pitching forward again and wrapping Johnny up with both arms in a clinch. He leaned everything on Johnny, but he wasn't too heavy. Johnny was glad to know it was puppy weight after all.

When the ref stepped in to break them up, the kid whipped his head around and butted Johnny good on the crown. Maybe it was accidental. Maybe it wasn't. Either way, Johnny lost his balance for a split second before throwing a weak left jab and following it up with a clinch of his own. The crowd booed this clutching and grabbing, but Johnny didn't care, he was too busy holding tight for five stinging seconds as his head cleared. Once it did, he knew better than to get close again.

Johnny picked his shots the rest of the round, staying back to pelt the kid with left jabs to the belly, rights to the ribs. He felt the effects of these punches all the way up his arms and into his chest. He wondered how many rounds he had left before he punched himself out. The honest answer wasn't comforting: maybe five if he didn't push.

Knowing how to counterpunch a man, when, and in what spot was to know his rhythms and weaknesses more intimately than even a lover might. It was a bond of fighting rarely discussed and not easily described. Most people never understood that it was all intuition until a punch landed—and landed right—and then, it was just a fact, something to be exposed.

And the fact here was the kid hated body shots. He was already fussing with his beltline, dropping his left shoulder to make sure he could cover himself, just in case.

For its part, the crowd didn't appreciate Johnny's tack. They wanted him to fight with his head on the kid's shoulder, trading sloppy uppercuts in what his old trainer would've called a 'phone booth special' because both fighters would be close enough to almost fit in one together. That didn't suit Johnny though, not with his arms getting heavier. He revised his estimate to four rounds.

Which is why the end of the first couldn't come sooner. Johnny ducked a wide, looping hook and snapped a hard combination to the kid's body when the timekeeper banged on the canvas three times to let everybody know there were only ten seconds left. Johnny felt it in his feet and pivoted. It was a perfect time to wheel away, making like he was content to run out the rest of the round. When the kid threw his hands up to protest, the crowd booed right on cue.

That was when Johnny went back in. He covered two yards in three quick steps and dipped low, feinting the same hook to the body that had been turning the kid's ribs to mashed potatoes all round long. It was enough.

The kid bit on the fake, dropping his elbows in anticipation for the blow-that-never-came as Johnny went upstairs to the kid's eye and fed him a left hook that cut him before a straight right hand smashed his jaw at its socket and almost made him lose his mouthguard.

The crowd sure didn't boo that.

When the bell dinged its ding, the fighters went back to their corners.

***

Takanori was the first to meet Johnny there. His eyes gleamed as he slapped Johnny's back too hard.

"Ban no Yoshio!" Takanori's Japanese was violent in Johnny's ear. "Give him a disease with your fists!"

Johnny shook his head at that and the blonde medic told Takanori to get out. She didn't say anything to Johnny about his fighting, but she sure had an impressed grin on her face. Behind her, a leggy ring girl went by with a Round 2 card held high. Johnny rolled his neck and wondered if she was a solider too.

Across the ring, the kid fronted good but he had eyes like prey. He grimaced as his cutman pressed the cold metal of the enswell to his right cheekbone, a q-tip already sunken into the cut above the eye. The kid said something, but his heart wasn't in it. He was too busy staring at Johnny across the ring, trying to figure out how to get hurt less.

Johnny took a sip of water, swallowed half, and spit the rest into the bucket. He had a strain high up in his right shoulder but otherwise he felt okay. If he limited his rights and focused on the kid's eye with short left hooks, he'd be done early.

The blonde worked more Vaseline over his brow and on his head where he'd been butted before straddling the ropes and ducking out as the bell went.

***

Round 2

Johnny switched it up. He stormed across the canvas and belted the kid in the mouth with the same straight right that ended the first round, one that jarred his shoulder something serious. It was stupid of him.

When the shot landed, the crowd rocked back with a collective, "Oh!"

Johnny had done it to show the kid he could, and then, he backed off again, because he was disciplined and smart, and he wanted the kid to know that too. Once the kid understood that, he'd understand that Johnny Ban had already won, and every extra second he stayed in the ring he was just making it harder on himself. It was a message he had to send, because Johnny wasn't sure he had three full rounds in him.

The kid didn't understand though. He got mad instead, mad Johnny wouldn't fight him inside, mad he kept eating jabs, mad his eye was bleeding again, and mad Johnny angled out of his flapping clinches by sidestepping.

The crowd agreed with the kid. They felt they'd been duped by Johnny's sudden aggression only for it to be followed by tactics and yelled as much.

What the crowd didn't understand was that the power in Johnny's right arm was shot. Every time he threw it, it felt like getting knifed in the shoulder socket. The left would have to do. He jabbed and moved, taking it to the kid's bleeding right eye. He kept throwing the same left jab-left hook combination and the kid couldn't stop it. By the fifth time it landed, Johnny knew the kid couldn't see it through the blood.

That didn't stop him from lunging for Johnny though, and when he did, Johnny turned his ribs into a xylophone, hitting three solid notes on the left side and one on the right while gritting his teeth through the pain. The kid took a step back from the middle of the ring and dropped his hands to his belly, which leaned him forward and put his chin on a platter, so Johnny hit that too, 1-2. Left, left. Pinpoint shots. Johnny breathed hard through his mouthguard, but it felt good to be in the ring again, to be in control, not taking orders. As the kid's hands went upstairs to cover, Johnny went downstairs. Ribs again, 1-2 with left hooks.

The crowd erupted as the kid staggered back into the ropes, arched his back against them, and shot forward into Johnny's arms. Toe to toe, leaning his head on Johnny's shoulder, trying to find leverage in the phone booth, the kid was heavy with sweat as he tried to wrap both arms around Johnny to make the punching stop. But Johnny was too quick. The kid never saw it coming. Neither did the crowd, despite being on their feet, jockeying for a clean view.

It was the uppercut that froze him. What the kid didn't know, what the crowd didn't know, what nobody in that tent knew, was that Johnny Ban wasn't an outside fighter when he got started, he was a 'hurter,' as his old trainer would say, one of only a handful of non-Mexican lightweights on earth who wanted to stand on your doorstep and punch you until all your ribs broke. And maybe Takanori was right. Maybe there was some benefit to growing up hard, as an outsider in the most homogenous country on earth. After all, those experiences had turned Johnny Ban into a 24-karat finisher.

Johnny's left uppercut hit the kid's chin so squarely that it wobbled his legs. The kid gave up tensing his body after that and set to flexing his legs so he wouldn't lose his balance and fall forward. There was only one problem: Johnny was waiting for it. He stepped to his left and ripped a perfect left hook to the liver. The kid's face contorted like he'd been electrocuted, and when he tumbled to a big wet smack on the canvas, the tent practically exploded.

Johnny went to a neutral corner and tapped his right shoulder to make sure it hadn't fallen off yet. He put his arms up on the ropes for the count but everybody in that tent knew the kid wasn't getting up. When the numbers finally got to ten, the bell made it official: a technical knockout at 2:08 in the second round.

***

When Johnny made it back to his corner, Takanori grabbed his ankle and shook with all his might. Johnny let him. The crowd threw a wave of applause his way, more in atonement for doubting than as adulation for his skill. That didn't matter to the Japanese servicemen rushing the ring though. Johnny saw in their faces that they had won, Japan had won too, and he still didn't know how he felt about that exactly. Exhausted mostly, and glad the kid hadn't hung in longer.

At the center of the ring, the kid's cutman coaxed him into a sitting position and the blonde medic busied herself with getting his gloves off.

"Good fight," Johnny told him.

"Yeah," the kid replied with a pained smile, "I'm gonna look *real* tomorrow."

"Tomorrow?" Johnny patted the kid's shoulder with the cushion of his glove. "You look real right now."

The kid chushed his lips like he was letting off steam. "Man, I better run into you again. You gotta teach me some of that stuff."

Johnny gave the kid a look that only someone who had been taught everything he knew by someone older and better could give a younger man in need of schooling.

"Sure," Johnny said. "Anytime."

***

These weren't idle words to Johnny Ban, he'd meant them, and in the heat of the briefing tent, with the autopsy picture staring up at the ceiling, Johnny interrupted Major Ross's lecture about materials procurement to ask what the kid's name was.

Major Ross's shoulders sagged, but he spoke without hesitation. "Raul Ibanez, Lance Corporal, United States Marines."

After that, he looked at his watch. "That's eighteen hundred, gentlemen. We'll reconvene tomorrow at oh-six-hundred."

Everybody stood. Salutes were exchanged.

Major Ross paused a moment before bowing. He didn't wait for it to be returned so Lieutenant Takanori and First Sergeant Ban bowed to his back as he whipped through the tent flaps and out into the hot blanket of sunset draping itself over the base.

Johnny finished writing the kid's name and place in his notebook before shifting his sore right shoulder. If he ever got back to America, Riverside was the first spot he'd visit. Outside the tent, soldiers talked and laughed as they passed, whether on their way to or from the mess tent, Johnny didn't know.

"You miss the honesty of boxing." Takanori kept his eyes on the cigarette he was rolling. "You prefer hurt to come straight at you and look you in the eye."

Johnny tapped the photo of Raul with his index finger. He said, "As an alternative to sniper fire, I recommend it, sir."

It wasn't meant to be a joke. But Takanori threw Johnny a half-smile anyway as he exited the tent.

Beyond the flap, Johnny saw the sun flash twelve different kinds of orange before it was covered again. He was glad Takanori had gone. There would've been no use telling the man the other version of Ban no Yoshio's tale. In the one Johnny knew, the counselor felt he'd made a grave mistake in setting fire to a city gate and blaming a political rival for it. For this, he was truly remorseful and welcomed exile. But in order to further atone for his crime, he sacrificed himself so that he might lobby for the health of the country even in the afterlife. His wish was granted, but it came with a price: whomever he touched as a god of pestilence would die a horrible death. And this was why the cook, the one Ban no Yoshio famously told about an epidemic being reduced to nothing but coughs because of his lobbying, died in bed some days later—a victim of the plague that was spread to him only by proximity to Ban himself—and this was why the god had not shown himself since.

Takanori must not have known that one. Otherwise, he could have seen that the same thing had happened to Raul, in its way. The proof of it stared lifelessly up at Johnny, frozen, with a beetle on its brow, a question mark for a neck. It wasn't plague that had done it this time. First it was punches, and then it was a bullet that made two holes. And maybe, Johnny allowed himself the thought in the quiet of the empty tent, he was a lot more like Ban no Yoshio than he'd care to admit.

He too was a destroyer, despite his best intentions.

Ryan Gattis is the author of the novels *Roo Kickkick & the Big Bad Blimp* and *Kung Fu High School*, which was acquired by The Weinstein Company and chosen as a Barnes & Noble Discover Selection. Raised in Colorado, he holds an MA in Creative Writing from the University of East Anglia in Norwich, England, and lives in Los Angeles. Inspired by the city, his latest work is a 1-2 combination of *noir* novellas in the Johnny Ban Series: the jab of *The Big Drop: Homecoming* and the right cross of *The Big Drop: Impermanence* - back from Iraq after being injured in the line of duty, Johnny finds himself lured into a search for the only woman he ever loved in L.A.'s Little Tokyo.

Joseph Goodbye
Jeffery Deaver

At last they were close.

Thirty-two men were closing in on their prey.

The soldiers were armed with M4s and H&Ks, sweaty fingers nervously clenching trigger guards, not triggers, for fear of accidental discharges if they stumbled or lurched. Which happened frequently. The rainforest ground was uneven, the foliage and vines thick as tangled cables. And, of course, they would intentionally dive to cover when the HRA soldiers turned and fired on them from positions unseen, spattering automatic weapons rounds in their direction.

At the front of the main contingent of the pursuing soldiers, Colonel Frederick Lazlo glanced around him and was pleased with his troops' performance. They were soldiers by profession, yes, but soldiers from nations that had seen mostly peace during their lifetimes. Belgium, France, India, Ghana, Canada, and, of course, Bangladesh— the largest percentage of UN peacekeepers. Most of the men making up Lazlo's force here in the Northern African Republic this searing summer had fired their weapons only on ranges.

But despite their combat inexperience, twenty minutes ago, when Mtombe's first mortar rounds fell on the compound outside of Ouham City, Lazlo's men had instantly donned their blue helmets and flak jackets, charged their weapons and assembled at the front gate to meet the assault. Lazlo put into place one of the defense tactics he had planned out and ordered his troops to rehearse dozens of times.

The firefight had been brief. Mtombe had made no real strategy for the attack, whose purpose apparently was to seize the UN armory's weapons. The rebels had approached on the main road in mid-morning, perhaps anticipating little resistance. And typically, given the warlord's massive ego, he'd come with only a small portion of his army, perhaps 50 soldiers, men mostly, though a few women and, heartbreakingly, some of the child soldiers he was fond of "recruiting."

It was nearly a rout. By the time Mtombe's force had turned and fled, only three peacekeepers had been wounded, none seriously. There'd been some minor injuries too among civilians: two patients had been hurt by mortar shrapnel in the overcrowded hospital located within the compound, the only medical facility for miles around.

As for the Heavens' Resistance Army casualties, however, five soldiers had been killed and a half dozen others wounded. Lazlo and the UN troops had watched in horror as Mtombe, protected by covering fire, executed his own injured men with his gold-plated pistol as they lay on the ground, begging for mercy. Lazlo had learned that Mtombe frequently did this because he considered being wounded in battle a personal betrayal.

Then the HLA force had fled and Lazlo had immediately ordered his troops to pursue the retreating rebels.

They were now closing in.

"UN Two to UN One" clattered through Lazlo's radio, the voice tinted with a South Asian accent.

"Yes, Captain. Where are you?" Lazlo's voice was modulated by gasps of breath as he slogged through dense rain forest at the head of his contingent of troops. They were on foot and moving for the most part uphill. The fifty-four-year old US Army officer was stocky and didn't jog or workout as much as once had.

"About a half click northwest of you." M.G. Rahman, a captain in the Bangladeshi army, was commanding the second UN force, which had split off, an attempt to overtake and flank the rebels from the west. While Lazlo's contingent was on foot, because of the dense vegetation, Rahman's platoon of peacekeepers was speeding in jeeps and an armored personnel carrier through the grassy savannah.

"No sign of him breaking west?" Lazlo asked.

"None. A mystery. He keeps north."

Lazlo warned, "Watch him, Captain. It might be a feint. We're split now. He could come out of the forest at any minute and engage."

"That's what we are hoping for, Colonel." The Bangladeshi chuckled. "We're not in NAR to see the sights. We're here to rid it of vermin. UN Two out."

Lazlo urged his own force forward even more quickly. He wasn't going to miss this unbelievably fortuitous opportunity. The peacekeepers had anticipated that some unit of the HRA might attack their compound but had never imagined that an assault would be headed by Mtombe himself. The sole purpose of Operation Guardian was to arrest the warlord, or kill him, and since the inception of the operation three months ago, they'd never gotten closer than five kilometers from the man.

And now they were within 500 meters of capturing the sadistic rebel.

Lazlo heard a voice from beside him.

"Colonel, don't get his strategy." James Prescott was a British Special Air Service officer, assigned to the UN force. He and Lazlo had fought side by side in Fallujah and later outside of Kabul. Prescott was younger and in much better shape (SAS, after all, was in many people's opinion the best special forces groups in the world). Still, he too was out of breath. The temperature was close to 100 F and the incline of the jungle floor nearly as steep as a flight of stairs in places.

"Agreed," Lazlo said. "It's odd." Mtombe's men were escaping due north toward an imposing line of cliffs. They'd be sitting ducks on the rock face if they tried to climb. As for the east: that was no easy escape route either; the Katto River featured a dangerously swift current in midstream and the hungry crocs on the shore. And M.G. Rahman and his heavily armed vehicles were in the west.

Prescott asked, "Why didn't they turn south after we drove them off? They could get lost in rain forest for months."

"That's what I would have done. But—"

"'You're not psychotic demigod,'" Prescott quoted, offering the line that had become *the* catch phrase of Operation Guardian.

Lazlo laughed. Then asked, "What's your hostile count, captain?"

"I make it fifty, maybe a few more."

"Weapons?" Lazlo asked.

"Nothing too exotic. Chaps seem to have scrounged up quite a few M16s. I *do* wish you Yanks could screw down the lid on those things."

"I'll tell you about the Second Amendment someday, Captain."

"You cowboys."

Lazlo now directed his men up a hill. A few random slugs zipped their way. They were ignored. At the crest he ordered everyone into defensive prone, while he surveyed the landscape. They were in the selva, rain forest. Light and shadow vied, thanks to the layers of trees, some several hundred feet high. He noted evergreens too and furniture wood trees, teak and mahogany. A few ebony. Rubber plants, oil palms and orchid. To the left, west, where Rahman was engaged in his flanking movement, Lazlo could see shea trees rising from the savannah, as well as acacias and erythrianas and whimsical, eerie baobabs.

He saw no signs of immediate threat and ordered his soldiers to continue the pursuit.

Again Lazlo wondered why Mtombe was headed north. Under other circumstances that might have made sense; there were clearings where he could arrange for an extraction. But not now. The Department of Peacekeeping Operations' mandate for Operation Guardian did not permit airstrikes—Mtombe tended to hide out among innocent civilians—but it did establish a no-fly zone over the areas where rebels were located. No helicopters would be plucking Mtombe from his predicament.

"Ah," Prescott offered wryly, "I've sussed out his strategy."

"Which is?"

"He's counting on divine intervention."

The comment was not as facetious as it might seem. Behavioral analysts working for the UN had diagnosed Jean-Pierre Mtombe as a delusional paranoid personality. He claimed he'd been anointed by Jesus to reclaim control of the despotic Northern African Republic and establish a new holy land. The warlord conveniently ignored the fact that the NAR was one of the few truly democratic countries in sub-Saharan Africa and was working toward a sterling human rights record. Still, Mtombe had managed to cobbled together a thousand or so fanatical followers by asserting his claims to divinity and some bizarre mystical connections to great political and artistic figures from the past. (Lazlo's personal belief, however was that the biggest draw in HRA recruitment was the carrot of raping and plundering, and the stick of severed limbs if one didn't join up when asked. Those brought more into Mtombe's flack than his spiritual connection to Shakespeare and the Roman Emperor Tiberius.)

Ten minutes later, they'd closed the gap to within two hundred meters of Mtombe's rebels forces.

It was at that moment that the thought came to Lazlo.

And he suddenly understood why Mtombe was going north.

My God, the commander thought. His camp is here!

Mtombe and the main HRA contingent had set up a command post an hour's hike from the compound of the very UN peacekeepers trying to find and arrest him. A brilliant strategy. Mtombe had been right under their noses for months; Lazlo's troops had been searching for him in locations much further away.

But then he realized something else.

"My God," he said, stopping.

"What?" Prescott asked.

"Everyone! Stop moving."

"Why? What do you see?" The SAS soldier turned, stepping to the side, lifting his weapon.

"No!" Lazlo called to him. "Freeze!"

But too late. The piercing explosion shot upward, shredding the Brit's left leg, turning it into jelly and flecking the foliage and Lazlo himself with bits of camo, skin, muscle and blood. Screaming in pain, Prescott fell backwards. He stared at the bone, oddly white, stark white, fleshless, protruding ten or twelve inches from the pulpy stump of his thigh.

Then the blood, gushing, filled the ground beneath him.

"Please," he mouthed, "tell…" He stopped speaking. He shivered once and lay still.

Lazlo ripped his tourniquet kit from his backpack but before he took one step forward he saw that Prescott was gone.

The commander shouted, "Mines! Nobody move!" He grabbed the radio. "M.G.!"

"Colonel, we heard an explosion."

"Stop. Immediately. Retreat the way you came. Mtombe's mined the whole area."

"Will do, Colonel."

Lazlo snapped, "I wasn't thinking." Furious with himself.

"Who was hit?" Rahman asked.

"Prescott."

"Is he—"

"No. He didn't make it."

Lazlo could hear the man's sigh.

"Back out and regroup."

"Yes, Colonel. Now, perhaps, the DPKO will agree to an airstrike."

Maybe, Lazlo thought. But by the time the Department of Peacekeeping Operations considered the matter and worked out details with member nations, Mtombe would be long gone.

"We'll meet you back at base, Colonel."

Lazlo called to his men, "We're retreating. But move carefully. Study the ground at your feet. Look for any disturbances at all. Any mounds of earth."

Lazlo shucked his back and carefully walked forward toward Prescott's body.

"Colonel," one peacekeeper called. "Leave him. It's too dangerous."

But Lazlo kept walking, slowly, making his way along patches of dirt, where he could see any evidence of mines—he hoped. He made it safely to Prescott's body, unhooked the man's backpack, and, summoning all his strength, hefted the corpse to his shoulder. He felt man's warm blood soak the back of his uniform.

He turned south and, with his troops, retreated, moving, literally, inch by inch to safety.

***

"They were expecting us."

"That Lazlo, he is devil, a demon," replied Jacob Bedaya.

"Expecting us," repeated Mtombe, lounging restlessly on the dozen massive silk pillows he preferred to chairs. The two men were in the opulent tent in the center of the HRA camp. "You could see, couldn't you? They were prepared."

Bedaya, one of the warlord's senior aides de camp, recognized the mood. Tread careful here. Very carefully.

"Yes, the blue hats were prepared. Can I get you something, Lord General Othello?

Mtombe didn't answer. He frowned suddenly and asked, "Do you smell that, Jacob?" He inhaled hard through his broad nostrils, which were set in a broad head. The warlord was large everywhere, from a neck like a tire to man breasts to massive calves.

"Smell what, Lord General Othello?"

"It is the smell of perfume in the raw. Ambergris, the vomit of whales. It occurs to me, though, that perhaps it is not just whales that generate the essence of frankincense. I believe it must be all large animals. Are there elephant here?"

"No, Lord General, I think not." There had once been many pachyderms in the Northern African Republic, but only a few remained in the wild, thanks to ivory poachers. As for the nation's pride—the black Rhino—they were gone completely now. And all because of fools in Asia who clung to a superstitious believe in the power of ground-up horn.

Mtombe turned his wide face to Bedaya's. "No? You think not? No elephants?"

"Well, I'm not sure, Lord General."

"I smell them."

"Then you're probably correct."

"Perfume." Mtombe's dark eyes widened. He often displayed a childlike fascination with the most curious things. "This is a very good idea I have just had. I am thinking the HRA will start a perfumery operation. Massive. Perfume from large animals. Buffalo, elephant, hippos. Perfume is what the wise men brought Mary and Joseph."

"Frankincense."

"Ah, you were listening to me."

"Sir, I always—"

"Enough." Mtombe lifted a bottle and sipped the warm Coca-Cola that was the only beverage Bedaya had ever seen him drink in the two years since the man had emerged from their village as a self-proclaimed rebel leader in the Northern African Republic. Mtombe then ate handsful of dates and nuts imported from South Africa. He believed the food gave him unlimited sexual prowess.

At least the warlord chose to believe that fruits and nuts, not rhino horn, were his personal Viagra.

"So, you will look into that."

"Yes, Lord General. Look into what exactly, sir, if I may ask?"

"The Chinese will buy it. Our perfume. They will buy anything from Africa."

"I will be sure—"

"Who betrayed us, Jacob."

"Betrayed?

"What I was telling you a moment ago! They were expecting us. How did Lazlo know we would be coming for the weapons?"

"He has observers, he has spies."

"I think he has *traitors*," Mtombe spat out. "Traitors within us."

"Lord General Othello, your soldiers are as loyal as the sun to the stars. They—"

"What does that mean? Sun, stars? Astrology?" He growled, "What are you saying?"

"I misspoke. Forgive me. Your soldiers? They revere you."

Better than saying they piss their pants in fear.

"Lazlo…Now he knows where our camp is. We will have to move again. Soon."

"Yes. Lazlo might go to the UN and get permission for airstrikes."

Silence for a long moment from Mtombe.

Bedaya wondered, as he often did, if he'd just committed a mortal offense.

Then Mtombe smiled. "You think my perfume business will do well? We will make aftershave too. It will drive the women crazy."

"Yes, Lord—"

"Ah, quiet." Mtombe ate another handful of dates and picked the residue in his teeth with one of his long fingernails. Another swallow of Coke. "Jesus has spoken to me. Just now. He has given me a plan. I need one of our soldiers to help us. Someone who is young. Not threatening. We can trust completely. There will be money involved. Gold. A lot. Who among us can we entrust this mission to?"

"Joseph Goodbye, perhaps."

"That scrawny little thing? He's a chicken. How old is he?"

"Eleven, I believe, Lord General."

"Good. I think he will do. Bring him here. Now."

***

Bedaya ushered the boy into the tent.

"Ah, ah, ah, it is Joseph Goodbye," the warlord said, smiling his famous smile, broad as his shoulders.

The child was about five feet high, thin as reeds. His round head was shaved and his skin was unblemished by combat scars, unlike most of the soldiers in the HRA. Like all the child soldiers, Joseph had killed in battle. But he wasn't suited for that life and Mtombe kept him mostly in the office and kitchen. Bedaya was pleased at that. As a regular soldier, the youngster wouldn't last long.

He wore a tattered beige and black plaid shirt and cargo pants. Both garments were far too large. On his tiny feet were tiny Nike running shoes.

Joseph was looking everywhere but at the man himself. He glanced at Bedaya, who nodded some reassurance. Joseph turned toward Mtombe again but could not hold his eye.

"I have an important job for you."

The boy said nothing.

"Yes, I have picked you of all my soldiers."

Joseph Goodbye gave a faint smile. Then remembered, it seemed, that he was frightened, or should be frightened, and looked down once more.

"Do you know why I picked you?"

The eleven year old merely shook his head.

"Because you are among the most loyal in my army. I have been good to you, no?"

Now, a nod.

"You work in my office. You don't have to carry packs and RPGs and guns and get shot at. And when I came to your village and enlisted you in the service of God, I did not kill your family. I left them all alive. You mother and father and your sister, too. I was generous, even though I do not think they love me.

Finally the boy spoke, in a voice that was nearly a whisper. "No, Lord General Othello, they do love you."

Mtombe didn't seem to hear. He watched a fly for a moment, a large one, buzzing loudly. Then a baboon call filled the air. Finally the warlord lifted the bowl of dates and offered them to the boy. He took one.

"Take more!" Mtombe boomed.

Joseph palmed a large handful and shyly put them in his pocket.

Mtombe roared with laughter.

"Why did I treat your family so well...? Because you're destined for greatness. You know 'destined'? That means you are intended to do good things for me, for Christ, for our cause. You will help?

Another nod.

"We are in a difficult position here. The blue hats know where we are. We need to escape but they will be looking for us. So we need to lead them off. There is a man I know in their compound who is willing to help us. His name is Peter. He will mislead Lazlo and the blue hats. That will give us time to get across the river and back to the villages in our part of the country."

The boy took this in for a moment. Bedaya had no idea if he understood what Mtombe was saying. But then Joseph asked, "He believes in our cause, Lord General Othello? This man?"

"No, he believes in something else, Joseph Goodbye."

Bedaya's heart pounded hard as Mtombe looked his way. "What does he believe in, Bedaya?"

Please let me answer well. "I would think he believes in money."

"Yes, yes, that's what he believes in. He is not a son of Christ but he has agreed to help those of us who are. But I must pay him first. And you are the one who will get his gold to him."

"Yes, Lord General Othello."

"Now. Hold your arm out." Mtombe walked to the corner of the tent and picked up a rusty machete.

Joseph Goodbye stared at the blade. He didn't cower. He didn't whimper. But his lips trembled.

"Hold your arm out!"

Tears began to flow, glistening in twin trails down the boy's round cheeks.

"Are you loyal to your Lord General Othello?"

Bedaya began, "Lord General—" And was silenced with a fierce glare.

Joseph stretched his hand out. Mtombe rested the blade on the back of the boy's hand and then slowly drew it back, slicing into the skin.

"Ah," he gasped at the pain.

The cut was shallow but blood spread abundantly, crimson on black, and dripped to the floor.

Mtombe tossed the weapon on the ground. "My brave Joseph. I am proud of you."

The youngster stared at the cut.

"Does that hurt?"

"No, Lord General Othello. Maybe a little."

"Bedaya. Bind it with a bandage."

"I'll go get—"

"Your shirt!" Mtombe raged. "Cut part off your shirt! Didn't you hear me say we must move fast?"

The aide ran forward, picked up the machete and awkwardly sawed off the tail of his gray blouse, then bound it around the wound.

"Now, Joseph. Here's what you will do. You will go to the blue hats' compound. They will see you are injured and take you to the hospital. No one will be suspicious of a young boy who is injured and needs medical treatment. When you get into the hospital, call me on this phone."

For the first time since he'd been in the warlord's tent, perhaps the first time in years, Joseph Goodbye showed some emotion. His eyes marveled at the white mobile. He nearly smiled. "It's an iPhone, Lord General Othello."

"Yes. And you may keep it afterward."

"Oh, thank you, Lord General Othello!"

"So, I was saying. You will call me when you are there. Then I will call him and have him meet you in the hospital. You will give him the gold. Then you leave the hospital and come back here. You understand?"

"Yes." Joseph Goodbye rubbed the phone and put it into his pocket. Bedaya noted that he kept his uninjured hand over that portion of his cargo pants, making sure, perhaps, that the phone did not fall out or that he would feel a hand trying to steal it.

"Come with me." With some effort, Mtombe rose and the three walked from the warlord's tent to the one beside it, which served as the HRA's office.

There, at a table, was a flabby, gray-complexioned man of about fifty. He featured a massive, ugly scar on his cheek, which kept you from looking at his crooked nose and bug eyes.

"Ah, Lord General Othello!"

"Emmanuel. This is Joseph Goodbye. He has agreed to help us in our escape from the blue hats."

"Soldier Goodbye! A hero."

"Yes, he is," Mtombe agreed. "Now give him the gold. Emmanuel opened the safe. Inside, Bedaya could see hundreds of small gold bars. The soldier extracted a money belt and handed it to Mtombe. From the weight, Bedaya guessed it was worth a hundred thousand dollars.

"Pull up your shirt."

The boy did, revealing an emaciated waist. Mtombe fixed the belt around Joseph's midsection and tugged the shirt down.

"Good. Are you ready?"

"Yes, Lord General. I will do what you say."

"I know you will. Because you are a loyal soldier of the Heaven's Resistant Army...*And* because you will want to see your family again. See your family as alive and happy as they are now. You don't want anything to happen to them."

"No, Lord General Othello."

"Good. Now, go."

***

The hike from Lord General Othello's camp to the blue hats' compound was only five kilometers but it took Joseph Goodbye four hours to get close. The early part of the journey was slow because he had to make his way carefully around the land mines.

Weaving, moving in a tiresome zig-zag pattern. He'd pause occasionally to remove the iPhone and look at it. Then carefully replace the device in his pocket, which he'd button shut. And start off on his hike once more.

The mines scared him. He had been close when one of the New Resistance Army soldiers, drinking, had stumbled off the path and stepped on of Lord General Othello's mines. A bang had resounded through the jungle, but not ear-splitting. A small puff of smoke. The solider and fallen back, stunned and looked down at his right leg. The cargo pants had been blown off up to the thigh. His flesh—red and black—remained pretty much as it had been, though his foot was gone and the calve up to the knee was split right down the middle.

The solider had screamed for only sixty seconds before Mtombe shot him to death for disloyalty.

Finally, now, Joseph Goodbye was out of the mined area and moving more quickly. When he entered a clearing, he could catch a glimpse of white smoke from the blue hats' camp, adjusting his course to steer for it. He looked around him carefully all the time. The blue hats didn't seem to shoot unarmed soldiers but there were poachers, gangs and other warlords, in this portion of the Northern African Republic.

Buffalo too, the most dangerous and unpredictable of the animals here. And time to time a big cat would attack, grip its prey's head and shoulders in its front paws and yellow teeth and strip away at the belly with the rear claws. (Joseph Goodbye had seen that happen too; he feared cats as much as land mines.)

But today, it seemed, he had the jungle to himself.

Was that a sign?

Perhaps it was. That he was on his way to glory.

Destined...

Please let me succeed, Jesus our Lord, he prayed. And Joseph Goodbye also said asked for help from Brekyirihunuade, too, the Cote d'Ivoire god, whose name meant the All Seeing, All Knowing. Though if Lord General Othello Mtombe knew he was praying to that god, he would be beheaded in an instant, if not crucified. Still, Joseph could not help himself. This was the god that his family had prayed too. He wondered if they still did. He thought of his sister. He—

Then he heard voices!

He dropped down in a bed of jungle shrubs, a bright green one with red, paddle-shaped leaves and a stark spiky plant he recognized. It had pods that oozed a sweet milk when you sliced them. This reminded him of his hand. The bandage was now dark red with drying blood.

The voices grew louder.

Blue hats?

Or poachers or gangs, who would slice his throat in a moment and steal his phone and the gold?

He peered out.

Ah.

Rising.

He chose English, not French. "Please, sir! Please. Can you help me?"

The two blue hats, skinny men, with machine guns and wary eyes. Approached.

They saw he had no weapons but looked carefully through his backpack, which contained only water, a raspberry yogurt energy bar and a Justin Timberlake CD. They glanced at his phone but handed it back.

"Who are you?"

"Joseph Goodbye."

"Ah, son, that is a good name. *Non*, Pierre?"

"It is. What happened to your hand?"

"I fell, running from some of Mtombe's men."

"That son of a bitch. *Merdre*. Well, come with us. We'll get it all taken care of. There's a hospital in our compound."

Together the threesome turned and walked down the path. They'd gotten only ten meters before they startled a huge parrot, who winged off into the sky in a fierce rush of color.

Joseph Goodbye took that as a sign that Brekyirihunuade or Jesus or perhaps both were looking after him.

***

"Where do you think our little chicken is, Jacob? He's such a skinny boy. He should eat more if he wants to grow into a man."

"I would guess nearly to the blue hats camp by now Lord General Othello. May I ask, who is this person you will be bribing for information? This Peter, the traitor to the blue hats? I don't recall him."

"You don't recall him? You mean you are angry I didn't mention him to you?" Mtombe asked, his voice like oil.

"No, sir! No. I was merely curious who he might be. A matter of curiosity only."

The warlord rose from the pillows and strode to the mesh window in the side of the tent. "Well, the fact is, Jacob, my friend, that there is no Peter and there is no deal to mislead the blue hats. I have put in place another plan entirely."

"A plan? What would that be, may I ask?"

Mtombe explained. The belt that Joseph Goodbye wore contained not gold but several pounds of C4 plastic explosive.

"*What?*"

"Yes, yes, a good plan, don't you think? Our little chicken will be taken to the hospital. Once he's there he will call me on his iPhone to tell us he's arrived. I will then place another call—the number of the mobile attached to the detonator in the money belt. That much explosive will surely kill anyone for ten meters around and probably bring down the entire wing of the hospital, if not the whole building."

Bedaya masked his horror as best he could. "Yes, yes, Lord General. A brilliant plan. I wondered why Soldier Emmanuel gave Joseph the belt. He has little to do with the business side of our operations."

Other than buying arms and landmines.

And he'd thought it odd too that the plan he'd laid out to Joseph Goodbye had certain Biblical tones: betrayal for gold, the name Peter.

Mtombe turned his eyes on Bedaya. "There is something about your face, Soldier Bedaya, something that seems troubled."

"No, no—"

"Don't be afraid to tell me your opinion."

"Opinion?"

"Of my plan. To meet Frederick Lazlo head on. To show him he cannot toy with us."

"Just, with all respect, Lord General Othello, I'm wondering if blowing up a hospital will only make Lazlo angrier."

Mtombe raged, "Why do you care if he's angry? *I'm* angry! I am the one who's angry! Who are you tell me not to be?"

"Of course, I didn't mean that."

"Then why did you mention it? Why does no one understand me? The hospital blows up and Lazlo will see we are a force to be reckoned with. He will probably surrender."

"Surrender?"

"Yes. To make sure such an event does not happen again. He will likely pay reparations too. When he sees we are—"

"A force to be reckoned with."

"Yes, and if you are ever ironic with me, Jacob, I will cut both your arms off in a hair of a second."

"No, no, Lord General!"

"Now, I am going to pray. Leave me for five minutes."

"Yessir."

Mtombe eased his massive frame down on his knees, clasped his sausage fingers together and began muttering, "Dear Jesus, who watches over me and embraces me with His arms, so that I may guide our magnificent country to greatness. Please, Jesus, help us prevail with this, our glorious quest, and guide Joseph Goodbye on his mission…"

Bedaya stepped outside into the camp, hazed with wood fire smoke. He looked over the hundred or so HRA soldiers, most as skinny as Soldier Joseph Goodbye. Like many of them Bedaya was here because Mtombe knew where his family lived and would, without a moment's hesitation send soldiers to murder them.

Why don't I have the courage to simply grab the machete and slice his throat?

What madness have I fallen into? Bedaya thought. He gripped his phone. He could call someone. The police in the capital. Maybe he could even get through to the UN. Or at least call the hospital directly. He could warn them.

But he thought of his wife, his sons, his teenage daughter. At home now, fifty kilometers away. Missing him. Yet safe.

And put the Nokia away.

Some minutes later: "Jacob!" Mtombe called from the tent.

And, shamed by cowardice now and for the past three years he'd associated with the HRA, Bedaya rejoined his leader.

"He spoke to me, Jacob."

"He…Jesus spoke to you?"

"I heard his words. He told me we will succeed. Does Jesus speak to you in English? Sometimes he uses French with me. Sometimes a language I don't understand. Well, answer me."

What is the right answer? "English, Lord General Othello."

Mtombe turned to him quickly but whatever reaction had been forthcoming was derailed by a humming of a cell phone.

"Ah, see, Jacob. You of little faith."

"I have faith, sir. I—"

Mtombe hit the speaker phone. "Hello, Joseph Goodbye."

"Lord General. I'm in the hospital."

"And you have the gold with you?"

"Yes, some blue hats looked in my backpack but they didn't search me. I thought they would take my phone but they didn't."

"Where are you exactly?"

"In a ward on the ground floor. Ward A. I'm waiting to see a doctor about my hand."

"I will call the man you are to give the gold to. Peter. He will come to see you. But tell me, is it crowded there?"

"Yes, Lord General Othello. That's what's taking so long. There are many people here. Some sick. Some injured by the landmines."

"Men, women and children?"

"Yes. Mostly woman and children.

"But how *many*?" Mtombe snapped.

"I would say fifty."

"And how many doctors and nurses."

"Ten, maybe more. I didn't the difference between a nurse or a doctor. Everyone is wearing white or blue smocks."

"Wait where you are and I will call Peter. He'll come and you will give him the gold belt. Then you will slip out and return to us. You will be a hero."

"Yes, Lord General."

Mtombe gave a vague smile to Bedaya, who felt sick at the thought of what was about to happen. He glanced at the machete on the floor. But it was far away and, as if sensing his thoughts, Mtombe kept his eyes glue to his aide. The warlord could draw his pistol and fire it in a fraction of a second. Bedaya had seen it happen often. He remained where he was.

"Remain talking to me, Joseph Goodbye. I will call Peter on my other phone."

Mtombe picked up a second mobile and dialed a number. His thumb paused over the last digit. "Now, we shall see." He pushed the button.

Joseph Goodbye's phone went dead.

And a moment later there came a distant boom of an explosion.

No, no, no!

Mtombe laughed in delight. "Ah, see, you didn't believe me, Jacob, but my plan worked. Jesus is proud of me now. I can tell you. He is praising me in heaven." Then the man's dark eyes swiveled to Bedaya. "I am so pleased to learn the news."

"The news?"

"My friend, my friend, my friend...I have to tell you. I *did* worry that you were the traitor. The one who'd warned the blue hats about our assault this morning."

"I didn't! I swear!"

"I know that now. I've eliminated you. You see, that was really the point of my plan. If you were the traitor, when I sent you outside you would have called the UN or someone to warn them. If the explosion had not happened you would have been the one. But you didn't. The hospital's been destroyed and you are in the clear."

"You mean, you killed Soldier Goodbye and those people simply to test my loyalty?"

"What other reason would I have? Did you really thing I believed Lazlo would surrender if I blew up his hospital? Pay reparations?"

Bedaya could say nothing. He wondered if he was going to be sick.

Mtombe said, "Now, we must get to work and find the real traitor. The explosion occurred so it's neither you nor Soldier Emmanuel. But what are your thoughts on Solider Hrakaal? I have not been liking the way he regards me when I give my sermons."

Bedaya sputtered, "I...I don't know. It could be."

"Well. Perhaps I will simply say I have discovered that Hrakaal is a traitor and behead him in front of everyone. That should discourage the real traitor. Buy us some time to find his identity. Now, while the UN peacekeepers are busy rescuing patients at the hospital, we must escape here. We'll go west and then north." He walked to the tent flap and called, "Soldier Akiba!"

A moment later a tall, somber soldier appeared. He was not from the Northern African Republic, but from Congo; keloid scars, dozens of parallel lines, marked his arms. This seemed blasphemous to Mtombe, Bedaya knew, but Akiba had saved the warlord's life once and so he was tolerated.

"Yes, Lord General Othello?"

"Marshal the men and tell them we are moving out in an hour. Bring me the minefield maps and I'll plot our escape route. They're in the first file cabinet next to the desk in the office."

"I'll get them now."

But before the solider turned, there came the sound of automatic weapon fire, masses of it, from all directions. Two slugs popped through the tent walls and struck a pillow, sending a cloud of feathers into the air.

"No!" Mtombe cried, his face twisted with rage. He drew his pistol and ran to the tent flap, flung it open.

Bedaya and Akiba joined him.

The blue hats were overrunning their camp. Some HRA soldiers were fighting back, but firing blind. Most were dropping their weapons, raising their hands. A few fell spread-eagle on the ground.

Mtombe lifted his pistol to fire at a cluster of the blue hats.

Bedaya and Akiba looked at each other.

Together they charged forward and tackled the warlord.

Some minutes later, the UN peacekeepers had to pull Jacob Bedaya off Mtombe's chest, on which he knelt as he pounded his fist into the round face again and again and again. It took three blue hats to drag him off.

Mtombe cried out for Jesus to help him, but no heavenly assistance was forthcoming. Like the others, the warlord, Bedaya and Akiba were bound with plastic restraints, ankle and wrist, and popped into sitting positions against nearby trees.

A few moments later Bedaya noticed a small entourage break from the jungle into the camp. He was not the least surprised to see that the leader of this group was the UN peacekeeping force commander, Colonel Frederick Lazlo.

He was, however, shocked to who was at his side. Joseph Goodbye, wearing a flak jacket and a blue helmet, strode into the clearing and walked up to his former leader, gazing down at the bloodied warlord. Though the protective equipment hung comically on the eleven-year-old's minuscule frame, there was nothing at all amusing—or childlike—about Joseph Goodbye's eyes, which bored into Mtombe's like lasers.

***

"Joseph only agreed to help you," Lazlo explained to Mtombe as the UN medics treated his battered face, "so he could get the land mine maps to us."

"What?" the warlord muttered.

Lazlo nodded at the boy. "Seems he'd made a copy of them when he was working in your camp office. He knew the mines were the only thing keeping us from attacking you here. But he'd been waiting for a way to get it to us. As soon as the patrol that picked him up brought him to the compound a couple of hours ago he asked to see me in person."

"He knew you?"

Lazlo laughed. "You're surprised at that? You put a price on my head. Literally, of course. Ten thousand dollars if somebody brought it to you on a spear. All of your people know my name."

"But he's a boy."

"How can you say that, Mtombe? You didn't give him a *chance* to be a boy."

The madman gazed at the commander as if he'd been speaking a foreign language. Lazlo then continued, "He handed me the maps and the belt, telling me about your plan to bribe somebody named Peter. I knew it had to be a trap and that the belt was an improvised explosive device. We played along. Our demo people got the IED into a pit away from the compound and we coached Joseph on what to say to you. Then he called, and you detonated the bomb. I shut his phone off right away, so you'd believe you'd succeeded.

"Then, thanks to the maps," Lazlo said lightly, "we came a'callin'." He shrugged. "Interesting—you relied on the minefields and didn't bother to post sentries. We wouldn't've had quite so much surprise if you'd followed classic textbook defensive tactics."

Joseph spoke for the first time. "He thought Jesus would look for him."

"You! Soldier Goodbye! You do not know the trouble you've made for yourself, chicken boy. When the revolution succeeds, you will be the first to die. And very slowly." The warlord's rage amped up further: "I gave you *everything*, and this is how you repay me? Judas! What did the bastard blue hats the promise you? An Xbox? A Kinect?"

"They promised me a gift I'd been dreaming of for two years, Lord General Othello. They promised me you."

"I treated your family well!"

When he replied, the boy's words were flat; the monotone was chilling, more eerie than if he'd shouted. "Treated them well? You cut off my father and mother's hands. And my sister? You had her dragged to the soldiers' barracks. She was there for a week. Fourteen years old. She has never been normal since then. She sits by herself most days and stares at the wall."

"Which is what you're going to be doing for the rest of your life," Lazlo told the warlord.

Captain M.G. Rahman joined them. The slightly built, handsome soldier said, "The entire camp is secure, Colonel. I have teams out marking the positions of the mines. The sweepers will be here in a few hours."

"Any intel on the HRA's other camps?"

A glance at Mtombe. "Yes, yes. It took all of ten second to find them. He didn't encrypt his computers."

He thought Jesus would look out for him…

"Probably two hundred other soldiers total in three other camps. None of them know about the operation here. I've got somebody manning Mtombe's radio, as if it's business as usual. They're in the dark."

"You're fools!" Mtombe growled. "The people will rise up when they hear what you've done. They'll come to my—"

"Give it a rest," Lazlo said. He nodded his head to several beefy UN peacekeepers, who hauled the man to his feet—they grunted under the effort—and led him away to a prisoner of war transport vehicle.

Joseph Goodbye pointed to a man who'd been identified as Jacob Bedaya, one of Mtombe's aides. "He was forced to help the Lord General. He is not a bad man. He was good to me and the other child soldiers."

Bedaya looked up at Lazlo and said nothing.

The colonel said, "There's no warrant for him, but we have to detain everyone in the HRA until the tribunal looks over the evidence and decides what to do with them. If he's not guilty of war crimes he'll be released."

Then the boy was glancing at an AK-47 machine gun, lying on the ground.

"I will fight with you," he said. "I will come with you and help you kill the other HRA soldiers. I've killed before. I know how."

"Sorry, Joseph. Can't do it. Our charter's clear. No civilians in combat. Only consultants. You know what a consultant is?"

"I don't know that, no."

"Someone who helps by giving information."

"Well, I will be a consultant on how you can kill the HRA."

Lazlo smiled. He studied the skinny youngster. He assayed the eyes, the posture, the tone of his words. He decided that Joseph Goodbye was not lost forever. Teetering on the brink, yes, but not lost. "Maybe we'll talk about that. But don't you think you should get home to see your family? I'm sure they miss you. Your sister needs you. You can help her get well."

The boy's eyes, still flat, scanned the smoke filled clearing of the HRA camp. "I *would* like to see my family again. Yes."

"Good. I'll have some of my men drive you to your village. You have your iPhone that Mtombe gave you?"

"Yes." The boy added reluctantly, "Do you want it?"

"No, you keep it."

"Really?"

"Yes. I have the number. I'll call you soon. To see how you are doing. You and your family."

"Yes, Commander. You can call me. I will be proud to consultant for you."

"That's a plan, Joseph."

Lazlo gestured to a pair of peacekeepers, standing nearby. They slung their H & K machine guns over their shoulders and approached. "This's Joseph Goodbye."

"Hey, you're the kid who helped us."

They both shook his hand. The boy seemed embarrassed. He looked down.

Lazlo said, "He'll tell you where his home is. Take one of the armored jeeps and drive him there."

The other peacekeeper said, "Sure thing, Colonel. Come on, son. This way." The three of them walked away. At the clearing, Joseph Goodbye stopped and looked back. His dark eyes, still flat, still very, very adult, caught Lazlo's. The boy gave a salute.

Lazlo restrained the smile and reciprocated. The boy nodded and turned, and he and the two peacekeepers disappeared into the rain forest.

Jeffery Deaver's novels have appeared as #1 on bestseller lists around the world, including the *New York Times*, the *Times* of London, and the *Los Angeles Times*. The author of thirty-three novels, two collections of short stories, and a nonfiction law book, his *The Bodies Left Behind* was named Novel of the Year by the International Thriller Writers Association, and his *The Broken Window* and *Edge* were also nominated for that prize. His most recent novels are *The Other List*, a thriller told in reverse, *The Kill Room*, a Lincoln Rhyme novel, and *XO*, a Kathryn Dance thriller, for which he wrote an album of country-western songs, available on iTunes and as a CD. Before that, he penned *Carte Blanche*, the latest James Bond continuation novel. Deaver has been nominated for seven Edgar Awards from the Mystery Writers of America, an Anthony, a Shamus and a Gumshoe. His book *A Maiden's Grave* was made into an HBO movie starring James Garner and Marlee Matlin, and his novel *The Bone Collector* was a feature release from Universal Pictures, starring Denzel Washington and Angelina Jolie. He was born outside Chicago, and holds a bachelor of journalism degree from the University of Missouri and a law degree from Fordham University. Readers can visit his website at www.jefferydeaver.com.

The Rain in Eritrea
Richard Peabody

Tim was eating ice cream. He was talking plans. "So next weekend, how about a B&B in Charlottesville? We can ride horses at my friend Nancy's farm. Or maybe kayak some?"

Janet didn't know how to break it to him. The ticket for Eritrea in her Polartec vest. The haunting photos of land mine victims. Kids. No eyes, no arms, no legs. There was widespread famine, hundreds of rape victims due to Ethiopian incursion, and a general sense that everything she'd seen being built during her years as a foreign correspondent was rapidly being torn asunder. She wanted to get back and see for herself. "I was kind of hoping—"

"Oh, don't say it." He held the spoon upside down in his mouth, the chocolate sauce dripping, barely visible, sliding over his thin moustache. "We can't just spend the entire weekend in bed. We have to get out and do something. The weather's supposed to be phenomenal," and he rapped the spoon against her right knee.

He was protesting too much. Janet knew he'd like nothing better than an entire weekend in bed. And the chocolate sauce would play into his fantasies. How to tell him. Just do it.

"Look, Tim, I've made arrangements—"

"Work?"

Janet nodded, brushed some vanilla from her lap.

"You're leaving?"

She nodded again.

"When?"

"Tomorrow. I'll be gone two weeks."

She knew Tim was pissed. Another assignment in Eritrea. More planes. More excuses. He was frustrated. So was she. In the past he'd have dragged her to bed and growled like a wild animal while marking every square inch of her body with love bites and hickeys. No longer. Tim stared at her for a second, licked his spoon, got up from the couch and went into the kitchen. The frequent trips, the trashing of his plans for the two of them, were all taking their toll, and she knew it. And the hardest part was not knowing whether she wanted out of the relationship or not.

***

The Land Rover was bumping along like an amusement park ride. A few years ago Janet had ridden with the rebel Eritrean People's Liberation Front, watched them capture Russian tanks, rocket launchers, artillery pieces, trucks, and anti-aircraft guns, and imprison the Ethiopian soldiers of the Derg regime, who by daylight waged air strikes against this tiny country in the horn of Africa. Those were heady days and Janet had marveled then at how the little guy had won, had stood up to the bully. They'd gained their freedom only to get dragged into a prolonged series of border disputes with the new rulers of Ethiopia—their counterpart the Ethiopian People's Revolutionary Democratic Front. Trenches on both sides now stretched from the Sudan to Djibouti, about the length of Pennsylvania, and to complicate matters they also had a Sudanese-backed Islamic guerilla force nipping at their heels. Ato, the driver at the wheel today, was new. Only fifteen, but with the hardened face and vigilant eyes of a war veteran. Janet watched the mountains fading on the horizon and remembered her first trip to North Africa. She'd assumed everything in the desert was flat. Nothing could be further from the truth. Every bump amplified by the lack of suspension. The Land Rover was going to own her kidneys before the week was out.

The hospital building in Mendefera had been rebuilt many times. Recent air raids had left nothing but rubble. The two kids in one of the surviving rooms were in amazing spirits considering the damage. They told their stories through Blatta, her interpreter on most of her past visits to the country, on whom she depended for food and comfort and insulation against daily vicissitudes. And Janet took it all down with speedy dispatch and carefully detached emotions. Once a journalist always a journalist. Just like her father.

"I was walking with my cows," the boy said. "One of the cows stepped on a mine."

The cow had been obliterated. Shrapnel from the anti-personnel mine taking the brother next to him, and ripping off one leg and forever darkening an eye. The other boy's story was similar. Both waiting to be fitted for their artificial limbs. Both not even born when Eritrea fought Ethiopia for liberation.

Land mines. Perfectly patient killing machines. And Eritrea had one of the deadliest land mine infestations in the world.

How to explain? How to say, look Tim, I've watched these people struggle and suffer and succeed. They've beaten two super powers. They're part of me now and I'm part of them. The eyes. The smiles. She'd been snapping photos of kids in Asmara. The sheer joy now that they were free to simply walk around. The U.N. Peacekeepers a visible presence in the capital city. They'd be patrolling the border with Ethiopia by the start of the new year.

***

"You know you could get killed don't you?" Tim had driven her to the airport. He hadn't given her that kind of time lately. Janet thought it was because he was afraid he was contributing to what he regarded as her journalistic vice if he aided and abetted her. Tim had never traveled out of the country and it was becoming clear that he felt threatened any time she did.

"Yes, I know."

"You better be home by Christmas."

"I promise."

"Is it really worth it Janet?" He was squeezing the steering wheel so hard his hands were white claws.

How to explain to her lover why she is so moved by a country being born? How to get that across? Communication was her talent and yet with Tim she was incapable of communicating how much this meant to her. To go, to see, to witness. He'd accused her of being an ambulance chaser. She'd begun to wonder about that herself.

"Is it?"

"We've been over all of this before Tim, I'm scared of course. I don't want to die. But I'm well aware it could happen." Her friend and mentor Larry Shapiro had been killed in Kosovo. Janet knew death was sometimes par for the course. "I'm not suicidal if that's what you're getting at." And she was amazed just how angry and defensive she was becoming. In a blink they were at the airport and Tim was embracing her and helping her with her black duffel and then she was in the terminal and when she turned around the beat-up blue Toyota was no longer at the curb. And it was at times like this, standing alone among a host of strangers, that the prospect of living together under one roof, having wills and life insurance and a family, looked particularly comfortable.

***

Nothing ever prepared her for the flies. They were everywhere. Blatta, Janet's interpreter, told her that the Land Rover had been delayed. So she tried to listen over the buzzing while he elaborated between bites of Birsin, the veggie stew he cadged for her whenever they actually found time to eat, about his sister who'd moved to Seattle. The famine and the war had cut down on the availability of the beef and lamb dishes that made up most of the country's cuisine. And God only knew where Ato had actually gone after dropping them off. Half-tracks and soldiers had surrounded a shed. In the shed a stack of land mines. Brightly colored square boxes. Janet realized that they bore an eerie resemblance to her laptop. The writing on the land mines claimed them for the EIS, the Sudanese-backed Eritrean Islamic Salvation bandits. So that was true. Janet had no reason to doubt. A civil war raged in the Sudan between the Arab-Muslims in the north and the black Christians in the south. This spillover of additional death-dealing hardware into Eritrea was hard to stomach. In Eritrea, miraculously, the half-Muslim, half-Christian country made up of nine ethnic groups, simply got along. She took photos of the land mines. How many were there? She lost count at one hundred.

***

The broiling hot sun and lack of sleep blurred the days together. They were on a rutted track to Barentu and the sky had turned gray and menacing. Janet was half asleep, her head bouncing against the window frame, almost in tune to the roaring engine and the shaking vehicle, and she oddly found herself daydreaming about Tim decorating his bookshop for the holiday season. Why wasn't that enough for her? She thought about her father, how he'd been gone for weeks at a time, how he'd missed her birthday, her graduation.

An explosion pounded her awake. They weren't moving. The Land Rover was parked. What was going on? Janet jumped down, her boots sinking into the ferruginous sand. Goats bleating. Animal gore on the hood. Goat innards littered all over the landscape. Land mines. And the remaining animals could easily trip another one or two. Ato, the driver, was helping somebody up just a few yards off the dirt track. Blood everywhere. Blatta. She grabbed a towel and a canteen and in a completely adrenaline-fueled lapse of common sense raced over in time to see her friend collapse and breathe his last before she could touch him, make eye contact. Thousands of bloody pinpricks in his chest, his face, his arms. Janet didn't know how long she cried in Ato's arms. She couldn't tell whose keening was the loudest.

***

Rain was falling and Janet sat under the tin roof of a ruined Tukul, a mud/wood/stone hut, listening as the drops rattled and pinged. Ato was in the half-track smoking with a friend. She could see the two boys through the open door. She wondered who had originally planted the land mine that killed Blatta. Could have been Eritrean, Ethiopian, even Sudanese. Hell, it could have been Rommel or Mussolini. Leave it to the Italians to name the place Eritrea, Classical Greek meaning Red Sea. A sea of blood, Janet thought. And every single drop shed was due to the imposition of colonial borders, imaginary lines on paper, lines between ethnic peoples who had been at war for generations.

The rain felt good mixed with her tears. Janet couldn't remember the last time she'd actually seen it rain in Eritrea. She rarely ventured along the Red Sea coast. The water ran in eddies and currents around the wheels of the Land Rover and the half-track, picking up speed down the incline toward the ocher plains, rolling on to the Sudanese border, and into the endless desert sand.

***

Janet can't reach Tim when she tries him from the airport in Asmara. The phone rings and rings. On the flight she drinks too much so she can stop worrying. He's left her and moved out, or he'll be there when she calls from Dulles. The "will he or won't he" game distracts, dulls her pain. Until she honestly hopes he's not there because she can't imagine having to explain anything. Doesn't want to explain. Maybe after she sleeps for a year. Maybe then. And then she discovers that their relationship simply isn't big enough to share her sense of outrage at injustice.

Janet tries to ring Tim again once she's inside the people mover. She lets the phone ring six times, seven, and the answering machine doesn't pick-up. His answering machine. Maybe he's really gone? Or maybe he's waiting right outside? She walks in front of the porter who pushes her baggage. She wonders if she'll be happy to see him or if her heart will sink. No matter, he's not in sight. The busy Sunday terminal oddly quiet and cavernous.

***

Janet draws the first cab in the airport queue. The driver's features are chiseled. He is from the horn of Africa for certain. Is he Oromo blood?

"Are you Eritrean?" Janet asks, making eye contact for a moment in the rearview mirror. The Redskins game playing on the radio, a surprise in itself.

"There is no such country," the driver says, his eyes two icy tunnels meeting Janet's in the mirror.

Richard Peabody is a French toast addict and native Washingtonian. He has two new books out—a book of poetry, *Speed Enforced by Aircraft* (Broadkill River Press), and a collection of short stories, *Blue Suburban Skies* (Main Street Rag Press). He won the Beyond the Margins "Above & Beyond Award" for 2013. He has edited *Gargoyle Magazine* since back before Elvis died.

Toys of Death
An Excerpt from *Rambo III*
David Morrell

A note from David Morrell:

"In 1972, I published a novel called *First Blood*. Ten years later, it was adapted into a hit film starring Sylvester Stallone as Rambo, a decorated Vietnam veteran whose emotional scars from the war draw him into a private battle with a small-town police chief.

"The international popularity of the character prompted three film sequels, in one of which, *Rambo III*, he journeys to Afghanistan to rescue his mentor, Colonel Trautman, from a Russian military base where Trautman is being held captive. World politics have changed a lot since 1988 when the film was released, but somehow Afghanistan continues to be a hot spot.

"The following is from my novelization of *Rambo III*. In several places, my plot differs substantially from the movie. One example is this section in which an Afghan guide instructs Rambo about the toys of death in Afghanistan.

"Unfortunately, Afghanistan isn't the only place in the world with these toys."

* * *

In the glint of dawn, they felt rested enough to continue. Under Rambo's expert care, the horses had regained their strength. Mousa said his prayers. He and Rambo ate, then buried the crates the packhorses had been carrying. Mousa marked the spot with a good-sized rock but looked worried. "If black wind come before we return, it bury rock. We never find this place."

Mounting their two remaining horses, they continued. The wasteland became more dismal. Rambo saw bomb craters, the rocks around their edges blackened and scorched. He rode past skeletons of oxen. He passed the burnt-out hulks of Soviet tanks and armored personnel carriers.

As they neared the far end of the plain, approaching rugged foothills, Rambo noticed something he'd never seen before. It so puzzled him that he stopped his horse and dismounted for a better look. Ahead, on a slope of rocks, small green objects were scattered in profusion. There seemed to be hundreds of them. They looked like toys, like small green tops of the sort he'd spun on the ground when he was a boy. He led his horse toward one and stooped to pick it up.

"No!" Mousa yelled.

The alarm in Mousa's voice made Rambo freeze with his hand above the toy.

Mousa jerked his horse to a stop and quickly dismounted. "See."

Mousa warily picked up the toy and inspected it as he would a loathsome insect. Then using a cautious underhanded motion, he threw the toy toward the wasteland behind them.

The toy exploded with a roaring flash, stones and shrapnel pelting the dirt.

Rambo steadied his startled horse.

"Enemy leave toys for children," Mousa said. "Toys green, the color of Islam. Children trust. They spin tops. Bang! Hand gone, foot gone. Everywhere these. Russians not want kill children, just want wound so parents take care of them instead of fighting. To be wounded in Afghanistan is to die. Slow. Very slow death."

Rambo swelled with outrage.

"You saved my life," Mousa said. "Now I saved yours."

"We make a good team."

"*Inshallah.*"

"Yes," Rambo said. "God willing."

David Morrell is the author of *First Blood*, the award-winning novel in which Rambo was created. He holds a Ph.D. in American literature from Penn State and was a professor in the English department at the University of Iowa. His numerous *New York Times* bestsellers include the classic spy trilogy *The Brotherhood of the Rose* (the basis for the only television mini-series to premier after a Super Bowl), *The Fraternity of the Stone,* and *The League of Night and Fog.* An Edgar, Anthony, and Macavity nominee, Morrell is the recipient of three Bram Stoker awards and the Thriller Master award from the International Thriller Writers organization. His writing book, *The Successful Novelist,* discusses what he has learned in his four decades as an author. His work has been translated into twenty-six languages. His novelizations for *Rambo (First Blood Part II)* and *Rambo III* are available as e-books and have long introductions that discuss the Rambo phenomenon as well as the drama behind each film. His most recent novel is *Murder as a Fine Art.*

Of Mice and Mines
Nathan Grady

"Fuckin' mice!" complained Neil, but the other three people in the rumbling train's private compartment ignored him. Neil, mid 20's, wore tan cargo pants, boots, and a gaudy Hawaiian T-shirt.

Patrick read his book.

Derek rested his eyes.

Maria looked out the window at Vietnam's scenery whizzing past.

"I can't fucking believe it," griped Neil. "We take a six hour plane ride, all because Stacy *says* this secured transportation gig pays and is low risk even with its proximity to the Golden Triangle, but what do we find when we get to California? Mice!"

Neil paced back and forth in the train's cramped compartment. "Then another 12 hour flight, this time in a sweat stinking freight plane, to courier lab rats to a contact in, *what was it?* Sapa? And why did we land in Saigon anyway? What was wrong with Hanoi? It was a shorter train ride."

"Stacy told you already," responded the spectacled Patrick, not bothering to look up from his four decade old book *The Politics of Heroin in Southeast Asia*. "There was no way to be sure our cargo wouldn't be seized in a phony security inspection at Hanoi. Our contact has stronger influence in Saigon."

Patrick, also mid-20's, wore black slacks, a collared white shirt, a skinny black tie and a threadbare black sports coat.

"But *their* government hired us to do this chicken shit job, why would their own customs try to screw it up?" Neil stopped pacing. "And why the hell do they want these stupid mice anyway? U.S. customs says they're not carrying some militarized pathogen, they're just stupid lab mice."

Patrick looked up from his book. "Quit complaining. Think of where we are. Even with most of the heroin business now coming from Afghanistan, the Golden Triangle trade amounts to roughly 64 billion dollars a year. Most of it runs through Thailand, but for that kind of money even the communist government of Vietnam isn't beyond corruption. *Anything* that might connect to the Golden Triangle, no matter how small, won't go unnoticed. These mice are worth enough for somebody to hire us to bring them to the border of the Triangle, so they must be important. All that really matters is we get to our contact in Sapa with the cargo intact. Besides, you wouldn't even know they were mice if you hadn't opened the case in California. For someone imagining a militarized pathogen, that's an idiot move."

Neil changed his tone to a child trying to come up with a new excuse. "Well, there were air holes in the box, I thought it would be some rare exotic animal."

"Why bring a rare exotic animal to the Golden Triangle?"

"Maybe as a bribe to some eccentric drug smuggler, I don't know. What's up with these mice?"

"Don't know, don't care, don't have to. Just have to deliver them."

Derek stood. "That's it! No way I'm going to get any rest in here. I'm going to the dining car, see if they got booze."

Derek was a gruff man in his late 40's wearing military camo cargo pants and camo flack vest. He slid open the door to their compartment and started down the hallway toward the front of the train.

Patrick called after him: "Remember, this job isn't done till the package is delivered!"

Derek didn't slow his pace for the middle dining car.

Patrick turned back to Neil: "He's right, you haven't stopped complaining since we left the station. Relax. You're in a foreign land. Enjoy its majesty. And if you can't do that, just go explore the train. D's not the only one sick of your bitching."

Neil threw out his arms. "Fine. I'll take a walk."

Neil left and drifted toward the front of the train.

The express train from Saigon to Hanoi featured a dining car, four semi-private passenger cars, two in front of the dining car, two behind, and four open public cars, two on each end of the semiprivate cars. The last car carried the train's cargo. All livestock had to be kept in the cargo car. Patrick had booked the semiprivate compartment closest to the rear of the train, but there were still two public cars between his party and the cargo car.

Now only Patrick and Maria were left in the compartment.

Clack-clack-clack

Maria wore her long black hair in a ponytail. Growing up as an enforcer in the street gangs in Venezuela, she didn't know her exact age, but dummy documents Stacy cooked up for her said she was 23. That didn't feel far off. She'd only recently joined Neil and Patrick's band. She still felt uncomfortable. Alone with Patrick, Maria started to fidget.

"You know," said Patrick, noticing Maria's discomfort, "we've pulled out of the station. The mice carrying case is like a small suitcase, and they don't make much noise. I don't think anyone would mind if you brought them back to our compartment. We're supposed to keep a close eye on them anyway."

Maria, grateful to have a reason to leave this cramped quarters, nodded, took the claim ticket and left the compartment, headed for the back of the train.

"And with that," muttered Patrick, "maybe I can get some reading done."

Clack-clack-clack

Neil moved to the next semiprivate car, just as Derek made his way to the dining car through the door at the other end. A Vietnamese man wearing a green coat left his compartment and drifted behind Derek. Neil slowed his pace.

Most compartments in this car were empty, with their doors wide open—until halfway down the train car. That compartment held an attractive European woman wearing a red dress, high heels, and cute glasses. She was reading her iPad, glancing out the window. As Neil strolled past her open door, he shot her a smile. She politely returned one of her own.

Take a chance, thought Neil.

"Hey."

"Hey," she responded with a European accent.

"Sorry for presuming, but it's a long train ride, and you don't look local either. What brings you to this lovely country?"

"That's observant of you. And you're right, I'm an agriculturalist here collecting soil samples. What about you?"

"I'm in charge of delivering a secure package in Vietnam."

"So, you're some sort of FedEx man?"

Neil smiled. "Actually, I'm a contractor. A mercenary."

Clack-clack-clack

Maria made her way toward the back of the train. The public car held few passengers. Mostly locals, some tourists.

Maria knew Patrick and Stacy chose a usually deserted midday train. Her bosses even timed it so their team had to rush straight from the plane to the station. Not stopping to gear-up after their flight was risky, but moving quickly with no side stops made intercepting the group or its package difficult, and spotting any sizeable opposition was easy when in small crowds.

Few passengers on the train gave Maria comfort. Her years as a cartel enforcer made her wary of crowds. Though proficient with a pistol, she didn't like guns. They gave away position with every use, and silencers were clunky, cutting her mobility. Her talent with a blade had kept her from being made into a high-price whore. She would have spent her life killing for the crime family that owned her from youth, but a rival cartel eliminated her bosses. They would have killed her, too, if not for the coincidental arrival of Patrick, Neil and Derek.

They rescued her from her country's blood-soaked streets.

Maria made her way to the back of the second public car: Two elderly Vietnamese couples enjoying the scenery. A napping business man with a suit but no briefcase. A small Vietnamese man wearing a too big green coat that looked like a trench coat. A blond American man, probably an English teacher in one of the Southeast Asian countries.

A train porter in an ill-fitting uniform sat in the last seat in the train and looked bored out of his mind. As she got close, he stood up, blocking the door to the cargo car.

He barked a command in Vietnamese.

"Sorry, *no comprendo*, I don't understand." Maria attempted to move past him.

The porter stood firm and switched to English.

"No access when moving. Only at station. Please return to seat until train stops."

"I need a case from the back. It's small, *poquito*. No trouble."

"No access when moving. Only—"

"I have a claim ticket." Maria fumbled for the paper from Patrick. "I just need the case."

"Policy says no access. Wait till Hanoi."

"Please, *por favor*, the case is important."

Maria's boss was expecting the case. Although he wasn't as unforgiving as her last boss and the consequences of failure were likely not harsh, she didn't want to botch so simple a task.

The blond *gringo* had been watching the attractive South American woman in cargo pants and black tank top. Now he stood and walked to the back where she—luckily for him—seemed to need help.

Maria stopped her pleas with the porter as she detected *approach* behind her, turned, ready to assault both the *gringo* and the porter.

The blond *gringo* fixed his eyes on the official. "Come on man, let her in the back to get her thing. What harm could it do?"

"No access while—"

"Look around," said *Gringo*. "It's not as if you bending the rules will piss off the few other passengers."

Now *Gringo* and Maria stood almost side-by-side, in reach of the door leading to the cargo car blocked by the small official.

Maria was tense: Why had the *Gringo* to come to her aid? Back in Venezuela, the only men who'd tried to 'help' her really just wanted sex or subservience.

Gringo focused on the porter who was not enjoying being outnumbered.

"No access when moving. She wait until Hanoi."

"Tell you what," said *Gringo*. "You don't have to do a thing. I'll let her through."

Gringo grabbed the handle and jerked the door.

The porter caught *Gringo's* arm, stopping him from getting the door all the way open. Their struggle created enough space for Maria to slip through the door.

The porter dropped *Gringo's* arm and reached for Maria.

Gringo stopped him. "Might as well let her get her case."

A few seats away, the man in the green coat pulled out his cell phone, texted.

Clack-clack-clack

In the dining car, Derek downed a gin and tonic. He'd already had a few, but knew he wasn't too drunk to do his job. Neil and Patrick recruited this veteran soldier in a bar in Iraq after a bandit gang decided not to hand over their prisoner for the ransom Neil and Patrick brought. Derek rescued the two American novice mercenaries. Patrick offered him employment. Almost dry of funds and in danger of running dry at the bar, Derek took the offer. His drinking never stopped.

The bartender looked at his watch, called out that they were fifteen minutes away from Da Nang, first in Vietnamese, then English, then French.

The other man sitting at the bar who arrived after Derek checked his cell phone texts. He was wearing the same style bulky green coat Derek had seen on a few other passengers. The coat was hardly fashionable. Derek figured it was a local trend. The man read his text, responded, and put his phone away.

Figuring that Patrick would begin to worry, Derek signaled the bartender.

"Here," Derek put money on the counter. "And get me a fresh bottle to take back to my car."

The bartender gave him as much of a disapproving look as he could get away with without risking his tip, but brought Derek a fresh bottle.

Derek opened it, took a swig, got up from his stool and headed back to his car.

As Derek passed him, the man in the green coat stood to leave.

Derek got to the door first. The man was close enough behind that Derek left the door open for him. The space between train cars was small. Hip high guardrails on each side protected the passageway from the passing scenery. The sliding doors between cars had smoky glass windows with almost no transparency but some reflection. This blurred mirror showed Derek an abrupt change in motion of the man behind him.

Derek thrust the bottle in his right hand backward. The bottle rammed into the man's thumb, made him drop a serrated combat knife he'd shoved at Derek's back.

Derek back-stepped with his right leg, shoulder-checking the stranger, knocking him off balance. Derek swung the gin bottle into his assailant's face. The man stumbled, hit the guardrail—flipped over.

Suddenly, all there was between the cars was Derek, the bottle, and the knife.

"Whoa." What could Derek do now? The man had left the train. He looked at the bottle in his numb right hand. The glass hadn't broken. Derek picked up the knife, tucked it into the front of his pants, and continued toward his companions.

Thought: Just a robbery gone wrong.

Clack-clack-clack

In the cargo car, the porter pushed past *Gringo* and Maria and rushed to the back door. He spotted a huge stained box with "Tow Chain" written on it in several languages. He opened the box, releasing a pungent odor of grease, and pulled out a large chain and an old lock with its key on a small, discolored rope loop. To the passengers' surprise, he chained the rear door shut. He tried the door. It wouldn't budge. He took the key on a rope and tied it around his belt loop. Turning back to the bewildered pair, he grinned.

"No access to back door, no throwing cargo from the train, no suicide jumper and no stowaways through back."

"Oh come on!" said *Gringo*. "That has *got* to be a safety hazard. Nobody's here to jump off a moving train."

"No matter, can't happen now. Woman, get your case and go."

Maria hurried to a shelf in the back of the cargo car and grabbed the silver combination lock case dotted with air holes.

As the three of them left the cargo car, the porter barked: "Claim ticket!"

The porter grabbed the ticket Maria showed him, then the claim tag on the case, grunted. "Take case. No coming back. Keep case until leave train."

The porter tore the claim ticket into pieces.

"Thank you." Maria turned to *Gringo*. "Thank you, too, *estranero. Gracias.*"

Maria ignored *Gringo's* smile as she hurried back toward her car.

He called after her: "Don't lose that case. After all our trouble, that would suck."

Maria didn't answer.

Behind her, she heard *Gringo* say: "And my name's not '*Estranero*.'"

But she hurried on.

As she walked past the man in the green coat, he pulled out his phone, texted.

Clack-clack-clack

The case was small enough to carry one-handed, but large enough that opening a door by herself was difficult, so when Maria arrived at their semi-private car she was relieved to see Derek approaching from the other end.

Inside their compartment Patrick was still reading, while Neil sat with his arms crossed, his legs up, an expression between a frown and a scowl. When Maria and Derek entered, he lowered his legs so they might sit, but kept his foul expression. Patrick took the case from Maria.

Derek frowned at Neil's ire. "You still whining about this lab rat delivery job?"

Patrick spoke for Neil: "No, now he's all pissy because he struck out with some European chick in another car."

"Hey, she would have loved me if I'd run my game I use in the States, but *no*: I decided to be honest. Figured I might as well tell her the truth, that I'm a bad ass mercenary."

Derek snorted.

"Wait D," interjected Patrick: "It gets better. Go on and tell them."

Neil blushed. "Not only did she think my true job was just me running a game, 'turns out she works with humanitarian aid programs, so the whole *gun for hire* thing was a minus. After that—"

Neil blinked. Stared at the combat knife thrust in Derek's belt.

Patrick and Maria noticed it too.

"How the hell did you get that?" Neil asked Derek.

"Every crook targets the American tourist. Some little guy in a green coat tried to knife me between cars. You might say he took a tumble over the side."

Patrick glared at Derek: "We don't need this. Bodies call attention, and we're supposed to be keeping a low profile. Throwing people from the train is—"

"I didn't throw him. You've seen the sorry excuse for a guardrail this train's got? Fool tumbled over on his own. He probably ain't even dead, unless he went under. Besides, in the struggle he took about a shot of my gin on his clothes, so if he is dead, he'll smell like a drunk fell off the train, 'least without a blood alcohol test, and by the time that's done, we'll be long done. We're fine."

Patrick frowned. "Bodies attract attention. Plus, I understand if you couldn't, but you should have tried to grab him. Then you might have learned why he targeted you."

"I already said why! He came in right after me, saw me putting 'em away at the bar. Little guy probably saw the moment between cars as his chance to take my wallet, throw me off the train."

"Wait," said Neil: "The little guy with the green coat who came into the bar right after you? I saw him follow you in there. He came from a private car. If he was short enough on cash to try to pull a fast one on you, why blow money on a private car?"

Worry furrowed Patrick' brow.

Derek continued: "Then he did it for the kick. Hell of a price to—"

The compartment door flew open.

A man in a green coat thrust a blade at Derek's face.

Derek barely grabbed the attacker's arm, stopping the two handed thrust. The man freed one hand from his knife and made a grab inside his coat. Patrick kicked the man's hand, pinning it against the attacker's chest.

With the speed that kept her alive in her hometown, in one smooth motion Maria jerked the knife from Derek's belt and stabbed the steel into the intruder's eye.

He dropped to the floor the compartment like a stone. Dead.

Patrick spoke first. "Close the door. Bandage the wound."

"Why?" Neil said, sliding the door closed. "It's too late."

"For him, maybe, but I don't want to wade through an inch of blood."

Patrick looked at the man's green coat. "D, you said he wasn't on the train anymore."

"This ain't the one who tried to get me."

"I know him," Maria said as she tore the dead man's shirt to bandage over his oozing eye. "He was in the last car, by the baggage car."

Patrick paused a moment. "Check the body."

Derek opened the man's coat and patted down his pockets. Found his train ticket, a silencer and the pistol he'd tried to grab.

"What the fuck?" exclaimed Neil as he took the gun from Derek. "If he was carrying, why the knife first?"

Patrick picked up the knife the man had dropped when he died and compared it to the one Maria had that Derek brought earlier: they were the same.

"I don't think this was a robbery. If he knew we came straight from the airport, unarmed, all he'd need is a knife." The phone in Patrick's pocket rang. Patrick answered the phone, said: "Why isn't this contract as simple as it should be?"

"What's going on?" Stacy asked at Patrick from their warehouse headquarters in Florida. Stacy was the group's technical support, with skills that would put her on the NSA hacker watch list if she didn't also freelance for them and other federal agencies.

"We've had two assaults by men with issued weaponry."

"Shit," said Stacy. "I called because my program monitoring old CIA short wave scanners picked up that radio traffic tripled since you guys landed. Are you on your train?"

"Yes, but I don't think we were the only ones. The guys who are after us are organized. Who would want to stop us from delivering these mice, and what's so special about them?"

"Hold on"

Patrick waited.

Maria and Derek propped up the dead man in the seat.

Derek stood with his back to the door, holding it shut.

Patrick told Stacy: "If it helps, the men who attacked us came at us with knives, even though the second one also had a silencer and gun."

"Hold on a...Oh, look at that."

"You realize I can't see what your looking at."

"Those aren't ordinary mice."

"Really."

"They are GM mice for ordinance detection. Mice that have been 'genetically modified' to react to land mines. They can clear a field three times faster then a dog team, and are small enough not to set them off. They're easier to manage and care for too. They're quite revolutionary."

"But why try to kill us over them?"

"All I have now is our employer. I knew I should have looked deeper when we took the job, simple delivery my ass. Sorry, but here's what I'm getting now:

"We were hired by a political coalition within Vietnam. The coalition is attempting to remove minefields in the north. Their main opponent is a Colonel in Vietnam's air force. The Colonel is publicly claiming that the minefields are to suppress guerrilla terrorists, but the coalition has shown that really the minefields are in place to protect poppy fields. The Colonel is probably on the take for major heroin smugglers, if he isn't one himself. And...*uh-oh.*"

"What?"

"I hacked his office e-mail. Today he approved a light equipment package release for a four-man team, with a special amendment for silencers. Sound like your guys?"

"A four-man team? Then why not come at us all at once? And why the knives?"

"Well, if you get sliced up instead of shot..."

"Then it would look like a civilian robbery gone wrong instead of a hit. Must be an individual bonus for whoever brings back the case, or they'd all have come at once. There's still two more on the train. I don't think they'll stick to knives."

"Patrick, the colonel probably knows when you arrive in Hanoi. He'll have people waiting, and now with dead bodies, he has a legitimate excuse to hold you."

Patrick hung up. He brought his fingers to his temple. The others had overhead the conversation.

Derek looked at the blood spattered green coat. "Should have known. Typical soldier thugs, even undercover, they like uniforms."

Patrick turned to Derek. "What proof are you drinking?"

"What?"

"Your drink, what proof is it?"

"85, I don't drink the cheap stuff."

"Hand it over." Patrick loosened his tie. "Maria, use the knife to pry out a couple staples or nails. Try the window frame or the upholstery. Anybody have any string or rope? Hell, dental floss will do."

"I have a cord garrote," said Neil. "It was the only weapon I could think of that I could keep while going through airports."

"Hand it over. Derek, you still smoke?"

Clack-clack-clack

Two green coat clad thugs flanked the troop's private compartment door, guns drawn. One grabbed the door handle, nodded to his partner, jerked the door open. His partner zeroed his aim. Only a bandaged man was in the compartment, slumped in the seat. The lead man entered to check the body. As he did, he caught a wiff of smoke. Suspended above the door was the gin bottle, the garrote tied to the base, wrapped over a pounded-in nail, and lashed to Patrick's tie, now a stopper for the bottle. Affixed to the doorframe via an upholstery staple was a matchbook strike pad. Fixed to the door was a match. Lit when the door was opened, the match ignited the gin-soaked tie. The flame quickly burned through the garrote cord. The cord snapped, the bottle dropped, broke open. The compartment roared into flame.

Fwoom-clack-clack

Derek, Neil, Patrick and Maria hurried toward the cargo car.

Patrick carried the bulky silver case. "If we have any luck, our green coated fellow passengers were only given basic information: a small group of Americans transporting an important case to Hanoi. They probably don't even know what's in the case. We didn't until Neil looked. They spread themselves throughout the train, so I don't think they knew which car we were in. That would mean that the two we met were the two in the back half of the train. If our luck holds, the two from the front will check our compartment as they pass."

They made it to the last public car. The porter recognized Maria and the silver case.

"No, no, not again! I told you no access when train moving!"

Not stopping, Patrick told Derek: "Take him out. Gently."

Before the porter could react, Derek grabbed him by the temples and slammed his head into the wall of the train, startling the other passengers. The porter went limp. Derek controlled his fall so he landed sitting on the rear bench. The key tied to his belt loop clinked as it hit the bench.

The door between cars flung open. A man with a burned green coat and covered in soot aimed a pistol at Maria's back—fired.

Bang-clack-clack

Gringo had seen Maria enter with the others, was about to call to her when Derek took out the porter. When the burned man charged in with a gun, *Gringo* lunged to pull Maria down—but acquired a hole in his chest.

One old lady screamed.

Maria caught *Gringo* as he fell.

Patrick ducked.

Neil fired three rounds from his scavenged pistol into the burned man's chest.

Maria held *Gringo* as he gasped for air.

"*Por que?*"

"Jimmy."

"*Que?*"

"Name. Jimmy. Thought you should know..."

Jimmy went limp.

The train whistle blew. The cars lurched, began to slow.

"Come on," said Patrick, "we have to keep moving. We don't know if the fourth one is coming. Even if he isn't, there is probably a huge welcoming committee in Hanoi. By now they likely have a description of us and the case."

Maria looked up from Jimmy's body. "We'll be trapped in the last car. The train man, he chain the back door when Mister Jim and I were back there before."

"Then we have to be prepared to fight. The opposition at the station probably won't give up without the case...or..."

Patrick blinked. "Or maybe we just give them what they want.

"You said *he* locked the back door?" Patrick pointed at the unconscious porter.

Clack-clack-skreeeeee

The train pulled into Hanoi. Military Police blocked all passenger exits. The soldiers orders, issued by top brass under an hour ago: *Find the air-holed silver combination case and arrest any American who has it.* They searched the train. Found two charred bodies in a burnt-out private compartment, a third body in the area between the last and second to last passenger cars, and a fourth body, an American. In the last passenger car, under the arm of the unconscious rear train porter, was the locked silver case with air holes.

In the last car of the train, the cargo car's rear door was barred by a tow chain. Though the chain hung slack enough to open and reach through the door, the gap was too narrow for a person. When the solders woke the porter, he said he chained it shut long before he got knocked out.

The Military Police set up barricades to contain the exiting passengers for interviews. Now in possession of the all-vital case, orders obeyed, the officers failed to notice four people walking toward the station along the tracks.

Climbing onto the platform, the three men and one woman made their way into the station. Patrick took out a key on a discolored rope and dropped it into a trashcan. As they walked to the taxi stand, a small creature poked out of Neil's cargo pants and made a jump for it. Neil caught the creature before it hit the ground and jammed the little guy back in his pants pocket.

"Fuckin' mice."

Nathan Grady's work has been published in AOL's *Politics-Daily.com*, *Huffington Post*, and the *Journal of Asian Martial Arts*. He has lived inside D.C.'s Beltway for most of his life. He comes from a creative family: His father, James Grady, is a bestselling author and contributor to this anthology, his sister Rachel Grady is an Academy Award-nominated documentarian, and his mother Bonnie Goldstein is a private eye turned journalist. Nathan, 25, is eagerly working on his career in fiction.

Tan
John Sayles

Con Tinh Tan sits in the waiting room. She avoids looking directly at the other patients. The Americans. She can see them partially reflected in the mirror that is the back pane of the fish tank. She can look past the underwater flash of lionfish, saltwater angels, yellow tangs, rock beauties, sea robins, past a ceramic replica of the Golden Gate Bridge, to watch the Americans, sitting and waiting.

There is music playing around Tan, music so quiet and without edge that sometimes it is like she is humming it to herself, though none of the songs are familiar. A single receptionist shuffles file cards at a desk. The window behind her overlooks the Golden Gate Park. The receptionist has large, blue eyes, made rounder and bluer with liner and shadow, made larger still by the tinted aviator glasses she wears. Tan wonders if the receptionist could ever keep a secret, could ever hide a fear behind such open, blue eyes.

Tan can see a small boy reflected from the fish tank, half obscured by a drowsy grouper, a small boy with a harness strapped around his head, cinching into his mouth. When he turns to talk with his mother his lips stretch far back over his gums and he looks like a small muzzled animal. He seems not to notice or care.

In 1963 Tan was thirteen and in the mornings would bicycle with her two younger brothers along the walls of Huế to the nuns' school. Her little sister Xuan went to grammar school closer to home, inside of the Citadel, and her older brother Quat crossed the river to go to high school. The nuns taught Tan poetry in Vietnamese, prayers in French, mathematics and history in English. She was a good student, which pleased Father very much. Your father expects you to do well in school, he would tell them at dinner. Only the educated person can save himself. Father never said what the person was saving himself from. Tan believed it was the lake of fire the nuns warned about, and she worked very hard.

Each night they faced the family altar to think about their ancestors, beginning with Mother. Then they'd say French prayers. All of Tan's ancestors, back as far as Father knew, had lived in Hue. But none lived and worked in. the Citadel like Father did. Father had grown up with the Ngo family, had been a high-school friend of Ngo Dinh Diem. When Diem received the Mandate of Heaven he remembered his friend, and Father was given an important job in the city government. In Tan's house Diem was always spoken of in the same tones as the ancestors. They called him the Virgin Father and he was included in Tan's nightly prayers.

Tan liked mornings best, when she could take her time riding to school, surrounded by the high walls and the moats, the tiled roofs and gardens. She could look over the walls to see the mist rising off the Perfume River, could stop and rest by the Emperor's Gate and watch the city waking up. Hue was a walled garden.

The ride home was too hurried to enjoy. Tan was the eldest daughter, responsible for dinner and cleaning. It never bothered her. If she waited around school too long the boys' section would let out and they would tease her. Monkey. Tan had an extra pair of canine teeth that pushed her upper lip out, and made her nose look fatter. Face like a monkey! the boys would cry and bicycle circles around her. Monkey-monkeymonkey.

But sometimes Tan would sit with the picture of Mother they kept on the altar and see the same teeth, the same lips and nose. It was her connection with Mother. It was her face.

Quat mostly stayed out with his friends from the high school. He came home just before dinner, tried not to get in an argument with Father, and then went out again. Father was a quiet and gentle man but Quat always managed to make him angry. Quat did well in school but didn't like the priests. Quat would speak against the priests or the government at dinner and Father would remind him where he was. They would begin to shout and Xuan would cry and then they would stop speaking to each other. Your father has work to do, Father would say to them, and move to his desk facing the far wall. Your brother is going out, Quat would say to them, and he would leave, grabbing a few last bites of food.

When they were younger Quat would sit with Tan in the walled garden behind the house and tell her stories. He told of the wars with the Chinese, and the one Tan liked best was about the Trung sisters who rose up to fight the invaders on elephant-back. She felt very safe and very peaceful, sitting inside the garden behind their house in the Citadel of the walled city of Huế. The stories Quat told were often bloody and terrible, but the Chinese had been defeated long ago.

Father arranged to have Tan's teeth taken care of. Their own dentist had said there was nothing to be done, but Father went to the Americans.

The Americans were there to fight the country people. The Virgin Father had allowed them to come. They lived in a place beyond the walls and across the river and weren't allowed to come into Huế. Tan had seen people who weren't Vietnamese, like the French priests, but she hadn't ever seen an American. She had heard stories, though, and was scared of them.

Father worked with the Americans sometimes. Sometimes he did favors for them and they returned the favors. He said they were very strange people, always laughing, like children. Father did some favors and arranged for an American dentist to work on Tan's extra teeth.

Father went with her the first time. The American was a young man who laughed and made faces for her, like a child. He was so big she didn't know how his fingers would ever fit in her mouth. He gave her shots till she could no longer feel any of her face but her eyes. She was too scared to make a sound or move. She felt that if she closed her eyes she might disappear. Though she studied English in school the American mostly used a kind of sign language with her. He slipped tongue sticks under his lip for fangs and made a deep monkey growl. Ugly. Then he yanked them out with a pair of pliers and smiled, showing all his white teeth. *Dep*. Pretty. That was what he was going to do to Tan.

Tan lay back and watched the huge fingers work over her and tried to keep her eyes open.

When she came home that first time her lip and gums were so swollen that she looked more like a monkey than ever and Father let her stay home from school for two days. Quat had an argument with Father about the Americans. But on the third day most of the swelling had gone down and Father was very pleased. He told Tan that she would go back to school, and that she would go back to the American for follow-up treatments.

She got used to eating and talking again and the boys no longer called her monkey. The nuns said it was wonderful. Tan was not so sure. Looking in a mirror, all she recognized were her eyes. The American had taken her face.

It was after the last visit to the American that Tan saw the bonze. He was trying to sit on the sidewalk just outside of the gate to the American compound. American soldiers were forcing him to move away and a crowd had gathered around. There were three or four other bonzes in the crowd, sunlight flashing off their shaven heads. Tan rode closer on her bicycle. The monks scared her, scared her even more than her Catholic nuns did. Father said that the Buddhists would never get ahead, would never move into the twentieth century, and that the monks were traitors to their people. The bonze who was trying to sit was very young, no older than Quat. Tan could see that he had let the nails on his little fingers grow long. The American soldiers pushed gently with the sides of their rifles and the bonze and the other Vietnamese moved across the bridge.

Tan followed, pedaling slowly. The crowd grew as the bonze walked through the edge of the city, they whispered and kept their eyes on him. He walked solemnly, looking straight ahead.

The bonze tried to sit in front of a huge pagoda. The people inside came out to watch but government soldiers roared up in a truck and began to push them away. The soldiers jabbed and threatened with the barrels of their rifles, and soon the bonze had to get up and move again.

He was crying a little. The crowd began to drop away. He no longer looked straight ahead, he wandered in a wide arc looking about for a place to sit. The section of town was familiar, he was leading Tan home.

He finally settled by the Emperor's Gate. He sat and began to pray and the crowd ringed around him. Three of the other monks sat to pray a few feet away from him, while another placed a metal gallon can at his feet like an offering. The bonze finished praying and dumped the contents of the can over himself. The crowd stepped back a few paces, and Tan held her breath against the fumes. The young man burst into flame.

Tan watched. No one in the crowd spoke. The bonze was the black center of a sheet of flame, he began to rock forward, began to fall, then straightened *and* held himself upright, still praying. The only sound was the burning. Tan watched and wondered if it was a sin to watch. She smelled him, meat burning now and not gasoline. He fell over stiffly on his side, a crisp sound like a log shifting in a cooking fire, and as if a spell had been broken sirens came to life and the crowd moved away. Tan pedaled home as fast as she could. She didn't tell what she had seen. She fixed dinner but couldn't eat, saying that her teeth hurt from the American.

Shortly after that the Virgin Father and his brother Nhu were murdered in Saigon. People shouted in the streets, honking horns and raising banners and the nuns kept Tan's class inside all day and told them stories of King Herod. Father was put in jail. He was a loyal friend of the Ngo family. Some government soldiers came during dinner and drove him away for questioning. Quat tried to stop them but Father told him to sit and finish his meal. He would be back after the questioning. He told them all to pray for him. The soldiers took Father away. Quat sat at Father's desk, facing the wall, and cried.

One of the office doors opens and a doctor walks into the waiting room. He nods to the boy in the face harness. The boy closes his mouth tightly and shakes his head. His mother whispers to him. He won't go. The doctor leans down next to him, talking in calm, fatherly tones. The boy's face turns red, he presses his knees together and clamps his fingers to the edge of his chair. The mother whispers through her teeth, the doctor takes hold of the boy's arm and squeezes. The boy goes with the doctor, looking to his mother like he'll never see her again.

The sergeant major darts after the Moorish idol, seeming to nip at its tail. They shoot through the tank in jumps and spurts till finally the bigger idol turns and chases the sergeant major all the way back under the shelter of the Golden Gate.

When Tan was sixteen she lived in the Phu Cam section of the right bank with Dr. Co, one of Mother's brothers. He didn't allow Tan and Quat and the other to call him Uncle. Always Dr. Co. He was older than Father. Father died in the jail from tuberculosis. A man came from the government and said that was what happened. Father was buried in the Catholic cemetery.

Most of the Catholics in Huế lived in Phu Cam. Dr. Co was political chief of their ward. He had eight children of his own and now five of his sister's to care for. The house was very crowded. Sometimes Tan rode her bicycle back into the center of town, to their old house in the Citadel. She would watch it from across the street until she saw someone moving around in it. Everything had to be sold or left behind, there wasn't even room for the family altar. Dr. Co kept Father's desk.

It wasn't good living with Dr. Co and his wife. Their children teased the younger brothers and Xuan all the time. Tan was the oldest girl and had to work hard in the house. Quat and Dr. Co hardly spoke to each other. Quat was going to Hue University with the money Father had put aside for him, money that Dr. Co thought should be used to run the combined family. Quat drove a taxi and brought some money home but it didn't seem to please Dr. Co. He said the university teachers were Communists. And that the Communists were responsible for Father's death. Quat spent much of his time with his friend Buu, who was working in the Struggle Movement. Dr. Co said the Struggle Movement was backed by the Communists, and that Quat or Buu or anyone else who got involved with the crazy Buddhists and their burnings and demonstrations would end in serious trouble. Quat never argued, he just walked away.

Tan went to the Dong Kanh girls' high school. She would ride along the river on Le Loi Street on school mornings, enjoying her freedom from the Co house. She did well in her studies and was considered one of the prettiest girls. The boys from Quoc Hoc would say things sometimes when she rode past but not in a mean way.

Dr. Co had late-night meetings at the house. All the children would be crowded into one room and Madame Co would go to sleep, but Tan had to serve the men. There were politicians from the ward and men who must have been doctors or worked at a hospital. They spent the night buying and selling medicines. Tan was tired at school the next day and she hated the way the men looked at her and made jokes when she brought them their food and drinks.

Tan tried to be obedient and agreeable in the Co house and tried to make sure everyone got enough to eat. Quat had his dinner out and the younger brothers could fight for themselves, but Xuan was small and thin and Tan had to save something out of her own bowl to give to her when the rest were sleeping. They would sit up and Tan would try to tell the stories Quat had told her, but the only one she could remember completely was about the Trung sisters. Xuan loved that one and always asked for it. Tan left off the last part, the part where the Chinese came back and the sisters had to drown themselves.

One day in the spring Tan and her classmates were let out of school early. People were milling in the streets, radios blasted news at every corner. Everyone had a different rumor about what was happening. Tan tried to bicycle home, but the way was too full of people. They were crowded around an old man carrying a radio and Quat's voice was coming from it.

Tan was excited and scared. Quat said that the Struggle Movement was coming to fruit all over the country and that here in Hue the Buddhists and their friends had control of the city. Control that they meant to keep until their demands for reform were met. After each demand that Quat read, the people in the street cheered.

It was a strange kind of control. There weren't soldiers in the streets with guns like there had been after the Virgin Father was killed. The soldiers were all staying in their barracks in the Citadel. The city-government people were staying inside too, and there was no one guarding them. There were Buddhist flags flying everywhere. The Buddhists had the radio stations and the people in the streets. Tan had never seen so many people outside at once in her life.

The people in the streets were saying that they couldn't be beaten, the soldiers in the barracks were on their side and the Americans wouldn't dare interfere. The generals in Saigon would have to have elections, for none of them had the Mandate of Heaven.

In Phu Cam people were in the streets too, but they were much quieter. Trucks drove through with loudspeakers saying not to worry, they wouldn't be hurt. No one seemed to believe them.

There was a meeting at the Co house late that night. The doctor and his politician friends from the ward were there. Quat was there, and Buu, and several other people from the Struggle Movement, including two bonzes. They talked about peace, talked about how to avoid having people get hurt. Tan listened from the next room. Buu explained how the Buddhists had control of the city, how the First Division was staying neutral and the Americans were all hiding in their compound. He explained that it was important for the city officials to cooperate if they were going to avoid violence. That much of the violence might be directed at the city officials themselves. Dr. Co and his friends pledged to do anything they could to help in the difficult times ahead.

People waited to see what would happen. There were demonstrations but no government soldiers to break them up. Tan went to school, people went to their jobs, but there *was* a feeling of waiting, that no normal routine could be taken up till the demands were resolved one way or the other.

Quat started coming home for dinner. He talked openly about politics, about what he thought should be done to choose new leaders. Dr. Co hardly spoke. Quat talked constantly and in ways that were not right in front of one's uncle. It frightened Tan. Often at night now she could hear through the wall that Dr. Co was hitting his wife. Tan felt like she did after Confession, waiting to hear the Penance the Father would give her.

The rumors came first. Ky. Ky was coming to attack them. He was coming, closer, closer. It was hard to get reliable reports. They lived in a walled city and were afraid to travel far. They waited. They wondered if the Americans would let Ky come. One night when Quat was out Dr. Co said that Ky was a good man. He might not have the Mandate of Heaven but he knew how to get things done.

Buu brought the news that General Ky was in Da Nang, fighting the people there. So close. Ky's men were fighting the soldiers who had been stationed there, were shooting civilians in the streets and in the pagodas. The Americans had helped them transport the troops and weapons. Hue would be next.

Dr. Co didn't say anything. He went to bed. Madame Co looked relieved and said maybe the best thing would be to surrender. Quat and Buu talked late into the night. The only way to *save* it, to keep the Struggle Movement alive, was if Hue could present a united front against Ky. The Buddhists and the Catholics and the soldiers in the Citadel and the city-government people—all standing together.

School ended for Tan. Ky was coming, he had cut off food and supplies. Dr. Co brought home some bags of rice and boxes of medicine one night and hid them in the attic. They were for the siege, he said. When things got really tight he would ration them out to the people in his ward. He didn't tell Quat about them. Every day people said that Ky would come tomorrow. They waited. Rumors went around about killing in Da Nang. But Da Nang was different, people said. Da Nang was crowded with refugees and Communists and Americans. The Americans walked around in the city like they owned it and dumped mountains of garbage alongside the roads. It was the kind of place you could expect a lot of killing. Ky would never dare to do the same thing in the Imperial City, would never march shooting into Hue.

A nun burned herself. Somebody burned the American library, and the American consulate. The leader of the Buddhists, Thich Tri Quang, told people to pray and be very holy. Buddhists planned to put their family altars out on the streets to stop Ky's tanks when he came. Everyone listened to the radio station. Quat spent most of his time there, and Tan heard his voice often.

One day Quat gave her a message to bring to Dr. Co. The doctor was gone when she reached home. She tried the house of one of his political friends. The friend's wife said he had left with Dr. Co, in a hurry. Tan tried the ward hall. No one was inside but an old man who said Dr. Co had been there with the other politicians but had left.

***

Tan rode into the center of Hue, to the city offices. There was no one but janitors in the City Clerk office and the District Court was empty. Tan went to the soldiers' barracks.

The soldiers were gone. The people in the streets in the Citadel said the soldiers had gotten into trucks and jeeps and driven northward out of town. Ky was to the south, in Da Nang.

Tan started back to the station. Thich Tri Quang was on the speakers telling people to stay off the streets. Ky was on this way and there was no one left to stop him. They had been betrayed. Tri Quang told people not to resist, he didn't want Buddhists killed like in Da Nang.

Before Tan reached the station the talking had stopped and there was music playing. When she arrived there were government soldiers standing guard at the entrance with their rifles pointing out.

Dr. Co came home three nights later in a very good mood. He said the traitors would be taught a lesson. He said that he was glad that order had come back to Hue. He didn't mention what he was going to do with the supplies in the attic. Quat didn't come home. Dr. Co said he must have run off to join the Communists. He was lazy, he wanted other people to do all the work, then come along and take it over. Dr. Co had a lot to drink and said more about Quat. Quat was twenty years old, he said, and yet without a wife or a job. He would never amount to anything, never be able to take care of a wife and twelve children, four of them orphans, like Dr. Co did. When Dr. Co and Madame Co went to bed there was noise, but not because he was beating her.

A week later a boy gave Tan a note from Buu. He had hidden in a Catholic church when the soldiers came and now he was going into the country. He had seen Quat captured by the icy soldiers and taken away for questioning. When Tan went to the soldiers they said she should try the city police. The city police had a record proving the existence of a Con Tinh Quat, but had no idea of his whereabouts. He was wanted for questioning.

Quat didn't come back. Sometimes late at night Tan and the younger brothers and Xuan would sit facing each other in a small circle and pray for him and cry. But quietly, so as not to wake Dr. Co.

Tan sees a little girl watching her in the fish-tank mirror. The girl is maybe five years old, sitting with her mother. One side of her face is puckered with burnt skin, a nostril and the corner of her lip eaten away. Her blond hair is tied up in pale blue ribbons. She smiles at Tan through the fish and plastic eelgrass and Tan smiles back. The little girl takes her fingers and folds her lids down to make thin eyeslits like Tan's. The mother looks up from her magazine and gives the girl a quick slap on the wrist.

Tan was eighteen. It was very early morning, only a few hours into the Year of the Monkey, when she was wakened by the popping. Close, a sporadic hollow popping and flashes like heat lightning in the sky. Dr. Co had just come back from a Tet party at the ward hall, he was still in his rumpled street clothes when he wandered out from his bedroom. It was monsoon season and had been drizzling on and off all night. Dr. Co held newspapers over his head and went out. He came back without the papers, hair plastered to his head, looking very pale. The Communists were attacking all over, he said—trying to take over the city. It would be best to stay in and wait for the Americans to come out of their compound and chase the Communists away.

They sat in the dark, no one sleeping, no one speaking, and listened to the popping. The sounds grew very close, the house shuddered a few times, and then they moved away. That was the Americans, said Dr. Co from the corner he was huddled in. When the ground shakes like that it is the Americans chasing Communists with their big guns.

At dawn Dr. Co and Tan went out to look. It was very quiet, raining lightly. Soldiers walked in the street carrying rifles— Vietnamese soldiers. They weren't the ones from the Citadel though. These men wore khaki uniforms and green-and-red armbands, and called to each other in the rapid dialect of northerners. Dr. Co hurried Tan back inside.

Dr. Co sent Madame Co and the young children to shelter at the Phu Cam Cathedral, a little ways across the railroad tracks. The soldiers wouldn't bother a woman and children. Tan had to stay and help him gather their valuables. When it was dark they would try to reach the Cathedral.

Now and then Dr. Co had Tan peek into the street. There were people with rifles in everyday clothes, and the people with their hair in buns, the country people in black pajamas. The popping and explosions came from up by the American compound now, and from the walled city across the river. The Communists were in control of Phu Cam.

Dr. Co cursed the Saigon generals and the Americans. This was what came of declaring a truce with the Communists. Dr. Co gathered his papers and money and some of the medicines he had stored in the attic. Ever since the Struggle Movement failed, Dr. Co had been bringing home supplies and storing them in the attic. Things he said the Americans had given him. He put the medicines and a few cartons of cigarettes in his suitcases, but he left the American ham and beef upstairs.

In the early evening someone pounded on the door. Dr. Co told Tan to say he had gone to the hospital to treat casualties, and ran up into the attic. The pounding continued, someone yelled that they should come outside, that no one would be harmed. Dr. Co was called by name. Tan sat on the floor, too scared to answer the pounding. It stopped. After several quiet hours Dr. Co came down.

They tried to sneak out late at night. At the railroad tracks someone called for them to stop and searchlights came on. Dr. Co ran into the darkness and Tan tried to follow. The suitcase she'd been given was heavy and when she heard men close behind her she had to drop it and scurry away. Tan spent an hour squatting in the shelter of a small pagoda and then found her way home. Dr. Co slapped her for leaving the suitcase behind. How would the family eat, he asked, now that she had thrown all their money away? Tan saw no sign of the suitcase Dr. Co had been carrying.

They lay on mats in the children's room, several feet of darkness between them. They didn't speak for over an hour. Neither slept. Then there was pounding on a door down the street. Voice shouting. Screaming, and a shot, very loud, very close, and a woman wailing on the street. Pounding on a door, closer. Dr. Co came over and lay by Tan, putting his arms around her. She couldn't tell which one of them was shaking so hard. Pounding right next door, more shots, more crying. Tan held her breath. She felt Dr. Co's heart beating against her back. The pounding came again, on the other side of the house. They had been passed over. The pounding moved on down the street.

Tan felt Dr. Co's breath hot on the back of her neck. He pushed his face through her hair and kissed her there. She was the one shaking now, she was sure of that. He rolled her onto her belly and pulled her clothes up. The northerners were near, she couldn't cry out. She couldn't think who she would cry to.

Tan felt crushed under his weight, the matting dug into her breasts. She tried to think of prayers. She was glad she didn't have to see his face. Tan bit her lip against the pain and he pushed into her from behind. That evening, frightened by the pounding, she had forgotten and not called him Dr. Co, had not even called him Uncle. Father, she had said, what will we do?

Dr. Co lay still on top of her when he had finished. He lay so still and so long that Tan thought he must have fallen asleep. But then he rolled off her and she groped her way to where she could wash herself. Tan sat shivering under her father's desk until dawn.

It rained heavily all morning and the fighting sounds were muffled. Dr. Co didn't meet her eyes or speak. When Tan looked out she saw a few of the country people riding by on bicycles. They didn't seem to notice how wet they were getting.

The pounding came in the afternoon. Dr. Co was called by name. He went up in the attic to hide. The people outside said they would start shooting if no one came out. Tan opened the door.

There were country people and a few people dressed in city clothes. They all wore red armbands. One was a girl who went to the Dong Kanh high school with Tan, a very pretty, popular girl. She wore a pair of pistols in her belt. Another of the people was Buu.

He looked much older. He held a clipboard in a hand with only one finger and a thumb on it. He pretended he didn't know Tan.

Buu asked where Dr. Co was. Tan said he had gone to the hospital. Buu said they knew that wasn't true. The people stood in the house, dripping, and told her not to be afraid, they were here to protect the Vietnamese from the Americans and the Saigon generals. Tan was too frightened to speak. Father, her uncle, the nuns in school—all had told of the terrible things that the Communists did to people.

Buu sat on the ladder leading to the attic and asked if they were hoarding meat in the house. Tan shook her head. Buu said he had learned about decay since he had been away from the city. If you lived too close to it you never noticed the smell, but any outsider could tell right off that things were rotten. Buu led the people up into the attic and they found Dr. Co hiding behind containers of American beef.

Dr. Co cried and pleaded. They bound his hands behind his back with wire, told him not to worry. They were only taking him for questioning. Buu told Tan to stay in the house until told what to do by the People's Army. The country people carried the meat out into the rain. Dr. Co didn't say good-bye.

Tan dressed in black and waited for night. There was no trouble at the railroad tracks and she reached the Phu Cam Cathedral. Women inside were wailing, beating their faces with their hands. There were no men. No men and almost no boys.

The Communists had come that morning, sobbed Madame Co, and had taken all the men and boys away. Just to a political meeting, they said, and then they would be brought back. They had taken Madame Co's four sons and Tan's two brothers. No one had returned. Xuan had volunteered to go for help to the government soldiers. She knew her way in the Citadel.

Tan told Madame Co her husband had gone to work at the hospital.

She started after Xuan in the morning. Rain beat down and there was fighting everywhere. She ran north toward the river, ducking between buildings when the fighting came close. She saw northern soldiers. She saw Americans. Loudspeakers said the People's Army was winning. A sound truck blared that the government soldiers were in control.

Tan was knocked to the pavement by an explosion. Her head hurt. She went on. Somebody shot at her. She felt the bullet pass, dove to the ground and cut her hands open. She stumbled onto a man lying dead in a puddle on the street. Tan crawled off him and ran for the river. The fight roared around her, trucks burning, houses burning, flames sizzling up to meet the rain. Tan saw blood running through the gutters with the rain. A flying piece of brick hit her, her side burning, and an old man fell in front of her, bleeding, tangled with his bicycle. It was the lake of fire the nuns had told of, it was the Day of Atonement. Her head hurt. Tan ran upright down the middle of the street, knowing only that she had to reach the river.

The bridge was gone. There was no way back to the Imperial City. Her head hurt. She had to get across. She held her head in her hands, tried to remember. She was the sister of—there was someone floating by in the water, facedown. She was the daughter of—the water was gray, its surface alive with rain. Glowing embers blew from the fires in the walled city and died as they landed on the water. She held her head and sat on the bank of the Perfume River, trying to remember who she was.

The air conditioner blows on Tan, her nipples stand up and hurt a little. She folds her arms across her breasts. They are so big, so hard, since the Chinese doctor did them. She is a tiny, thin woman with huge breasts. She wonders if they'll ever be small again, be soft. If she gives him her eyes maybe he'll let her have her body back.

There are pictures on the wall. Chins pushed back or strengthened, noses straightened and reduced, harelips mended. Oriental eyes made round. Before and After, say the pictures.

When Tan went back to the Co house it was full of government soldiers hiding from their commanding officer. They sat half-naked on the floor with their clothes hanging to dry, eating what was left of the food, cooking on a fire made from Father's desk. They called for Tan to come in and sleep with them. She ran. The Americans and Communists fought in the Bien Hoa suburb to the north. The Americans built a pontoon bridge and Tan crossed with thousands of other homeless people. The people said the Americans would feed them.

Tan wandered in the walled city, looking for Xuan, looking for food. Thousands wandered with her. The walls had crumbled under the bombing, half the houses were knocked down. People looted what they could before the soldiers came back. The soldiers had guns and took the best of everything.

The sun came out for one day and the bodies in the streets began to stink. Families, dressed in white for mourning, made circular graves for their dead in the red earth of the parks and school yards. The bodies were wrapped in black cloth, then in white, and buried in the mud. The Americans wrapped their dead in green plastic bags and left them on the curb for trucks to pick up.

Tan found Madame Co at a refugee center the government soldiers had set up. There was no food. Dr. Co had been found with his hands still bound behind his back, buried alive. There was no word of Madame Co's sons or Tan's brothers. No word of Xuan.

Tan wandered in the monsoon. Sometimes Americans would give her food. She was afraid to approach them alone, but joined groups of begging children. Tan found the men gave more if she talked like the little children. Hey, you, GI, she would call, you numba one. You give gell to eat, yes?

The Americans would smile if they weren't too tired and hand out a little food. People cooked what they could beg or steal right on the street, in water pots made from artillery shells.

The first time Tan saw Supply Sergeant Plunkett he was wrapped around a case of Army K-rations. He grinned at her as he hurried across the rubble, rattling his cans of beans and processed ham. Care for a bite? Tan was too hungry to be scared. His legs were so long that she had to run to keep up with him.

You, me, pom-pom, he said to her in the abandoned house they sheltered in. Boom-boom. Fuckee-fuckee?

He seemed very pleased when she didn't understand what he meant.

You vir-gen gell?

She told him she was.

Vay good. Me show you boom-boom. Then you eat. Beaucoup food.

He did what Dr. Co had done to her, but he looked her in the eyes afterward and smiled.

You no vir-gen now. You Plunkett gell.

Tan smiled back at him like she had learned from the young children, smiled and said you numba-one GI. Numba-one boom-boom. Me eat now?

The Communists disappeared and bulldozers came to bury the walls and buildings that had been blown down. Tan went with Plunkett to Da Nang. He would give her money. If the Communists had taken her brothers and Xuan she would become wealthy enough to buy them back.

Plunkett set her up in a house on the edge of the sand flats in Da Nang, close to the refugee camps. There were four other girls who had American soldiers. Plunkett paid her rent and gave her money for food and clothes. She sewed most of it into a chair. It was nice having the other girls to talk to, there was a mama-san to keep the house and always enough food. Plunkett visited at least twice a week.

There was garbage everywhere in Da Nang, small mountains of it that little boys fought and played on. People in the camps sat all day waiting for food, crowded together like insects. There were girls on the streets, country girls who had sold eggs and produce in the market before the fighting. Buy me, buy me, they said. Me numba-one gell, suckee-suckee, six-hundred pi.

Plunkett would come to drink and for boom-boom. He liked how thin her body was, how her breasts barely stuck out. My little girl, he called her. He asked if she had a little sister he could meet. Tan said she had no sisters. He showed pictures of his little daughters back in America. Plunkett didn't like the name Tan, he called her Betsy. It was the same name as one of his daughters.

He smiled and laughed constantly, like a child. He said he didn't like her eyes. They looked like she was hiding something from him. You trick me, he would say. Alla time same-same. You Betsy unscrutable gell. He gave her money to have the round-eye operation like Madame Ky, like the other girls in the house. She sewed it in the chair.

Tan had been in Da Nang three months when the word came about the men and boys taken from the Phu Cam Cathedral. Their bones were found buried together in the jungle a few miles from Hue. Most shot, some buried alive. Over four hundred men and boys. Plunkett gave Tan money to send to care for her brothers' bones.

Her belly grew. The other girls noticed first, then Plunkett. He was very angry and took her to his friend Dr. Yin.

Dr. Yin was Chinese and smelled of ammonia. Tan was terrified. Plunkett reassured her that Dr. Yin was an American, a soldier, and his friend. But Chinese was Chinese. Tan screamed and had to be given a shot when the young doctor approached her.

She was thin again then, but Plunkett didn't seem to like her so much. He brought her a Catholic-schoolgirl's uniform, like she had worn when she was little, and had her put it on for the boom-boom. Sometimes he made her bend over so he could hit her with his belt. He didn't smile or laugh so much anymore.

Plunkett left things at the apartment, medicines, food, sometimes guns. He ordered Tan not to touch them. She listened for hours to the American radio he had given her. She would lie in the dark at night twisting the dial back and forth, listening to all the different languages, all the voices blending into each other. She felt like she was floating, hearing everyone's private thoughts. When she woke the batteries would be dead and she'd be without radio till Plunkett came. He always had batteries with him.

Tan was twenty, had been in Da Nang two years, when she saw her sister on the street. Two Americans were walking with their Vietnamese girls. One of them was Xuan. She looked like all the other street girls, looked like she could take care of herself. Her American called her Sue-Anne. Tan followed, listening to her sister laugh at what the Americans were saying, and then let them walk out of sight. A moment later she thought better of it and tried to catch up, but Xuan had turned some corner and was gone.

Plunkett said he would send Tan to America. She would help him be a rich man. He explained that in America opium was used just like money, better than money. But government police would steal it from you, just like in Vietnam. It was hard to bring opium to America, but Tan could help him.

He took her back to his friend Dr. Yin. They explained how much just a little opium was worth if it was pure. She watched the doctor put it into the implants. They would be like a cyst, he said, like a thorn that the skin grows over. Harmless.

Tan lay on the slab and remembered all the stories Quat had told her. Dr. Yin put her under. She dreamed of riding a bicycle in a quiet, walled city.

When she woke her breasts felt mammoth, they jutted out stiffly from her body. The skin was stretched taut, the nipples pointing up and out. There was a scar in the crease beneath each breast, creases she had never had before. The breasts didn't feel a part of her. They belonged to Plunkett. He loved to grab them in bed. The future is in my hands, he would say, and smile like he used to.

He arranged for her to go to the American city of San Francisco. He would come later. Tan was afraid to tell him about the money she had hoarded, afraid he wouldn't understand. It was in piasters, and wouldn't be any good in America. It wasn't opium. The day before the plane took her, Tan ripped the money out of the chair and gave it to the other girls in the house.

It would be good in San Francisco, she thought. No one was fighting and there was always enough food.

A nurse, a young American girl, calls Tan into the office. She is seated in a leather reclining chair. Doctor is in the back washing his hands, says the nurse, I'm his assistant. The nurse asks Tan if she is sure she wants to go through with the eye operation, says she is a very pretty woman already. Tan says she wants to go ahead. The nurse leaves.

There are more pictures on the walls inside the office. Before and After pictures, profiles of breasts enlarged or made smaller. A picture of the doctor in Army fatigues sitting on a pile of sandbags. Tan closes her eyes, tries to steady her heartbeat.

Tan lived in a bad-smelling Mission Street hotel run by an old Thai man. The rent seemed high, but that was something the nuns hadn't taught about in English. Tan avoided talking to anyone, she took all her money with her if she went out and never walked more than a few blocks from the hotel. She waited for Plunkett.

A young brown-skinned woman with a little baby lived in the next room. Sometimes at night she would play her radio, slow, sad songs in Spanish to keep her baby from crying. Tan would lie in bed, listening through the wall, and think how nice it would be if she could be friends with the woman.

Tan waited. Her American money began to run out. She ate rice at a Vietnamese restaurant on Powell Street. On the sign out front was a map of Vietnam with the northern half painted red and the southern half painted green and all the major cities labeled. Young American men would come by with their girls and point to spots on the map, but very few came inside. Mr. Thuong, who ran the restaurant, would talk with Tan while she ate. He had come to America during the fighting between the French and the Communists. He seemed very kind, but Tan was careful not to tell much about herself. Her bill never came to what it said on the menu.

Tan waited in her room on Mission Street. She was afraid. Afraid of the Americans, afraid of being alone, afraid of being caught with the opium. They had searched her when she got to the Hawaii airport, a woman had put her hands up in Tan's private parts.

Plunkett wrote her a letter saying when he was coming. He wrote in the child-language he had used to talk with her. It was very hard to read. Tan went to the docks to meet him.

Passengers came off the big boat, but Plunkett was not among them. Tan asked a man from the boat, who took her to a policeman. The policeman said that Plunkett had been taken for questioning. He asked Tan's name and address and she gave him false ones. Plunkett never showed up at the hotel. Questioning meant the same thing in America that it did in Vietnam.

Mr. Thuong gave Tan a job at the restaurant when her money was gone. She made salads in the kitchen and tried to avoid the busboys and dishwashers, who were all Chinese. Mr. Thuong couldn't pay her much, she didn't have a Green Card, but if she ate at the restaurant she had enough to pay her rent.

One of the waitresses, a Korean girl named Kim, was friendly to her. Kim had another job, being a girl in a Chinese bar on Pacific Street. The Chinese men would come in a little drunk and Kim would sit by them and talk and they would buy her drinks. It made more money for the bar. The Chinese tried to do more and you could make extra. Kim let them touch her breasts. Kim said she was willing to sell her breasts but nothing beyond that. The girls in the bar were all Koreans and had American boyfriends or husbands. They had come over from their country with soldier husbands. Kim said it would pay much more than making salads, said the Chinese men would like Tan. She was small and delicate but had big breasts for them to touch.

Kim told her to have the round-eye operation. If she ever wanted to get an American boyfriend, to be able to become a citizen and get papers so she could have a nice job, she would have to have her eyes changed. That was how they wanted it. Tan said she was interested, but kept putting it off.

One morning Mr. Thuong came out from listening to the news and began to paint the bottom half of the Vietnam map red. There were tears in his eyes as he painted. At least, he said, it is all the same color now. It was that morning Tan decided for the operation.

Kim showed her the ad for the plastic surgeon in the yellow pages, a big ad with a picture of the doctor. Tan recognized his face.

Tan lies in the reclining chair wondering what he'll do. If he'll remember her. If he'll steal it from her or give her to the police. But one way or the other, she'll be free of it. The last of Vietnam locked inside her, next to her heart, will be gone.

The doctor comes in rubbing his hands on a towel. Tan catches her breath, tries to look calm. She wonders what she'll do when her eyes are round and unguarded.

Hello Tan, says Dr. Yin. I've been expecting you.

John Sayles began his career writing fiction, including the novels *Pride of the Bimbos*, *Los Gusanos*, and *Union Dues* (a nominee for the National Book Award), as well as the short story collections *The Anarchists' Convention* and *Dillinger in Hollywood*. This led to work in Hollywood, penning such cult classic screenplays as *Piranha*, *Alligator*, and *The Howling*. As a director, he has been a seminal force in American independent film with such classics as *The Return of the Secaucus 7*, *Matewan*, *Lone Star*, and *Eight Men Out* (to name only a few). 2014 will see the production of his 18th directorial work, *Go for Sisters*. More information can be found http://johnsaylesblog.com.

The Mermaids of Clintonville
Will Huston

Marina turned twenty-one yesterday. The celebration with co-workers wasn't much, modest at best. A plain yellow cake. No icing. And two wax stubs posing as candles. But that was life here, the kind of life that one grows accustomed to after years of civil war. The war was over now, it had been for a few months, but the effects were still in full tilt. Stores and pubs were open but mostly for show. Shelves empty, cupboards bare. If you wanted something stronger than coffee you drank homemade rakija. The sputtering economic engine of post-war Serbian life was fueled by the street merchants, their thread bare blankets spread out on the sidewalks, littered with cheap bangles and bobbles from China, pirated CDs and DVDs from the West, Turkish cigarettes, and whatever unrotted food could be scrounged from outside the back doors of government mess kitchens, provided the packs of mongrel dogs weren't competing for it. One had to make do with whatever was at hand. Until yesterday, none of this really concerned Marina. Until yesterday, everything, including her mother and young son, was taken care of. But today was different. Today, after six years, Marina was out of a job.

She woke early, thankful that she had been allowed to spend one last night. She quickly gathered up the scant belongings in her cubicle. Then, without fanfare or good-byes as to not wake the others, Marina walked through the building one last time and met Lubija at the front door. Lubija had been kind to her. Not in a maternal sense, but protective nonetheless. That protection profited them both very well during Marina's time there. Sometimes the soldiers or police would get a little rough with the girls. Sometimes beyond rough. But Lubija would have none of it. And she paid the authorities very well to see that no harm came to her stable. Sure, there had been an incident or two. The occasional girl injured, or dead, but that was rare exception to the rule. Besides, if a guy wanted to get rough or kinky, he could always visit the mermaids of Clintonville. In Clintonville nothing was out of bounds.

***

"I wish you could stay, Marina, but you know the rules." Lubija said as she pressed the ten hundred dinar bills into her hand. Marina took the severance pay and yes, she knew the rules. Once a girl reached her twenty-first birthday she was considered too old to work the brothels. The soldiers, cops, politicians, and diplomats liked them young. That's why she ended up here in the first place. She was young. Fifteen, in fact. Marko had just been born and she needed to find a way to care for him. Marina wasn't sure who the father was. How could she? The nearest candidate she could narrow it down to was one of the six Croat soldiers who grabbed her off the streets, took her to a back alley and proceeded to joyously rape and beat her for over twelve hours. They left her there. It took another twelve hours to limp the eight blocks home to her parent's flat.

When her mother found out what happened she wanted to disown Marina, the shame brought to the family would be too much. But in the end she didn't. Shame to what family? Two years earlier, on Christmas Eve, her father complained aloud on the job about the eleventh hour notice that he would have to work at the power plant for part of the holiday. After finishing his shift he called to see if he needed to bring anything home. He was last seen alive when he stopped for milk at the local magazin. Two days later he was found face down in a drainage ditch next to his car, a bullet to the back of the head. The milk bottle was lying next to him, empty, unbroken. Her brother, Dzjura, didn't fare much better. He got caught up in the patriotic zeal that disguised the real cause of the war and enlisted in the infantry. Four weeks after boot camp a sniper's seven point six two found its way into his chest. No benefits, no life insurance.

Marina had to find a way to make ends meet. And she had to find a way fast. A new mother at fifteen doesn't have a lot of choices or skills to rely on. The only thing she felt she knew how to do was what she learned from the at the hands of whomever Marko's father was and his companions. So, she went to Lubija's and became very good at it. So good in fact, that she quickly became quite popular. The highest rollers from the local military and government asked for her first. But no more. She was too old. At twenty-one. She looked into Lubija's indifferent eyes one last time. "Good luck, Marina."

Marko felt good in her arms as he slept. It was nice to feel the warmth of his little boy body next to hers. Nice to smell the little boy smell of his hair. Nice to hear the airy metronome of his little boy lungs. It had been over five years since they had done this together for any longer than a few minutes on the Sunday visits they had at Lubija's. Now she could bask in the comfort of being with her little boy as much as she wished. It was a dreary comfort but a comfort nonetheless. She wished for eternity. She also wished to shed tears, tears of joy. But tears were something she left mixed in the pool of blood and semen in the grime of some random back alley seven years ago. Eternity was cut short by the knock on the bedroom door, her mother reminding her that she had to be in the bread line before seven. Being late for the bread line was a harsh affirmation of you snooze, you lose. Marko stirred from the noise. She gave him a reassuring hug to let him know he was fine right where he was. She kissed his forehead and cooed a motherly goodbye into his ear. He cooed back. That made her smile. It didn't make Mother smile.

Marina felt almost alien as she walked home, the bread in hand. She hardly recognized the place any more. A neighborhood once bursting with life and color was now devoid of any such pleasures. The blue sky replaced by gray, laughter and music replaced by sobs of despair and the whistle of the biting wind. Pastel building facades were painted over in gray. Even the people were gray. Everywhere, everything, everyone, gray. "How could this happen?"

When Marina came in her mother already had Marko up and dressed. Mother had been dressing him every morning for nearly his entire life. She had no intention of handing the duties over to this newly arrived intruder. Marina set the bread on the counter, then took a DVD from her coat. She had picked it up from one of the thread bare blanket vendors on the way home. She offered it to her son but Mother intercepted. "He already has this one." The chill was as icy here as it had been waiting in the bread line. She took a knife from the drawer and cut into the bread. Two slices each. She spread one with lard, the other with fruit preserves. Food at Lubija's was never this meager. "Want some tea with this, Mom?", she asked as she served breakfast. "That would be nice." "What about you, baby?" Marko nodded yes.

Marina turned the electric burner on high, quickly filled the kettle, then returned it to the stove. She had to hurry as it was ten minutes 'til eight. At eight the power would go off for four hours, then on for the next four, off four, on four, and so on. Forever. At seven fifty-eight the kettle whistle violently shattered the silence. While she prepared the tea she thought of how it would take time to reestablish herself. But just like the power intervals, time was precious and finite. She had to do something, and do it quick, or they would all be out on the streets. One had to make do with whatever was at hand. And that hand was time, each tick dimming the lights of what few rays of hope there may be. Mother's unexpected reception didn't help either. In truth, Marina didn't know how her mother would react to her return, but hostility was near the bottom of the list of unknown expectations.

The school bus rattled and squeaked as it pulled away, leaving Marina and Mother blanketed in a belched out cloud of diesel fumes. By the time the smoke cleared the bus and Marko were out of sight. "Let's go back inside before we freeze," Mother said. "We need to talk." Marina had other plans. "You go, mom. I have something I need to do." When her mother wanted to know what that something was Marina balked. "Go. I'll be back. And we'll talk. I promise." Like so many times in the past, Mother didn't like Marina's attitude. But she accepted it. And at that moment she had a realization. Her daughter was no longer a defenseless little girl. She was a woman. A woman with resolve. This softened Mother's attitude a bit. "Okay. I'll be here when you get back."

Vlad, a weasel-eyed bear of a man, was playing poker with a couple of his underlings in a back corner of the dusky bistro. Before the war he had done quite well in what could kindly be called the information business. How many dozens of people were imprisoned or executed due to his observations was unclear. But it was a lot. Rumor had it that he may have played a hand in the Christmas deaths of some disgruntled power plant workers. Spying on your neighbors was big business back then. When the conflict broke out he shifted his occupation to facilitation. You needed something, he could get it for you. Didn't matter what but he preferred the basics, weapons and drugs. Vlad had made a lot of connections over the years and that's why Marina came looking for him in the dingy yellow air of the coffee house. "Would you like something? Espresso? Rakija? Whatever you like." Marina wasn't there for socializing. She came right to the point.

"I understand you know the General."

Her directness took him by surprise. "I might. How does that concern you?"

"I want to meet him."

"Why?"

"I want to be a mermaid."

This surprised him even more. "Do you know what you're saying?"

"I know exactly what I'm saying."

"But you don't have the qualifications."

"I know that. But that's my concern, not yours."

"Five hundred dinars."

Marina took what she had left from her severance at Lubija's and laid it on the table. "I'll see what I can arrange," Weasel-eyes snarled as he clawed the money and stuffed it into his shirt pocket. "Come back tomorrow." He focused on her ass as she navigated through the tables on her way out. That made him leer. "Nice, huh?" It made his underlings drool.

After they finished their ham and cheese sandwiches Mother told Marko to go get ready for bed. "I'll be in to tuck you in." After the boy left the room, Marina chided Mother. "I'm here now, Mom. I should be the one doing the tucking. I mean he's my son, not yours."

Mother bristled. "Oh, really? What kind of mother does what you did? Lying on your back, selling your dignity is hardly what I would call being a good parent. Who was it that changed his diapers, heard his first words, watched him take his first step, picked him up when he fell? That was me. Not you. Me."

"Selling my dignity, as you call it, put clothes on your backs, fed you, and kept you warm with a roof over your head. That's more than I can say you ever did for me."

The wounds of having lost the men of the house were still fresh for both of them. While Marina's father was alive Mother didn't have to worry about providing. And she didn't have to worry about providing during Marina's years at Lubija's either. Marina was right. But it hurt. Marina could see that, too. "I'm sorry, Mom. I didn't mean to be so cruel, but what would we have done if I didn't make the sacrifice I did? It's not like I wanted to."

"We could have done something."

"Like what?"

Mother had no answer. She sat there, deflated. "So what do we do now? Two weeks and rent is due."

"I'm working on something. I'll know more about it tomorrow."

"Mee-maw," Marko called out from his room.

"You go."

"You're not upset?"

"He's your son, not mine."

Marina got up to go tuck the little boy in. Sitting alone in the near dark, Mother sobbed.

"Sit. Please." Marina took the invitation. "Would you like something? Espresso? Rakija? Whatever you like." She shook her head. Vlad dismissed the underlings so he and Marina could speak alone.

"I spoke with the General. He agreed to consider your request."

"And?"

"And, since you don't have the right qualifications you have to tryout. You understand what I'm saying?"

"Of course I do."

"You have more courage than most, I'll give you that."

Marina could care less about Vlad's praise. She was there to get this done. "When can I meet him?"

"Five hundred dinars."

"I already gave you five hundred."

"That was for me to relay your request. It's another five hundred for instructions."

Her heart sank. "I don't have it."

Weasel-eyes smirked.

"A rakija now if you don't mind." she said. "A double." She was counting on the homemade hooch to make her woozy.

He lasted no more than twenty seconds. Marina was thankful for that. She was also thankful that he kept it clinical, taking her from behind as she bent over the rear boot of the car. She pulled her panties up from around her ankles as Vlad took out a Gitane and lit it, then tucked his penis back into his pants. She laughed to herself, amused by the smallness of his manhood. She wasn't even sure if he had entered her. She was right about that double shot of *rakija*. Not only did it make her woozy, it numbed the sadness of the situation.

"Six tomorrow morning on the west side of the building."

"Do I tell them anything?"

"No. No need. Who else would show up there so early? He had a point. "They'll know who you are and what you're there for. You know where it is?"

Of course she knew where it was. Everybody knew where Clintonville was.

"Maybe, if you make the tryout, I will come see you."

"You have that kind of money?"

"No. Maybe you give me a discount."

She laughed. "This was your discount."

"Good luck, bitch," he growled as Marina turned, leaving the large man and his small penis behind.

The lights came on, telling Marina and her mother that it was eight. Marko was already in bed so she could tell Mother about her plans without fear of him overhearing. "I have a tryout in the morning. At Clintonville." Mother didn't know much about the sex trade in the area but she sure as hell knew about Clintonville. Everybody did. Even though the American president was responsible for countless bombing raids on them he was forgiven due to the reputation of his sexual appetite. And because of that sexual appetite the Serbs embraced him as being a normal man. Just like them. They understood that his position of power had provoked the bombings. That was part of his job. But he was forgiven because he, like them, loved sex. They loved that he loved sex because they loved sex, too. It was only fitting that the most expensive whorehouse in the country, housing the most desired women, be named after America's most famous pussy hound. They were sure he would feel honored.

Mother listened in horrified disbelief as Marina recounted what she was going to have to do to become a mermaid. Neither of them had ever known anyone else who had sought to work at Clintonville. That was because if you did pass the tryout you were never seen again, except by the brothel's clients. If you didn't pass, you more than likely died in the process. "If I can do it, money will never, ever be a problem again, Mom. We will all be taken care of. I've heard that I can make ten times what I did at Lubija's. You and Marko will never want for anything again."

Mother nearly choked on her next question. "But what happens if you don't?"

"I don't know the answer to that. I just know that I love you and I love my baby. And someone's got to provide. If I can't take care of my family, then what good am I?" There wasn't much more to say so they sat there until the power went off. Marina lit a candle. She grabbed Mother's hand and squeezed it gently. "Don't worry, Mom. Whatever happens will be for the best." It sounded like a cliché but it wasn't meant to be. Marina stood and kissed her mother on the forehead. "Goodnight." She stepped to the doorway. "Mom."

"Yes?"

"I meant it when I said love you."

"And I love you, Marina."

Marina disappeared into the hallway. Sitting there in the near darkness, Mother sobbed. A few minutes passed before she got up to go to bed herself. She picked up the candle to light the way to her room. She stopped at Marko's door and peeked in. She was overwhelmed to see her daughter and grandchild wrapped in each others' arms. Marina may have been a disappointment in the past, but not now, not here. Mother could see that Marina loved her baby more than anything in the world. And that that is the way it should be. It pained her to think that she would never see Marina again. She quietly pulled the door shut and went on to bed.

The General was already there when she arrived fifteen minutes early. He had two junior officers with him, along with a distinguished looking older civilian man holding a medical bag. "Good morning. We've been expecting you. Turn around please."

She did so.

"Vlad was right. You do have a nice ass." The men chuckled in agreement. The General wasn't really a general. In the war he was a sergeant assigned to oversee the hospital for war-wounded women. Most of the victims would not have survived transport so instead of taking the wounded to the hospital, the hospital was taken to the wounded. It started as a large tent but had since been replaced by an actual two story brick and mortar building. It was expensive to care for the victims and most of the money had to go to support actual combat operations. Barely any left for medical expenses. So the sergeant came up with a very lucrative and enterprising idea to make the hospital pay for itself.

"So, what do you want me to do?"

"It's very simple. All you have to do is go to the front door."

"I don't understand."

"Don't worry, you will. Just walk to that door. It's only thirty steps."

***

She stood there in the cold dawn, not wanting to do what she was about to do. But she had to do it. Was she going to die? Was it going to hurt? A memory came to her. A memory that gave her faith that she was doing the right thing. It was the memory of a song, a child's song that she loved to sing and have sung to her. It was from an old American movie that her mother took her to see when she was Marko's age. She never had the chance to share the movie with him; the vendors never had a copy of it. She remembered how the song always brought her hope. Hope was abundant until the war came and brought the brutish opportunists who exploited anyone and everyone for their own gain. She sang it silently to herself as she prepared to walk the short distance to Clintonville: "*Somewhere over the rainbow, way up high.*'" This made her feel good; that everything would turn out as she wished.

She was ready now.

"'*There's a land I've always heard of, once in a lullaby.*'"

She took the first step. Then the next. And the next. So focused. Oblivious to the men behind her. Laying down bets. Calling out numbers.

"Two."

"Eight."

"Ah, no. Fourteen

Back when the war was raging, the sergeant's idea to turn patients into prostitutes was considered bold and brilliant. After all, the women couldn't go anywhere, nor did they have the ability to defend themselves. It was the perfect business opportunity.

Word spread like wildfire about the place and when he considered the instant riches he took in, the sergeant felt entitled to start calling himself the General. His time in the military had taught him that those in the highest positions with the most wealth were also those with the most perverse of deviant sexual fantasies. The more perverse the better, price be damned. And deviance with a mermaid of Clintonville cost a fortune. Just the thought of sex with a limbless woman drove the power brokers crazy.

Living. Breathing. Sex toys.

When the war ended, the General saw no reason to close shop. The mermaids had nowhere to go and couldn't really take care of themselves, so it made perfect sense to stay in business. And business was even bigger and better than ever. If he wanted to call himself the General, who cares? They didn't care if he wore the garb either. As long as he supplied the demand he could wear any damned thing he pleased.

"Mom!" Marina screamed. It was too late. Mother was well into the minefield by the time Marina got there. "It's okay. It's okay, sweetheart. Everything is going to be fine. You'll see." It was then that Marina realized that another mother loved her baby more than anything in the world. The way it should be.

For Amy

Will Huston is a filmmaker, author, and self-proclaimed assessor of human behavior whose work has taken him around the globe. His time in the post-war Balkan Peninsula inspired "The Mermaids of Clintonville." He previously worked with EJP as the writer of "A Hundred Bucks Is A Hundred Bucks" for the anthology *Help! Wanted.* Will is currently in pre-production on the film *Frenemy*, an excursion through the mind of a mass murderer. He lives in Los Angeles with his cats, Ricky and Lucy.

Damaged Goods
Quintin Peterson

Once again Luther Kane finds himself wearing his UN Police uniform winter gear and rocking his blue peacekeeper beret, walking slowly across that same old snow-covered, war-torn field in Pristina, Kosovo. Again he steps on the landmine and the blast flips him like a coin. His ears ringing, he stares at the ragged stumps of his muscular legs on the bloodstained snow, both torn off roughly at the knees, steam rising from the wounds. And though he does not recall anyone screaming that fateful day some three years ago, always in this agonizing reliving of the horrific incident, manifested nightly in his dreams, he hears someone screaming like a banshee…

As usual, he woke with a start from this recurring nightmare drenched in cold sweat, but this time he wasn't lying in his warm, cozy bed but on a cold, hard floor.

As he rubbed the back of his aching head, where a lump had erupted, he thought, *What the hell? What happened? Where am I? Shit, who am I? Oh, yeah. I'm Luther Kane…*

Kane noticed then that he wasn't wearing pants and that his prosthetic legs were missing. He still wore his tailor-made black suit jacket and button down gray dress shirt and black tie, and white surgical gloves, but his father's crumpled and mashed-in black fedora was lying on the floor next to him near the bottom of a staircase.

"Looked like you were having a nightmare," said someone with a thick Russian accent.

Luther Kane focused through squinted eyes on the man who had spoken. It took him a moment to recognize him: Ivan the Terrible Sizov, Russian Mob Boss. Castrating his enemies and even subordinates who merely disappointed him was this sadistic psychopath's signature, Kane instantly recalled.

Kane thought, *Fuck me.*

As he stared in dismay at Sizov, it all came rushing back to him:

A short time ago earlier that cool spring night he had hacked into and overrode Ivan's security system, bypassed the alarm, made brief recordings of the home's empty rooms and empty periphery and set up loop recordings and fed the images back to the video cameras so that the house and its grounds would appear to be empty during his intrusion. Afterward, he broke and entered through the back door of the vicious criminal mastermind's luxurious home.

He'd crept upstairs and burglarized the floor safe inside of the walk-in closet of the fiend's master bedroom to get what he needed to pull off his plan. However, when he'd crept back downstairs to leave the way he had come, someone had hit him on the back of the head with a blackjack or a baseball bat or a 2 by 4 and put out his lights. Ivan had been the electrician, no doubt. Funny thing was Ivan was supposed to be out of town for the weekend, according to Nadia, and yet here he was. It was as if someone had ratted Kane out.

As Kane endeavored to serve his client Nadia Kurylenko and free her from Ivan's clutches, old friends at Interpol and the Department of Justice had given Kane the skinny on Sizov:

Ivan the Terrible was born in Novosibirsk, Siberia some forty years ago and had spent half his life in Russian prisons, antisocial networking and cultivating mutually beneficial relationships with countless minions of the underworld. Those life-long relationships had helped him build his criminal empire, making him a fortune through narcotics, gambling, human trafficking, arms dealing, murder for hire, and whatever criminal enterprises that would keep him seated on his throne. His booming prostitution business, which spanned the entire Eastern Seaboard, was all that Kane had been concerned with however.

Kane had figured a way to free his client and to bring Sizov to justice at the same time and had bypassed the barbarian's security system to loot his floor safe. Using the ledger he'd lifted from the safe Kane planned not only to expose Ivan as a pimp but to get him arrested on RICO charges and drag him kicking and screaming into the light of day. The domino effect would topple Ivan's entire empire and in the chaos, Nadia would be able to escape to freedom. That had been the plan, anyway...before he woke up and found himself helpless and at the mercy of the merciless.

Luther Kane had hoped that saving Nadia would be a cakewalk, even though he knew better. If life had taught him nothing else it was that nothing worthwhile is easy.

"You were having a nightmare about losing your legs, I'll bet," Ivan continued. He smiled. "That's nothing compared to what I have in store for you."

Kane sized up Ivan Sizov. The barbarian with the smug look on his craggy face had long, dark hair streaked with gray, stood 6'4" or 5" tall, and was clad in what appeared to be tailor-made black slacks and a snug-fitting royal blue Izod Polo shirt showing off his Russian prison tattoo-covered muscular arms. He had Kane's Colt .45 Model 1911 tucked in his waistband and was searching Kane's pants pockets.

On the floor next to Ivan was Kane's black leather tool bag filled with the loot he had pilfered from Ivan's floor safe and leaning against the wall behind Ivan next to the tool bag, standing tall as though they were going somewhere, were Kane's state-of-the-art **Ottobock®** prosthetic legs, complete with 1C50 foot shells shod in black Florsheims, useless to him now. They might as well have been in Anacostia.

As though he'd read Kane's mind, Ivan said, "Nice legs. They must be the Cadillac of bionic legs."

Indeed they were. Kane's bionic legs with gyroscopes and accelerometers and state-of-the-art microprocessor-controlled knee joints, which utilized a complex sensory system and sophisticated rule sets to mimic natural gait more closely than any other prosthetic knee, were the latest from Ottobock®. They delivered unmatched functionality, including special features to help step over obstacles and ascend stairs. He'd like nothing better than to kick Ivan in the ass with one 'em right now.

"You are a well-dressed burglar, my black friend," Ivan observed. "You people are always overdressing for the wrong occasions. But then again, this *is* your funeral after all."

The simple truth was that Kane had a date with his client later that night after he straightened out this mess and wanted to look his best.

Ivan looked through Kane's black leather ID folder.

"Luther Kane, Jr." Ivan read, eyeballing Kane's military ID card. "Army vet. A war hero by the looks of it." When Ivan came across Kane's private investigator license, he cooed and added, "Private investigator, too, license issued by the Washington, DC Metropolitan Police Department's Security Officers Management Branch. Then that means you are not really a burglar. The question is who would hire a crippled black detective to break in to my safe?"

Ivan seemed to be lost in thought for a moment. Finally, he turned his attention back to Kane. "I was going to fly out of town to attend a business meeting, but just before I boarded the plane, I got a call advising me that the meeting had been postponed due to…a death in the family. I am fortunate that I did not have to leave town and returned home or you would have gotten away with this."

"Lucky you," Kane said.

Ivan smiled, nodded and replied, "Unlucky you. Come to think of it, that is the plight of your entire race, no?"

Sizov tossed aside Kane's slacks and picked up the black leather tool bag Kane had been carrying when Ivan had clocked him. He opened it, dug inside and removed what had been the contents of his floor safe, all still inside the weathered brown leather folder he'd stored them in: cash, negotiable bearer bonds, blackmail materials, and the handwritten, green leather-bound ledger containing the record of his payoffs to police and government officials Ivan kept because he distrusted computers and digital data storage devices. Ivan left the burglary and safe-cracking tools inside; including the iPad Kane had used to hack into and override Ivan's security system, and dropped the tool bag back to the floor with a clank. He unzipped the brown leather portfolio, checked its contents, and then placed the leather folder on a phone table in the foyer next to personal items he had taken from Kane while he was unconscious.

"What is odd is that you don't have a driver's license or any keys on you," Ivan continued. "And no cell phone. If you did not drive here, you must have an accomplice who dropped you off ...but how could you let him...or her know when to pick you up without a cell phone? You surely would not use my landline. This is very odd indeed."

Kane's driver's license was in his wallet, stowed in the glove box of his imported from Detroit fully loaded gloss black AWD Chrysler 300 5.7L HEMI® V8, parked two blocks down and one block over. His cell phone was also in the glove box and his keys were in a magnetic key box which he'd stuck to the undercarriage of his car near the driver's door. The Wireless Remote Control for his bionic legs, which allowed him to activate different modes for special activities such as cycling and cross-country skiing, was also in the glove box. He only wished he hadn't forgotten to toss his ID folder into the glove box as well. What a rookie move. He must be getting old.

"Regardless, it is obvious that someone hired you to rip me off," Ivan continued. "And believe me, sooner or later, you are going to tell me who. Sooner is better for you. But of course, I don't expect a hard case like you to answer me without some persuasion. It will probably take hours, but I am going to enjoy making you talk."

"You seem to enjoy talking too," said Kane. "Do what you gotta do, Ivan. What are you waiting for?"

"My men," said Ivan. "I'm waiting for my men, Luther. What, you think I am going to make a bloody mess here in my home? Are you shitting me? No, me and my men are going to take you someplace where we can interrogate you undisturbed for as long as we want, a place where the mess won't matter.

"One of my men is getting the workshop ready and three are on their way here now. As soon as they arrive, we're going to strip you naked, wrap you up in a neat little package, and throw you into the trunk of a car. Then we are going to drive you out to that workshop, way out in the woods, where no one can hear you scream."

"What are you going to do," Kane smirked, "make me listen to Russian opera?"

Ivan threw back his head and laughed from deep within his belly.

As Ivan laughed Luther considered his plight. He could see no way of getting out of this alive. But no matter what Ivan and his henchmen did to him, he would never give up Nadia.

When Kane had taken this cockeyed case, he shrugged it off that he owed Claire Bradley for all the rehab sessions and for getting him back on his feet, so to speak. He'd probably still be in a wheelchair were it not for her, still bitter and idle. When he'd met her, he had been at his lowest point, wallowing in self-pity, mourning the loss of his legs. After all, he had been a law enforcement officer, first an MP and then an MPDC officer; a captain in the U.S. Army Reserve; a soldier of fortune, and an athlete extraordinaire with the physique of a prizefighter and now was just a useless cripple. Oh, how the mighty had fallen.

The straw that broke the camel's back came when he'd returned stateside half the man he used to be and his ex-wife Laura had him served with divorce papers while he was still wheelchair-bound in a hospital. She'd tossed him away like refuse. But at least she didn't take him for half of his net worth, which was decent of her, he thought, considering that she could have just for spite. Hell, she was well off to begin with, but she had a new husband lined up: Rick "The Brick" Jones, owner of Brix Construction Company, who was erecting more than half D.C.'s new office buildings, condos, and all of the new single family homes on the prime real estate of the former site of Walter Reed Army Medical Center on Georgia Avenue, N.W. Still, it was nice of Laura not to kick a cripple while he was down.

Kane was withdrawn and did not speak to anyone at the hospital, not even when spoken to. And then Physical Therapist Claire Bradley came along, the Ottobock® Bionic Legs his soldiers-of-fortune friends had purchased for him in tow. The first thing she said to him was, "Feeling sorry for yourself, huh? Snap out of it, soldier. We're going to get you up out of that wheelchair. See these?" She pointed to the bionic legs. "These bionic legs are better than the ones you lost and I'm going to teach you how to use them. Now, repeat after me, soldier: These are my new legs. There are many like them, but these are mine. My new legs are nothing without me and I am nothing without them."

Kane laughed and Claire joined him. That did it. He opened up to her right then and there.

Over the course of his rehabilitation and training on operating and fine tuning his bionic legs to suit he's needs, he had recounted to Claire his history as a soldier, a police officer, a mercenary for U.S. corporations, and a private contractor for black ops in war-torn countries commissioned by federal agencies.

Finally, he'd told her the story of how he'd lost his legs working for the UN Police, training police officers and helping build a police department in Kosovo.

As usual, he had been awakened at 0615 hours that fateful morning by men praying in the mosque near the flat where he lived. He'd even taken the time to describe his flat to her: one big bedroom, living room, dining room/kitchen, with Turkish rugs on the wood floors, heaters in every room, big bathtub with shower, and a Turkish balcony. The men were still praying after he'd bathed and gotten dressed and exited his flat and walked past the huge mosque on his way to work at Main HQ for the Kosovo Police Service, about a ten minute walk from his flat. At the base of the mosque was a general mercantile store and grocery, which he'd dubbed Allah's Five and Dime. He'd stopped by there after work when he needed fresh bread and milk and other food items A huge loaf of bread cost 25 cents/Euros, he reminisced, milk about 55 cents/Euros, a single service of juice about 19 cents/Euros, and an Espresso about 20 cents/Euros. The equivalent of a personal cheese pizza cost $1.50/Euros.

He had been admiring the beautiful Šar Mountains when he stepped on the landmine. Funny, he'd been walking pretty much that same route to and from work for months.

He'd shaken his head as he'd reflected aloud how he hadn't gotten so much as a scratch while working the mean streets of D.C. as a cop, or in all those combat situations in Iraq, Afghanistan, Angola, and Somalia, only to be mangled in peace time by a leftover landmine from a war that ended long ago.

In response to his griping, Claire had recited the opening sequence of ABC TV's The Six Million Dollar Man: "Steve Austin, astronaut. A man barely alive. Gentlemen, we can rebuild him. We have the technology. We have the capability to make the world's first bionic man. Steve Austin will *be* that man. Better than he was before. Better... stronger...faster."

It was a hoot.

Yeah, Claire had brought him back to life, so he owed her big time. When she'd brought the case to him, he'd taken it, no questions asked. He wouldn't even be a private dick if she hadn't suggested it. Not that he needed the money. He had his generous pension from the District of Columbia Metropolitan Police Department, as well as a pension from the U.S. Army Reserve; and had close to one million Euros stashed in a Swiss bank, wages he'd earned tax free in the four years since he'd retired from the police department, working as a private contractor in Iraq and Afghanistan for Halliburton and Blackwater, et al; and a group of his buddies who'd worked along with him as contractors for black ops abroad commissioned by the alphabet soup of federal agencies (DIA, DoD, CIA, CTU, etc.) had chipped in and bought him his expensive new legs and saved him a shitload of cash. What was important is that P.I. work gave him something to do; made him feel as though he served a useful purpose. After all Claire had done for him, taking Nadia Kurylenko's case was the least that he could do for her.

Besides, the case was right down his alley.

Sitting across the desk from him in the office of the Intrepid Detective Agency, just down the street from his Camden South Capitol residence, located atop the Last Stop Liquor Store on South Cap, Claire told him the sob story of Nadia Kurylenko, a one-legged streetwalker she'd been rehabbing and training how to walk on her new bottom-of-the-line artificial leg, one step above a pirate's peg leg. According to Nadia, her pimp had taken the limb because she had tried to run away from him. She offered him the job to free Nadia and bring her pimp to justice. He took the job, with pleasure. Pro bono. He'd agreed to meet the client the night of the same day Claire offered him the case.

Due to the fact that the pimp had his men keeping an eye on Nadia, Kane agreed to pick up the streetwalker like a john on the 400 block of New York Avenue and take her to the nearby crappy No-Tell Motel she operated out of. There they would conduct a consultation under the guise of a sex trade business transaction.

Claire told him, "When she comes by for her session this afternoon I'll let her know you're coming tonight around ten. You can't miss her."

Claire was right. There was only one peg-legged streetwalker on New York Avenue that night; just one broken doll crammed into a red tube top and Daisy Duke coochie cutter faded blue jean shorts clip-clopping along the avenue. It was heartbreaking. Funny thing was that when he pulled over to pick her up, he was shocked to discover that he knew the broken doll.

Raven-haired Romani beauty Nadia "Gypsy" Kurylenko, mouth open, stared back at him wide-eyed with surprise through the open passenger window of his pristine black Chrysler 300.

"Сукин сын!" Nadia exclaimed. "You're Luther Kane, Claire's friend the P.I.?" Nadia opened the door and hopped inside. She punched Kane's shoulder, hard, and asked, "What's with this Steve Austin bullshit?"

Kane winced, rubbed his shoulder, and countered, "Well, what's with this Gypsy bullshit?"

"Gypsy is my nickname at least," Nadia retorted. "But you lied. Steve Austin, investment banker my ass. And where the hell have you been? You didn't even say goodbye."

Luther said, "It's a long story."

Nadia said, "I've got all the time it will take you to tell it."

Luther shrugged and said, "Well, it's like this..."

As he fabricated an excuse for his behavior, he put his ride in gear and pulled off.

In his rearview mirror, Kane immediately spotted the gray Lincoln Town Car tailing them.

Nadia Kurylenko turned out to be a call girl Kane had known as Gypsy. He'd encountered the pretty little gypsy girl a couple of years ago, back when he'd first gotten back on his feet, so to speak. He'd picked up the leggy call girl the first time—back when she still had two beautiful legs—almost two years ago in the CityZen Bar of the Oriental Mandarin Hotel on Maryland Avenue, SW in Washington, D.C.

His buddy John Mayfield, a retired D.C., homicide detective who had taken the gig as Chief of Security for the hotel, had advance knowledge of an investment bankers' convention coming to the Oriental Mandarin and had talked Kane into taking the Presidential Suite at a discount before all the rooms for the event had been booked and also had convinced him to masquerade as an investment banker. Mayfield had told him:

"Man, top-shelf hookers work all the conventions, but they eat up investment bankers. Just dress for success and you'll blend in. Then all you have to do is hang out at the bar. Before too long, a hot little young honey will sashay up to you and slam, bam, thank you ma'am. C'mon, Luther. You deserve a night in heaven. Welcome home, hero."

Mayfield was right.

Luther Kane, Jr., decked out in a Field English Custom Tailors of Georgetown black suit, starched white Paul Frederick dress shirt, burgundy Calvin Klein silk tie, and wearing upon his well-combed crown his late father's black fedora, swaggered into the CityZen Bar at around 2000 hours on Friday the 13th and ordered a Vodka Martini, shaken not stirred, with two olives. By 2007 hours, a Raven-haired-swarthy-complexioned- shapely-young-beauty crammed into a red dress that fit like an Italian leather driving glove was at his elbow, eyeballing him with arresting peepers the color of honey and chatting him up. Gypsy she said her name was.

He took her hand and said, "I'm Steve Austin. What are you drinking?"

The same as you, she'd told him.

They chatted over drinks for a while. She told him he smelled good and wanted to know what he was wearing. "Lagerfeld," he told her and then said she smelled good too and wanted to know what she was wearing. She smirked, looked him in the eye and told him, "Me."

When they'd finished their drinks Gypsy asked him if he wanted a date. He nodded and said, "I surely do."

He paid the bar tab, tipped the bartender with a one hundred dollar bill, and they left the bar, arm in arm.

On their walk from the hotel bar to the elevator to the Presidential Suite, his gait was flawlessly natural, because he'd worked hard it, the desired effect being that no one would ever suspect that he ended just above the knees and was riding atop mechanical legs. His stride was strong, assured, but on the inside he felt weak and insecure. And yet once they were in his suite and the truth was finally revealed, his impairment didn't seem to faze Gypsy; she was all over him like a cheap suit. But that's just because prostitutes are jaded, he figured. Hell, they see it all, right? Still, there was something magical about the night he spent with her. And so using the alias of Steve Austin, he'd seen her for some time after their first encounter at the Oriental Mandarin, frequently spending nights with her at several five-star hotels in the Washington, DC metropolitan area, but not once at his residence in the Camden South Capitol building, just up the street from his business office located atop The Last Stop Liquor Store, right across the street from his second home, Nats Stadium. He did not want to take the chance that a neighbor or something in his condo would reveal his true identity.

From their second "date" to their last, whenever Investment Banker Steve Austin was "in town on business," he brought along to whatever hotel they happened to be staying his Apple iPod Classic 160GB and Bose SoundDock® Portable digital music system docking station to provide the mood music: mostly Oldies but Goodies R&B love songs, Smooth Jazz, and the collected works of Frank Sinatra. Once she'd even performed an impromptu exotic dance for him. Dressed in a Victoria's Secret Red Satan Slip and Kimono, the Raven-haired Romani beauty gyrated, pelvisized, and grinded to the pulsating rhythm of Shahin and Sepehr's The Last Goodbye when he'd accidentally selected the tune on his iPod. Before he could make another selection, Gypsy had caught the groove, held up a finger and said, "Wait." And with that, she belly danced on the floor at the foot of the bed.

Her exotic dance to the pulsing rhythm of The Last Goodbye was extremely erotic. She was mesmerizing! Gypsy was sexier than any pole dancer he'd ever seen at the Ragin' Cajun Supper Club strip joint up on Mount Olivett Road, that's for sure. It was quite a treat.

Gypsy seemed to like the music he liked almost as much as she seemed to like having sex with him. But then again for a successful prostitute, that was the trick, wasn't it? It was just instant intimacy, a trick of the trade, nothing more. He tried to convince himself that there was nothing wrong with that, but just when things seemed to be going so well between them he had abruptly stopped seeing her without a word.

The bitter truth was that he had ditched Gypsy for the same reason he'd been so obsessed with her: she'd made him feel whole again. He could not afford a fantasy like that, especially not one manifested by a prostitute; could not, on top of everything else, end up a pathetic, turned out trick. Such a prospect certainly did not suit a man like him who'd dedicated his life to higher standards. Gypsy was damaged goods and he deserved better. She couldn't be his Bacall, uh uh, no way. So he'd dumped her, despite the fact that he did not have anyone to replace her or even a remote prospect for a meaningful relationship with someone worthy of the effort. That didn't matter. What did matter to Kane was that being in love with a hooker could only end badly for a man like him.

In the shabby motel on New York Avenue, Nadia recounted to Kane how Ivan the Terrible had kidnapped her near her Romani encampment somewhere in Albania some thirteen years ago when she was only twelve. She had been his favorite ever since, up until she'd tried to escape, and he had kept her with him always, only letting top-dollar clients have a crack at her occasionally. She had been living with him in his Fall Church, Virginia home when she'd gotten her chance to make a run for it. Ivan and two of his henchmen, Anton and Boris, had tracked her down in no time and then they'd taken her to a cabin in the woods where he ordered Boris to blast off her left leg with a shotgun. Ivan had had a surgeon standing by who sutured the stump, without anesthetic, and" nursed" her back to health, without pain medication. (Gypsy did not know the doctor's name, but to Kane, only one name suited the butcher: Dr. Mengele.) And after she'd healed, Ivan had sent her to rehab to learn how to hobble about on the cheapest prosthetic leg money could buy. He might as well have given her a table leg.

She recalled that at one point during the couple weeks she had been bedridden, Ivan had stood over her and said, "I gave you everything and you spat in my face. You had the privilege of living with me and of having all the comforts of home. I dressed you in the finest clothes, fed you the finest food, and made you a top-dollar call girl, sharing you only with the best of my clientele. Now you will work the streets for pennies as a one-legged streetwalker, the plaything of scum, and you will live in a crappy motel, and eat only fast food until the day you die!"

Anton and Boris had grinned and licked their chops when Ivan added, "And Boris and Anton get all the sex they want, whenever they want and however they want it…for free."

Key to pulling off this job was that Nadia the Gypsy had lived in Ivan the Terrible's home and knew his operation and all of his secrets, including the contents of and combination to his floor safe and had spilled it all to Luther Kane, P.I. As she'd spilled her guts to Kane, he had figured out how to save her. In the days following their meeting he'd plotted his risky scheme very carefully.

Kane had been looking forward to not only bringing Ivan down, but to making him suffer, as well. He'd picked up a little something extra special for Ivan from his buddy Kelly McMurry, the arms dealer. Kelly owned a gun shop on Marlboro Pike in Forestville, Maryland and sold specialty items to special clients in a back room of the store. There Kane had picked up the perfect gift for Ivan the Terrible. Kane prayed that even if he didn't make it out of this alive, Ivan's gift would still be delivered...

Ivan's smartphone rang and pulled Kane from his thoughts.

Sizov answered his phone, "Где - Вы?" He listened briefly and then replied, "Хороший."

Sizov disconnected the call and told Kane, "They will be here in a few minutes. I'm going to put my stuff back in the safe where it belongs. Be right back." And then he laughed and added, "Don't go anywhere."

Ivan Sizov snatched his brown leather folder from the phone table and sprinted up the steps. Luther Kane immediately seized the moment he'd been waiting for, praying for. He quickly soldier-crawled across the shiny hardwood floor over to his black leather tool bag. He dug into the bag and pulled back a Velcro strip that concealed the zipper to a secret compartment on the right side of the bag's interior. He unzipped the compartment and drew from it his Charter Arms 5-shot snub nose .357 Magnum Bulldog revolver with a hot-load of 250-grain Hydrashok hollow-point ammo. Like his Colt .45, his Bulldog was untraceable. Controlling his breathing, he aimed at the staircase and waited for it...

The explosion followed by the high-pitched wailing informed him that his booby-trap had been effective. He grabbed his bionic legs, put them back on, slipped back into his tailor-made black trousers, and then stood tall. He buckled his black leather belt and then took from the telephone table his ID folder, black and red *Anarchy* Zippo lighter, and black pack of American Spirit 100% natural tobacco cigarettes, and put them all back into his pants and shirt pockets before he walked upstairs.

He found Ivan the Terrible on the floor of his walk-in closet, the air thick with the stench of Sizov's blood and sweat and the spent explosive. A victim of the castration mine Luther had rigged to be triggered the moment Ivan stepped into the closet, Ivan the Terrible, his eyes closed tightly, was drenched in sweat and moaning and writhing in agony, both hands gripping the singed, ragged and bloody crotch of his tailor-made slacks, clutching the shredded remnants of his mangled manhood.

Sizov swore, "Трахните меня! О, Трахните меня!"

Luther Kane reached down, snatched his bloodstained .45 from Ivan's waistband, and wiped the blood off the gun onto the shoulder of Ivan's Polo shirt. He tucked the gat into his waistband at the small of his broad back and then reached down, picked up off the closet floor Ivan's brown leather folder containing the loot, and then flung it from the closet to the bedroom floor.

Kane stood over Ivan, smirked and said, "I see you met Bouncing Betty. She's a real bitch."

"Fuck you!" Ivan screamed. "I'm going to kill you, you black motherfucker!"

"Not likely," Luther countered.

Ivan spat in Kane's general direction and once again yelled, "Fuck you!"

"The plan was to let you live," Kane confessed. "It would have been the best punishment and justice would have been served. You would have suffered for the rest of your life, an emasculated pimp, and you wouldn't have had a clue who to blame; who to pay back. But now that you know who it was that did this to you, I'd been signing my own death warrant if I let you live. And that's a real shame because I wanted you to suffer for a long time. It's what you deserve."

"Fuck you, neeguh!" Ivan wailed. "Fuck you!"

Kane snatched a ¾ length sable coat from a hanger, put his right hand—the one holding the gun—through the left sleeve of the garment, and strategically draped the coat over himself to shield his shoes and clothes from the forthcoming blowback of Ivan's gray matter, blood and bone. He pointed his .357 Magnum at Ivan's head. The Bulldog barked once and Sizov fell silent.

Luther tossed aside the soiled sable coat, exited the walk-in closet, and picked up Ivan's brown leather portfolio before he ran back downstairs. He tucked the folder under one arm, picked up his fedora, brushed it off, put it back in shape, and then donned it gingerly, careful of the sore lump on the back of his head. He unlocked the front door and then doubled back, picked up his tool bag, and stuffed in Ivan's leather folder. He then walked back and positioned himself near the front door, just outside the foyer. He squared his shoulders and stood tall, .357 Magnum at the ready. He didn't have to wait long before there was a knock on the door.

Kane heard a couple of people on the front porch and though he could not make out what they were saying, they sounded jovial.

"Откройте дверь, Ивана," someone yelled on the other side of the door.

"Входивший," Kane beckoned them.

The door swung inward and three men standing one behind the other on the porch, about to walk in single-file, came into view. The first gunsel in line saw Kane holding the hand-cannon and realized the big mistake they'd made. He fumbled for the Glock 9mm tucked in his waistband...

Luther said, "Crime doesn't pay."

Kane took aim and the Bulldog barked once. The slug passed through the chests of all three of the thugs like a hot knife through butter. They all instantly dropped like sacks of potatoes.

He tucked the still-warm Bulldog into his waistband and set down his tool bag. He peeled the surgical gloves from his sweaty hands and shoved them deep into a pocket of his suit jacket.

Kane removed his lighter and hard pack of cigarettes from his shirt pocket, and shook one loose from the box. He stuck the cigarette between his full lips and fired it up. He put away the pack and lighter and exhaled blue smoke as he looked the dead men over. Anton and Boris were not among the departed. He picked up his tool bag, stepped over the corpses, and walked down the front stairs and out of the front yard.

The case wasn't closed just yet. He had one more thing to do tonight before Nadia would be safe and secure; he had to get rid of one, maybe two more of Ivan's henchmen: Nadia's watchdogs, Boris and Anton.

Kane knew well the car Anton and Boris drove because he'd spotted it tailing them the first night he picked Nadia up on New York Ave. For a few nights after that he had watched them while they watched Nadia clip-clopping along the avenue.

Tonight as Boris or Anton kept an eye on Nadia while she worked New York Avenue, Kane would stake him out. When the time was right he'd use his .45 to take out the thug(s) sitting in the gray Lincoln Town Car and then leave the .357 magnum on 'em before he picked up Nadia.

Ivan's ledger and blackmail materials targeting government officials and influential private citizens would be delivered the next morning to a stand-up guy Kane knew at the FBI, anonymously of course, but in the meantime, while the feds built their case against Sizov's criminal empire, Kane figured it couldn't hurt to provide a red herring to occupy the law folk and the Russian Mafia; something to distract them and boggle their minds as they tried to fathom just what the hell had happened at Sizov's house. The corpse(s) of Boris and/or

Anton in possession of the murder weapon used at Sizov's house would serve that purpose nicely…

Of course, the cash and negotiable bearer bonds from Ivan's floor safe were for Nadia, so she could start over somewhere, fresh and clean. And buy a new leg. Definitely, she needed a new leg. A top-of-the-line Ottobock® Bionic Leg, for sure. On second thought, her new leg would be his treat. He'd even throw in the foot.

Seated in his black leather upholstered Chrysler, Luther Kane glanced over at Nadia "Gypsy" Kurylenko's bag of loot resting on the shotgun seat and then leaned over and opened the glove box. He withdrew a sterling silver flask filled with John J. Bowman Single Barrel Bourbon Whiskey, unscrewed the cap, and took a deep swig. He closed his eyes for a moment and sighed. He reclosed the flask and tossed it back into the glove box, closing the compartment's door after it.

Kane turned over the powerful V8 engine and Frank Sinatra belting out Luck Be A Lady emanated from the radio via his magnificent machine's Beats Audio 10 Premium Speakers. Kane smirked and nodded his approval as he basked in the glow of the catchy tune.

He turned on the headlights, put his ride in gear, and drove off into the night.

Sometime during the drive back to D.C., Luther reconsidered his position and had a change of heart. He decided that it really might not be such a bad idea to hook up with the broken doll. Both of them were damaged goods after all.

Perhaps together they both could feel whole again.

Native Washingtonian **Quintin Peterson** is a retired D.C. police officer who served the public for more than 28 years. He is an artist and award-winning writer who has authored three DC-based crime novels, a book of poetry, several short stories available via Amazon Kindle and BN.com Nook Books and has contributed to six crime fiction/noir anthologies and to *SANITARIUM* and *eNoir* magazines. He is currently employed at the Folger Shakespeare Memorial Library in Washington, D.C.

MILONGA MINEFIELD
Yvonne Seng

Milonga: a fast-paced tango; a gathering of tango dancers; a style of tango music

Frydy Bascom shoved her spare leg into her gym bag and threw it in the back of her pickup. The mangled bumper wore three stickers barely visible through the red dust. *Get Lost in Montana*. *Cowgirl Up*, a bucking cowgirl on a candy pink background. And *Trout Dancer*.

Life in a nutshell. Montana chic.

She right turned past the Man Store and honked at some damn fool who'd cut her off in a hurry to get his cheap beer and smokes, drove past the homeless outside God's Love and set a bead down Last Chance Gulch towards an A-1 parking spot that spanned storefronts of the Indian Alliance, No Sweat Café and the pole dancing studio.

"Feckin' A!" she shouted out the window and flipped a good-humored finger at the designer sports vehicle that nosed into her space. "Find your own goddamn spot!"

She edged forward in front of Aunt Bonnie's Used Books and Helena's only Thai restaurant, reversed up real tight to the gold-rimmed SUV and jumped out. Slammed the door.

"Don't work for you any more, Judge Janson," she said and gave her old boss a hug that almost rocked him off his stack heels. "Gotta learn to get along without me, JJ."

"Girl Friday," he replied. "Nev-ah."

The middle age man with the steak-dinner and two-whisky paunch gave her a long, affectionate squeeze. His nose came up to her breasts and that's where he liked it. He buried himself in her long lush hair, dark and glossy like melted chocolate, 70 percent cocoa, and sighed.

They both wore chambray shirts, blue jeans and hand-tooled cowboy boots, but that's where it ended. Judge Janson, JJ to select friends, wore a silver bolo of a bear around his fat little neck and a tweed jacket—business casual. Frydy had a turquoise, freeze-factor 8, hooded Pata-Gucci ski jacket that matched her cat slanted eyes. His rodeo belt buckle was made in China. Hers was real.

"Fry-dy," she enunciated slow-ly, white teeth bared between cracked red lips. "Two Ys."

"Yeh, yeh, I remember," he said. "Too wise for your own good."

Frydy's name was the legacy of an illiterate, good-for-nothing, good looking loser Argentine ranch hand who'd knocked up her

Basque cook of a mom and signed the paternity papers after a few too many drinks and before he'd left town. Town being Wolf Point, Montana.

"Should be happy he gave you a name, love," her mom would say whenever they shared a couple of drinks, mother-daughter like.

"And that you wasn't born on a Satur-dy." Frydy would chime in with their well-worn ritual. They'd laugh and snort real unlady-like, and clink glasses.

"To life," they'd toast. "To life."

"Lock up the bag?" Judge Janson nodded to her gym bag in the back of the pickup.

"Nah," she said. "Anyone who steals it is in for a big surprise."

"Lock it up," he said. "I'll buy you a drink."

The Last Chance Bar was as dark and desperate as the old gold mine it was named after. The lunch crowd, which actually began at breakfast, had thinned out and would reappear after a nap. The rowdies and daring college kids had a few more hours to get their courage up. They had the place pretty much to themselves.

"Well if it ain't my favorite bull roper," Mike shouted from behind the bar.

"And my favorite bull-shipper," Frydy threw back. "Hi Unk."

She balanced on the metal rung of the bolted down bar stool and air kissed him across the sticky bar.

Frydy's legacy from her dad was more that her first name. Her mother's side was short and dark, like Uncle Mike at the bar: they'd given her their coloring and temper. Her dad contributed the height and panther build, a fancy dance rhythm and an uncanny nose for trouble. He'd thrown in the love-'em-and-leave-'em for kicks.

"Look, number one bull roper it says right here!" Mike slammed the gilded trophy on the bar beside a Pabst and a Bourbon ditch, a finger of whiskey and whatever water you can find in dryland Montana.

Judge Janson raised an eyebrow as Frydy took a long sip of ditch, leaving a bright red kiss on the glass.

"Little early for the heavy stuff?" he said. Looked at his watch. Three o'clock.

"Celebrating," Frydy replied. "Birthday. Sort of. Dutch courage."

They both saluted the rodeo statue.

"Barrel racing," she added. "Not bull roping."

Five years ago, Frydy had graduated from the University of Wyoming law school where she'd begun undergrad on a rodeo scholarship. She was the sweetest barrel racer Montana had known. The slightest squeeze of her thigh and a thousand pounds of horse would turn on a toothpick. Two perfectly tuned bodies pressed into one.

They could milonga through a minefield.

Five years ago, she'd followed Kurt, her international law professor, to Angola—as far away from his wife and kids as they could run, they'd laughed—to work with war victims. Good ideals. Wrong reason. Maybe the gods gave her credit for being in love and naïve: they didn't kill her.

While Kurt gathered data and turned people into numbers, she threw her cowgirl heart into broken, smashed up, blown apart kids. Kids who woke up in hospital tents with limbs missing, blown away by land mines, by machines and politics they didn't choose. Worse, kids used as bomb dogs. When all the real dogs had been eaten or blown to bits, the kids were force-marched ahead by bands of enemy vigilantes, their small bare feet detonating the land mines. They were expendable.

While her two-bit, adulterous lover boy churned out statistics and yelled into his satellite phone to international aid agencies demanding more money and hot showers, Frydy entered his notes into the solar-powered laptop and went to check on the kids in the tents. God damn! she'd curse, but there was no god to curse. How could there be?

She threw her mind into devising ways to help the kids walk. After the surgeons and reconstructive specialists had done their job, she helped the kids to eat without arms or hands. To pee and crap however they could. She pushed them. She willed them to live. She nursed her anger with a killer smile.

She never knew what hit her. Stretching her long legs after another fight with that sonofabitch. The locals were morons, he yelled. The doctors were worse than useless. The aid agencies were fools. She was a bitch. No one gave him respect, he yelled at her.

She took a familiar pathway, safe, already cleared. Just needed to walk it off. Walk him off. Hot and humid, beginning of the wet season. Sun setting rapidly as it always did in that part of the world. Total drop into darkness. Maybe she just wasn't thinking clearly.

The heel of her cowgirl boot triggered the mine. Right leg. Above her knee right down to her boot. Gone. Total drop into darkness.

He left her there. Took the first plane out, back to his hygienic life with its hot showers and cold wife.

First time she hadn't walked out on love first.

Always a first.

She stroked the trophy her uncle proudly kept at the bar among the clutter of old neon signs and bounced checks.

First in barrel racing. Last in love.

"Five years, then," JJ said. "Let me warm you up."

He plugged a few dollar's worth of change into the juke box. The same old dance tunes slid across memory's cracked linoleum.

Fryday shed her jacket and pulled her hair up into a ponytail.

Alan Jackson started them two-stepping.

"Where I come from…," he twanged.

"Tell me about today," Frydy said. "What did she get?"

"Like you," he replied. "Life."

"Hmmh. No leniency?"

Slow. Slow. Quick-quick. Slow.

"*…it's cornbread 'n chicken. . . . ,*" JJ sang off-key.

Judge Janson was smooth on his small, pointed feet. Like a lot of rotund men, his center of gravity was low. He could boot scoot like a plaid-shirt ballerina.

"Jury didn't buy her insanity plea," he said. "Shot her husband and his girlfriend in bed. Fully dressed."

"Her?"

"Them. Cold blood."

"Separated, what, a couple of years?" she said. "He asked for a restraining order, right?"

"It's not over if I'm not over you." Vern Gosdin moved them into a seamless cowboy waltz

"Didn't do no good. What can I say? She broke into the house in the middle of the night. Used her old keys. He was going to get the locks changed the next day. Crept around downstairs while they slept upstairs. Brought guns with her. Sat in his favorite chair. Ate candy bars. Waited until just before dawn then went upstairs, shot him in bed."

"The girl?"

"Weren't no girl we're talking about, here," JJ said. "All of them, mid-fifties. Not kids here, hon. Goddamn mess. Older ain't smarter."

"Emergency services got it all on tape?" Frydy asked.

"Some. Got the struggle on cell. Girlfriend managed to push the wife out the door. Locked it. Called 911. Both the ladies, both of them called 911 to save their man. You believe?"

"Nope."

"Yup. Could hear the sirens in the background. Stereo. Then the shots. Pow. Pow. Pow. Bitch shot her right through the door. Pow. Shredded her."

"Shit."

Frydy paused, waiting for the next tune to drop.

"You can't stop a woman when she's out of control," Rodney Crowell pitched it from the juke box.

"You nailed that one," she said.

"How's your new leg?" he asked. "Haven't heard any clicks."

"Worked the bugs out, real smooth. I'm a good guinea pig," Frydy replied with a grin.

JJ glided her around the floor.

"Like driving a Porsche," he said. "Nice."

"Top of the line carbon," Frydy replied. "High tech minimalist work of art. Could hang it on the wall and charge admission."

"Gonna show me?" JJ asked.

"Pervert."

She patted his firm little butt.

"Time to go," she said, nodding toward the door. The evening crew was starting to crowd the bar, encroaching on their private dance floor. "I'm meeting Annie for a burger."

"Not eating at the Club?"

"Lost the expense account," she replied. "I'll meet you there later?"

It was winter dark outside, streetlights pierced the leaden sky. Hardened drinkers propped up the brick wall, sucking up some nicotine, their faces flickering red then orange in the old fashioned neon. JJ walked her to her pick-up, past the brown garden beds littered with butts and broken bottles.

"Looks like snow," she said as she hefted herself up into the cab.

He rolled down his tinted window as he came up level.

"I'll bring the wife," he said. "Show her how the big girls do it."

Frydy parked outside the Montana Club and walked down Last Chance Gulch to Big Dorothy's Saloon, a legendary brothel that had toned down and straightened up.

Fat snowflakes covered the walkway and caught in her eyelashes. Maybe she'd get some skiing in this weekend. Try out the new leg. Beautiful sleek machine. Not the flesh-colored prosthetic that desperately tried to imitate her lost limb.

No, this leg was beautiful. Lean and honest. The way life should be.

Truth was Frydy was in love with her new leg. Maybe as much as with her Blue Heeler, Rusty, who waited at the cabin.

"What should I name it," she asked out loud as she approached the old arch commemorating the long-gone Chinese community from Helena's gold rush days.   "What should I name you?" she corrected herself and laughed. "Listen to me talking to a metal leg like it's my new best friend."

She pulled out her lipstick and plumped her lips, checking her reflection in the rug store window. The owner, a Turk with the beautiful eyes, waved at her through the glass. Yesterday his toddler son had used Frydy's new leg as his personal jungle gym to climb up into her ever-loving arms.

Snow had begun to pile up outside Big Dorothy's. Annie was sitting at a small table at the back of the bar, her dark hair buried in a book. A kick-ass sass-mouth, a hummingbird on caffeine, Annie waitressed at the bar's restaurant. She was meeting Frydy between shifts.

A slow Wednesday with snow coming down like a ticker-tape parade. The non-profit and hiker crowd wouldn't be there until the Blackfoot Brewery closed at eight, if they came at all. Annie didn't care. She looked up from her book and squinted when she heard Frydy's name being shouted.

"Frydy! Girl! What's it going to be?" Lisa, the red-headed Amazon behind the bar, yelled out. She pointed to the craft beer on tap— Moose Drool, Bitterroot IPA, Beltian White—and raised her hands in question.

"Blue Dolphin," Frydy replied, indicating the water pitcher. "Double."

"Heard there's an old flame in town," Lisa shouted.

Frydy grimaced and continued towards the back.

"Word's out," Annie said after the ritual hugs.

"Yeah, word's out, hon," Reba the head waitress said as she slid in beside them with her order book. "Sorry to hear."

"How's the grandbaby?" Frydy replied.

With her blonde curls and devilish grin, Reba looked hardly out of high school, but that's life along the Great Divide. She pursed her lips then grinned, admitting defeat.

"Yeh. Sure," she said.

She pulled out her iPhone and scrolled through the images, pulling up a video of her golden, punk-haired grand daughter crawling through the dog door of her cabin.

Frydy belly laughed. It felt good.

"The usual?" Reba was back on task.

"Blue cheese burger. No onions. Fries. No ranch." Frydy repeated her mantra. She looked up at Annie who was biding her time. "Anything?"

"Steal some fries. I've eaten."

"Bring some ranch, then," Frydy added.

They both stretched their backs then leaned over the table towards each other. Old friends. Old running partners. Knew each other's rhythms. Been through hell together.

"What are you reading?" Frydy asked, nodding towards the paperback on the table.

"I heard he's in town. Kurt," Annie replied.

"Yeah. Well."

"You okay?"

"We do what we do," Frydy replied. "You?"

"They found her body, you know," Annie replied, strangling the neck of a paper napkin.

Frydy looked at her, puzzled.

"The teacher that went missing. Wolf Point. Where Jake's staying. Man camp. Hello?" Annie said.

She had forgotten that Annie's 19-year old son lived in a man camp outside of Wolf Point and drove 90 minutes each way through the dusty plains over the border into North Dakota to work the fracking fields in Bakken. Overcrowded primitive camps sprung up everywhere, chasing the oil boom. Men cramped together. Sleeping in shifts. Snuse. Red Bull. Dope. Drugs to keep you up. Drink to bring you down. It was the Wild West all over again.

"Oh, shit, yeah," Frydy replied, softly cursing her lack of eloquence. News of her Kurt's arrival in town had unsettled her world. That it had spread over town was equally unsettling. Montana is one small town, her mom used to say.

"Word is she was strangled," Annie said. She dated a cop and had the latest. "Threw her in a ditch outside of town, covered her with trash. Goddamn shits."

Kurt was in Helena on official business, visiting the governor. Something about shipping cheap coal to China and the problems with the western seaports. Or was it the pipeline from the tar sands in Canada? It didn't matter. He was in town and asking about her. Bragging her up.

His best fucking student. His joke, not hers.

"Kidnapped her. Two shitheads on meth on the way to the Bakken," Annie said. She practically swallowed a French fry whole and thumped on her bony chest to dislodge it. "She went for a jog, Frydy, a frickin' jog in the morning. A teacher, can you believe!"

"Was she raped?" Frydy asked.

"Raped? Raped? Who gives a fuck!" Annie fumed. "She was out jogging."

"Of course," Frydy said and placed her hands over her friend's.

"I need a smoke," Annie said.

"Poor kids," Frydy added softly, thinking of the school children who'd come face to face with violence.

"Predators. Just like that guy today. Raped a six-year old girl. Did you read it?"

Frydy nodded.

"Claims he was innocent. That she had initiated it! She initiated it? Goddamn, I want to kill him."

A froth of fury rose in Frydy's gut. Images of the children in the rain-soaked tent cities of Angola. Mutilated. Their wounds were visible.

But this six-year old girl? How would her wound show itself? And when?

"Gotta go," Frydy said sharply and slid off the stool. She held onto the edge of the table to steady her anger.

Annie glanced at the clock above the bar.

"Me, too," she said.

Sadness clung to them as they did a pat-hug.

"Almost forgot," Annie said. "Good luck tonight."

"Hang in there," Frydy replied.

Snow was coming down with a fury. Frydy strode the several blocks along the Gulch. She pulled her gym bag out of her pick up and took the stairs to the second floor of the Montana Club two at a time. She stowed her jacket on the coat rack with the strappy red dress she unfolded from her bag, and took a deep breath.

More than a century of old wood and cigars, rare steak and whisky, met her nostrils. Built for bank barons and overnight millionaires who struck gold during the city's heyday, to entertain opera singers and show off fancy East Coast wives, the Montana Club groaned with atmosphere.

She paused in the doorway before making her entrance. Flurries of snow danced outside the floor-to-ceiling windows, a surreal backdrop to the tropical palms that lined the room. The strains of jazz saxophone filtered through the clink of glasses and raised voices. Milo and the quartet were playing tonight. Maybe KC would sing. Yes, that would be good.

She looked at her watch. She had one hour until the milonga, the gathering of tango dancers. And to her own, personal celebration.

Five years since her leg was blown off.

Smiling, she headed to the long, carved bar with its gleaming mirrors and top shelf bottles. She edged through the crowd and finger-waved briefly at silver-haired Lennie in his tuxedo coaxing a sexy lament out of his jazz guitar. His son on the piano flashed her a welcoming wink, while Milo, finished with his solo, let the alto hang by his side, his eyes closed while he tapped the beat against his thigh. The short trombone player in the tux and military buzz cut transported the room to Brazil.

Better than good. It was perfect.

"Lagavulin." The young bartender in the crisp white shirt slid the heavy glass across the polished bar with a lovesick smile and a small ceramic pitcher. "And a splash."

Frydy dipped her long fingers into the water jug and flicked the droplets into the single malt. She raised it to her nose and breathed in the released aroma of smoky peat. She closed her eyes and took a sip, let it roll over her tongue, down her long, ready throat, and work its magic. The young bartender and several men at the bar watched closely, forgetting to breathe.

She listened as Milo announced that KC would sing. A woman's velvet voice fingered the crowded room. Conversation dropped. KC had them in the palm of her hand. Oh, she sang, she sang just for you. Just you. Oh, honey.

Frydy had her back turned to the bar the first time she heard KC sing. She had heard this voice, this luscious voice, and expected to find a tall willowy seductress in black satin. She had searched the band. There, in the center, the short trombone player with the boyish face, the military haircut and man's tuxedo. K.C. Kasey. The sultry voice flowed from her soul.

Frydy exhaled the whisky fumes through her teeth and opened her eyes. Now she was ready. She turned to face the room. Tonight, this was her room.

Five years ago in rehab at the Mayo, the psych had asked her about her goals. The PT crew listened in. Well-intended. Nice people. They'd been with her through surgery and got her back on her feet. Foot, that is. Now they were ready for the next stage. The prosthetic.

"Goals?" Frydy repeated.

"Yes. Do you plan to ride again? Run a marathon?" The doc had asked. "You're an athlete. You were once, what, a bull-roper? You're tough. Over-achiever. Use your anger. I know you set goals."

Frydy had snorted.

"Barrel racer," she had said wearily. "I was a barrel racer."

She had pushed off the wave of depression that threatened to suck her down again. God damn it. Her whole goddamn life was a goddamn mess. She'd run off to Africa with that sonofabitch and he'd left her. Left her. Crippled. Anger was brewing wild. Her thoughts switched to the children. Their blown apart little bodies. The determination in their eyes.

"Tango," she blurted. "I'm going to dance the goddamn tango."

The medical team had looked at her in disbelief. Then nodded.

"You watch. Five years. I'll be dancing the tango at the Montana Club in a little red dress. And I won't miss a goddamn step."

She had looked them in the eyes.

"You can bet on it."

Frydy looked around the Montana Club. The velvet couches and club chairs had been cleared in front of the band for the milonga. The oriental rug rolled up. A couple of dancers were already wandering in, their elegant gowns and tight black suits under their ski jackets.

The second half of the room was taken up by diners. Ranchers, legislators, the city elite. Behind them tall mullioned windows faced a fairy tale snowscape. Heavy woodwork. White tablecloths. Flowers. Chandeliers and fireplaces.

Yes, tonight is my night. Frydy patted her leg as she joined the room in applauding KC.

And then she saw him.

He sat at the table of honor, smack up against the dance floor. He was staring into the aging cleavage of the plump platinum blonde on his right. The woman, a few drinks in, was massaging his thigh, her piranha smile working overtime. It wasn't his wife. That grey little mouse sat on his left.

Frydy froze. He hadn't seen her. She blinked, slugged back the whiskey, and made for the door.

"Howdy, Fry." The voice came through a haze. She was bent over double by the coat rack and slowly looked up.

Chad. Her dance partner. All suited up and looking impossibly handsome. A diesel mechanic by day. Tango dancer by night.

She slid down among the coats and rested her head on her knees.

"You got a bad case of the jitters there, Fry," he said and stroked her head. "Get you some water? Something stronger?"

His hand smelled of strong soap and industrial strength cleanser. She allowed him to pull her up.

"Come on, Fry," he said. She allowed that firm hand that gently guided her around the dance floor to wipe that one stubborn tear from her cheek, but she flinched at its touch. "Time to knock 'em dead. Go get changed and I'll warm up the bar."

He handed her the red dress hanging on the coat rack.

She grabbed her gym bag and went up to the ladies' room. Someone was in the stall peeing, so she wedged off her boots and stripped off her shirt and jeans. She hung her red dress over the edge of freestanding mirror, washed her face and rooted around in her gym bag for her toothbrush and makeup.

Janey, the bookseller, came out of the stall, washed up at the sink next to her and went about repairing her makeup. She'd been crying. Frydy half-listened as she cleaned her teeth.

"Rafael was rejected for probation today," Janey said.

"Aarrgh," Frydy replied as she picked at a shred of lettuce stuck between her molars.

She knew Rafael from the hippy health food store where she bought her bulk spices. He had an after school job there.

"I was his tutor, you know. Sweet kid, but he had dyslexia," Janey said, talking to Frydy's reflection in the mirror. "I mean, that's not the reason he killed his friends. Not even the girl they were fighting over. No. Something just snapped."

Frydy spat and rinsed her mouth.

She put her hand on Janey's shoulder.

"All I know is that he set his friends up, ambushed them, and shot them. I didn't know him like you did."

"He'd get depressed, just like my nephew," Janey continued. "My nephew could've gone either way. We all could've."

She looked Frydy in the eyes.

"Rafael went the other way."

Frydy stared at herself in the full-length mirror. Black strapless bra. Black thong panties. Shiny robotic leg.

She reached into her bag and pulled out her spare leg. Flesh colored plastic, a perfect match for the shapely long one, still part of her body. The fake leg, she called it.

Her fake leg was already sheathed in a sheer black stocking. A thin black pencil line ran from its stocking heel to the lace-topped garter that held it up, dressed and ready for her to attach to her stump, once she removed the metallic prosthetic.

She pulled a matching stocking out of her bag along with her black, heeled tango shoes. She propped her fake leg against the mirror next to her red dress and sat on the stuffed and ruffled vanity chair.

Janey looked at her. Looked at the half-naked rag doll of a cowgirl staring at herself in the mirror.

She put her hand on Frydy's shoulder.

"Thanks for listening," she said. "It helped. Enjoy tonight."

Frydy continued to stare at her reflection, at the plastic, stockinged leg propped up against the mirror. This is what she always wore to tango. She had trained it to dance with her. She got her nerve endings to talk to it, do what her brain wanted it to do. Nobody could tell it was a fake leg unless they were told. But some people knew. And stared.

The one-legged tango dancer.

She knew the whispers.

Fuck 'em.

She thought of Kurt out there in the dining room. The betrayal she thought she'd forgotten had risen to the surface. He had left her. Mutilated. He'd run away.

She stroked her beautiful new robotic leg before preparing to release the suction that kept the nerve receptors in place.

It was a work of art.

Honest and lean.

Life.

"We all could've gone either way," Janey had said

Frydy looked at her own long, nut-brown flesh-and-blood leg. She looked at the plastic fake in its lace stocking. The tight red dress hanging from the mirror.

She thought of the jazz siren with the velvet voice in the boyish tuxedo. Her honesty.

And she made a decision.

Strains of Astor Piazzolla met her as she slid through the staff door into the bar. Chad was waiting, leaning nonchalantly against a stool, his upper body swaying with the dancers already on the floor. She rested her hip next to his and absorbed the vibration that passed between them.

He turned to claim her, to ask permission to dance, but she raised a finger to her freshly reddened lips. She was not ready to be led. She glowed, almost a fever glow, and he was ready for the passion of her dance. But she half closed her eyes and looked away, a soft intoxicated smile across her lips. She was not ready to accept.

The other dancers continued. They nodded for Chad and Frydy to join them. Made room on the floor, subtly opening and closing a space, inviting them in.

But she waited. Chad waited. The band waited. The room waited. And she knew that Kurt had seen her, and also waited.

She stood against the bar in her red dress with its bared back, her chocolate curls pulled up in a dramatic sweep, her long, drop earrings that caught the light, and waited. She waited until the room fell silent. Waited until it rang with tension. The tension of a tango.

She nodded to the band. To her partner. To the room.

Chad placed his hand on the small of her back and with the slight pressure of a finger, guided her onto the empty dance floor.

They moved as one body, yearning and yielding, their eyes both searching and blinding. They moved with slow longing around the floor, feeling, not hearing, the music. They danced the exquisite pain of desire.

Slowly a quiet buzz began to fill the room. Whispers and short gasps.

She slid the beautiful new leg across Chad's calf. They paused, and the languor of a hot, summer afternoon settled on them. Beads of sweat pearled on her naked back. He slowly pivoted her, his hand supporting the ripple of her spine as she arched away, their bellies joined. She articulated the knee, enjoyed the pleasure of its smooth transition, and wrapped the sleek metal sculpture around Chad's thighs. Finally she extended her new leg high into the air, bared through the slit in her red dress as she arched backwards, and raised her tango shoe to the gods.

Frydy didn't see the patrons stand. She didn't hear the gasps or the applause. She never saw Kurt stand up and quickly leave the room.

She only heard the music change tempo.

Milonga.

She quickened her step under Chad's direction and they both opened their eyes. The other dancers joined them on the floor.

"You're something," he whispered.

She followed his gaze down her body.

Her new leg.

A work of art.

Lean and honest.

You can bet on it.

She didn't miss a goddamn step.

Australian-born author **Yvonne Seng** worked and lived for many years in hotspots of the Middle East and North Africa, where she daily faced the issues of landmines, and in Turkey. She is the author of *Men in Black Dresses* (Simon & Schuster, 2003). Seng lives a stone's throw from Last Chance Gulch, Helena, Montana, where she currently works on an historical crime novel.

No Pasaran
Heywood Gould

This was told to me by Ben, a burly old guy with ink-stained hands, who sold anarchist pamphlets from a bridge table in Union Square Park, New York City, early '60's. A young reporter, eager for a story, I scribbled hastily while he was talking so any mistakes are mine...

In 1936 the world was going to shit. There was a Depression, millions out of work. Hitler was screwing the Jews, Mussolini massacring the Ethiopians, the rest of the world watching on the sidelines.

We believed the Revolution would bring equality and brotherhood for all. When word leaked out that Stalin was starving farmers in the Ukraine, we dismissed it as Capitalist propaganda.

Our one great hope was the Spanish Republic. The military dictator had been deposed. The Bourbon Royal family offered to come back, but didn't get any takers. Socialists, anarchists, liberals, even reactionaries got together and wrote a new constitution with freedom of speech, woman's suffrage and civil rights. It was the first victory for the people among many to come —or so we thought. But in '36 Franco's Nationalist army landed on the mainland from Spanish Morocco. Hitler, and Mussolini kicked in weapons and logistics. Hitler even sent a Luftwaffe company for ground support. Salazar, the Portuguese dictator, let the Germans smuggle tanks and heavy artillery across the border in violation of international agreements.

The Loyalists appealed to the Socialist countries. Russia sent weapons and a few tanks, Mexico old rifles. France gave lip service but actually stopped aid convoys at the Pyrenees. The French said they had to live up to the Non-Intervention treaty the Europeans had signed, but meanwhile they knew the Germans and Italians were violating the treaty so that was all bullshit. The so-called democracies felt more comfortable with the fascists, but would never admit it.

Thousands of young people dropped everything to join the International Brigades on the Loyalist side. I was studying civil engineering at Cooper Union. I was ready to die for the Republic, but afraid to face my girflfriend Sylvia so I sneaked out early one morning and left her a letter, saying I would return in triumph in time for a June wedding. I had this idea that we would get a ticker tape parade like they gave Lindbergh. I was a kid, you know...

Christmas Day 1936 three hundred of us sailed from New York. I was surprised to see how many Negro volunteers were on board. First night out a colored guy got up and said: "Fascism is the enemy of all black aspirations. I can't wait to get to the front and kill those fascist bastards." We cheered and yelled and hugged each other. Spent the rest of the trip, drinking wine and singing Commie songs in every language. Wanna hear "The Internationale?" How about "Avanti Populo"? Or "Union Burial Ground" by Woody Guthrie? I still know them by heart.

We landed in Le Havre and took the train to the Pyrenees. We had to split up and pretend to be hikers or students because they said the French weren't letting volunteers cross the border.

We worked our way south to Albacete. First day we saw a bunch of manacled guys being marched into this big barn outside of town. "Enemy prisoners?" I asked. "No, our guys," they told me. "Drunks or deserters or counter-revolutionaries. Watch what you say around the Commissars."

No matter what side you're on the army is always the same. Our commanders were the meanest guys I'd ever met. They drilled us all day and lectured us about signals, strategy and ideology—a crapload of that—at night. If you disagreed or said anything they didn't like you got a political trial in which they made sure you were a good brain dead Red, sorry for what you had done or said, before they sent you back to your unit.

They gave us World War I Remington rifles, which had been lying disassembled in Mexican warehouses for years. We were supposed to fieldstrip them, clean them, load them without blowing our heads off. Try to aim it and you become a target, they said. Just pop one and duck. Don't look to see if you hit anybody or you'll be the one to get hit.

Greasy food and not much of it. Cheap cigarettes made out of tobacco shreds, but that's where I picked up the habit. No women, not even pros. I was starting to worry if Sylvia had gone back to her old boyfriend.

One day a Russian came in. "Any engineers here?"

I raised my hand, first mistake. They brought me to see "Luigi." That's what he called himself, although he had a Brooklyn accent and talked like a high school teacher.

"We're gonna stop the fascist advance with mines," he said.

He gave us a little history lesson. They were called mines because they had been dug under besieged cities in Biblical times to make the walls collapse and a thousand years later had been filled with explosives. We would be among the first to use "portable" mines.

"We're gonna cripple the fascist war machine dead in its tracks," he said.

You didn't need an engineering degree. It was like playing in the sand at Coney Island. We used buckets, cans, tins, old helmets, filled them with gunpowder, tamped them down and stuck in a detonator attached to a spring that Luigi had invented. Seven of us kept at it until we had over a hundred. No time to see if they worked. They loaded us into a truck and headed north to Madrid. They didn't tell you much, only that Madrid was the beating heart of the Republic and we couldn't let the fascists take it.

It was about two hundred and thirty kilometers on the map. We kept stopping, huddling in the dark, hearing artillery and machine guns up ahead. We got to Madrid before dawn. There were big banners with the Republican motto "No Pasaran." They Shall Not Pass. We kept chanting it— "No Pasaran." People waved to us from the windows.

We stopped on a narrow cobblestone street. "They have to come this way to get to the center of town," Luigi said. Another Commissar showed up, a big slob American who looked like my Uncle Mo, the butcher. He told us were were going to ambush a German armored column that was coming from the north. This wasn't just a skirmish, he said. This was the Worker Davids against the fascist Goliaths...

We started chanting "No Pasaran" again and drowned out the rest of his speech.

Luigi was yelling in Spanish and people came out of the buildings with picks and shovels. We dug up the cobblestones and planted the mines in the holes. The Spanish people were crying, shaking our hands. A big woman built like Mae West kissed me on the lips. I tried to see where she lived so I could go up and see her.

When we were done they sent us to a neighboring street. When we ran out of cans people brought food tins and buckets out. When we ran out of powder we were done.

They put us on a roof at the end of the street. We stayed there, freezing, all night and most of the next day. There were volleys of rifle fire. "Paseos they call it," Luigi said. "Executing fascist soldiers and spies." We heard shots on the next street and got nervous, but Luigi calmed us down. "Curfew violators..."

I was surprised. "They're on our side. Do we have to shoot them?"

"They're told to stay inside," he said. "If they come out they could be spies, Fifth columnists..."

"I thought the people wanted us here."

"The Revolution begins as civil war," he said . "The workers against the priests, the proprietors and the parasites." The way he was stringing all those p-words together, it must have come from some speech he had made a hundred times before.

The Germans weren't taking any chances. They spent the whole night bombarding the area with artillery. Buildings around us took direct hits and burst into flame. People were screaming, babies crying. Everybody trying to get away. We heard a horse neighing. Then a loud popping noise like a balloon bursting. Luigi threw his helmet. "Shit! They ran over one of our mines." He leaned way over the roof. "Get those people off the street!" Two Spanish guys from the FAI—that's the anarchist group—went down. People were running out of the burning buildings. A guy pushed a barrow out into the street and BOOM right over a mine. "Keep them on the sidewalk," Luigi yelled. "Don't let them walk in the road."

We were shivering in the dark, our fingers in our ears. Another hour and I would have gone nuts. When it got light we heard the tanks rumbling into the city.

There were bodies in the road. That poor horse, its guts leaking out. "Leave them there to block the tanks," Luigi said. The guy with the barrow had lost part of his leg, and screamed until he passed out. Our snipers were on roofs and in doorways. They were trying to set up a machine gun on a roof but couldn't get it to stay on the tripod so just propped it against the ledge.

A few tanks came down the narrow street one at a time. We lay flat and waited. Nothing happened. Luigi peeked over. His face got all twisted and he started crying like a little kid. "We put the goddamm mines in the middle of the road. The tank treads aren't hitting them."

The tanks bumped over the horse, then squashed one of the bodies. But kept going like nothing had happened.

Down the street, one of the snipers chucked a Russian grenade off a roof. The first was a dud, but the next one blew pretty good and tore some treads off the one behind it. The turrets started turning. One of our guys ran out of a doorway and rolled another grenade. It hit a tread and tore a chunk out of that Panzer, but it fired anyway and blew a hole in the building. The tank ahead of it fired into the buildings on both sides and kept rolling.

A tank turned the corner with a squad of troops behind it, hunched real low and looking around, scared shitless. Behind them was a truck towing the biggest cannon I'd ever seen—an .88 I found out later. Behind that was a covered truck. And another squad, behind it, marching close together, which is the worst thing to do, but they were Spanish farmers probably and didn't know no better. The 88 rolled right over a cluster of our mines. Nothing happened and Luigi started crying again.

"I swear I'll shoot the sonofabitch who made those."

A truck swerved to avoid the dead horse and BAVOOM. The mine ripped right through the front end and the truck caught fire. All of a sudden it was like a chain reaction. The mines blew the wheels off the cannon carriage. Fascist troops panicked and ran right into the snipers down the street. The machine gun started, but jammed after a couple of rounds. The driver jumped out of the burning truck waving and yelling to the covered truck behind him. That guy tried to turn and back up and went right over a mine. It blew a ball of flame sky high. "Ammo truck," Luigi screamed. Everything went up like fireworks on the Fourth. Luigi was waving his rifle and yelling out of his mind. We had to pull him down because it was raining stones and wood and burning shrapnel.

People were running around like chickens without heads. You couldn't tell who was who through the smoke, but we kept shooting. At least I did until Luigi grabbed my arm. "You're wasting bullets." The first tank made it through, but the one with the broken tread was disabled. A guy popped up, hands high, but they cut him down before he could climb out of the hatch.

Somebody whacked me on the head. "Let's go..."

We had to jump from one roof to another, holding our rifles in front of us at full port. Some kid got nervous and threw his rifle onto the roof before jumping. It went off and hit another guy in the leg. He almost rolled over the ledge, screaming.

We went to a staging area in the Centro. Luigi was telling everybody "we captured an 88." You get excited and you don't feel anything, not even fear. But when it's over you see what happened to you. I was okay, but I felt like somebody was sticking a toothpick in my ear. Turned out I had a punctured eardrum.

They gave us bread and coffee. I just wanted to go someplace warm. They loaded us into trucks. Luigi hopped in as we pulled out.

"You're a full-fledged squad of sappers now," he said.

One of the American guys didn't know the word. "Saps is right," he said.

We found out that the fascists had used prisoners and local people and horses and anybody they could find as shields. Sent them down the mined streets to get blown up. Some Brit yelled at Luigi: " We're killing our own people."

Luigi got that high school teacher look again.

"These are effective tactical weapons," he said. "Nothing can be totally controlled."

Later we got a hold of some captured German Tellermines they were using against our Russian tanks. In those days you could just dig up a German mine and and replant it against the Panzers. The Germans got wise and put in anti-handling devices in the next war.

They made a lot of mistakes in Spain. We could have beaten them. But nobody wanted us to win...

"What are you blabbing about now?"

A woman with weary eyes and white streaks in her gray hair was standing there with a lunch box and a thermos.

Ben put his burly arm around her like he was posing for a photo.

"This is Sylvia," he said. "The girl I left behind."

My story never made it into the paper.

Born in the Bronx and raised in Brooklyn, **Heywood Gould** got his start as a reporter for the *New York Post* when it was still a pinko rag. Later, he financed years of professional and personal rejection driving cabs, assisting morticians, tending bar, and writing screenplays. He is the author of eight novels, among them *Fort Apache, the Bronx*; *Double Bang, The Serial Killer's Daughter*, and *Greenlight for Murder*. He has also written nine movies, including *Cocktail*, *The Boys from Brazil*, and *Rolling Thunder*, as well as directing four feature films. He lives in Southern California.

The Landmines of Beverly Hills
Terrill Lee Lankford

His fingers trembled as he rolled the joint. The last one he would be rolling until who-knew-when. She didn't like him sparking up and he always tried to avoid it whenever they were together. He had even given it up completely for a few years to make her happy, but lately he had been backsliding. And stress always made the backsliding easier. She would be landing at LAX soon and arriving at the hotel soon after that, so he needed to get a little buzz on before she got there. The trick would be in the timing. Could he mellow out just enough to be chill without her noticing he was stoned? They hadn't seen each other in almost a month. The reunions were always fraught with peril. She often came back from her "missions" exhausted and cranky. And he often said or did the wrong thing upon her arrival, which would make things worse. It usually took three or four days before they could get back into the rhythm of living together again. And those three or four days could be hell. If not for the kids they would have split up years ago. The kids and the press. The kids and the press and the public. The kids and the press and the public and the world. The kids and the press and the public and the world and *her*. Her will was too strong. They would separate when *she* decided it was time and not before.

He loved her of course. But he had had no idea what he was getting into when they fell in love. Her reputation had preceded her. She was wild. Intense. Talented. Beautiful. Many called her the sexiest woman in the world. And since he was also considered by many (or at least by People magazine—twice!) to be the sexiest man in the world, it was only natural that they would be together. No matter how much chaos it would create. It had been difficult in the beginning. The world seemed to turn against them for a while. After all, he had left America's Sweetheart for America's Super Vixen. The world couldn't know what he knew—about BOTH of them. The world couldn't understand. So there was a lot of hate out there. But the heat of their passion blinded them to the controversy. When the smoke cleared and everyone settled down about the scandal, they were still together. That was when he realized that she was far more than he thought and that things were going to be far more complicated than he could have imagined. He had also, of late, realized that time is a much more brutal mistress than the press. Time is a bitch. Time takes its toll on any relationship, no matter how magical it may seem at the beginning. Living with her was the first time he actually realized how much *work* a relationship required. And he had been working his ass off for years now.

Sometimes it didn't seem worth it. A *lot* of times it didn't seem worth it. She really was just a person when you boil it all down. Not a Goddess. Just another human being. Beautiful, yes. Talented, yes. Kind, yes. But there were many beautiful and talented and kind women out there. He could, for the most part, take his pick. He could be with just about any of them if he wanted to be. He chose her. Or maybe she had chosen him. He wasn't completely sure how it had happened. At the time he *thought* he was the one who had made the first move, but in retrospect he realized that was probably not the case. Women can sometimes seduce you without you ever realizing it. She made him think it was all his idea but now that he knew her well he knew better than to believe she had ever been anything less than in charge. While it was exciting it was very exciting. But excitement fades and then there is the work, which is to be expected, but he could never anticipate what she had in mind for them. Something had happened to her on her own wild journey to fame. She had gotten *good*. She had turned her fame into a weapon for righteous causes and she had taken him along for the ride. *Together*, she had said, *we can really make a difference.*

He hadn't understood that at first. Not the magnitude of it at least. He didn't realize how all-consuming these missions would become. He always considered himself an okay guy. He never wanted to harm anyone (at least anyone who didn't have it coming) and he liked to do charitable things, but he also liked to chill out when not "working." And being famous was a lot of work. Now it was like he had TWO full time jobs. Being famous and doing good deeds. Making the movies was the easy part. That was like play. And he didn't have to do it that often. But being famous was hard work. And it was 24/7. When you added the missions to it all there was very little time left to chill. Sometimes it seemed ridiculous to expect so much out of an Oklahoma boy. Who was he to be trying to fix all the problems in the world? One of his favorite lines in the movies he had made was, *"We're all monkeys,"* and deep down he believed that. We are all just monkeys. Why not just do as monkeys do? Be natural. Keep it local. He used to sing a few lines from a Stones song to her during trysts: *"I am just a monkey man and I'm glad you are a monkey woman, too."* She would laugh, but she never took the concept to heart.

She had been in Cambodia for the last three weeks, detonating landmines and visiting maimed farmers and their children. In the meantime he had been left in L.A. to care for their own brood. He didn't mind it at all. He preferred hanging out with the kids to being out in the public. He liked people. Most of them, at least. But he didn't like what his fame had done to the worst of them. The paparazzi. The hustlers. The haters. It was hard to be around people like that. He understood what Sean felt and the way he behaved around them. He envied Sean's ability to kick ass when cornered, but he couldn't carry on like that. Angie had always insisted he be on his best behavior in public. *"If you are an asshole, people won't love you. And if people don't love you we can't get good things accomplished."* Her eye was always on the big picture.

Yes. It was full time work being him. Half of a power couple. *The* power couple. The power couple all other power couples envied. The one that set the gold standard for power coupling. He had only wanted to be an actor. To make a little money, smoke some good weed and meet beautiful women. He could never have imagined that the plan would be so incredibly successful. Or what dark price he would have to pay for that success.

His cell phone buzzed. He looked at it. She was texting him. "Just landed. See you soon."

He fired up the joint and took a toke.

It was dangerous, this most recent plan he had hatched. He had taken their favorite room at the Beverly Hills Hotel. The one they had spent the most time in when it had all began. Before the missions and the kids had entered their lives. He had loaded the room up with flowers and champagne and sent the kids and the nannies and the teachers and the bodyguards to the beach in Malibu for the day. He wanted to have a few hours of alone time with her before the circus began again. A little romance. But this was a risky move and he knew it. She would want to see the kids immediately upon returning. But once that happened it would be a long time before they would be alone together again. He was hoping they could get reacquainted before the mayhem set in. He missed her. He missed her body. He missed the intimacy they once had. And he had felt outside temptations lately, so he needed to get himself right. He needed to focus on her again. Because if he couldn't get his act together, madness could ensue. Chain reactions that could go nuclear.

He looked down at the pool area. There were only two girls down there now, both asleep on their thin, empty bellies and their full, voluptuous breasts, basking in the waning sunlight. Long gone were the days when he could stroll down there and start a casual conversation with them. Fame had taken that privilege from him. Fame and *her.*

His cell buzzed: "Carl says you got our room at the Beverly Hills. How sweet."

He took another toke. But a small one this time. This shit was *strong.* It was that Godzilla shit. And she was in the car now, heading this way. He would have to be sharp by the time she got there. And clear eyed. He stubbed out the joint and put it in his wallet.

His cell buzzed: "On the 405. Can't wait to see the kids!"

Shit! He got the joint back out and fired it up again. This had been a mistake. And he was going to pay dearly for it. He took a long toke and felt the wave wash over him. If he was going to get an ass kicking he wanted to be mellow so he wouldn't fight back. She was like a bear. She would bite and maul him when he had been bad, but the less resistance he presented the less chance of her crushing his tiny skull in her powerful jaws.

His cell buzzed again. It was a text, but not from her this time. It was from George. It read: "FOR YOUR EYES ONLY" and then there was a link to a web address. He clicked the link and watched as a Beagle moved a chair around in a kitchen, climbed up onto a counter, and stole a tray of chicken nuggets out of a toaster oven. The first two minutes were a little slow. It took the dog a while to figure out his game plan and where exactly to put the chair to create stairs leading to the proper spot on the counter so he could reach the toaster oven without falling into the sink. But once he was on that counter it was funny as hell. He nuzzled the toaster door open and pulled out a few hot nuggets and they fell on the floor. He ran down his homemade stairs to retrieve them, then climbed back up and pulled the whole pan out of the oven and dropped it to the floor with a crash. He scrambled back down and ate every last one of the nuggets, leaving his masters to go hungry. It was too much! He laughed so hard at the dog's antics that tears filled his eyes. "Fuckin' George," he said when it was all over. He texted him back: "LOL."

There was an immediate text reply. But it wasn't George. It was her. "LOL what? That I'm on the 405 or that I can't wait to see the kids? What's so funny?"

Ho-lee shit! He had somehow mixed up the texts and replied to her last one instead of George's. What to do now? How to fix this? The truth! Always stick to the truth or as close to it as humanly possible. That's what his dad had taught him.

He texted her back. "No, Hon! I was texting George. Or thought I was. He sent me a funny link and I just wanted him to know I liked it. I'll forward it to you right now."

He hit send so the fire could be extinguished immediately, then found George's text and forwarded it to her, adding a note at the top of the message: "I love you, honey. Can't wait to see you!"

As he hit send again he realized that it was possible that she could misconstrue the note he added as actually being a note George had sent to him with the link. Had he just made things worse? He prayed not.

The joint suddenly burned his fingers. During the chaos he had ignored it and it had burned down to a roach. He tapped it out on the railing, touched it to his tongue to make certain it was all the way out, then flipped it into a nearby palm tree. He went into the room and got a glass of water from the sink, drank it down in one gulp. Then he splashed water in his face and dried it with a towel. It was time to suit up. He went into the bathroom, brushed his teeth, scraped his tongue, and took a mouthwash chaser. He wanted her to smell no weed on his breath.

His cell buzzed: "Cute video."

That's it? "Cute video?" She didn't think it was LOL? Now he felt stupid. But at least she didn't make a mean remark about George sending him another love note. So she must have understood that what he had written at the top of the text was meant for her.

He opened the refrigerator and got out a bottle of champagne. Maybe if they *both* got a buzz on quickly all would go smoothly. He hoped she was mighty thirsty.

He felt guilty not going with her this time. He had said he had a lot of work to do for his company. And while that was no lie, the real reason was much more shameful. He couldn't handle it any more. He couldn't handle meeting the men and women who had been mangled by the landmines. It was too much for him. Their pain and disfigurement was unbearable to him. But it was nothing compared to meeting the children. The children broke his heart into a million pieces. Legless, armless, sometimes even faceless children. Children who had had their reproductive organs demolished. Children who pissed and shit into bags, but still managed to smile when they met a stranger. Their pain and misery made it hard for him to enjoy being alive. To enjoy being *him*. Being strong and healthy and rich and beautiful and most of all *whole*. He couldn't deal with the guilt anymore and it made him feel so very, very ashamed. But he didn't know what to do about it. She was so much stronger than him. She always had been, but for a while he had put on a good show. Now his heart and mind were scarred by what he had seen and experienced. She was no stranger to the pain either. He had held her on many a long night while she sobbed uncontrollably because of what she had seen during the day. But somehow in the morning she would be back to normal. Ready to continue the battle. Stronger than ever. She seemed to feed on the horror and turn it into iron will and fierce resolve. The *mission* remained clear to her. But for him it was taking a massive emotional toll. It was making him feel empty and helpless. He didn't know if he could do it anymore.

His cell buzzed: "Pulling up to the hotel! Very excited!"

Would she be as excited once she saw that the kids weren't there? Could he convince her it was all okay? Could they have a few hours to themselves to make love and to heal without dealing with the circus that was their lives? To find out if they were still who they used to be? To find out if it was all still worth the work?

He felt like was stuck now, in this bizarre life they had constructed, like a Cambodian farmer standing in the middle of a mine field. To make any kind of move, forward, back, or even sideways, could result in a crippling event. But move he must. She was coming. He heard the elevator ding out in the hallway. Heard her footsteps approaching.

He moved to the door cautiously. From this point forward he would have to be extremely careful. There were a lot of landmines ahead.

Terrill Lee Lankford is a novelist and filmmaker. His novels include *Earthquake Weather*, *Blonde Lightning*, and *Shooters*. He recently directed the feature film *Christmas with the Dead*, and wrote *The Reconstructionist* with Michael Connelly. He is currently working on unnamed projects in an unnamed city to be released at an unknown time in distant future.

Idyllwild
Michael Hemmingson

1.

Ex-cop Sean Talmadge—retired five years now—wouldn't let it go, and continued to harass me over a missing persons case he was convinced I was guilty of, going back seventeen years. When he was a homicide detective with the Hermosa Beach Police Department (northwest of Los Angeles), he followed me in his off hours and kept me under surveillance, albeit any evidence pointing toward the disappearance of my ex-lover, a friend of Talmadge's daughter. He retired three years ago but continued to haunt and harass me; he was no longer with the police department and claimed he was a licensed private detective and working for a client to find out what happened to Nicole Rense—that's the name of my ex-girlfriend. Talmadge's "client" was himself; the man was obsessed with me in a most unhealthy manner.

I moved from Hermosa Beach to the mountain community called Idyllwild in Riverside County. My father owned a pre-fab trailer in the retirement community Pine Grove and when he passed, I inherited the place. I am not retirement age but the park allows those under fifty-five to live there if a property is from inheritance. Six months after I moved to the quiet, cozy Idyllwild community, Sean Talmadge, age 65, moved into a trailer on the other side of the golf course from where I lived. I tried complaining to property management and they said he purchased the lot and pre-fab with a solid bank loan and he had every right to live here; more, in fact, because he was a senior citizen and I, age 44, was not.

I would have moved to another state, or across the country to the east coast, but I did not have the finances. I lived off disability benefits, the pittance the government allotted me, for injuries in the first Gulf War. With a prosthetic right leg and right arm, I was not exactly employable in the real world. Even if I could move far away, Talmadge would most likely follow me. He followed me when I flew to Las Vegas once; have no idea how he found out I was there and what hotel I was staying at—but there he was, in the casino in Circus Circus. "Oh, hey, Steven Vance," he said, acting surprised, "what a *coincidence* running into you." Right. "So," he said, patting me on the back, his breath smelling of vodka, "you here for some gambling or did you stash

Nicki's body somewhere in Vegas? Lots of unsolved murders here in Vegas, eh?"

He was a heavy drinker. When he was still a cop, I filed several harassment complaints with the Hermosa Police Department. I had one interview with some lady from Internal Affairs; I suggested his drinking problem had made him delusional and obsessed. Talmadge did not stop bothering me; I knew his friends in the department simply looked the other way, and Talmadge most likely convinced them I was responsible for whatever happened to Nicole Rense.

2.

I met Nicole a year before I joined the Marines and was shipped to Kuwait in 1991. She was 20, second year of college, and I was 22. We had a rollercoaster relationship: one week madly in love, the other vehemently fighting. The passion made for some memorable times in the bedroom. She was angry and upset that I had joined the Corp. *"Why* do you want to be a stupid *jar*head?" she asked me with confusion. "You're gonna get *killed* over there," she said with concern. "Don't expect *me* to wait for *you,"* she said with spite.

I told Talmadge many times: "She broke up with me. She said she met some guy and was taking off to Vegas with him."

"So who is this 'guy'?" he would ask.

"I have no idea."

"Because he doesn't exist."

"She could have been lying."

"He's a fabrication of your imagination. What did you do to Nicki?"

"Nothing."

"Where is her body?"

"I have no idea."

"We're going to find out the truth eventually."

"When you do, let me know."

I was free of him when I went to the Middle East; there, I lost an arm and a leg from a landmine that the HumVee I was in drove over. Two men in my platoon died. For a long time I wished I had gone with them. I had to come home a crippled "hero." I did nothing heroic in Kuwait and Iraq. No one did.

3.

My handicapped status did not deter Talmadge from continuing his harassment, surveillance, and constant questioning and badgering. He was convinced I had something to do with Nicole's vanishing because his daughter, Lisa, told him so; she said Nicole was afraid of me, that I had physically hurt her.

"Something you must understand about Nicole," I said one time, when he brought me into the station and put me in an interview room, "she was into the rough stuff. She was into BDSM. She was *kinky.*"

The look on his face was priceless: the shock, the disgust. "You're making that up," he said, making a fist; I knew he wanted to punch me in the mouth.

He refused to believe the truth about a young woman who had been friends with his daughter since they were both nine. I should have told him some dark nastiness I knew about Lisa, things Nicole had told me...

4.

I could feel his eyes whenever I took to the golf course. When I went to the community pool and relaxed in the Jacuzzi, he would show up and swim laps. He always kept his distance, never engaged conversation. I didn't know what he thought he'd find; perhaps he expected me to fall apart, drop to my knees and confess my crime because the weight of guilt was too heavy on my heart and I needed forgiveness.

When I drove into town for groceries and a liquor store run, or to have a burger and beer at the local grill, he would follow me in his beat up flatbed truck, do his shopping at the same time, or having a steak and vodka tonic at the local grill.

One day I decided *enough,* it was time to confront him.

5.

I drove east, on the highway, and headed down the mountain for the desert. I looked in the rearview: he kept his distance, but his truck was there, pacing. I pressed on the pedal and lost him for a while; I slowed down and let him catch up. I speeded; slowed down, let him come back. I toyed with him for three hours, wondering if he had enough gas for this, if he kept a full tank like I did.

I drove through Palm Springs, then to Indio, and headed southeast toward the Salton Sea. It was four in the afternoon and the sun was blazing hot. The car thermometer read 113. I had AC. Did Talmadge? Was he sweating it up in that old truck?

We were the only vehicles for miles in both directions, in the middle of the desert, the rancid smell of the Salton Sea muggy and thick. I was looking for a certain mile marker. When I passed it, I drove two hundred feet and stopped. This was the place I wanted.

This was the exact place I had planned.

I got out of my car and he got out of his truck. His skin was bright pink and his body covered in sweat. He approached me quickly, stomping his feet on the scorching hot pavement. He had a revolver in his hand, a .38 Smith and Wesson. He pointed the weapon at my chest, hand shaking. I worried he would accidentally pull the trigger.

"Did you hide her body somewhere around here?" he demanded. "Is that why you stopped?"

"I stopped because you've been following me, Talmadge. Why won't you let this go?"

"I loved her," he said like a croak, and then he began to cry. The heat and stress was too much for him. "God help me, I loved that sweet beautiful girl."

So that was it. I remember Nicole telling me about an older man who was obsessed with her, in love with her. She never said who it was. "It's really kinda sad," she'd said.

"Something you should know," I said slowly, "I had a threesome with Nicole and Lisa. That's right: I *made love* to *your* daughter. Once. Just once, with Nicki there."

That was a lie but I knew it would strike him deep. I should have told him this before. His face paled. "You…" He couldn't speak. His eyes bulged. "No," he moaned. He dropped the gun and fell to his knees, grabbing at his chest, trying to breathe.

I moved toward him. "Something the matter, old man?"

"My…in my…cab," he wheezed. "Pills. My…nitro…please…"

I walked to his truck. I took my time, hobbling on my prosthetic leg. I opened the cab door and spotted a pillbox on the passenger seat. I opened it. There were eight sections for vitamins and medicine: iron and calcium, Vicodin and nitro.

Talmadge was lying on the ground. I stood over him, holding the pillbox over his head. He reached up and pleaded, "Pill…please…"

"First I want to tell you something," I said. "I'm going to give you the confession you've been waiting seventeen years for. Yeah, I buried Nicole near here. Sweet little beautiful Nicki." I gestured. "About half a mile out there, middle of the desert. You've been right all along, Sean. You can die knowing that, and knowing you won't be able to do a thing about it."

He began to violently shake. He wanted to get up. He wanted his gun. His heart would not cooperate with his desire for justice.

I picked up the .38.

"I should show you mercy. Instead, I am going to stand here and watch you slowly die. For the seventeen years of hell you gave me. I lost two limbs for this country and what do I come back to? *You.* Was Nicole there for me? She said she loved me, she said we were soul mates, until I joined the Marines. She broke up with me; said she met some guy at a party and was going to Vegas with him for the weekend. I'm sure it was a lie to hurt me, to show me she was serious about letting me go. She came to my apartment to tell me that. I was hammering some nails into the wall to put up a painting and I used that hammer, slammed it into her head. I crushed her skull. I put her body in the trunk of my car; it was easy, she was petite and skinny, as you know. I drove out here, I knew the desert, I knew I could bury her out here and no one would ever find her. And that's what I did. Her bones are out there, buried. I could go out there and dig her up, you know. I left a large rock on her grave, in case I ever needed to move her body."

By the time I was done talking, he was dead.

I leaned down. "Goodbye, Detective Talmadge."

I left him there. I got into my car, taking his gun, and drove back to Idyllwild.

6.

A trucker came across his body and called the highway patrol. I saw a news item on TV and word around the retirement community was that Mr. Talmadge had died of a heart attack out by the Salton Sea. There was an obituary in the local weekly.

I thought I was free now; I could live my uneventful life in peace. The first visit I received was three weeks later, by his daughter Lisa. I had met her a few times when I dated Nicole. The years had not been kind to her; the sprite teenage girl in my memory was now a tired, plump real estate agent and mother of three, two husbands behind her.

"Hello, Steven," she said.

I acted like I didn't know her.

"It's me, Lisa Talmadge. Well, Harrison. That was my second married name. I was Talmadge."

"Oh yes. *Lisa.* How are you doing?" I pretended: *How strange this is.*

She gestured behind her. "I'm collecting my father's belongings. He passed away...did you know that?"

She was playing me. I replied, "Yes, I heard. My condolences."

She stood there, waiting for me to invite her in, the civil thing to do. So I did. She walked past me and looked around, taking inventory of my Spartan existence. She saw the extra prosthetic limbs leaning against a bookcase. "So you were injured in the war," she said.

"Yeah. Some war."

"It must have been painful." Her voice was cold.

"Can I get you something? Soda, water, soda water? A beer?"

She turned and glared. "Let's cut the bogus nicey-nice, Steven."

"Let's."

"I know why my father moved out here."

"To stalk me."

"Not *stalk*. Investigate."

"Your dad was a sick man. Senile, delusional. You must know this."

"What I know," she said, "is that you did something to Nicki. My best friend. I knew about your violence."

"And hers? You must have known she was…"

"I *knew* what she liked." She was uncomfortable saying that, her face going red. "I know she went to see you, to dump you in person. She thought you deserved that much, no Dear John letter or a phone call."

"She never came to my apartment to tell me anything," I said calmly. "She broke up with me on the phone. I told your dad this—hundreds of times."

"I talked to her the night before. I didn't hear from her again. No one did, not her folks, other friends. *No one.*"

"She took off with some guy."

"Yeah, she said she met a new guy but she didn't go anywhere with him."

I felt a tinge of pain—so the other guy *was* true.

"My dad talked to that guy and the guy said she never showed up for the Vegas trip."

That bitch…that cheating bitch…

"What happened to my dad?" she asked sharply.

"He had a heart attack."

"My dad checked in every day on what he was doing. 'Just in case' he always said. He was determined to find out the truth and put you away."

"Like I said, he was a disturbed man with an obsession."

Should I tell her what her father confessed, that he "loved" Nicole in a way a man should not love his daughter's friend? I could say maybe he killed Nicole and was trying to pin the old crime on an innocent man…

"He called from his cell phone and said he was following your car," Lisa said. "The same day he was found in the middle of nowhere, rotting in the hot sun."

"Lisa, I'm sorry, but that is not true. I have not been out of this trailer in three months, other than to go into town for groceries."

If anyone in this park saw me drive out of town, saw Talmadge follow me in his truck, noticed that I came home late, my alibi would shatter. This was a community of tired old people, however, who were lost in the past or preoccupied with their favorite TV shows.

"He was on to you and you knew it."

"I'm going to have to ask you to leave," I told her.

I held the door open. She walked out. The tension off her body was like a wave of knives.

"Your day will come, Steven," she said.

I sighed and feigned weariness. "Again, my condolences about your father. He may have been mentally ill, but deep down he was a good man."

"The hell with you," she said, walking away fast, back to her father's trailer, back to picking up what was left of his life.

7.

I had committed no crime, unless withholding medication from a heart attack victim was a crime. No one could prove that; there were no witnesses on that empty stretch of road. I did steal his registered handgun, and that could be construed a criminal act. That night, after Lisa's visit, I dismantled the handgun and drove back to the desert, burying the pieces every five miles.

I kept one bullet as a trophy, like I had kept Nicole's hair clip.

Hindsight: perhaps I should have broke into Talmadge's trailer; he most likely had a file on me, surveillance photos, notes on his theories. Then again, if I had removed anything like that and his daughter knew about it, suspicion would fall on me.

I was surprised that Nicole's remains had not been found by now. I had waited for it all these years, for the warrant and handcuffs, if her bones could even be identified. The crushed skull would indicate murder. Maybe one day she would be found, and I would be long gone from this earth.

I simply wanted to live the rest of my days in peace.

8.

Five months went by. I expected another visit from Lisa. Her father's trailer went up for sale and was purchased by a couple from Canada. They were nice people and I chatted with them by the pool a few times. They had always dreamed of retiring to nether regions of California.

Five months, and then I was paid a visit by a Los Angeles County Sheriff's detective named Harold Kent. He gave me his card, showed me his badge and ID. He asked if he could come in and talk to me. I said certainly. "How can I help you, Detective Kent?"

"May I sit down? It's pretty damn hot out."

"I have AC," I said. I reached for the control on the wall and turned on the cold air. "Can I get you anything? Water, soda, soda water? Beer?"

"If you have some cold water," he said, sitting at the card table in the living room area. An antique manual typewriter was on the card table; one day I would write a memoir about the Gulf War and Nicole.

I got us both small bottles of water from the fridge. I sat across from him.

"Thank you," he said, gulping the water down. He was a heavy-set man in his mid-50s, probably more used to deskwork than the field. I looked at his card: he was in the economic crimes division. Deskwork, tracking down embezzlers and bad checks.

"You were a Jarine in Gulf One," he said. "I was there, manning radar at CentCom in Saudi Arabia."

"Army?"

"Reserves."

"Would you like another water?"

"Eh? I'm fine, thanks. Let me get to it, Mr…"

"Call me Steve."

"It's about Sean Talmadge. You know who he is—was."

"Yes, he lived across the golf course."

"Sean and I were good friends; we were partners in a patrol car twenty-five years ago. He trained me, had seven years seniority. He made detective before me, the smart bastard. He wanted homicide; I wanted white-collar kicks. I knew he was keeping an eye on you, convinced you had something to do with a girl's disappearance. His daughter calls me, she says you had something to do with her father's death."

"He had a heart attack is what I heard."

"Yes, a massive coronary. It was bound to happen, he didn't take care of himself."

"She came to see me and made accusations," I said. "I did not cause her father's heart attack."

"She's upset. She also thinks you are responsible for her missing friend."

"Is that why you're here? Are you investigating me now?"

He held out his hands. "Not my jurisdiction. And I'm not homicide. I'm just here to get Lisa off my back. You must understand, she won't stop bugging me unless I came out here and had a talk with you."

"I understand," I said.

"I'm sure she'll come to her senses, that her dad died naturally and these things happen."

"I feel for her loss."

"Hopefully she'll be satisfied when I tell her my opinion is: you're a wounded vet living quietly out here."

"That's me."

He stood up. "Thank you for your understanding."

"Anytime."

We shook hands.

I didn't believe him. Never trust a cop.

I watched him from the window. He was taking a good look at my plot, my car. He looked back at my trailer.

9.

I was on my guard. After six weeks, I again thought this mess was done with. Never underestimate the determined. Lisa Harrison neé Talmadge broke into my trailer, a gun in her hand. She wasn't stealth about it; I heard the sound of glass breaking, my side door opening. I grabbed the baseball bat I kept by the bed and rushed to the living room. Lisa turned on the light and smiled at the sight of me, holding the bat, she holding the gun: a .9mm Glock. She probably found it with her father's belongings when she came by to pick up his stuff.

"I know how to use a gun," she said, "Daddy taught me."

"What's the meaning of this?" I asked, wondering if I should rush her, if she had it in her to shoot.

"Drop the bat, you murderer."

I saw in her eyes intent. Yeah, she would shoot me; it had taken her months to get up the nerve to come here.

I put the bat down. "Take it easy, we can talk about this…"

"Oh yes, *we will talk.*"

"I know you are upset about your father…"

"I have been *upset* nearly two decades about my friend. *My best friend.* That you took away from me. What did you *do* with her?"

"Lisa, look," I said, stepping forward.

"One more step and you're dead."

"All right then, you want me to say it? I killed her. I killed Nicole. I didn't plan to; it just happened; I lost my control. She broke up with me and I had a hammer and I used it." How strange it felt, a relief: to say it out loud, to tell someone my darkest secret, like I had told her father out by the Salton Sea.

She wasn't expecting my confession. "Just like Daddy said."

"That's right, Lisa. Sean Talmadge was correct all along. But did you know your father was in love with Nicole? Your best friend? That he wanted—"

"Shut up with your lies!"

She stumbled. Was she drunk? Her father was a drinker; I remember Nicole mentioning that Lisa liked her wine a little too much.

"What did you do with her body?"

"She's out in the desert." I had an idea. I said, "I can take you to her."

"What?"

"I can take you to her grave, and you can vindicate your dad. You'll be the hero. I want to turn myself in and confess," I lied to her. "I want to pay for what I did. Your dad will be a hero, so will you. It is time for me to do this."

"Okay," she said. "Is it far?"

"Not far," I lied again.

"I'll shoot you, I really will, if you try any monkey business."

"We'll just need a flashlight and a shovel, okay? Don't get nervous."

She followed me as I got a flashlight from the kitchen and a shovel from the back of the trailer. I could smell booze on her breath.

"We can take my car," I said.

"Wait, I don't know," she said, "let's wait until morning when the sun—"

She stumbled on one of her feet. Drunk. I swung the shovel around, hitting her on the side of the head. She dropped the gun and looked at me with surprised terror. I swung the shovel again.

10.

I took Lisa out to the desert to be with her friend. I could not find the exact spot in the dark. It was close enough. The sun was just coming up when I finished digging a hole. I dumped Lisa into the hole and covered her up.

I stopped for breakfast driving back to Idyllwild. I would have to pack some things, go somewhere else, another state. Or I could just stay put and play dumb. I would need to wipe the trailer down for prints, fix the broken glass on the side door; look for her car in the retirement park, or outside it, wherever she left it. I didn't know what she drove; I would need to keep an eye on a parked car in the same spot over the next week. *This could be done, this will work...*

11.

"Don't join the Marines," Nicole had said. "Stay here with me, or go and never have me. Your choice."

12.

Choices, I thought when I arrived home, to find several Riverside Sheriff vehicles and one unmarked car parked around my trailer.

Harold Kent was there, sporting a glib smile. The sheriff deputy handed me a warrant, giving them carte blanche to search my trailer, which they had already done when I was gone.

Kent held in his hand what they were seeking: a cell phone. Another deputy had two items bagged: Nicole's hair clip, Talmadge's bullet: my momentos.

Lisa had left her phone on when we had our exchange, placed on the card table by the typewriter and I had not noticed; everything I said was on Kent's voice mail at the LAPD.

My lawyer is working on getting the recording tossed out: it was obtained by a citizen, there was no warrant for such, and a recording in possession of the LAPD was out of jurisdiction—they did not know where Nicole was murdered, she vanished from Hermosa Beach, and they had no body—for a cold case crime and the case of the now missing Lisa Harrison. Search parties were sent into the desert, but the desert was too vast, no graves, body or bones turned up.

Nevertheless, I have decided to confess. It is time. I will give my allocution to the court: my crime seventeen years ago, what really happened with Sean Talmadge, where I buried both Nicole and Lisa...

13.

Or maybe not.

The judge has excluded the voice mail as unlawfully obtained evidence. Without it, my lawyer says, they cannot hold me. The lawyer is filing a motion to have charges dropped. I will be back home soon, in Idyllwild.

Michael Hemmingson lives in southern California and Baja California. Some of his books include *Pictures of Houses with Water Damage* (Black Lawrence Press), *Wild Turkey* (Forge), *Hard Cold Whisper* (Black Mask), and *The Chronotope* (Wildside Press), among others.

PAT in Love & War & Soccer
James Grady

Long before Amin learned about love and soccer, PAT—the "Policy Activation Team"—met without him on a spring morning in the Eisenhower Executive Office Building that looms like a gray castle beside the White House.

Rick, the National Security Council staffer who ran PAT, sagged under another day of hoping for the best as he loosened his tie, told the two men and two women sitting with him at that conference table: "Are we ready?"

"PAT is all here," said Valerie, who became a lawyer for the Justice department because of its name and hid dreams *he's married* Rick inspired.

On the other side of the globe, Amin grew up hearing how his father and uncle built the hiding space under their house that was actually two spaces—the up-top space filled with valuables to appease any marauder, the second even more secret cinnamon-smelling space below those false floorboards to hide his sister and mother and Amin.

On that PAT morning in D.C., Rick asked: "What's our status?"

Harris, a thin man in a blue suit represented the State Department on PAT. "Our allies are Green Light on a multi-national coalition intervention force. They want our men, money, materials. Some of them went with us into Afghanistan and Iraq, work with us on transnational terror groups, trade, China. If we tell them *no*, we might get the same answer the next time we need to ask."

Leah Kim represented the CIA. L.K. never mentioned her previous assignments. No one ever asked. "No other hope for those people. Their government—"

"Are crooks!" snapped bulldog-like Colonel, the Pentagon's PAT man.

"True." A faint lighting bolt scarred L.K.'s tan forehead. "But as bad as that government is, the northern warlord Kax and his Movement of the Faithful are worse.

"MOF is like a clone of the Khmer Rouge or Uganda's Lord's Resistance Army. They claim to be 'true fundamentalists'—blended Christian and Muslim, resolve that by fanatical faith in Dear Leader Kax. His *zombinaters* run rampant: looting, burning, rape, child soldiers, slave labor—you name the horror, they're eager for it and good at it."

Amin's uncle and aunt worried for his whole life about whether to get him to talk about the day when he was 5 and his father only had time to push the children into the bottom secret cinnamon hole while MOF zombinaters pulled their mother onto a truck. No one who loved her ever saw her again. Amin could never remember her face.

PAT's conference room smelled like old stone and lemon furniture polish.

L.K. said: "For the last three summers, MOF has roared out of the north through the only mountain pass. Each year, Kax returns stronger, kicks that government's ass harder, savages more people. CIA's assessment is the government in the south can only repulse Kax and MOF for this one last summer. Next year, barring outside intervention, the fanatic crazies will oust the corrupt government, take over the whole country."

Amin was 6 before he realized his father would never again do more than stare off into worlds only he could see. Amin's uncle and aunt moved in to take care of him and his sister, a necessity little Amin tried to apologize for, but his aunt shushed him with a wistful smile, said: "We live the lives we get."

Rick asked PAT: "What are our obligations?"

"Legally," said Valerie, "no treaty binds us to do anything. But what's important are our human obligations."

Like a protective bulldog, the Colonel leaned across PAT's table.

"I'll tell you what's fucking important," growled that bulldog. "My boss, this Secretary of Defense, is not going to stand on some runway watching flag-draped coffins get shipped home to mid-America. After nearly 7,000 of those from Afghanistan and Iraq since 9/11, the American public isn't going to stand for a combat deployment in a far-off civil war between monsters and crooks."

L.K. shrugged her CIA shoulders. "There are no good guys in that fight."

Valerie said: "But there are innocents."

"I say we do nothing," said the Colonel. "No flag-draped coffins."

Valerie had to say it: "Whatever we do builds some kind of coffins."

The Big Picture strained the thin face of Harris from the State Department: "Our allies are going in."

L.K. said: "They're going to need help. Once MOF's *zombinater* army breaks free of the pass, they scatter into small raiding parties, keep in touch via Facebook and cell phones, crowd swarm then... Poof! Gone."

"Like ghosts," said Rick who couldn't find the woman he married in who his wife had become, a stranger who didn't understand why he didn't just finish punching his ticket at the NSC and grab a big dollars job or prestigious professorship.

The Colonel turned to the scarred woman from the CIA: "Can't use drones against Kax. Too many mountains up north, his forces scatter too much once he fans out in the south, plus you never get real-time crosshairs intel' about the sky above his head. But CIA has some left over millions from Afghanistan bribes you could put on the table."

"Perhaps." L.K. flashed on her grandfather fleeing to freedom across a moonless night's river. "And while you won't want to use Special Ops commandos to parachute in and take out Kax, the Pentagon could send Green Beret trainers and advisers to help our allies whip the government's army into shape."

"No combat troops!" said the bulldog Colonel. "Advisers only."

L.K. smiled. "Them also setting up listening posts and scouting recruits for our global intell' needs gives us at CIA even more reason to help our allies."

"But bottom line," said Rick. "Can we stop Kax?"

Amin was 7 and walking with his uncle past the boarded-up school. A rumbling SUV packed with government secret police thugs clutching AK-47s didn't even slow down for the man and boy in the street. Amin's uncle swung him safely out of the way. The road dust kicked up by the secret police machine made Amin sneeze.

His uncle said: "Someday will be better, different."

Amin asked: "What if someday never comes?"

Uncle shrugged. "All we can do is all we can do."

Far away in time and space, in a gray castle on a bottom line morning, there sat PAT:

Rick with his loosened tie.

Valerie shoving her personal dreams behind her dreams of what's right.

The bulldog Colonel.

L.K. with her scar and visions of refugees running in a moonless night.

Diplomat Harris picturing warm handshakes or cold eyes, mushroom clouds.

"Bottom line," said the Colonel who knew his duty, "war never works like you want. We can back our allies, but even with our help, their intervention force won't contain Kax after he comes through the mountain pass. If they could deny him mobility, lock him onto a defined battlefield, they could smash him, they have the firepower. But if he fans out like he always does...Best we can hope for is to buy time and get lucky."

Rick thought: *God help us, we're the invisible faces behind someone else's fate.*

Processed air circulated through PAT's concrete room like the whoosh of a river.

L.K. said: "I've got an idea!"

All her colleagues leaned across the table toward the scarred woman spy.

"Even with our allies' coalition force and an upgraded military, that government needs to lock Kax onto a battlefield," she said. "Deny him the ability to diffuse, swarm.

"So when Kax comes roaring out of that pass, what if he can't fan out? What if he has to stay on the highway, can't send his *zombinaters* off the road?"

The Colonel said: "What are you're talking about?"

She said: "Landmines."

They all blinked.

L.K. said: "I'm talking about mining the fields along that lone highway out of the mountains to keep Kax's monsters from going off-road to loot, to rape, to kill."

"We haven't used landmines since the Gulf War in '91," said the Colonel.

Diplomat Harris checked his IPAD, said: "Or produced them since '97, exported them since '92. The U.S. has paid more to clear minefields than any other nation. We're one of 36 countries that hasn't signed the Mine Ban Treaty. The Administration said they'll decide about signing 'soon.' The treaty's got solid Congressional support, but..."

Rich muttered: "Good luck getting anything through Congress that the other party can claim 'weakens' our military and defense options. Especially because any and every *no* they win bolsters their case that we can't get anything done."

Harris said: "The world will object if we use landmines."

"No matter how good the cause," added Rick.

"While it's technically not illegal for us to do," said Valerie, "it feels wrong."

A whisper escaped from Rick: "What else works that feels right?"

The river of processed air whooshed over PAT.

"Militarily," said the Colonel, "the strategy is classic."

"Politically," said Harris, "we could sell our allies on landmines— if we'd give them cover to say it wasn't their doing, because lots of them signed the treaty."

L.K. frowned. "There's gotta be a way to get this done."

"Wait!" said the Colonel. "We've got thousands of landmines stockpiled in Tooele, Utah. Have our aid package to our Allies funnel CIA cash to that government. Those crooks will rip some off, cost of doing business. But they then also hire a contractor to buy surplus from our Pentagon's Excess Defense Articles program and pay for C-130's to fly into Tooele one dark night, load cargo.

"That government takes delivery over there and owns the mines. Then it's not us, we're only helping them do better what they're going to do anyway with what they've got. We're clean, our allies are covered. Cycle ordinance guys into our trainers and advisers. Plant the mines along the highway out of the pass far enough and thick enough to trap Kax's *zombinater* invaders into a targetable on-the-highway battlefield."

"Landmines don't care who they explode," said Valerie. "Wherever they are, they become a way of life."

Diplomat Harris said: "Sounds no worse than the way of life those people got today and can expect tomorrow from a psycho warlord."

The scarred CIA woman whose job it was to know the secrets of the world said: "Sometimes you need to risk a lot for a little good."

"Put fences around the fields," said the Colonel. "Hell, mines work best when they're not secret. They'll protect the people of that town by the pass from sneak attacks—maybe from any attacks. No more Kax and his looting, raping, killing."

On the day the schools re-opened, Amin's uncle nodded toward the barbed wire fence stretched across a field by the highway: "Yes, now you can come out here, but—"

"—I know," said Amin. "Don't go there."

"Bottom line," said the Colonel, "if Kax roars out of the pass, the mines trap him on the highway, a defined target. If he doesn't invade, there'll be time for the coalition to make that government stronger, mount an offensive into the north, get him there."

"Either way," said the persuaded diplomat Harris, "it's a win."

Valerie said: "What about afterwards? With the mines?"

The Colonel said: "Our allies' coalition force and that government can hire contractors—we can specify only U.S. contractors—to clear the minefields when it's safe, send some CIA dollars back to Uncle Sam in taxes."

H.K. said: "Plus the Treasury would get the dollars earned from selling surplus in Utah before we can't sell it anymore. Won't solve the national debt, but it won't hurt."

"So," said Rick, "the policy package PAT's going to recommend is CIA black money plus Special Ops advisers and trainers with an intel' component augmented by ordinance guys. Surplus sale with clean-up provisions so that government is the one using landmines and we're just there to make the job the best it can be."

"Works for us at State," said Harris.

The Colonel shrugged. "With the understanding that the first flag-draped coffin home to America is followed by all the rest of our troops."

L.K. said: "Depending on circumstances."

The Colonel blinked. "Acceptable."

Ever so slightly, the scarred CIA rep' gave her nod of approval.

Justice department lawyer Valerie sighed. "Lots of *t*'s to cross, *i*'s to dot, but...If we keep it legal...Justice wants to stop the bad guys. Or at least the worst ones."

"So *yes*," said Rick.

Valerie shrugged—then nodded, her brown hair brushing her shoulders.

She understands, realized Rick, she gets what and why, then he said: "The only way to say *no* is to commit to something better. I got nothing, so...That's that."

The Colonel hurried out of PAT's conference room, drove to the Pentagon and into a Florida retirement five years later with a General's star on his uniform he never felt he deserved because even though he transferred from PAT and the strategy wasn't his command cross to bear, the allied coalition needed four years and thousands of casualties (but only nine red-white-and-blue flag-draped coffins) to triumph over MOF, a war that ended only after a disillusioned *zombinater* shot Dear Leader Kax in the head.

CIA star L.K. and the State Department's Harris drifted out of the conference room behind the Colonel, wandered down the corridor of that gray castle next to the White House as they whispered back channel gossip about the three maddest dictators on our blue stone spinning through space. They both transferred out of PAT before MOF's defeat and the cuts in foreign aid that ended efforts to clear the minefields.

Rick and Valerie stood alone by PAT's table after the meeting.

She said: "Do you think we're doing the right thing?"

"There are some choices you've got to make," he said.

Then oh so slowly, his fingers reached toward her hand as he said: "And there are some choices you get to risk."

She felt his touch, their love and the swirl through his divorce, their wedding, two kids and cheap cake at retirement parties when they left public service decades later.

Amin was 11 when he glimpsed such love. For children younger than him, Kax and MOF zombinaters were then mostly boogeyman stories. He and his buddies played soccer on the outskirts of their then peaceful but poor town as the girls in their class watched. A wild kick sailed the soccer ball over the rock sideline markers. The black & white soccer ball rolled across a barbed wire fence that had rusted and fallen over.

In the cool breeze sun, under the blue sky, Amin felt the brown eyes of Shana. Knew only the brave win such love.

Just like he knew where the ball had bounced and rolled and gone without anything bad happening, so he knew where to step to rescue the ball, be the hero.

Onto the field he ran.

James Grady's first novel became the classic Robert Redford movie *Three Days Of The Condor*. Born and raised in Montana, Grady has received Italy's Raymond Chandler Medal, France's *Grand Prix Du Roman Noir* and Japan's *Baka-Misu* literature award, and been an Edgar finalist from the Mystery Writers of America. Along with more than a dozen novels, his film work includes stints with Steven Cannell, HBO, FX, and CBS on TV dramas and feature work. In 2008, London's *Daily Telegraph* named Grady as one of "50 crime writers to read before you die." After Watergate, Grady was an investigative reporter for muckraking syndicated columnist Jack Anderson, freelanced for THE WASHINGTON POST, THE NEW REPUBLIC and was a cultural columnist post-9/11 for AOL's PoliticsDaily.com. Grady and his wife writer Bonnie Goldstein live inside D.C.'s Beltway. Their daughter, Rachel Grady, is an Academy Award nominated documentary maker. Their son Nathan Grady is a writer who also has a story in this volume.

LOST DOG
Laura Lee Bahr

I put up flyers all around my neighborhood. It's right off of Pico Blvd and there are never any places to park for the people who live here. People generally have to park blocks away from their destination. All that pedestrian traffic—somebody might have seen Irene.

I didn't lose her in the neighborhood, but I figured maybe she had tried to make her way back. I've heard of dogs doing that, going across states to make it back to their homes. Not that Irene would be able to make it across traffic and wait at the gate for me, but I was desperate to do something. I had already hit all the animal shelters in a twenty-mile radius. I had already put up flyers at every business and everyplace in the canyon where she'd disappeared.

I didn't know what else to do.

I put up my last flyer, trying not to look too closely at the bad color print job of her face because I didn't want to lose it on the street. Irene looks part beagle, part English bulldog, all mutt. She looks like something in between Snoopy and an Ewok. She's like the cutest thing ever. And she's little, too. She loves to sit on anybody's lap and you can just rub her belly. And most dogs have that kind of dog smell, but not Irene.

It was my fault she was gone. I let her off the leash. I'd thrown a ball too hard and it had gone deep into the brush. She went for it and didn't come back. After about a minute, after calling her, I went after her.

I couldn't find the ball. I couldn't find Irene. I looked for eight hours. I spent the entire day until dark looking, talking to hikers as they came up and down the hill, person and after person. "Have you seen my dog?" I asked everyone I saw.

I even asked a guy who was clearly homeless, with a sleeping bag and a Carl's Jr. cup. This guy seemed flattered I'd asked him. He said he'd help me, he'd help me look. But by that time night was falling, and I was already numb with desperation, so I didn't even properly appreciate the joke of a homeless crazy guy being my only viable assistance. Then I got the idea of the flyers. That's what you do, right? "LOST DOG."

Anyway, I'd put up the last flyer, and I bit down hard on my tongue so I wouldn't burst into tears, and I thought about hiring a private detective. Do detectives look for dogs? Would they? I had a reward posted for $1000. For that much money would a private detective get involved?

And then my cell phone buzzed. A number I didn't recognize, and I had this leap in my chest. Maybe someone had found her.

"May I speak with Tom Harmon?"

I just had "call Tom" on the flyer, but I wasn't thinking all that clearly or I would have noticed the clipped, professional tone.

"Yeah?" I said, waiting—every part of me waiting.

"This is Rachel Friedlander from Los Angeles City University, calling for Dr. Julian Johnson from the Mass Media & Photojournalism Department. Dr. Johnson would like to talk to you about acquiring your father's photographs."

She spoke so fast and all I was thinking was—*wait, this isn't about Irene?*—so all I could manage was "huh?"

"Can you hold for Dr. Johnson?"

"Uh…"

She was waiting for me to say yes or no. Since I didn't follow my "uh" with anything more she continued to wait another five seconds before asking it again. At that point, my disappointment fully registered and I said, "I'm sorry, I am really busy right now."

"Is there a better time to call back?"

I couldn't think about that right then so I just hung up.

***

Losing Irene had been the most terrible thing that had ever happened to me. Much worse than losing my last girlfriend who I thought was 'the one,' worse than losing my job and being unemployed these past six months, worse even than losing my Dad.

Of course, I was a kid when I lost my Dad. Didn't know what death or grief or losing really meant. He had been gone a lot anyway, so for a while it just felt like he was gone on a really long assignment. It had always been surreal when he was home anyway, like he was just waiting to leave again. Then he and my mom got divorced, and I barely noticed the difference. He just didn't sleep at home on occasion any more.

He died in the field, so to speak. My dad was a photojournalist. It was a pretty big deal—his death. It was in all the major papers, which my mom had kept. I looked through them briefly, a couple years back.

One of the newspapers reported at how "gentle" people said my father was. How much he 'cared about the people' he photographed. "He was very concerned with the struggle of the everyday people," another one of them had said. I can remember, too, his lanky body, his blue jeans and kind of shoulder slumped curve. He never raised his voice. He never seemed mad, even with the whole divorce. He just had this look like he understood something about you that made him want to just be silent and witness. Everything about him was like that. Yes, "gentle."

He and two other news people were trying to cover a story in Central America between the Nicaraguan and Honduras side. The car they were in exploded on the road and killed them all. They said ("they" being witnesses reported in the papers) the Nicaraguan side had placed mines to stop supplies being trafficked and the car hit one. Other witnesses said it wasn't a landmine at all, but a grenade launcher that was deliberately fired at them. There was some controversy over which, mainly because of intent and someone purposefully killing journalists. But however it happened, he died there in a big mess of 'boom.'

If this were a movie, I would have this life-mission of finding out what happened to my Dad and why, or maybe I'd be working to bring about a better world through volunteering at some important organization, trying to change the world for justice or something because of his legacy.

But I am not going to do anything like that.

I don't care. More than don't care, I don't want to do 'good.' People don't deserve good. People deserve this messed up place.

Maybe my Dad would be ashamed of me. I guess I've never really cared, though. If it had been so important that he be proud of me he should have lived so he could be. He decided that capturing images of people in war-torn places was more important. And left behind what he thought was most important.

All of his negatives and pictures are my inheritance, so to speak. They were left to me. They are in unceremoniously marked, dusty boxes in the basement of my mom's house in Downey. I've never even really gone through them. Some inheritance. But I guess a university thought it was worth something.

So I now had to think about those pictures again, and whether or not I wanted to donate them to someone who would do something with them. I thought maybe I should drive to Downey to look at the pictures and see what I had before I gave it up, if I even wanted to give it up.

At this point, Irene had been missing now for two days and I couldn't bear the lengthening shadows and the thought of sleeping with her not in the apartment.

But then I thought about Irene finding her way home, about her maybe yelping at the door. It was impossible, but it seemed too real for me to go anywhere.

***

"I got your dog."

It was 10:07 and I was five beers in and feeling really shitty when I got this text.

I almost fell off the couch I was sitting on in the dark.

I texted back:

"Where are you?"

"Where did you find her?"

"I am so relieved!"

"Where are you?"

"When can I pick her up?"

I sent one right after another. I would have continued to send them forever if I hadn't gotten this reply:

"Do you have the reward money?"

I stopped and took a deep breath, feeling that sick-full feeling from the beer and bad news.

"Of course," I wrote back.

"Cash?"

I felt so sorry for myself right then, knowing I was about to walk into a trap, but that I'd do it just for the slight chance that it wasn't total bullshit. "Of course," I texted back.

"Meet me at the corner of Pico and Robertson."

I stumbled to my feet, pulled out some pants, emptied the pockets of any change or cash, and walked into the night.

There was a halo of light beneath a street light, and beneath was a thin girl with bleached white and green hair. She had in ear-buds and had her phone out and was playing on it or something. She was wearing a t-shirt with a monkey face and the monkey's eyes were all blacked out with x's.

I didn't know if this was my contact or not. She certainly didn't have my dog. But she was the only person out right now at that corner, even with all the traffic on both Pico and Robertson. Nobody walks in LA—right?

As I came closer to the halo of light she took out an ear-bud and I could see her little elfin face and that it was covered with acne. She didn't look older than sixteen.

"Are you the person who texted me about my dog?" I asked, trying to not let my voice shake. I was angry right now. Really angry. I knew she didn't have my dog, and if she did, I knew she had taken her. Stolen her. But that wouldn't make sense. I had lost Irene ten miles from here.

She nodded, her eyes showing that she was probably high or cranked up on something, and scared. I didn't care.

"Where is my dog?" I asked, loudly.

She motioned for me to follow her.

Stupid move, I knew, but I did.

She walked fast and turned into the alley behind the closed drug store. I could make out the edges of several dumpsters.

I stopped then, couldn't will myself any further.

"Your dog is down here," she said, too loud. She was already into the darkness and standing there, like a wraith.

I didn't answer and I didn't move. Dogs were like that, too, when they sensed danger. They just stopped and waited, sniffing the air.

She turned and barreled toward me quickly, one ear-bud in, one out, her mouth making an angry shape as it spewed, "I said your dog is down here, jackass!"

I slapped her across the face. Her face recoiled hard and fast like it weighed nothing and the other ear-bud fell out of her ear. Then I grabbed her, fast, and pulled her into me with arm behind her back.

She smelled like stale body odor and cigarettes and cheap perfume. Her body was little and I felt like I could snap any of her bones or even her head straight off. This wasn't a fair fight with her, but my guess was that she wasn't alone or preparing for any sort of fight that was fair.

I couldn't see them, but I could sense them, out there. An ambush waiting to happen.

As I held her there, they started to come out of the shadows behind the dumpsters.

I thought about two things. One, they had my dog. The other, they didn't. Chances were they didn't have my dog. They were going to mug me for the supposed grand of cash only an idiot would have. Chances were they were kids on drugs and didn't know any better on how to do this.

So, I could let her go and run and be back in full light in a manner of minutes and have full cops in two. Instead I pushed her in front of me and then kicked her, hard in the back, toward them. She screeched out but moved away and into the edges of the shadows fast.

And I waited.

The shadows kind of moved toward her as she swore a blue-streak at me. I won't repeat what she said. But then she yelled at them to "kick his fucking ass and take his money" and started swearing and yelling at them. There were three of them. Three of them could have taken me. Easy. But they didn't want to come out of the shadows. They were scared.

They wanted to run away.

So I ran toward them, and then they did run. All of them.

I was yelling and swearing a blue-streak now, too. I won't repeat what I said, I don't even remember what it was, but I can remember being surprised at the sound of my own voice as the last of them disappeared over the dumpsters. Everything in me felt on fire. I was disappointed they were gone. I wanted them to come back. I wanted blood.

I walked back in the dark toward the halo of light. I heard something crack.

I had stepped on her phone.

I picked it up. If I could have ripped it in two I would have. Instead I threw it as hard and as far as I could.

I walked back onto the streets near my apartment. I wasn't thinking anymore. I was just tearing down the flyers I had put up hours earlier, one after another. I tore each flyer down with a violence that felt like I was using someone else's arms. *What a stupid idea. What a meaningless, mindless, ridiculous idea. Yeah, 'do something.' Something stupid!*

I pulled off the last one and dumped them into a blue bin some homeless guy would dig cans out of early the next morning. Then I thought of something that made me feel almost better. *I wish I had chased those kids down. I wish I had hit the girl, slapped her harder. I wish I had broken their bones. I wish I had fucking killed them.*

***

Day three that Irene was missing I stopped by the shelter closest to the canyon again. Nobody was saying yet, "maybe adopt another dog," but it was hard looking at all the faces of those dogs in cages. None of them did anything to deserve death. None of them did anything to deserve to be in a cage. I was feeling like my insides were full of flies looking at them. I ached for them. But I left them in their cages like they were death-row criminals.

Rachel Friedlander called again, and I realized it was time to assess the situation of the boxes. It was weird but thinking about my Dad made me feel better. Like somebody slamming something into your face when your stomach hurts real bad. Focus on something else.

I called my Mom first. She re-married about ten years ago. She married this guy named Jake who is all right. They both work in the school district. She teaches fifth grade but is going to retire soon, and he is a vice-principal at another school. They don't work at the same school or anything. Anyway, I called her and asked if it was okay if I let myself in because I knew she was at work and she said sure.

All of my Dad's stuff—my inheritance—is in the basement. My Mom is an amateur photographer—she was once a pro too but let it go when I was born to raise me and stuff, and then she changed careers, but she has lots of stuff set up in the basement. It's pretty creepy down there, actually. There is a light box that you put negatives on so they illuminate, and this little spy-glass thing you look through to look closer at pictures. Now everything is digital so all that stuff that is there is like a ghost town of the way things used to be done.

I let myself into the house. My Mom has a cat named FluffBall that is always mewing around somewhere, but I didn't see her when I first walked in. I went to the fridge first thing, just like I always used to do. Didn't even think about it. There wasn't much in there, but I found some iced tea so I poured myself a glass. FluffBall came in then and ran around my legs, purring, thinking I might feed him.

I was really glad to see him. I've always liked cats, too, I guess. Animals are cool because they don't pretend to be anything than what they are. And they are always present, just where they are. I found a cat treat for FluffBall and then went down to the basement. I knew he'd follow me if I let him, but I didn't want him to come down there. He didn't usually go in the basement, and I was worried he'd get stuck in there or something. It was stupid, but so was losing your dog. So I ignored his meows wanting to follow me and shut the door and went down the steps, the little exposed bulb blinding me.

I turned on the light box and the fluorescents lit up. I put down my iced tea. I sneezed a few times.

I pulled down a box. It said, "1975- 77 Mexico City." I opened the box. I was greeted by the sharp smell negatives have. I didn't want to get fingerprints on them, so I tried to only touch the edges. Pictures of people. And more people. Sad people. Struggling people. Hurting people.

I pulled down another box. And another. And another.

"Guatamala"

"El Salvador"

"Honduaras"

I pulled out negatives at random from each box.

People with babies on their backs. People crouched, hiding. People washing clothes in a river.

At some point I heard the front door and my Mom's voice. She came down the steps, FlufBall following her.

FluffBall looked at me with accusing eyes when he got down the steps, but was on my lap quickly, purring up a storm. I told my mom about Irene. I hadn't told her yet. She gave me advice. I'd already done everything she suggested, twice.

My mom looked at the negatives I was looking at. She got something soft and sad in her voice. She looked at them with me, telling me stories about the pictures sometimes.

"These people were refugees," she said of the people washing in the river. "The government said there were no refugees so when he got these pictures it was a big deal."

Of people in front of a hut, children in the dirt. "He stayed with this family for days, he said. Can't you see how comfortable they are with him?"

Men in uniforms with guns. A woman with a face like leather, crouching, hiding, her face in terror. A naked baby crying.

Mom opened a box labeled the year he died. She sifted through it and pulled out a strip of negatives. "The magazine and the papers printed this one," she says, pointing to a picture of peasants. "And this one." Another picture of soldiers, posing with guns. "These were in his camera when he died. These were the last pictures he took."

"Did they kill him?" I asked.

"Who?"

"Whoever was on the other side of what he was showing?'

She thought for a moment. "I don't know if it was an accident that the journalists were killed or they did it to send a message," she said, "but whether or not they meant to kill *them*, they meant to kill."

The door opened, heavy steps. Jake came down, too. He muttered over the pictures as well. He seemed to feel no threat about the memory of my dead dad. He admires him. Maybe if they'd still been married when my Dad died, Jake wouldn't say words like, "so brave" and "such integrity" and other kind of meaningless phrases that just shows how comfortable he was with my dead father having some immortal alpha-dog status in show of public servitude. He is a principal at a middle school. Whoop de dee.

They asked me if I want dinner. I didn't but I said yes.

We all had dinner. It was a casserole type of thing my Mom makes special for me, it's like mac and cheese with potato chips on top. I ate enough to feel sick, but I felt better than I had in three days.

Jake was telling stories about crazy parents and teachers and we were all laughing. I could feel Irene disappearing in this make-believe: I am still a kid living at home. Nevermind that Jake was never here when I was a kid, and it was just me and Mom, toughing it out. We didn't even have FluffBall when I was a kid. But I am like a kid now, age 36, and these are the adults who are going to take care of me. And I lost my dog, but that's what happens when you are a kid. It's okay. It doesn't matter that the world is rotten. It doesn't matter that the world tortures and rapes and kills and hurts and all these people who are the machine of suffering. Right now, I am home and I have parents.

After dinner, my mom asked me if I want to spend the night. It seemed a lot better than going home so I said yes.

I went to the basement to put the pictures all back. I had already decided that Johnson and Friedlander can have them. I was already overwhelmed and I'd just started. I looked at the picture of the peasants again, in front of their home. The woman's face is easy and she looks happy. They all do. Stuck there in the dirt, but content at least, and like it's nothing for them to have their picture taken. I realize how long Dad must have waited with those people for them to feel that easy. And then it strikes me: The guy taking the picture is *one of them*. He couldn't pretend to be one of us when he came back here, to pretend he was home. This white man from California was never one of us.

My insides lit up. Someone like that- someone who felt more at home with the oppressed of the world, that was someone who might hear a prayer.

"Dad, I lost my dog," I said softly.

And then I cried, and realized I hadn't even cried yet in those three days. And then I cried harder.

"Dad, I lost my dog and I really wish I could find her,"

And then I started to sob.

And I know this is weird, but I feel like he heard me. And I feel like he told me what to do next.

***

I drive straight to the hill where I lost her.

I know the entrance is closed, but we always went up this back way, anyway, past houses. It's dark, so I have to use my phone as a flashlight, but then I get my eyes adjusted and it's fine. It's scary, all the shadows of the trees and brush. It's scary—the sounds of the night, and knowing I could fall and die and no one would know or find me for a while.

I am back to the creepiest part of the park, even in the day, where I saw the homeless man. I realize I am afraid of him, especially in the dark. But then, why I am headed there?

I stop. Everything is alive around me. Alive and dark and full of secrets of what they know.

I whistle for my dog.

And I hear something. A whine.

I call her name.

There is a movement.

I turn on my phone light and shine it out.

It is that man I met, who said he'd help me. He has eyes that look like they are full of water, they reflect in my phone-light. Like an animal. And he is not homeless. He lives here. This hill is his home.

He is holding her. Irene. She is whining and shaking for me, but cannot come.

"Her legs got smashed up," he says.

I am there with arms out for her, arms around her. I am hugging him to take her.

"I looked for her and found her, she got smashed up but I been keep her going."

I have my arms around her and him. He releases her into my arms and staggers back.

I am not dreaming. I got my dog back. He gave me my dog back.

"There's a reward!" I cry to him. "1,000 dollars!"

He moves from one leg to the next, like his brain is trying to figure it out.

"Use the money for her legs. She's smashed up. So she can run again. A dog should be able to run."

I have Irene in my arms, but I lean forward.

I kiss the man on the mouth.

Thank you, brother, I say.

And then we both disappear opposite ways into the dark.

Laura Lee Bahr is the author of short stories appearing in the anthologies: *In Heaven Everything is Fine* (edited by Cameron Pierce, *Eraserhead Press*), *Psychos* and *Demons*, winner of the Bram Stoker Award for best anthology (both edited by John Skipp, Black Dog & Leventhal press). She is the award-winning screenwriter of the feature films *Jesus Freak* (LA Film Festival) and *the little Death*. She is a multi-award winning actor, with a religious-like devotion to small theatre, and a long-time member of the Eclectic Company Theatre, where she co-wrote the book for the musical *Gothmas*. She is a director, musical performer, and a member of Creative Underground, Los Angeles. Her debut novel, *HAUNT*, won the 2011 Wonderland Book Award. She currently teaches math, drama and vocals to middle schoolers at a private school. She lives in Los Angeles with her sweetheart and two retired cats.

General Bongo
Lucian K. Truscott IV

General Bongo! General Bongo!

What was that? Was someone calling my name?

General Bongo! Esos say come quick! Beeg truck under beeg rock! Esos say come General Bongo!

The kid was about 10 years old and his eyes were a couple of shiny black holes in the night at the bottom of the Mahi Par Pass. It had been about seven hours since we had arrived at the top of the pass at dusk to discover that the entire gorge was bumper-to-bumper door-handle-to-door-handle stacked up with the biggest traffic jam I had ever laid eyes on, and having lived in L.A. for about 12 years I had been smack in the middle a few rather large ones. We—Esos my translator; Daniel, my photographer; and my driver Faraj—were on our way from Kabul to Jalalabad, and we had been warned not to travel the Jalalabad road at night. But there we were with the sun almost down and what would turn out to be about five miles of backed-up traffic directly in front of us. By the time we looked for a place to turn around there were about 200 cars, buses, and trucks behind us. We were stuck.

Dark shadows began to form on the walls of the mountains high above us, and here and there, we could see boys climbing the sides of the gorge gathering sticks for firewood they would sell to truck drivers who were already out of their cabs and laying out their sleeping bags and starting cooking fires, ready for the night. Or nights, as it would turn out. Esos asked one of the taxi drivers if he'd ever been caught in a jam in the pass before and he smiled grimly: many times. How long does it usually take for the police to untangle the jams? What police, the taxi driver asked. You see any police? I've been in one of these jams for 24 hours, once for more than two days.

Esos, Daniel and I had a summit conference. From our vantage point at the lip of the very top of the gorge, we could see what seemed like miles of backed up traffic. The road to Jalalabad was little more than a potholed dirt path barely wide enough for two cars to pass each other safely, littered with rocks and small boulders that had crashed down from the mountains lining either side. And let us not ignore the fact that the edges of the road were lined with piles of three rocks— two on the bottom, one on top—warning that mines laid during wars over a period of about 30 years were still out there along the roadsides as deadly as ever. We had already passed taxis changing tires in the middle of the eastbound lane because it wasn't safe to pull off the road. This was not good, we concluded. Especially not good was the fact that there were two Americans present in the pass as the sun went down—Daniel and me—and according to what Esos had been told by another taxi driver, it was not safe to be an American in the pass overnight.

What do you do when you're confronted with your imminent demise not righteously, journalistically while "covering the war," but instead Death By Traffic Jam? Well, you get your ass in gear and direct traffic, that's what you do.

Now it was seven hours later and Esos was down the road ahead of me the way I had planned it out. Esos worked the downside of each switchback corner moving the big eastbound trucks back so I could direct enough westbound traffic through to relieve pressure on the corner, and on we went, one switchback after another, over and over and over again.

Not speaking even a syllable of Pasto, what I'd been doing was jumping up on huge boulders drawing the attention of truck drivers and taxi drivers and bus drivers by making as if I was riding a donkey—spreading my legs like I was straddling the beast and pretending to slap its hindquarters with a whip, all the while screaming DONKEY DONKEY in English, obviously, and *HAAAGH HAAAGH* which I had been assure by Esos meant Donkey in whatever dialect Afghans were speaking. So I was up there on these boulders...and we're talking boulders the size of Volkswagens here...and I'm screaming DONKEY DONKEY...*HAAAGH HAAGH* and these people are actually paying attention to me, and moreover, they're howling their heads off with laughter.

You've got to know something about what you might call the Culture of the Donkey in Afghan life to understand why a looned-out American pretending to ride a donkey got their attention and caused uncontrolled laughter. All Afghans from rural areas—and that's most of the population—grow up around donkeys. They use them to carry firewood and hay and all manner of worldly goods. They ride them to and from school and from very early ages, they are tasked with driving their donkeys into the family's walled compound at night to protect them from predators. They love donkeys because they are so useful, and they hate donkeys because they are so stubborn and impossible. In fact, Esos explained to me that one of the worst things you can call someone in Afghanistan is a donkey. And here was this loony American pretending to ride a donkey, and oh, by the way, directing traffic by waving his arms wildly and ordering these taxis and busses and trucks around in the universal language of loondom.

BONGO BONGO! I'm signaling two cars to move forward and off to the side of the road.

MONGO MONGO! Now I'm backing-up a tractor hauling a wagonload of straw.

BONGO BONGO! Move forward!

MONGO MONGO! Back up!

When there was a lull in the action entire bus-loads of passengers made their way through the jammed-up traffic and gathered around my boulder and pointed at me and yelled: GENERAL BONGO! DONKEY DONKEY! BONGO BONGO! MONGO MONGO!

And I dutifully did my donkey dance and screamed DONKEY DONKEY! *HAAAGH HAAAGH!* until the time came to move another couple of trucks or direct a flood of westbound traffic through towards Kabul and freedom. Of a sort.

Everything was going swimmingly until Esos informed me that we had an al Qaeda intelligence operative riding on the bumper of our Suzuki four wheel-drive mini-SUV. The way the al Qaeda guy, as we referred to him, came to be on our back bumper is yet another story of the Mahi Par Pass, and like the rest of them, it had its own Interior Logic, as they teach in the Big Time Writing Schools.

It turned out that this character had been bugging Esos and Faraj for a ride to Jalalabad since we arrived at the top of the gorge, yammering yammering, can I have a ride? Can I have a ride? Faraj didn't like the way he looked, but to me, he appeared to be nice enough, trying his best of get into every photo either I or Daniel took. He looked like the kind of guy if you were an Afghan dad you'd want your daughter to marry. Or maybe not, given what we found out about him several hours into our labors. Or maybe he would appear especially wonderful to you as a prospective father in law. It all depends, doesn't it?

Then a couple of hours into our struggle down the pass, a taxi driver about 20 vehicles in front of us approached Esos with the news that our bumper-passenger was an al Qaeda operative on his way from Iraq to Peshawar. He realized that after we had untangled the about three or four switchbacks that he was actually going to make it to Jalalabad that night and became friendly with Esos and warned him that the guy had been trying to cadge a ride since earlier that afternoon, offering to pay when he got to Jalalabad and made contact with his al Qaeda boss. He cited his mission for al Qaeda as evidence that he was obviously a trustworthy guy, and a patriot to boot. Esos told me the news and I didn't give it much thought. I was too busy doing Donkey

Donkey and Bongo Bongo to pay much attention to the guy in the brown plaid headdress on our bumper. Then about an hour later, a mini-bus driver who was about 10 vehicles behind us going east volunteered basically the same information to Faraj. The two drivers had no way to know about each other, and yet there they were telling us the same story: the guy had been asking for a ride all night, promising to pay as soon as he got to Jalalabad and met up with his al Qaeda contact. Esos passed this second report about our passenger along to me and I made a snap command decision: Leave him on the bumper at least until we get to the end of the jam. He won't do us any harm if he figures he's on his way to Jalalabad and he's actually going to get there tonight.

The appearance of the guy was what confused me. I mean, have a look at the photo of me shaking hands with him. What? Me worry? It was the genius of al Qaeda to send an innocent looking kid on an important mission like carrying a message from Iraq to Peshawar. It makes sense, right? The guy was right for the job precisely because he didn't look right for the job. That's al Qaeda in a nutshell. They don't come to America armed with submachine guns to kill us. They come with box cutters.

So seven hours into traffic directing and Donkey-Donkeying, I was stage-managing the last switchback before the bottom of the gorge and things were looking pretty good. Or so I thought until the kid appeared out of the dark beseeching me to follow him to help Esos with the *beeg* truck stuck under a *beeg* rock.

General Bongo! General Bongo! The kid was still yammering at me as we made our way through the tunnel to the bottom of the gorge where I found a slammed-up insane mess of multifarious vehicles that would have done the Lincoln Tunnel proud on a Friday rush hour. And there waiting for me was Esos with a very serious look on his face.

General Bongo, he said levelly, using the nom de guerre awarded me hours before by happy drivers as they passed me standing on my boulder, waving them westward toward Kabul and freedom. Of a Sort. General Bongo, we have a problem.

You mean the truck? What's the story with the truck?

Yes, okay, the truck is stuck under a *beeg* rock hanging over the road and I need you to help me figure a way to move it. But we have another, *beeger* problem with those two buses. He pointed past a long jam of cars and trucks at two white busses idling in the dark with their headlights off. These buses are filled with Taliban fighters carrying AK's and they are on their way to Kabul to make *beeg* trouble.

Really, I said. We've got an al Qaeda guy on our back bumper, and now we've got two bus loads of Talibans in front of us. I considered my options which appeared to be exactly zero.

Esos said, I have talked to the Taliban commander. He knows about you, General Bongo. The Taliban commander looks up the pass from where he is stuck and he sees the traffic moving freely to the west and he sees the rest of us creeping forward to the east, and he has been told that an American is the one who is doing this. I told him that in order for us to move this traffic jam in front of him, you must pass his busses. I told him if he does not allow you to walk past his buses, they will spend the rest of the night sitting right where they are. So he has agreed, General Bongo. You can walk past the Taliban buses, but I must ask that you do so quickly, so we can get this *beeg* truck out from under the *beeg*rock and go to Jalalabad.

You think this thing is going to work? I asked Esos. Can we trust him?

Insha'Allah, said Esos. If it is God's will. But just in case, he said with a sly grin, I've got some guys on the hill above the buses, and they've got AK's and they will stand guard as you pass. Where did you come up with these characters and their AK's? I asked. There are many citizens with AK's in the Mahi Par Pass tonight, said Esos. The ones who are traveling to the east along with us are on your side, General Bongo.

So there it was. In order for me to get our asses out of the gorge and onward to Jalalabad, in order for me to fulfill my contract with the Big Time Magazine in New York and write something even marginally publishable, we first had to make a deal with the Taliban.

I have to tell you that I didn't even give it a second thought. Let's do it, Esos, I said. So forward we marched past the Taliban buses. I glanced into the buses and sure enough, there they were, heavily bearded, every one of them with an AK across his lap or between his legs. It wasn't until I got past them that I let it out. I mean, I was standing there behind those two buses full of Taliban fighters and I was thinking to myself, what in the hell is going on here? General Bongo? Donkey Donkey? Who are you kidding?

That's when I let out my howl—*When do I get paid? Where is my fucking check?* And suddenly, it came to me. I knew exactly how I had transformed myself into General Bongo and maneuvered myself and my guys to safety through five miles of hell. I was doing the same thing Bill Graham did the night I watched him maneuver himself and his entire paying audience to safety when the Lower East Side Motherfuckers attacked the MC5 and wreaked havoc at the Fillmore East. But Bill Graham was no General Bongo. He didn't need a nom de guerre. He was just Bill Graham, an ex-Marine sergeant and a veteran of the Korean war, just like my father. He was One of Us.

Just as it would be necessary in a discussion of the American hot rod to explore the inner-workings of the internal combustion engine, it will be necessary to briefly delve into the politics of Afghanistan if we are to tell the tale of General Bongo beyond his escape from the Mahi Par Pass. Politics was in the main the issue of the barrel of a gun in the spring of 2004. Legislative elections were upcoming later that year, followed by a presidential "election," which everyone already knew amounted to the crowning of Hamed Karzai. The country was being run not from Kabul but provincially by a cadre of war lords most of whom had emerged from the Northern Alliance in the Panshir Valley during the wars against the Russians and the Taliban over the past 25 years or so.

Jalalabad sits astride the road between Peshawar and Kabul, the main trade route through the region for the last several thousand years. It's the first trading town inside Afghanistan's border with Pakistan, the twin of Peshawar just across the border. Both towns were filled to the first-story windows with spies, insurgents, drug war-lords, ordinary criminals, fixers of every stripe and color, and a surfeit of government hacks and flacks on the take for everything from sewage permits—in a place where there was no such thing as an actual sewer—to phony visas permitting a stay in-country or travel to any country you cared to. The one major thing missing in Jalalabad was a sense of anyone being in control, because no one was.

It was true that Jalalabad and the provinces of Nuristan and Kunar had their own resident war lord, one Hazrat Ali, a pudgy 40 year old mujahideen commander with his own militia some 9,000 strong. Collaboration being the sincerest form of flattery, Hazrat Ali hadn't had any problem with getting U.S. help. His militia was fed, clothed and housed using United States dollars flowing downhill to the coffers of Mr. Ali from god only knows what stateside funding source. He had spent his youth in the Panshir Valley studying at the feet of the master, fighting the Russians alongside Ahmed Shah Massoud the famous Northern Alliance commander. Once the Russians had been ejected from Jalalabad, he moved into town and took his place as a militia commander until the Taliban drove him back into his mountain village of Daranuh. Once again he took up the fight alongside Massoud and when the Americans invaded in 2001, he seized another opportunity to move into Jalalabad, this time with stronger backing from the Northern Alliance. By the time I ran into him in May of 2004, the generally chaotic political situation in Afghanistan had left him a very, very powerful man in northeastern Afghanistan. Although his control of the region in and around Jalalabad was at best questionable, the strength of his militia army gave him enough power that he had been able to kill two of the brothers of the provincial governor, Din Mohammad, and drive him into a comfortable exile in Dubai.

We finally got out of the Mahi Par Pass around 4:00 a.m. and arrived in Jalalabad around 5:30 to be greeted by a roadblock manned by fighters loyal Hazrat Ali. Two words got us past the roadblock: General Bongo. They had been stopping traffic all night that had escaped the traffic jam in the Mahi Par Pass, and word of the miracles worked by General Bongo was apparently being spread far and wide. We woke up the desk guy at an old British colonial era hotel called the Spinghar, got a couple of rooms and collapsed.

The next day we headed for Asadabad, a smaller outlaw trading town about 30 miles north on the Kunar River. The road from Jalalabad to Asadabad, while lacking a 2,500 foot deep gorge and a seven mile traffic jam, was worse than the road from Kabul to Jalalabad. Much worse. Those 30 miles took us seven hours to drive. In case you're having trouble with the math, that's less than five miles per hour. The road wasn't rutted and pot-holed; it was cratered and strewn with boulders the size of compact cars. Not to mention lined with the requisite warnings against land mines and other high explosive roadside attractions. When we arrived in Asadabad, we had to drop off our little 4-wheel drive SUV at a local repair shack as all four of our shocks were bleeding hydraulic fluid that had leaked onto our brake shoes leaving us with no brakes whatsoever. I realize these vehicular details might seem inconsequential, but you have to consider the situation at hand: having gotten to a hellhole like Asadabad, the first thing you start thinking about is how you're going to get out. You need shocks and brakes to get out, trust me.

If Jalalabad seemed like an East Asian Dodge City, Asadabad looked like that planet Han Solo stopped at in the first Star Wars. The streets were crawling with malformed and disease-ridden Afghans using everything from push-boards to wheeled contraptions constructed of old baby carriages to propel themselves around. Polio was running rampant; people in various stages of decomposition from staph infection and gangrene huddled under shade trees and held out blistered hands, begging for hand-outs. Shop keepers and passersby were missing hands, arms, feet, legs…you name it…from land mine and unexploded ordnance accidents. Sewers, as usual, ran alongside the road or down the middle of smaller side streets. Rabid, foaming, bleeding dogs dug through piles of garbage alongside children who appeared to be in the same shape the dogs were in. Shop stalls sold hand-made poppy knives and various other tools of the opium trade. Healthier children carried bundles of dried poppy-sticks on their backs to be used as firewood and roof-thatch in their home compounds. And everywhere you looked, boys in dark blue pants and light blue shirts carrying Korans walked to and from a plethora of Madrassas that lined the roadsides everywhere, some of them openly sponsored by Saudi, Pakistani, and Iranian groups I recognized from anti-terror watch lists back home, such as the World Federation of Muslim Youth.

We ate a lunch of flat bread, rice and fried river fish and afterwards crossed the bridge over the Kunar River to find ourselves in…surprise!…Pakistan, the border with which was a good ten miles to our east running along the top of a ridge of mountains that formed the beginning of the Hindu Kush. All of a sudden our cache of Afghan currency wasn't good anymore. Shops accepted rupees or dollars, nothing else.

This was not a good sign. Already I could see that Asadabad was if not formally under the control of the Taliban, at least heavily under its influence. But the east side of the river was Taliban territory through and through. We had befriended a squad of guys from Hazrat Ali's militia on our way to Asadabad, and when they refused to cross the bridge over the Kunar, I should have known something was up. The American was drawing pointed fingers and whispered conversations, so we quickly turned around and crossed the bridge back into Asadabad proper and made for the auto repair shack and picked up our truck and headed south.

On our way up to Asadabad, we had stopped in the mud-hut village of Nachur to buy candy and oranges and bottled water from a little roadside shop tended by a very nice guy by the name of Matiz. On the way back, we stopped again and hung around for awhile talking. It seemed as if the brother of Matiz had been stuck in an eastbound bus in the traffic jam two nights before, and would not have made it to a big family wedding had it not been for this guy General Bongo who came around like a miracle worker and freed the lucky brother from traffic bondage. When Esos introduced me as General Bongo, Matiz grabbed me by the shoulders and wouldn't let go. He was running on and on, what a great thing I had done, and he had heard about donkey-donkey! Could he see General Bongo do the magic of donkey-donkey? Of course he could, so I stood out there on the dirt street and spread my legs wide and pretended to ride a donkey and flailed my right arm as if whipping the beast, yelling bongo-bongo-bongo! And Matiz went crazy with laughter, grabbing a bunch of little boys and sending them off into the dark to the compounds of the village elders to bring them to see General Bongo do donkey-donkey. It was already dark and getting late and it was known that the Jalalabad-Asadabad road had an even worse reputation than the Kabul-

Jalalabad road when it came to marauding bandits, but we hung around until Matiz had assembled about 40 of the men from the village in the street facing his little shop and I did donkey-donkey-bongo-bongo, and they went wild with joy. As it turned out, I was the first American any of them had ever met. None of the convoys running between base camps in Jalalabad and Asadabad had ever stopped. All they ever saw of Americans was a glimpse of helmeted faces going past in a blur of armored vehicles. Now here was the great American hero, General Bongo! In their village! Doing the magic of donkey-donkey-bongo-bongo! They practically wouldn't let us go.

The next day, we took off again in the morning going north on even worse roads through ever more narrow valleys into the region just around the valleys to the south of the Pech River where the famous documentary Restropo would be filmed a few years later. Even in these distant valleys, stories of General Bongo had been passed, and we were greeted everywhere as heroes, Esos basking in his share of the Bongo limelight. On the way up in the morning we stopped again at Matiz' roadside shop for some oranges and water, and I saw Matiz take Esos aside around the corner of the shop for a fairly lengthy conversation. I had meant to ask Esos about it, but forgot as we entered the badlands. On our way back south, once again just as it was getting dark, we stopped again in the village of Nachur to say goodbye to Matiz. This time he was ready for us. Nearly the entire village of 300 or so were out in the street waiting for us, the women in Burquas lurking at the edges of the crowd, little children scampering around chasing wooden balls with sticks. And now the greeting of the entire village was made clear. Matiz and the village mukhtar, the elder chosen as a de facto mayor, approached me and translated by a beaming Esos made me an offer. It had been decided not only by the village of Nachur but by several nearby villages, that it would be a good idea to have General Bongo on their side during whatever upheaval was coming their way as a new Afghanistan was taking shape. These people were peasants, but they were peasants descended from stock that had occupied that valley for several thousand years and had survived one despot after another. All they could see coming their way was another despotic regime like the Taliban, or the Russians or any other. What mattered wasn't Afghanistan the nation. It was their little league of villages, intermarried for centuries, as close to a "nation" as any of them ever expected to see. A good way to insure their survival as a tiny culture, a collection of villages, was to have General Bongo on their side. In this regard, they were prepared to give me my own mud-brick compound, a multi-family unit that had been abandoned by some local Taliban sympathizers after the Taliban had been driven out. Esos was uncharacteristically somber as he translated their offer. There would be the compound, and once the surrounding villages were taken into account, I would have a militia of about 600 men under my command. As many wives as I wanted to take would of course be arranged. This was a good life they were offering to General Bongo. Esos explained that they had spent most of the day in discussions about the arrangements. It was all agreed. All General Bongo had to do was say yes, and a celebratory feast would be laid out, and he would be welcomed into the village as its newest resident and military commander.

I can't say that "The Man Who Would Be King" didn't come to mind, because it did. I looked around at their faces in the gathering dusk. There wasn't a smile among the men. Even the children had stopped chasing their wooden balls and stood silently, sticks at their sides. Until that moment in my life, it was the single saddest thing I ever had to do, turning them down. It broke my heart and I know it broke theirs, but they recovered quickly enough, however. Matiz asked me if I would do donkey-donkey-bongo-bongo one more time, so the whole village could see. I did donkey-donkey, did I ever. I gave it my very best, pretending to ride the donkey, flailing away at his imaginary flanks with an imaginary stick, yelling bongo-bongo-mongo-mongo at the top of my lungs. The entire village erupted with laughter. Finally they had met an American and he was just like them.

Lucian K. Truscott IV is a journalist, novelist, and screenwriter based in Sag Harbor, New York. He is the father of daughter Lilly, 19; Lucian V, 12; and Violet, 6; the son of Colonel and Mrs. Lucian K. Truscott III; and the grandson of General and Mrs. Lucian K. Truscott, Jr., and Colonel and Mrs. Bartley M. Harloe. Mr. Truscott has no hometown. He is an Army brat who was the first American baby born in occupied Japan, and the son of two Army brats. By the time he left home at age 18 to attend West Point, he had lived in 22 different dwellings. He has spent most of the rest of his life moving around the United States and the world. He has written for the *New York Times* op ed page for nearly forty years, and for publications as varied as the *Village Voice, Rolling Stone, The New Yorker, Harpers, Saveur,* and *Military History Magazine*. He reported on terrorism in Israel and Beirut, and the wars in Iraq and Afghanistan. He has written five novels, and is at work on a memoir, *Dying of a Broken Heart*, which is available online at www.dyingofabrokenheart.wordpress.com.

Who Are You To Be So Brave?
Yvonne Prinz

I woke with a start. For several seconds I looked around the room for something familiar. Then I remembered I wasn't at the clinic anymore. I lay on my back and watched the ceiling fan turn big lazy circles. Filtered morning light stretched out across the floor. Had I closed the blinds last night? Already there was the relentless whine of the motorcycle rickshaws and the tuk tuks on the busy city street below. It was unfamiliar to me now that I'd been living rurally on the border. The room was warm and humid but after four months I'd adapted. I didn't flush as easily as when I'd first arrived. I'd stopped feeling swollen and peevish in the heat. My skin against the thin cotton sheet was golden and my hair was bleached from the sun and in need of a cut.

Adam's breathing was even. He lay with his back to me. The sheet clung damply to his hip. He seemed to be asleep but he may very well have been pretending. He may have been waiting for me to slip out of bed, pull on my clothes and drag my luggage out of this room, down the wide stone steps, enroute to the airport. Had I told him when my flight was leaving? I couldn't remember. A half empty bottle of Mekong whiskey sat on the bedside table with two glasses and an ashtray with an oily roach teetering on its edge. No wonder my mouth was parched.

Adam was the first person I saw when I arrived at the treatment center on the Thai/Myanmar border four months ago. I'd endured a string of missed connections en route and when I finally pulled up in the tuk tuk, I'd been traveling for 36 hours. I felt dizzy from lack of sleep. Adam stood on the porch watching me impassively. He made no move to help me with my bags. He wore pale blue scrubs with some distressingly large smears of blood on them. Still, he managed to look elegant. He looked like a man standing on the veranda of a chic Paris apartment, contemplating where he might get dinner. He did not look like a surgeon in a field clinic for landmine victims.

Most of our patients came from Myanmar, some of them had traveled daunting distances, bleeding and carrying the parts of their own bodies that had been blown off. Some didn't make it. Some were already dead when they arrived. To do what Adam did was akin to being a doctor in a hospital emergency room where every patient who walked through the door had suffered a terrible dismembering car accident and where most of the equipment was broken. And yet he seemed unflappable. His grey/blue eyes never registered the obvious stress of his days. He walked with a casual but measured pace from patient to patient, calmly instructing the nurses on what they needed to do first.

My job at the tiny crude clinic was in rehabilitation. I was a licensed physical therapist specializing in prosthetics. I worked far away from the blood and amputations and sewing people back together again. I dealt in stumps. Putting a leg (or an arm) where there was one missing and teaching the patient to walk again if that were even possible. It was grueling and emotional work. I became too involved with my patients. I knew too much about them even with the language barrier. They were peasant farmers, most of them, people with nothing much to call their own but they worked hard at every task I gave them. They smiled easily even though their lives would never be the same. I loved these people. I loved their families. I even loved the stray dogs that came around every day.

"Don't feed them," said Adam, in a voice tinged with classic British disdain. "They're filthy, and they'll never leave if you feed them."

"I don't want them to leave." I said, looking at him with an unwavering expression. What was there to do here, anyway? At night we watched movies, we read, and we played cards. What was wrong with keeping a few dogs from starving to death? The only place near the clinic to seek relief from the heat was a small natural swimming hole fed by a waterfall. We shared two motorcycles that belonged to the clinic and we went often to cool off. The local Thai kids entertained us, shrieking and dropping into the water from a rope that hung from a tree limb.

I saw Adam several times a day. We ate together, all of us who worked at the clinic: eight Thai staff members and five foreigners, in a dining tent. I was the only American, Betty and Jack were Australian nurses and there were two surgeons: Adam, from London, and Marco from Switzerland. I was eager to learn to speak some Thai and usually sat with the Thai staff to practice. Adam sat with the Australians and never looked my way. He never tried to speak Thai and his tone with the clinic workers always bordered on dismissive. Although I put some effort into ignoring Adam, I'd picked up a few vague details from the other workers. Apparently, Adam had worked in Afghanistan before this and before that he was in Iraq and before that he was in the Gulf.

Before coming to Thailand I'd worked at the VAMN in Minneapolis for five years. I was in desperate need of a change. The walls of my studio apartment were closing in on me. The winters seemed to get longer every year. I'd been trying to figure out how to break up with my boyfriend, Todd, who had broached the subject of househunting together. I couldn't think of a good reason to stay but I couldn't seem to leave. When the posting for this job appeared on the bulletin board in the staff room I jumped on it. I didn't care where I was going. I had to get out of there.

Days quickly turned to weeks and then I'd been in Thailand a month. I'd become accustomed to the heat, the cockroaches, sleeping in a tent, the squat toilets, and my roommate Betty's snoring but Adam's lack of compassion for his patients still rankled me daily. His work was top notch, better than the best surgeon's work at the VA hospital back in Minnesota and without any fancy equipment, but he went at it like a mechanic, working on a complicated engine: Get all the parts connected right, sew them up and send them on their way.

Pan was my favorite patient. Adam had amputated his leg above the knee. Pan had been caught in a monsoon and tried to outrun it. In his confusion he set off a landmine on the edge of a neighbor's field as he tried to find shelter. He had almost bled to death but he'd had the sense to take his shirt off and tie it around his mangled leg as he lay there in the mud, waiting for someone to find him. He should have died but he was thriving now, moving along like a person with two legs, thanks to Adam, but I was certain that Adam never gave him another thought after Pan was wheeled from the surgical unit.

Betty and Jack took care of the wounds and then, when the wound had healed sufficiently, Simon, a Prosthetist, who would fit the amputee with an artificial limb and then I would teach them to walk again, working on building up their strength and muscle tone. It was no surprise to me that most of them learned to walk very quickly. They were desperately needed back on the family farm. They intended to go right back to work.

One afternoon at the swimming hole I needed a hand getting myself out of the water. I pulled myself up as well as I could and flopped onto the sheer rocky ledge like a seal. I was well aware of ungainly I looked. Suddenly Adam's hand was there. I put my wet hand in his and he lifted me onto the rock.

"Thanks," I said, arranging myself to look more graceful. He handed me my towel and then he sat near me, watching the Thai kids play.

"When are you done here?" He asked, shielding his eyes with his hand, looking out at the water.

"A week."

"Can I come with you to Bangkok? I have some things I need to pick up. I'm here two more months and I'm desperate for some good coffee and cigarettes"

"Sure." I shrugged, trying to seem nonchalant, but I was puzzled at the request and already wondering how I would get through the journey with this moody taciturn man who hadn't exchanged more than a few words with me in four months and most of them had been unpleasant.

While the tuk tuk idled I said sloppy teary goodbyes to all the staff, put addresses into my phone, made promises to E-mail, Facebook, meet up again. Adam sat smoking in the back of the tuk tuk, idly gazing off into the distance, looking bored. Pan brought me a plastic bag of my favorite: Lychee fruit. I'd already started missing his broad, toothy smile and the way he said my name: "Kim-ba-lee".

The tuk tuk got us to Lampang and then we had a six-hour bus ride to Bangkok. Adam listened to music. I wrote a few E-mails and slept. We were overly polite to one another, saying excuse me too often, acting like we didn't know each other. When the bus rolled into the station I had expected we would find separate accommodations in Bangkok but Adam strolled next to me with his leather backpack slung over his shoulder.

"Do you know where you're going?" He asked.

"Yes, I have a reservation at the Buddy Lodge on Khao San Road. I'll need to catch a Rickshaw, I guess."

Adam stood in the street and waved with authority at an oncoming rickshaw. The driver pulled over immediately and we put my things inside. I was about to shake Adam's hand and wish him well when I realized he was getting in right behind me. The two of us and my bags were squeezed into a very tiny space now and I had no choice but to press my body against his crisp pale blue linen shirt. The motorcycle darted in and out of traffic, jamming my body repeatedly against Adam's. I was grateful when the rickshaw finally stopped in front of the guesthouse. Adam helped me out with my things and paid the driver.

"I'll help you up," he said.

"Oh, that's not necessary," I said. Truthfully, I wanted him to be on his way. I wanted to stop feeling the way Adam always made me feel. I didn't care if I was alone in Bangkok. I could eat alone, maybe walk around, check out a night market, buy some souvenirs to take home.

"Come on," He'd already picked up one of my bags and started toward the very modest lobby.

I suppose it was being away from the clinic finally. Maybe I'd been holding my breath, keeping up a brave face amongst all the suffering I'd seen. Maybe it had affected me more than I thought but I started to cry in a small café just off Khao San Road. The food had been delicious and I'd ordered a second beer. Adam looked up from his whiskey. There were tears rolling down my cheeks.

"What is it?" he asked. "What's wrong?"

"Nothing. It's...nothing. I'm feeling emotional, I think. All those people, they got to me, I guess, and now that I'm gone from there... silly, huh?" I dabbed at my cheeks with a paper napkin.

"No. Not at all." He looked around and signaled our waiter for the check. "Let's go."

Back in the room, Adam sat me down on the bed. He bent over me and placed his hands lightly on my shoulders. He pushed me back gently onto the bed till I lay looking up at the ceiling. He took a pillow and placed it under my head and then he took my right sandal off.

"Don't." I said, lifting my head

"It's okay." He ran his hand up along the back of my left leg and grasped my ankle with his other hand. He gave a sharp tug and my prosthetic leg released. He slid it carefully off and placed it on the floor next to the bed. Then he carefully rolled the liner down my thigh till the naked stump below my thigh was exposed. He bent over and kissed it. He looked up at my face.

"How did it happen?"

"A car accident when I was eleven. My parents were killed."

"I'm sorry."

I shook my head and automatically arranged my face the way I did when people tried to pity me.

"I wish I'd done it," he said, running his long fingers over the stump.

"What? Cut my leg off?" I made it sound raw on purpose.

"Yes." Now he looked critically at my leg from a surgeon's perspective.

"The man who did it was very kind." I said pointedly. "He was very compassionate. I'd just lost my parents. He sat with me for hours and comforted me."

Adam didn't respond. He took the rest of my clothes off with the same care as he had my prosthetic leg. My discomfort at being naked with my stump exposed diminished as it became less about the missing leg and more about us together and hungry for each other. Adam produced some good Thai pot from his backpack and there was a bottle of Mekong whiskey and glasses in the room. We were naked now and laying together under the cool white sheet.

"I do care, you know." He said, passing me the joint.

"Do you?"

"Of course. I'm a good doctor. I could have a practice in London and a wife with a hyphenated name and children in expensive boarding schools and invites to chic dinner parties." He paused a second. "I chose this instead. But if I'm going to do this I have to be careful not to let it affect me or I'd be crying into my Pad thai like you, Wouldn't I?"

Adam made love to me with great tenderness and I cried again. Tears streamed down my cheeks onto the pillow. I cried for Pan and those poor limbless farmers and my dead parents and my missing leg. I cried because I knew that my life in Minnesota was over and I could never really go back now. Adam dabbed at my tears with the bed sheet and kissed me but he said nothing.

We fell asleep in each other's arms, first Adam, then me.

After I left Thailand, I took one assignment after another, working in field hospitals and clinics all over Asia and Africa. I met a doctor named Howard from Boston in Ghana and eventually we were married. I moved with him to Boston and we had two little girls. I got a job working with amputees at Boston Children's hospital.

I never saw Adam again.

Yvonne Prinz is the author of several books for young readers including *The Vinyl Princess*, which has been described as "A dead-on portrait of a true-blue teenage music obsessive.", and was recently optioned for a feature film. She lives in San Francisco and is one of the co-owners and founders of Amoeba Music in Berkeley, San Francisco, and Los Angeles.

Six Days in May
Weston Ochse

*"We watch grainy reels of a fish flopping on concrete
arched, kicked, and nightsticked, rodney king.
Here I rub my own tender wrists,
ask my mother unanswerable questions - why are the cops doing this?
My mother will answer simply, and wisely, because those cops are bad.
Of the looters, because they are mad.
But why hurt us—she chokes Because, Ishle, we live close enough."*
—Sai-I –Gu, Ishle Y Park

Los Angeles, California—1992. Day 1

Momma Teta says that if you're good, you go to Heaven when you die. I love Momma Teta. She knows more about what we've forgotten about our lives in Sierra Leone than anyone. I asked her, *Momma Teta? Are my arms in Heaven?* She says to me *No*, with a long sad face. She says they're waiting for me. *Where are they waiting*, I ask her. *In the In-Between*, she says. *It is a no place. It's neither here nor there, both, neither.* Then I ask, *is that why I can feel my arms sometimes?* She smile so wide the clouds of my sadness are moved aside. And she nods so solemnly, it is as if I'd just spoken a grand secret.

!

The marine layer squatted off the L.A. shore like a bully, blocking any kind of breeze from washing away the stink and heat of Los Angeles. Those lucky million who lived west of the 405 got just enough to clear their precious air of most of the pollution that blanketed the rest of the city. But if you were unfortunate enough to live east of the 405 and anywhere south of the 10, the heat pushed you down like everything else in the City of Angels seemed to do; pushed you down and held you there, a boot on the neck until you final decided to leave for cooler climes… like Chino, Folsom or San Quintin.

"Fucking Korean has eyes in the back of his head." Rafiq steamed in the hot South Central Los Angeles heat as he scrunched against a building on the Vermont Avenue sidewalk, his back against a wall cast in shadow.

Jester chuckled as he picked at the dry skin on his hands. "You mean you're pissed that you can't lift another forty." He chuckled again, aware of the glares he was getting from his friend. "That mean old Korean won't let you steal his beer." He mocked Rafiq as he mimicked, *"Fucking Korean has eyes in the back of his head."*

Rafiq stood, his fists in tight balls.

Jester stood too, head and shoulders taller. "What you going to do with those, 'Fiq? You gotta calm down. Cops see you acting uptight, they gonna Rodney King your ass."

Rafiq glowered for a moment more, then stalked down the block. Jester shook his head and followed after him. They found a bench in front of Sampson's Barber Shop. A radio blasted Marvin Gaye from inside, occasionally cutting into a reporter, giving updates on the court proceedings from Simi Valley. Whenever she spoke, the barber shop would get quiet. When the music returned, voices raised, arguing the impossibility of an acquittal of the two white officers.

"Ain't that your cousin, Quasimodo?" Rafiq said, pointing with his elbow at a very thin young man, his head down as his feet shuffled towards them.

"Don't call him that." Jester's permanent smile—his namesake— grew wider. "Hey, Momodo! How's it hanging?"

The young man looked up, a shy grin appearing across a handsome, but scarred face with deep-set soulful eyes. As tall as Jester, he was preternaturally thin. Jester had a special place in his heart for his cousin. He'd only been in American for six months, and he was learning how to fit in, even though fitting in was difficult with his condition. Momodo's arms had been cut off by an RUF rebel with a machete. The loss of blood had almost killed him. If it hadn't been for the quick thinking of a neighbor and the field care from a United Nations doctor, Momodo wouldn't be here today.

"Hey, Jester. Hey, Rafiq," Momodo said, his voice barely audible. Dressed in dark T-shirt and black sweatpants, without arms he gave a crow-like appearance.

"What you doing out?" Jester scooted over and made room on the bench between himself and Rafiq.

Momodo sat. "Momma Teta needs some greens and pork fat."

"How you going to carry back the food if you get it?" Rafiq asked, his smart-assed question barely hiding true curiosity.

"I manage."

A fight erupted across the street between two men. It went on for half a minute, drawing a crowd that poured out of a nearby bar. When it was done, both combatants limped back inside.

"Do you feel it?" Momodo asked.

Rafiq looked a question at the other two.

"In the air," Momodo continued, "like in the village before the rebels came."

Jester nodded. "Things might just snap if we aren't careful."

"Only way they'd snap is if those *popo muthafuckers* get off."

Jester snorted. "You'd have to be blind not to have seen the video a hundred times."

Suddenly a roar went up in the barbershop. Jester turned around to see everyone on their feet, including two men with cutting capes still draped over them. Sampson himself, who usually only moved to go to address his lunchtime bowel movement, lumbered to his feet and stood in the middle of the room, fuming. Jester kept his eyes on him and watched as the normally sedentary four hundred pound man's face curled into a mask of rage.

"Get out!" he shouted. "Get out my shop!"

The other patrons stared at him. Rafiq and Jester exchanged worried glances.

"Get out, I said. Get to your homes. Go to your families. Just go! They just fucked us all."

The patrons and barbers jumped to grab their things and began hustling out the door.

The three young men spun as roar after roar erupted as the jungle of Los Angeles came alive behind them. Gin-fueled boozers poured out of the bar to meet a crowd gathered around a car, listening to the radio explain how an all white jury impartially let go free two white police officers for beating the fuck out of one of their kind. There were a hundred different shades of brown standing in the streets getting angrier and angrier until they became one unified color of red.

!

Breathless and sweat-soaked, the three young men came to a stop in an alley half a block down from the corner of Florence and Normandie. Flies buzzed around something dead near a trash bin. The stench of vegetables rotting in the May heat saturated the air. They exchanged wild-eyed glances as they gasped for breath.

"We gotta get the fuck home." Jester's smile was now somewhere a thousand miles away from of his worried gaze as he stared at the mouth of the alley where men and women were running either to or from something. The sounds of chants and screams were diminished by the brick walls of the buildings. An occasional shot rang out making them jump.

Rafiq straightened and dragged his forearm across his forehead. "Did you see that shit? See what Damian did to that white man?"

"I saw. I saw."

"Brother fucked him up."

"Brother fucked up, you mean. Ain't no reason to be attacking random white people."

"But we got to show them," Rafiq countered.

"They pulled him out of a fucking truck and beat him." Jester shook his head. "What's that going to show them? That they have a right to be afraid of us? Show them we're fucking animals?"

"Why're they looting their own stores?" Momodo asked, speaking for the first time in awhile.

"Brothers don't know any better," Jester said.

"Was the rebels who burned down our village. We tried to do everything to protect it. It's like the people are the rebels."

"Fucking frustration is what is it, Komodo," Rafiq said, ducking involuntarily as another shot rang out nearby. "Niggers get so tired of getting pissed on and getting taken from, they want to strike back. And if that's only a TV set and a box of soap, then so be it. At least it's something."

The armless Sierra Leonan shook his own head. "The people are the rebels," he said softly.

"They rebelling against the way things are," Rafiq said. "You're right, Komodo. We are the rebels. It's our turn to fight back." He stood and began to head back down the alley towards Normandy.

"Where you going?" Jester asked.

"Gonna join them. Gonna be a rebel until the all white empire strikes back."

Jester's eyes shot wide and his mouth gaped. "Are you kidding me, 'Fiq?"

"Hell, no. Come on, brother. Join us."

Jester didn't have to take a look at his cousin to know what he thought, but he did anyway. The young man's eyes were far away, probably in a place where rebels cut the arms off little boys who refused to fight with them. Jester put a hand on Momodo's shoulder. "You go on if you have to, 'Fiq, me and Momodo don't think the same way. We're villagers. This is our home and we don't want to see anything happen to it."

Day 2

When I was eleven years old, my father taught me how to be a poet. *It's not hard*, he said. *Take your emotions and turn them into words.* When they took my father the next year, I struggled to honor him. I composed my first poem sitting on the banks of the Bangasoka. It began with the words, *Carry him down to the depths of the river, so he can watch me walk along its banks.* It was a sorry effort that had no relation with how things really were, just a bunch of pretty words latched together that could mean anything. I constructed my last poem as I lay on a cot in a United Nations medical tent, flies licking at my bandages. *Never so sharp was the blade that cleaved my arms and circumcised my future; the best that I could ever do, left laying on the dust of a village where I once pretended to be a warrior.*

!

"This is like Sierra Leone," Momodo said, his eyes darting up and down the street.

Cars and trucks were overturned, some jackknifed intentionally at intersections. Vehicles, garbage cans and the occasional building raged with fire. People ran with such abandon, they often ran into each other, as often laughing at the convergence as they were angry. As they ran, arms laden with other people's things, they talked to one another. Momodo had only been in country for six months, but he'd come to know these neighborhoods. Sampson's Barber Shop was already gutted, the chairs stolen right before someone threw in a gas-filled bottle. Another grocer, one Jester's mom frequented, was fighting to keep his store, standing in a door and swinging a bat at everyone who moved. But he'd soon tire, and the determined crowd would get past him.

Jester peered around the corner, then jerked his head back. "Damn Korean's going to get shot."

"He's trying to protect his store. We tried to do the same back home."

"What would happen to him if he lived there?"

"They'd kill him," Momodo said matter-of-factly.

"Was it really that bad?"

"Not all the time. Only when the rebels wanted something. Mostly, they wanted more rebels. If you didn't join them, they did this to you," he concluded with a shrug, the best he could do in an effort to raise his non-existent arms.

"I still can't believe 'Fiq is part of this shit. And not just him. Almost everyone I know. I saw old Miss Scoggins running into her apartment with a case full of baby food and another case full of fabric softener. She don't have a dryer and she ain't got no babies."

"They so angry they don't know what it is," Momodo said. "I felt that way once."

"You the revenging type? Feel like revenging on someone?" Jester asked, trying to smile.

"Maybe those who took my arms."

"They a long way from here." Jester gave Momodo's shoulder a squeeze. "I wish I'd have been there, Cuz."

Momodo shook his head savagely. "Then we'd both have no arms. No, Jester. Wasn't your fault you escaped in time."

An explosion caused them both to jump. Gunshots rang out, then a cheer went up. The Korean grocer lay unmoving by his bat, the length of wood rolling back and forth as feet pounded past and into his store.

Jester closed his eyes and sighed.

Momodo had seen that reaction from his cousin before. Jester, nicknamed because of his constant need to make other people laugh, had escaped Freetown when he was eight. Arriving in Los Angeles, he quickly grew to match his father's six-foot-four frame and learned how to play American football. He was big and he was popular, which gave him an armor of protection that would come in handy, should they need it. Still, he was the sort who'd rather let someone do something that might be wrong than try and stop them. In the end, he believed in personal freedom. "Nothing you can do about it, Cousin."

Jester took a deep breath and opened his eyes. "Maybe there is. Remember that Korean 'Fiq was so pissed at?"

Momodo nodded as his eyes widened. "Think he's going to do something?"

"Who else would he do it to?"

Momodo felt phantom fists as the end of his phantom arms tighten into balls of resolve. "This isn't Sierra Leone," he said.

"No it isn't." Jester took off down the alley. "Follow me."

Momodo ran after him, his shoulders waggling from side to side in concert with his strides. He ran oblivious of the danger, not caring if he tripped, knowing he'd never be able to stop a fall without his arms. But this was more important than falling on one's face. This was about the fall of them all.

Traveling wasn't difficult. They saw one police car far in the distance, but no other sign of authority. They headed to Vermont, which had a preponderance of Korean businesses. Once they arrived, the atmosphere was completely different. Where before the looters had entertained an almost carnival-like atmosphere, this was more like combat. Momodo recognized the blue plaid of the Crips and the red of the Bloods, each huddled in groups, planning their assaults like it was a schoolyard football game. Where they'd previously been at odds with each other, their mutual enmity seemed to be the host of successful Korean businessmen situated along the length of the street.

The two boys stopped at the southeast corner of Manchester and Vermont, where a group of Crips waited, pistols held to the ground. Occasionally one would point towards a rooftop where a Korean aimed a rifle. There had to be thirty Korean businesses nearby. Several had been firebombed, but the rest remained unscathed, metal mesh and doors drawn across the windows like commercial castles.

"Come on," Jester said, as he crossed the street in a hunch.

They entered an alley, and ran west one block to Florence Avenue. As they exited into the street, they noticed a lessening of the tension. With fewer Korean businesses, there were fewer *gangstas*.

"What kind of revenge is this?" Momodo asked.

"It's not revenge," Jester replied. "It's opportunity."

They spied the sign for Empire Liquor on the corner with both English and Korean characters. Then they heard the shout. Looking south down Florence, they saw Rafiq along with six Crips. Their friend called out to them and waved his hand.

Jester and Momodo exchanged glances.

"Come on," Jester said.

They ran towards the corner where the Korean liquor storeowner stood in the doorway of his business glancing nervously up and down the street. Jester pushed him inside. Momodo followed after. The Korean began screaming at them. His wife cowered in the back. The place smelled like noodles and coffee with a pungent flare of ammonia

"Get the door," Jester ordered. Then he looked at Momodo. "Oh shit. I got it." He hustled to lock the door. The glass of the door and windows had already been reinforced with sheets of metal that had been affixed to the inside. He found a chain and secured it shut. When he turned around, he was greeted with twin barrels of a shotgun.

"I know you. You get out." The Korean man's eyes were wide with fear, but his mouth was a thin, resolute line.

"Listen, Mister," Jester began, but was cut off by the Korean's violent gesture with the gun.

A calm came over Momodo as he stepped in front of the gun. He let the Korean's eyes take in his missing arms. He willed his phantom right hand to reach up and push the gun down. Although it didn't move, Momodo tried none-the-less.

"Our friend is coming to rob you, maybe kill you. We will not let that happen," he said slowly and evenly. "Put the gun down." He willed his hand to move the barrels of the shotgun.

The man's wife said something in rapid fire Korean that had the man looking once again at his missing arms.

Momodo smiled. "It's going to be all right."

The Korean lowered his gun.

The door suddenly rattled.

"Jester, you in there?" Rafiq asked.

"Go away, 'Fiq. We got this one."

"No way. He's mine."

Jester shot a worried look back at Momodo, who smiled calmly in return. He'd seen worse.

Rafiq began arguing with the *gangstas* outside. Gunshots erupted. Bullets slammed into the metal of the door and the window like claps of miniature thunder. The Korean woman screamed. The glass on the door shattered, but the metal plates held.

When the firing stopped, Jester said, "We got our own guns in here, 'Fiq."

"What you gonna do with them? Give them to the cripple? What's he going to fire it with?"

"Come on now, 'Fiq. Ain't no call for that."

"I'm fucking sick of the way you and him pal around. And now you want to take my score."

Jester turned and whispered. "There a back door?"

The woman nodded, but the man stepped forward. "I'm not leaving my store."

He glanced at Momodo, then said, "I'll check the back."

Momodo stood with the two Koreans as Jester checked the back room, then the back door. The *gangstas* had begun to throw their weight into the front door, each crash causing them to jump with its impact. The interior of the liquor store was small. With one central shelf and wall shelves, it didn't hold much. The door to the back store room was beside a beer and soda cooler. The counter stood on the left, a plexiglass shield in place to protect the cashier, who in this case was the Korean man's wife. As he watched her, she said something to her husband.

"Your arms." The Korean man gestured nervously. "What happened?"

Momodo shrugged and put out his phantom hands in the universal sign of *it's okay*. "It happened in my country." He wasn't sure how much they knew about Western Africa. He'd yet to meet one of his new schoolmates who could place Sierra Leone on a map. "It was a war."

"W—were you fighter?" the man asked.

Momodo shook his head. "I didn't want to fight so they did this to me."

Jester rushed back into the room. "No one's getting in the back. There's another room behind this one in case things get real bad." He glanced at the front door. "They still there?"

As if in response, something heavy slammed into the door enough to rattle it.

"Looks pretty solid. Think it'll hold?" he asked the Korean man.

"Why are you doing this… helping us?"

Jester reached out and placed a baseball glove-sized hand on the Korean's shoulder. "Because we're all villagers." He reached out and grabbed a bag of potato chips. "Mind if I have some?" The man nodded. "Momodo, why don't you explain to them your philosophy of villagers and rebels?"

Jester pulled a Coke from the cooler, and sat down on the floor, facing the door. He ate mechanically as Momodo began to tell his story, explaining the vicissitudes of the eternal battle between rebel and villager.

Day 3

They stared into the mirror together: Momodo and the United Nations nurse.

"There was infection so we had to remove the arms all the way to the shoulders."

The rebels had severed his arms below the elbow. He'd imagined still using them, nubs instead of hands lifting things through handles, just like the others in his village did. It might have been an inexpert way to do things, but it was possible nonetheless. But now with no arms, with absolutely nothing below the shoulder, even that was impossible. For the first time he realized the enormity of what had been done to him. He tried to speak, but his voice cracked. He hadn't cried since he'd been brought in. He'd screamed, but never cried. Now, as he tried to find voice to his desolation, he couldn't help as the tears began to flow. Soon he was shuddering with sobs as the nurse put her arms around him. He wanted to put his arms around her, so without thinking he did, pressing and hugging her. She hugged him tighter then, but after a few seconds, she suddenly pulled away, her eyes wide. She disengaged and stood, confusion making her features ugly. He continued to cry as she stumbled out of the room. He never saw her again. A month later, they began the process of sending him to Los Angeles.

!

There'd been moments when they weren't sure if they'd make it through the night. Rafiq seemed so dedicated in his determination to kill the shopkeeper. The Koreans on the rooftops were a great help. They kept firing at the groups trying to invade their stores. Very rarely did they hit anyone, but the constant shooting made even Rafiq's group wary.

But at 3 A.M. it all changed when a car rammed the front of the store. Everyone except Momodo was dozing when the crash came. Glass showered all of them as they saw the front end of a Toyota breach the front. The door still held, if barely, but the glass was gone, as was the glass in the windows. If it hadn't been for the metal in front of the glass, the Crips would already be pouring in. But there was no doubt they would come soon. The metal looked like the inside of a Coke can that had been crushed by a divine hand.

Jester was the first one up. He grabbed Ms. Park, pulled her to her feet, and hustled to the back. He shouted for Mr. Park and Momodo to join them. Mr. Park refused to move. Seeing this, Mrs. Park shouted in Korean. Whatever she said was strong enough to make Mr. Park stumble backwards then join them. They all pretended not to see the tears in his eyes as they closed the metal fire door separating the store from the store room, locked it twice and stood back.

When the next crash came, they all jumped a little.

The Parks held each other.

Jester and Momodo exchanged worried glances.

A third crash was followed by cheers and curses as the Crips poured into the store. The sounds of their violence gave knowledge to what was being done in the store. The cash register smashed. Bottles hurled back and forth across the store, shattering more bottles. The rapid crunch of feet as they ran back and forth. Jocular cries as forties were opened, then silence as they were drank. Then shouts of triumph as they toasted one another for taking down the place, Rafiq's voice loudest and full of rebellious fire.

Momodo watched as darkness played across the light at the bottom of the door. The smell of liquor became heavy as clear liquid began to seep beneath and gather around their feet. Mrs. Park found several rolls of towels and began mopping them up. But then the light of the bottom of the door was gone. They heard a knock.

Mr. Park pulled his wife up and away.

"Hello in there," Rafiq said happily. "Why don't you come out and play?"

Mr. Park was about to say something, but Jester put a hand up and put his finger to his lips.

"Come on, Jester. You still in there playing the hero?" Rafiq laughed. "Listen, you did as good as you could with your rebel-villager bullshit, but now it's over. We broke down the door and are getting our revenge. Your job is done. We don't have any problem with you. Just leave us the Koreans and we'll let you go."

Mrs. Park's impossibly-wide eyes implored Jester and Momodo not to leave.

The sound of gun barrel rapping on the metal door. "Come on, Jester. Your time is ticking. These boys I'm with want Mr. Park for all the crap he's given them over the years. I convinced them to let you and the cripple Quasimodo leave, but it's not going to last forever."

Momodo kept his eyes on Jester, but his cousin remained implacable.

Voices began arguing on the other side of the door. Finally, a new voice. "Jester, open the fucking door or I'm going to bust a fucking cap in your boy, Rafiq."

"Wait. Wait," came Rafiq's suddenly terrified response. "You can't do that—" His words were cut off by a cry.

Momodo watched as Jester's fists balled. Momodo did the same.

"Listen, muthafucker," the voice growled. "This door ain't shit for us. We break through them every night all over this fucking town. All we got to do is cut down along the edge and separate the locks, then it's all over. You get one last chance." He pounded on the door with fists, making everyone jump. "Do you hear me muthafucker?"

Momodo examined the seam along the door jamb. He realized that the door opened from the inside of the shop, which meant the metal designed to block such a thing was on his side. Then he saw it. The Parks had built it this way to keep someone from breaking into the shop. They'd never anticipated these events. That the locks were operated by a key was the only reason they'd been able to lock it from the *wrong* side in the first place.

"Punching them out wouldn't help. They're deadbolts," Jester whispered to Momodo. He turned to the Parks. "I've seen them do this before. They're good—really good."

Mrs. Park hugged herself closer to her husband. "What do we do?"

Jester glanced around and seemed to come to a conclusion. "You stay here. Momodo, don't let them in. Their safety is yours. I'm going to break out the back and see if I can't get some help."

Momodo was about to say something, when the Crips began to bang on the door. Jester used the sound to cover his exit. He unlocked the door, peeked out, then slid out. Mr. Park ran over and slammed the door shut, and slid the locks back in place. When he returned to Mrs. Park, they both stared at him, their eyes taking in his empty shoulders, their unasked question *What do we do now* loud in their eyes.

!

Momodo spent three months in Hawaii before he landed in Los Angeles. The United Nations coordinated for him to receive rehabilitation at Tripler Army Hospital Center for Artificial Limbs. The first week he found himself in a long bay filled with American warriors who'd lost arms and legs while fighting. Many more were from Cambodia and Laos, legs forever removed by a mine they'd found from back when the rice fields had been Killing Fields.

With his wounds almost healed, he felt out of place among them. He'd merely been in the wrong place at the wrong time, while these men and several women had intentionally gone to a far away country to save people like him. Chaplains and their assistants came by several times a day, treating him like the others, the care and concern beaming from their eyes.

"You'll be able to wear prosthetics," a doctor told him one day. "The U.N. doctors did a remarkable job repairing and saving the nerves in the affected areas."

Momodo tried to imagine himself with prosthetics such as those worn by the patients who'd been there the longest. It was as if machines had been grafted to the skin. How much of one's humanity was lost because of this? How much less human were they? Although the lure of being able to use hands and arms just as he'd done before was strong, the longing for his flesh and blood limbs was even stronger. To accept a prosthetic would be to deny the hope that he'd ever be reunited with his arms, no matter how improbably that seemed. So when they'd approached him, he told them he didn't want prosthetics. After several days counseling, and several days of him rejecting the idea, they assented and began teaching him how to live without his arms. At first it seemed impossible, but shifting his body and with the creative use of his chin and his feet, he was soon able to dress himself.

It was both frustrating and funny. He still imagined his arms being attached to his body, and while his chin and feet did most of the work, he urged his hands to assist where they could. And although he couldn't prove it nor see it, he'd always been of the belief that they were there, just waiting and ready to work, if only he'd believe in them.

!

As promised, the Crips came back with a saw about an hour later. As it started and as the sparks began to fly, Mr. Park reached out and tried to appeal to Momodo.

"Maybe we escape out the back? Maybe we can make it?"

Momodo shook his head. "Too late. They're out back, I promise."

"How do you know?"

"I just do. See for yourself."

Mrs. Park stumbled to the door and put her eye to the peephole. She screamed and jerked her head clear just as a round tore through the slender glass tube.

The Parks ran to each other and fell to their knees in the middle of the store room floor. They grasped each other frantically, until they were certain they had good grips, unsure if this would be the last time they'd ever be able to hold each other.

Momodo spun as sparks began shooting sideways into the room from the door jamb.

Where were the cops?

Where were the other Koreans?

Where were the warriors to protect the villagers?

Unable to help, he felt the fear he'd felt when his own village had been attacked and the rebel who'd smelled like burned animal fat had thrust the AK-47 into his hands. Momodo had looked at it and known what it did. He'd known what it could do. He could have turned it on the rebel and killed him with it, but he'd too afraid. Not of dying, not of the rifle, but of what he might become if he accepted the rebel's invitation. It was this fear that had made him hurl the rifle to the ground. It was that fear that had caused them to remove his arms.

He felt fear now, but it was a different fear. He feared for these two Koreans—these villagers, who'd lived in peace all their lives, doing the right things, being the best persons they could be, only to become victims of events over which they had no control. Momodo suddenly realized that he was no longer a villager. He'd transcended that. By rejecting the weapons of the rebels, he'd become a warrior. And as the sparks met the ground and the saw spun dead on the other side of the door, he reached out, screamed out an unintelligible cry to purgatory, and seized the handle of the door. He pushed against the jamb on either side of the door with his feet, and held fast.

Laughter changed to confusion as they tried to pull the door open. His eyes snapped shut as he strained to imbue his hands with all the strength he had. He poured his need to save into his legs which straightened until his body was off the floor, held taught by his iron-fast grip.

They tried to twist the knob, but he wouldn't let them.

They pulled as one, but even with several of them, he had the leverage, he had the fulcrum, he had the hands.

Finally they fired at the metal door.

Momodo smiled, knowing they had no other choice.

His strength was legend.

His breath was furious.

His focus was pure.

They fired again, cursing and shouting.

His strength began to ebb.

His arms shook with the effort to hold the door.

He cried out as tears sprung to his eyes.

He couldn't let go. He couldn't give up. He had to hold on.

He felt the Parks getting to their feet, then felt their hands come over his. As the last of his strength left him, he let go, and allowed them to hold the door for a moment.

Then came shouts and screams from the other side of the door. Korean and English mixed with the sounds of gunfire.

Momodo scrambled to his feet and held his fists out in front of him. If they were going to come through the door, he'd be ready.

Suddenly, all was quiet.

After a moment, a small Korean voice spoke from the other side of the door.

Mr. Park replied and let go of the door knob. Mrs. Park did the same, grins removing the worry from their faces, like cloth to grime. The door opened slowly, revealing a young Korean, carrying a sawed-off shotgun. They embraced as the light of the morning revealed the awful evidence of the night. Dead Crips littered the glass smothered floor, their blood mixing with the liquid making everything the color of Bloody Marys.

The Parks turned and spoke to him.

He didn't understand, but he lowered his arms, and as they did so, they once again disappeared.

"How? How?" Mr. Park asked.

Momodo stepped between him and the other Korean. How was he to answer? How could he tell?

As he entered the shop, Jester came through the door, wearing a yellow bandana on his head.

"Momodo!" he ran and hugged his cousin. "You're alive."

They embraced for a moment, then Momodo stepped back. He pointed his chin at the bandana. "New fashion?"

Jester sneered. "Took some convincing. The other Koreans thought I was trying to fool them, but once they started believing, they formed a plan. This is so I wouldn't get shot." His eyes brightened. "You should see outside, Momodo. It was amazing. The villagers rose up."

The left together, limping down Normandie. If they kept heading west, they'd hit the ocean, where blonde-haired, bronzed people cavorted in the sun, unaware of the war raging just a few miles away. But instead they turned, heading to Vermont Avenue. Here and there were bodies. Storefronts firebombed. The streets littered with stolen goods.

Then they heard a strange sound, impossibly loud squeaking against the concrete.

They turned and saw the first of several in a line of tanks. They watched as one took up a post at an intersection, and the others continued towards them. The sight was amazing.

"Thought you fuckers would come this way." Rafiq stepped out in front of them.

"Fiq? What you doing?" Jester asked, letting go of Momodo and stepping between him and their one-time friend who now held a 9mm, sideways like a *gangsta*.

Rafiq was in bad shape. His face was a mass of bruises. His nose had been flattened. One eye was puffed shot, the other was scored with a black ring. He'd been shot in his left shoulder, which hung like it was broken. "Why'd you get involved? Why couldn't you leave it alone?"

"Take it easy," Jester said. "Let's just get home."

"Fuck getting home. You have a home. I ain't got shit and now the Crips have their mark on me."

Jester exchanged a look with Momodo. "Just let us pass, 'Fiq. We've been through enough, yo."

"It was that fucking cripple who ruined it all." Rafiq's gun hand began to shake as he tried to aim around Jester.

"Let it go, 'Fiq. He never done nothing to you."

"Nothing!" Rafiq screamed, his voice insane and quavering. "Nothing? Look at me? He did all this?"

Jester shook his head. "That was all you, 'Fiq. You made the choice."

Momodo became aware of the sound of the tanks getting closer. He couldn't tell how close. He didn't dare turn.

Rafiq lunged. Jester grabbed him. They fought over the gun for a moment, then it went off. All was still, then Rafiq fell to the ground. Jester turned, holding the pistol by its barrel. He was still turning when bullets from the tank stitched his chest, then crawled across the front of Momodo. They both fell as the bullets raked them again and again and again.

For a single moment, Momodo was an incandescent spark of pain, then his soul shot down a tube of cries and shouts, past the events of the past few days, and through a crowd robbing toys from a mega-store, past tanks, a bus with bright-faced children, and across the hood of a car with L.A. Laker bandwagon flags. A bright light urged him forward. He knew what was there. He felt them before he could see them. They wanted him as much as he wanted them. Their time in purgatory was over and in a quantum rush, he met his arms and he hugged himself into the light.

Day 4

More than four thousand soldiers patrolled the streets of Los Angeles. Among them walked Private Robinson, who'd stopped the robbery the previous day while riding in the M60 tank. Why the armless man was partnered with the other man, he'd never figure out, but the image of him as he lay in a pool of blood, his mouth fixed into a tight grin would stay with him forever. Now if only these people would stay inside and be peaceable, he could return to his apartment in Seaside and get back to playing his game. Soon he'd be a seventh level wizard and then he'd show them all.

Day 5

Moma Teta sat on her porch for the first time in days. She rocked and stared out into the bright clear day. They'd come to her and told her about her son and her nephew. She'd moved her boy across an entire ocean to get away from the violence. Momodo had come later—the poor boy—after he'd given part of himself so he might live. She guessed it wasn't enough. She guessed it was never enough. She rocked in her chair. A bus filled with peacekeepers rumbled by making her wonder if she'd left Africa at all.

Day 6

Mr. Park and his wife cleaned, then cleaned again. It took them most of the day. Every once in a while, they'd glance at the door to the storeroom. They'd never discussed what the boy had done. They had no way to talk about it. Park had seen many strange things in his fifty years of life, including the rescue of his country from the Chinese by men who didn't even know what a Korean was. Although that hadn't changed much in the forty years since the war, his silent appreciation for their desire to come to his aid continued unabated. During the rioting, just when he'd thought all was lost, two young men had come and saved them, duplicating what had happened during the war. It was hard sometimes to remember that America had a long history of supporting the Korean people.

He'd remember that.

He'd pass it on.

He continued cleaning and reminded himself that he still had to fix the peephole in the back door. Bending to his task, he worked at making his life that of a villager.

And life moved on.

Weston Ochse is the author of eleven novels, most recently *Age of Blood*, the sequel to *SEAL Team 666* which the *New York Post* called "required reading" and *USA Today* placed on their "New and Notable List of 2012." His first novel, *Scarecrow Gods*, won the Bram Stoker Award for Superior Achievement in First Novel and his short fiction has been nominated for the Pushcart Prize. His work as appeared in comic books, and magazines such as *Cemetery Dance* and *Soldier of Fortune*. He lives in the Arizona desert within rock throwing distance of Mexico. He is a military veteran with 29 years of military service, including work on information campaigns to bring mine awareness to Southeast Asia. "Six Days in May" was written while he was deployed in Afghanistan in 2013.

The Atlantic
William M. Brandon III

"Thank you. Yes, just leave it my cup. What's that? I've lost my sight, I rely on the sharpness of my other senses."

His sense of smell couldn't possibly be that sharp; the impenetrable stench of decay rose from the kneeling man as he clanked a few pieces of silver-coated currency in a small paper cup. The brittle fingers of his left hand positioned his collected belongings in neat rows along the small scrap of damp, sodden carpet he laid as his foundation on the warm, sunlit sidewalk.

"You are very observant; I can go nowhere else now, but I come from far, far away, near the Pacific Ocean, just above the old Los Angeles basin. I grew up there. Of course *after* the war; do I look that old?" The man laughed; his raucous, deprecated voice rose and fell between birdsong and the hiss of infrequently passing cars. "I can never go back."

The man's clothing was shiny at the joints, sullied with constant wear and he had unmistakably been using his trousers as an open-air lavatory for quite some time. Though his flesh had only seen fifty solar revolutions, his wearied countenance advertised the gnarled aftermath of exposure, disease, and absolute neglect. Though his eyes hid behind a milky curtain of cataract, they were alive and seemed to follow the trilling birds as they cautiously approached and sampled scattered pieces of a water cracker he had spread out for their convenience.

"Yes, I do miss it. Well, I miss what once was. After the Invasion, there wasn't much to love anymore. Everywhere one turned there was a stark reminder of a fallen city, long since infected by military patrols and remote-control centurions before my birth. Old Hollywood and Vine was as flat and overrun with vegetation as it had been before the masses began to arrive in the early twentieth century. Only the downtown landscape remained. Apparently, the Invaders decided to spare the skyline in hopes that the city could be remade in their image, a mockery of Western decadence, and a reminder to their own people to watch their step - to be wary of excess. Hypocrisy, if you ask me.

"That's a good question young man, I don't know why my father chose to plant roots on the western coast. Perhaps desperation of the sort that compelled the Colonists of old to murder and enslave in service of Manifest Destiny. After all, once the Invaders realized that the southern coast was dead and practically glowing with radioactivity from San Onofre, all potential profit dried up like Amanita in the high-desert. With the overlords absent, the families and prospectors of the basin were left to starve and fend off the myriad cancers and birth defects that became commonplace. Sure, it was, in good part, the fault of the Invaders, but it is folly to ignore the abuse our society sustained from our own government during our final decades as a sovereign nation. Of course I have an excellent vocabulary, does a man without a home have to be a bottled up ignoramus that imagines unicorns and aliens roam freely in the natural world?

"None of this can be news to you boy. Don't tell me you're one of them…yes, *them*…those that still refuse to take responsibility for our demise. Everyone wants to blame the Invaders, *it's their fault, we were perfect and pristine before their aggression*, but it's just not true. I guess you don't remember—of course you don't, I barely remember. And now, what's the point of remembering…"

The Old Man dipped his head in resignation, but his sullen eyes still moved frantically, in anticipation of an unseen attack. "We murdered our own beautiful world to protect it. The prevailing logic pushed its way to the forefront of the conversation, 'If we cannot protect our nation, we must mar it beyond any reasonable desire to possess it.' It was madness, but such was our thinking in that long gone era. Such was our drive to maintain our empire.

"Eh? No, no, we started on that path long before the invasion. For over a century we battered and poisoned our soil and our seas, long before the first whispers of insurrection we had already rendered our own homeland incapable of feeding its own people, and far before that, our water had taken on the pall of sewage and raw industrial waste. We sold clean water to the highest bidder until there were no more to sell. Our hubris cut us off from the Empire we had fomented—forced by violence, on the rest of the world. Like the Ancient Mariner, millions of cubic gallons of water licked our fouled shorelines daily, but 'not a drop to drink.'

"It was our own government that planted the deadly devices all over the basin, up and down both of our coasts, some far off notion that exploding soil would ward off the Invaders or at least compel them to move on. Maybe some young lieutenant even convinced his commanders that the devices would kill an acceptable percentage of the Invaders' forces, but that technology, if any of them cared to remember, had never worked. Instead, the devices sat inert waiting for the hapless citizens who returned to the basin to revive its lost glory.

"Citizens like my father."

For the first time the Old Man's eyes stopped darting back and forth and focused absently on the ground before him. His mind seemed to slide through the twin broken portals below his brow and surround him before waning and returning to a calmer, more resigned state. "I wish we had stayed in Nevada."

The Old Man gathered himself into a tight bundle and gripped his own shoulders before relaxing into a contemplative, meditative stillness. "There were no jobs, you see? Nothing my father could get anyway. 'Too educated, over-qualified, sorry we can't help but think that you'll leave in a few months for something better, so we can't risk wasting time and training on you.' The employers always said this with a straight face, as if a man coming to them, with hat in had, with desperation in his eyes and on his face, was anything but loyal in totality. There is something very cruel in the assumption that an educated man forced to take a menial job is somehow a turncoat and a traitor. By this time it took an undergraduate degree in Physics to garner a managerial position in a retail establishment. Yes, long before these fancy University boards devised the four divisions of post-doctorate credentials that the children in this town chase with their parents' money and blessing. You know why these education boards did what they did?" the Old Man looked up, perhaps rhetorically, but an answer would have been welcome. "Money, son. What do you do when an education becomes worthless? Simple, you create higher, more expensive levels of education so that the coffers remain full and the children remain unsatisfied - chasing the next level, endlessly praying to one day show their worth.

"So we set out, my father, his worthless Master's degree, and me, farther out west to the renewed outposts of the previously conquered continent. Leftist pioneers who still believed that home-schooling was folly set up a tiny four room 'school' on the edge of the basin. My father, himself an idealist, sent me to the tiny school. More, I believe, to force me to experience the lost art of socializing than to 'educate' me; so I went, everyday, absorbing the paltry crumbs available to those of us who were not University bound. Thirty total students were scattered between six grades, it was, in essence, a complicated daycare. Of course, this made for a very tight and asphyxiating *society* and the oppression of conformity was thick. There was no real room for the rebel or the outcast, hierarchy was self-imposed, the older and stronger had the rule of the roost and we younger lads and lasses had to fit in, on pain of returning each day to the nothingness of being cut out. Anti-social behavior was grounds for expulsion and none of us could afford to burden our struggling parents further by being an inhibition to their daily struggle to work and weekly struggle to receive compensation for their work."

Dense grey clouds began to gather in the skies above the Old Man's tiny rectangular compound. The birds had long since devoured his paltry offerings and scattered to nearby trees to wait for the dusk's thick curtains of unsuspecting insects to descend and fill their avian bellies. A thick, penetrating downpour began, and, as is the South's way, would end in a matter of minutes. The Old man raised his face to the sky, let the dense drops rain over his tired visage, and smiled.

"Never lasts very long. Not these days. Used to be, you could count on a soft rain all day and all night during the summer. Doesn't even rain in the Amazon anymore, so I hear.

"You don't have to tell me son, I know that a public education is a handicap, I lived it. What else could my father do? The prisons would not even accept us; they preferred those whose parents could be blackmailed to bankroll the inmates. Yes, I know, irony eh? The rich were the only suitable vestiges of incarceration, a depressing turn of events, nothing like the old vision of 'eating the rich' had dreamed of." The Old man reached deftly into a folded over wool cap and produced a scraggly, hole-ridden cigarette and a single match. Though his eyes remained blindly on the clouds above, he deftly licked the separating paper holding the tobacco to reform a seal - good enough - to light.

"You can barely get these things anymore. No such thing as tobacco, just strains of fluff that genetically mimic the old sacred plant, shot through with chemical nicotine - smart, those farmers, realizing that the plant was not the goldmine, but the drugs within. Hell, for all we know the nicotine is carried by tufts of rat hair dyed brown to increase the nostalgia and trick the mind. But you don't smoke of course, none of you young people do anything that might hurt you, might compromise your ability to live beyond a century. Who can blame you? These days people need at least seventy years of steady income to hope for a break, a relaxing of the body and mind, and even then, most people are hard at work until their dying day - my father certainly was.

"He died too soon; before I saw my tenth year on the edge of the basin. I was able to con my teacher for nearly a year, lied about my father's whereabouts, pretended that he was a workaholic and an alcoholic: couldn't come to meetings, couldn't send me money for lunch, couldn't raise himself from bed to look after his only son. None of it was true, and in the desperation to survive, to still belong to some group, I marred my father's reputation and disgraced his name. The small staff at the school took pity on me and I was permitted to sleep under my desk between sessions. More than ever I needed to belong, more than ever I was alone and belonged nowhere.

"In the summer I had to make my own way, with the tiny schoolhouse shuttered and the water and electricity turned off to save vital, dwindling funds, I found myself at the mercy of the basin's ever-changing weather and desperate roving bands of homeless, disenfranchised citizens. Suddenly I was a stark reminder to the other parents of what may happen to their children, I was no longer welcome in my schoolmates homes, suddenly I was a pariah, though I had done nothing wrong.

"One quiet evening I let the toxic waves of the Pacific overtake me, dreaming of a rapid and peaceful death in the over-salinated waters, and I was given a final vision of hope. As I slowly succumbed to the rhythm of the waves, a strong hand tugged at my hair. I thrashed and kicked in resistance but the hand drug me to the beach.

"'Are you crazy?' Ahmed asked me. 'I am no one,' I explained, 'I deserve death.' I began to walk back into the waves and he called out, 'Little brother, come with me, I have shelter.' I eyed him warily; I was not used to compassion and assumed it was a trick. Though he was just barely older than me, boys bought and sold other boys along the shore and I had to decide…was a life of servitude and degradation better than an early death? I made my decision. I walked back onto the sands and wrapped my arms around Ahmed.

"I was lucky, Ahmed had no need for my body, he was just a kind and giving soul. Though he had to keep my existence a secret from his father, he daily brought me food and on occasion scraps of clothing that he could no longer wear. Ahmed's grandparents had come to the former United States as refugees in the early part of the century, during America's wars against the Middle East. Decades later when the Invaders overtook the Western shores they began rounding up US citizens for trial and imprisonment. The irony of the "Good Americans" trials was lost on our citizens and they wailed that they did not deserve their treatment. Ahmed's father knew better, he knew that every single American deserved the long-withheld wrath of the rest of the world.

"Ahmed's grandfather had told Ahmed's father many stories about the Basin, stories about its former glory, it's past life as a beacon of entertainment for the world, a gleaming city which all of the world wished to emulate, from Mumbai to London. Ahmed's grandfather had been a student of American history as boy, all foreigners were in those times, and grew up with a distant respect for the bastion of freedom America presented itself to be. So Ahmed's grandfather dedicated himself to the practice of law; he was a bright and promising student and was able to gain acceptance on partial scholarship to Oxford. Once the bombs began falling in his country, bombs with the slogans from ignorant GIs scrawled in marker on the side—'Made in the USA', 'For Saddam with love'—Ahmed's grandfather returned to celebrate the fall of his homeland's dictator.

"Yes, that's true, the celebration did not last long at all, it became all too clear within weeks that the American armed forces meant great harm and would not listen to the cries of his countrymen until they had secured the very last oil field for Shell, Exxon, BP, and the rest. Ahmed's grandfather had read enough of the America's history to know that he needed to get his loved ones out of the country as soon as possible, so he gathered Ahmed's father, Ahmed's brother, and Ahmed's grandmother and fled via Paris to the United States. He hoped that they would be treated with respect: as stranded refugees who loved the United States in spite of the terror the American government was raining down on his people. Ahmed's grandfather was mistaken and he spent his last days rotting in a tiny cell on the western shore of Cuba along with countless, uncounted others. Ah, you do know the history, very good, young man, very good. Camp X-ray to be precise, a place of unspeakable crimes and the first of many chinks in America's slowly crumbling armor."

The Old Man shifted on his carpet and reached again for another small crumpled cigarette a passerby had tossed in his cup in lieu of money. "I don't mind when they put these in my cup; I'd spend the change on them anyway, so all the better they save me the embarrassment of imploring a shopkeeper for honesty in selling me these damn things. Sometimes a shopkeeper cannot be trusted; sometimes they pull a few loose cigarettes from the floor, or their own pack and toss them at me while they slide my change into their money drawer. I'm no fool, I know the difference between a pack of smokes and a bundle of refuse sold at top price to a crippled blind man."

The Old Man raised his head asking the sky for a bolt of lightning, just a little fire, couldn't the world give him just a little fire for his trouble? A young punk dipped at the knees and lit his cigarette without stopping, "Thank you," the Old Man cried after the vaporous youth, "you are a good man."

"Ahmed's father never saw his own father again. The American government had no intention of letting any of the people trapped in their torture chambers go, most died. Some were released, but they usually met their end in another prison nearer to their tribal lands or at the hand of the governments that finally agreed to allow them back in.

"Ahmed's father grew up in an impossible situation, he harbored intense hatred for the United States but had to seek it's refuge and provide for his mother and his younger brother until the day he could leave the United States for good. That day never came. More accurately, the day came and went as the whole world began the slow slide into regional and finally world conflicts. By the time Ahmed's father was a man, there was nowhere to go. To the South there was no longer a place for any person who had ever called America home, Europe was crippled by debt and austerity, Africa had become the Americans' new playground, the proud former Ottoman Empire had been destroyed, Asia rejected all refugees and Australia joined hands with the United States, once again playing colonial handmaiden as it once had for the United Kingdom. There was nowhere to run, so Ahmed's father stayed. After his mother's death, Ahmed's father moved farther west to the American desert. He and his brother became estranged; Ahmed could not release his anger toward the American government even though his brother had. Eventually his own brother considered Ahmed's father a traitor to their new home.

"Ahmed's father was able to attend small community colleges and eventually, through his own raw talent he was accepted as a professor at a tiny city college in the California desert. He met a woman, flattered by Ahmed's affections, and they had a single son. She soon grew tired of her exotic husband and left Ahmed and his father for the chaos of New York City. From his tenuous position on the board of the school's Ancient History studies department Ahmed's father watched the matured forces of Russia, South America and Asia encircle the United States. When the first Invaders landed in Los Angeles, Ahmed's father thanked the fates daily that they were far from any legitimate target.

"First came the showers of deadly missiles from offshore, tearing away at Los Angeles' paved hills and low-lying beaches. Before long the American forces pulled back beyond the hills and the invading forces began to infiltrate and imprison the battered and bruised inhabitants of the once proud metropolis.

"Perhaps as a sick, cynical joke, perhaps as a bitter last stand, the United States decided to make the same mistake they had been making for almost a century from Dong Hoi to Corinto. They placed the devices below the ground all across the basin. These devices, for a time, halted the push of the Invaders, exploding beneath caravans and supply lines, dismembering hundreds of invading soldiers, but eventually the Invaders abandoned Los Angeles and moved north and south along the Pacific coast. They only returned to Los Angeles on patrol to see that the city remained a burning hulk.

"As the invasion became normalized and the American people became resigned to their fate, the craven, and the starving began to repopulate the basin, slowly, carefully. The Invaders chose their seats of power far from the emaciated basin with it's thousands of sub-terra devices ready to spring forth and maim at the slightest provocation. Ahmed's father was dismissed from his position at the small college in the high-desert and after a long and painful exile packed their meager belongings and escaped to the no-man's land of former Los Angeles.

"Once there, Ahmed's father felt inspiration again, once again the broken, yet still compassionate man, brilliant man!" The Old Man raised his good arm high in the air in tribute, "collected what he could from the firebombed library downtown, rebuilt a small, abandoned storehouse on the outskirts of the old Skid Row, and welcomed the children of the city to come and study. He attempted to offer hope to a new generation who had known nothing but death and fear in their short and tragic lives. Such was Ahmed's father's compassion that he did not blame the young American children for the crimes of their fathers and forefathers, rather he felt an agony of untold seriousness when he saw them playing among the shattered metropolis, scraping together food and metals to feed and help enrich their families.

"When Ahmed found me, I was bound for death, I had no hope and I had no purpose; Ahmed finally presented me to his father and his father had pity for me. I began attending the tiny school on the edge of downtown, so different from my former school, and in order to repay Ahmed and his father for their charity I took to my studies with the passion of a starving child welcomed, finally, into a vast garden of delights.

"By my fifteenth year I showed undue promise, and alongside Ahmed, himself a gifted scholar, I made of myself a devoted apprentice to the old masters of Literature. Ahmed's father could barely keep up with my voracious need for more and his weekly trips - dangerous, I'm sure I need not mention - to the Library barely scratched my youthful itch. Soon I began to compose my own stories, rank plagiarism at first, to be sure, but over time, Ahmed's father saw in me justification for his efforts and pride in himself.

"On my sixteenth birthday Ahmed pulled me from my writing perch on the steps of their charred building near the dilapidated warehouse school. 'We will return to the sea, you, and I! To remember our friendship, to remember all that is good and proper in this dreadful life!' We told Ahmed's father that we had important things to attend to and he smiled proudly at our defiance and youthful pride. As we crested the hills dotted with sad ancient oil derricks the sea came into view and we paused. 'We should not stay long my friend, let's keep moving, we are not truly safe until we can smell the salt air of the Pacific.' Ahmed warned so kindly, but sternly, and I retorted that it was *my birthday*, not his and I wished to watch sun cast over the Pacific for a moment longer.

"As we shared a stolen cigarette on that blighted hill we heard the groans of an approaching vehicle. A warning to remain still and fall to our knees rang out from a great loudspeaker and we froze. 'On your knees rats!' the voice bellowed, echoing off the rolling grey hill and we hit the ground shivering in submission. When we saw the armored vehicle bearing the stark symbols of the Invaders we knew that we should have run; run for our young lives and risked a bullet in the neck, risked our deaths instead of cowering as we now were.

"The soldiers left the safety of their vehicle and pushed us to the ground shouting in a language neither of us understood—a favorite fear tactic of the Invaders when dealing with American children. They pulled us from the ground and began marching us toward a distant crest of the hill I had insisted we stay on…"

The Old Man's eyes shut and silent tears pressed down his weathered, leathery cheeks. When his sightless eyes opened he looked around for another cigarette, but there were none, only his paper cup that had been slowly filling with change. "They pushed us toward a large field that stretched down the hill and onto a long charred plain. 'You are just what we were looking for,' in English this time, so that we understood, 'we will not see our brothers maimed today by your sick government's tricks. Instead, we have you.' One of the soldiers patted Ahmed on the head condescendingly and Ahmed swung his fists helplessly at the armored tyrant. The soldier leveled Ahmed with the butt of his rifle. 'Both of you, run down the hill and across that field. If you survive, we will spare your lives.'

"In that moment we knew our fate: the field was an identified cluster of underground devices, our tormentors were a patrol sent to map the region and locate unexploded ordinance buried beneath the pockmarked soil. The soldiers had been sent to die by their commanders and we were now going to die so that their lives may be spared. In truth, it is difficult for me to blame them for their actions; we were all at the mercy of cowards who were willing to watch us die.

I began running first; Ahmed stood and followed behind me. I hoped that if either of us had to suffer it would be me; Ahmed and his father had sacrificed so much to show me a happy life, to give an orphaned street kid a chance at a beautiful existence. I reached the bottom of the hill and sprinted with all my might in a straight line, keeping the slowly rising horizon in sight. My mistake was not watching my young feet and I stumbled on the hood of an old truck half buried in the ground and crashed face first into the grey, dense mud. I heard Ahmed call out my name. As I turned to face him and raise myself from the ground, we both heard the click of the device. Ahmed was engulfed in an eviscerating white light. It was the last light my eyes would see. I awoke in Ahmed's father's bed, pain coursed through my body and terminated at my legs.

"'Be calm,' I heard Ahmed's father whisper. It was not a whisper, my ears were still vibrating, trying to repair themselves after the shockwave nearly ruptured the thin flesh of my inner ears. My legs, no mystery to you, were hanging dead from my hips and my arm lay stiff. The nerves in my arm were still quite alive and shrieked in pain, but I would never be able to life it again.

"Ahmed's father nursed me to health, he knew that if he took me to a medical facility that we would both be thrown in an Invaders' dungeon. In a year's time I was able to return to my studies, Ahmed's father focused on my future, it was perhaps the only way he could honor his son's memory, the only way he could suppress his rage and not leap into the sea in engulfing despair, as I had tried to so many years before.

"I sleepwalked through the following years, I was less successful at tamping down my rage, and I grew angrier and angrier as the occupation by the Invaders became our American reality. I blamed myself for Ahmed's death, no surprise to anyone, and I resented Ahmed's father for his total compassion. How could he not cast me out, the murderer of his only son? How could he torture me by showing me such unreal love and patience? On the sunrise of my twenty-first birthday, I left Ahmed's father's meager home near the tiny schoolhouse. I had no plan, no direction; I had no purpose but to run. By the time I was twenty-five I had lied to helpful strangers, been an adept thief, and murdered several unlucky travelers as they took pity on a crippled and blinded young man. I had wandered across this forsaken land seeking its eastern shore—a tired sign of self-retribution. Then, one day, enchanted by the smell of roasting pork and the calm, slow tones of this city's inhabitants and their undeserved charity, I placed this small carpet here, on this very corner, and have remained.

"I'm sure you're wondering, I know I have, why I did not keep moving. Somehow the prize, the release of reaching the Atlantic seemed too good, too wonderful a gift for me. A man who caused the death of his only friend and heaped shame upon himself with abandon, did not deserve the calm, warm waters of the sea, and so I stay."

The wind blew through the long matted strands of hair comprising the Old Man's beard. There was no one before him, save for a steady stream of young people hopeful for what their particular future held - be it a continuation of old money aristocracy, or the rebellious colors of subversive art. They lived in a world that only *remembered* the wars. He told his saga to no one, and in turn, no one listened.

The Old Man bowed his head in resignation.

William M. Brandon III recently relocated to breathtaking and traffic-free Athens, Georgia, from back-breaking and happiness-eviscerating Los Angeles, California, where he came mercifully close to making a living as a hired gun writing and editing copy for various commercial enterprises and creative endeavors. He began his lifelong road trip in the deprecated sands of Las Vegas, Nevada, and as a result of a military patriarch, and a subsequent unabated restlessness, has changed addresses fifty-six times in thirty-eight years. These days he earns his pittance from a real-life Kafkaesque nightmare and daydreams about sitting behind his typewriter working on his fifth novel, and conversing with his astonishing wife and his brilliant six-year-old stepson. His synaptic meanderings have appeared on his website (agentofdiscord.com) and in technical form on WIRED.com and THALO.com, in novella form in *Silence* (Transplant Press—2000), in memoir/novel form in *A Selfish Man* (Publish America—2003), in short story form in *Rain Crow* magazine (Athens Diptych—Issue #3), and finally, in voluminous letters to persons still enchanted with non-electronic communication. P.S. they almost never write back...

THE GHOST VILLAGE

Peter Straub

1

In Vietnam I knew a man who went quietly and purposefully crazy because his wife wrote him that his son had been sexually abused—"messed with"—by the leader of their church choir. This man was a black six-foot-six grunt named Leonard Hamnet, from a small town in Tennessee named Archibald. Before writing, his wife had waited until she had endured the entire business of going to the police, talking to other parents, returning to the police with another accusation, and finally succeeding in having the man charged. He was up for trial in two months. Leonard Hamnet was no happier about that than he was about the original injury.

"I got to murder him, you know, but I'm seriously thinking on murdering her, too," he said. He still held the letter in his hands, and he was speaking to Spanky Burrage, Michael Poole, Conor Linklater, SP4 Cotton, Calvin Hill, Tina Pumo, the magnificent M. 0. Dengler, and myself. "All this is going on, my boy needs help, this here Mr. Brewster needs to be dismantled, needs to be *racked* and *stacked,* and she don't tell me! Makes me want to put her *down,* man. Take her damn head off and put it up on a stake in the yard, man. With a sign saying: *Here is one stupid woman.*"

We were in the unofficial part of Camp Crandall known as No Man's Land, located between the wire perimeter and a shack, also unofficial, where a cunning little weasel named Wilson Manly sold contraband beer and liquor. No Man's Land, so called because the C.O. pretended it did not exist, contained a mound of old tires, a piss tube, and a lot of dusty red ground. Leonard Hamnet gave the letter in his hand a dispirited look, folded it into the pocket of his fatigues, and began to roam around the heap of tires, aiming kicks at the ones that stuck out farthest. "One stupid woman," he repeated. Dust exploded up from a burst, worn-down wheel of rubber.

I wanted to make sure Hamnet knew he was angry with Mr. Brewster, not his wife, and said, "She was trying—"

Hamnet's great glistening bull's head turned toward me.

"Look at what the woman did. She nailed that bastard. She got other people to admit that he messed with their kids, too. That must be almost impossible. And she had the guy arrested. He's going to be put away for a long time."

"I'll put that bitch away, too," Hamnet said, and kicked an old gray tire hard enough to push it nearly a foot back into the heap. All the other tires shuddered and moved. For a second it seemed that the entire mound might collapse.

"This is my *boy* I'm talking about here," Hamnet said. "This shit has gone far enough."

"The important thing," Dengler said, "is to take care of your boy. You have to see he gets help."

"How'm I gonna do that from here?" Hamnet shouted.

"Write him a letter," Dengler said. "Tell him you love him. Tell him he did right to go to his mother. Tell him you think about him all the time."

Hamnet took the letter from his pocket and stared at it. It was already stained and wrinkled. I did not think it could survive many more of Hamnet's readings. His face seemed to get heavier, no easy trick with a face like Hamnet's. "I got to get home," he said. "I got to get back home and take *care* of these people."

Hamnet began putting in requests for compassionate leave relentlessly—one request a day. When we were out on patrol, sometimes I saw him unfold the tattered sheet of notepaper from his shirt pocket and read it two or three times, concentrating intensely. When the letter began to shred along the folds, Hamnet taped it together.

We were going out on four- and five-day patrols during that period, taking a lot of casualties. Hamnet performed well in the field, but he had retreated so far within himself that he spoke in monosyllables. He wore a dull, glazed look, and moved like a man who had just eaten a heavy dinner. I thought he looked like a man who had given up, and when people gave up they did not last long— they were already very close to death, and other people avoided them.

We were camped in a stand of trees at the edge of a paddy. That day we had lost two men so new that I had already forgotten their names. We had to eat cold C rations because heating them with C-4 would have been like putting up billboards and arc lights. We couldn't smoke, and we were not supposed to talk. Hamnet's C rations consisted of an old can of Spam that dated from an earlier war and a can of peaches. He saw Spanky staring at the peaches and tossed him the can. Then he dropped the Spam between his legs. Death was almost visible around him. He fingered the note out of his pocket and tried to read it in the damp gray twilight.

At that moment someone started shooting at us, and the Lieutenant yelled, "*Shit!*" and we dropped our food and returned fire at the invisible people trying to kill us. When they kept shooting back, we had to go through the paddy.

The warm water came up to our chests. At the dikes, we scrambled over and splashed down into the muck on the other side. A boy from Santa Cruz, California, named Thomas Blevins got a round in the back of his neck and dropped dead into the water just short of the first dike, and another boy named Tyrell Budd coughed and dropped down right beside him. The F.O. called in an artillery strike. We leaned against the backs of the last two dikes when the big shells came thudding in. The ground shook and the water rippled, and the edge of the forest went up in a series of fireballs. We could hear the monkeys screaming.

One by one we crawled over the last dike onto the damp but solid ground on the other side of the paddy. Here the trees were much sparser, and a little group of thatched huts was visible through them.

Then two things I did not understand happened, one after the other. Someone off in the forest fired a mortar round at us—just one. One mortar, one round. That was the first thing. I fell down and shoved my face in the muck, and everybody around me did the same. I considered that this might be my last second on earth, and greedily inhaled whatever life might be left to me. Whoever fired the mortar should have had an excellent idea of our location, and I experienced that endless moment of pure, terrifying helplessness—a moment in which the soul simultaneously clings to the body and readies itself to let go of it—until the shell landed on top of the last dike and blew it to bits. Dirt, mud, and water slopped down around us, and shell fragments whizzed through the air. One of the fragments sailed over us, sliced a hamburger-size wad of bark and wood from a tree, and clanged into Spanky Burrage's helmet with a sound like a brick hitting a garbage can. The fragment fell to the ground, and a little smoke drifted up from it.

We picked ourselves up. Spanky looked dead, except that he was breathing. Hamnet shouldered his pack and picked up Spanky and slung him over his shoulder. He saw me looking at him.

"I gotta take *care* of these people," he said.

The other thing I did not understand—apart from why there had been only one mortar round—came when we entered the village.

Lieutenant Harry Beevers had yet to join us, and we were nearly a year away from the events at Ia Thuc, when everything, the world and ourselves within the world, went crazy. I have to explain what happened. Lieutenant Harry Beevers killed thirty children in a cave at Ia Thuc and their bodies disappeared, but Michael Poole and I went into that cave and knew that something obscene had happened in there. We smelled evil, we touched its wings with our hands. A pitiful character named Victor Spitalny ran into the cave when he heard gunfire, and came pinwheeling out right away, screaming, covered with welts or hives that vanished almost as soon as he came out into the air. Poor Spitalny had touched it, too. Because I was twenty and already writing books in my head, I thought that the cave was the place where the other *Tom Sawyer* ended, where Injun Joe raped Becky Thatcher and slit Tom's throat.

When we walked into the little village in the woods on the other side of the rice paddy, I experienced a kind of foretaste of Ia Thuc. If I can say this without setting off all the Gothic bells, the place seemed intrinsically, inherently wrong—it was too quiet, too still, completely without noise or movement. There were no chickens, dogs, or pigs; no old women came out to look us over, no old men offered conciliatory smiles. The little huts, still inhabitable, were empty—something I had never seen before in Vietnam, and never saw again. It was a ghost village, in a country where people thought the earth was sanctified by their ancestors' bodies.

Poole's map said that the place was named Bong To.

Hamnet lowered Spanky into the long grass as soon as we reached the center of the empty village. I bawled out a few words in my poor Vietnamese.

Spanky groaned. He gently touched the sides of his helmet. "I caught a head wound," he said.

"You wouldn't have a head at all, you was only wearing your liner," Hamnet said.

Spanky bit his lips and pushed the helmet up off his head. He groaned. A finger of blood ran down beside his ear. Finally the helmet passed over a lump the size of an apple that rose up from under his hair. Wincing, Spanky fingered this enormous knot. "I see double," he said. "I'll never get that helmet back on."

The medic said, "Take it easy, we'll get you out of here."

"Out of *here?*" Spanky brightened up.

"Back to Crandall," the medic said.

Spitalny sidled up, and Spanky frowned at him. "There ain't nobody here," Spitalny said. "What the fuck is going on?" He took the emptiness of the village as a personal affront.

Leonard Hamnet turned his back and spat.

"Spitalny, Tiano," the Lieutenant said. "Go into the paddy and get Tyrell and Blevins. Now."

Tattoo Tiano, who was due to die six-and-a-half months later and was Spitalny's only friend, said, "You do it this time, Lieutenant."

Hamnet turned around and began moving toward Tiano and Spitalny. He looked as if he had grown two sizes larger, as if his hands could pick up boulders. I had forgotten how big he was. His head was lowered, and a rim of clear white showed above the irises. I wouldn't have been surprised if he had blown smoke from his nostrils.

"Hey, I'm gone, I'm already there," Tiano said. He and Spitalny began moving quickly through the sparse trees. Whoever had fired the mortar had packed up and gone. By now it was nearly dark, and the mosquitoes had found us.

"So?" Poole said.

Hamnet sat down heavily enough for me to feel the shock in my boots. He said, "I have to go home, Lieutenant. I don't mean no disrespect, but I cannot take this shit much longer."

The Lieutenant said he was working on it.

Poole, Hamnet, and I looked around at the village.

Spanky Burrage said, "Good quiet place for Ham to catch up on his reading."

"Maybe I better take a look," the Lieutenant said. He flicked the lighter a couple of times and walked off toward the nearest hut. The rest of us stood around like fools, listening to the mosquitoes and the sounds of Tiano and Spitalny pulling the dead men up over the dikes. Every now and then Spanky groaned and shook his head. Too much time passed.

The Lieutenant said something almost inaudible from inside the hut. He came back outside in a hurry, looking disturbed and puzzled even in the darkness.

"Underhill, Poole," he said, "I want you to see this."

Poole and I glanced at each other. I wondered if I looked as bad as he did. Poole seemed to be a couple of psychic inches from either taking a poke at the Lieutenant or exploding altogether. In his muddy face his eyes were the size of hens' eggs. He was wound up like a cheap watch. I thought that I probably looked pretty much the same.

"What is it, Lieutenant?" he asked.

The Lieutenant gestured for us to come to the hut, then turned around and went back inside. There was no reason for us not to follow him. The Lieutenant was a jerk, but Harry Beevers, our next lieutenant, was a baron, an earl among jerks, and we nearly always did whatever dumb thing *he* told us to do. Poole was so ragged and edgy that he looked as if he felt like shooting the Lieutenant in the back. I felt like shooting the Lieutenant in the back, I realized a second later. I didn't have an idea in the world what was going on in Poole's mind. I grumbled something and moved toward the hut. Poole followed.

The Lieutenant was standing in the doorway, looking over his shoulder and fingering his sidearm. He frowned at us to let us know we had been slow to obey him, then flicked on the lighter. The sudden hollows and shadows in his face made him resemble one of the corpses I had opened up when I was in graves registration at Camp White Star.

"You want to know what it is, Poole? Okay, you tell me what it is."

He held the lighter before him like a torch and marched into the hut. I imagined the entire dry, flimsy structure bursting into heat and flame. This Lieutenant was not destined to get home walking and breathing, and I pitied and hated him about equally, but I did not want to turn into toast because he had found an American body inside a hut and didn't know what to do about it. I'd heard of platoons finding the mutilated corpses of American prisoners, and hoped that this was not our turn.

And then, in the-instant before I smelled blood and saw the Lieutenant stoop to lift a panel on the floor, I thought that what had spooked him was not the body of an American POW but of a child who had been murdered and left behind in this empty place. The Lieutenant had probably not seen any dead children yet. Some part of the Lieutenant was still worrying about what a girl named Becky Roddenburger was getting up to back at Idaho State, and a dead child would be too much reality for him.

He pulled up the wooden panel in the floor, and I caught the smell of blood. The Zippo died, and darkness closed down on us. The Lieutenant yanked the panel back on its hinges. The smell of blood floated up from whatever was beneath the floor. The Lieutenant flicked the Zippo, and his face jumped out of the darkness. "Now. Tell me what this is."

"It's where they hide the kids when people like us show up," I said. "Smells like something went wrong. Did you take a look?"

I saw in his tight cheeks and almost lipless mouth that he had not. He wasn't about to go down there and get killed by the Minotaur while his platoon stood around outside.

"Taking a look is your job, Underhill," he said.

For a second we both looked at the ladder, made of peeled branches leashed together with rags, that led down into the pit.

"Give me the lighter," Poole said, and grabbed it away from the Lieutenant. He sat on the edge of the hole and leaned over, bringing the flame beneath the level of the floor. He grunted at whatever he saw, and surprised both the Lieutenant and myself by pushing himself off the ledge into the opening. The light went out. The Lieutenant and I looked down into the dark open rectangle in the floor.

The lighter flared again. I could see Poole's extended arm, the jittering little fire, a packed-earth floor. The top of the concealed room was less than an inch above the top of Poole's head. He moved away from the opening.

"What is it? Are there any—" The Lieutenant's voice made a creaky sound. "Any bodies?"

"Come down here, Tim," Poole called up.

I sat on the floor and swung my legs into the pit. Then I jumped down.

Beneath the floor, the smell of blood was almost sickeningly strong.

"What do you see?" the Lieutenant shouted. He was trying to sound like a leader, and his voice squeaked on the last word.

I saw an empty room shaped like a giant grave. The walls were covered by some kind of thick paper held in place by wooden struts sunk into the earth. Both the thick brown paper and two of the struts showed old bloodstains.

"Hot," Poole said, and closed the lighter.

"Come *on*, damn it," came the Lieutenant's voice. "Get out of there."

"Yes, sir," Poole said. He flicked the lighter back on. Many layers of thick paper formed an absorbent pad between the earth and the room, and the topmost, thinnest layer had been covered with vertical lines of Vietnamese writing. The writing looked like poetry, like the left-hand pages of Kenneth Rexroth's translations of Tu Fu and Li Po.

"Well, well," Poole said, and I turned to see him pointing at what first looked like intricately woven strands of rope fixed to the bloodstained wooden uprights. Poole stepped forward and the weave jumped into sharp relief. About four feet off the ground, iron chains had been screwed to the uprights. The thick pad between the two lengths of chain had been soaked with blood. The three feet of ground between the posts looked rusty. Poole moved the lighter closer to the chains, and we saw dried blood on the metal links.

"I want you guys out of there, and I mean *now,*" whined the Lieutenant.

Poole snapped the lighter shut.

"I just changed my mind," I said softly. "I'm putting twenty bucks into the Elijah fund. For two weeks from today. That's what, June twentieth?"

"Tell it to Spanky," he said. Spanky Burrage had invented the pool we called the Elijah fund, and he held the money. Michael had not put any money into the pool. He thought that a new lieutenant might be even worse than the one we had. Of course he was right. Harry Beevers was our next lieutenant. Elijah Joys, Lieutenant Elijah Joys of New Utrecht, Idaho, a graduate of the University of Idaho and basic training at Fort Benning, Georgia, was an inept, weak lieutenant, not a disastrous one. If Spanky could have seen what was coming, he would have given back the money and prayed for the safety of Lieutenant Joys.

Poole and I moved back toward the opening. I felt as if I had seen a shrine to an obscene deity. The Lieutenant leaned over and stuck out his hand—uselessly, because he did not bend down far enough for us to reach him. We levered ourselves up out of the hole stiff-armed, as if we were leaving a swimming pool. The Lieutenant stepped back. He had a thin face and thick, fleshy nose, and his Adam's apple danced around in his neck like a jumping bean. He might not have been Harry Beevers, but he was no prize. "Well, how many?"

"How many what?" I asked.

"How many are there?" He wanted to go back to Camp Crandall with a good body count.

"There weren't exactly any bodies, Lieutenant," said Poole, trying to let him down easily. He described what we had seen.

"Well, what's that good for?" He meant, *How is that going to help me?*

"Interrogations, probably," Poole said. "If you questioned someone down there, no one outside the hut would hear anything. At night, you could just drag the body into the woods."

Lieutenant Joys nodded. "Field Interrogation Post," he said, trying out the phrase. "Torture, Use of, Highly Indicated." He nodded again. "Right?"

"Highly," Poole said.

"Shows you what kind of enemy we're dealing with in this conflict."

I could no longer stand being in the same three square feet of space with Elijah Joys, and I took a step toward the door of the hut. I did not know what Poole and I had seen, but I knew it was not a Field Interrogation Post, Torture, Use of, Highly Indicated, unless the Vietnamese had begun to interrogate monkeys. It occurred to me that the writing on the wall might have been names instead of poetry—I thought that we had stumbled into a mystery that had nothing to do with the war, a Vietnamese mystery.

For a second, music from my old life, music too beautiful to be endurable, started playing in my head. Finally I recognized it: "The Walk to the Paradise Garden," from *A Village Romeo and Juliet* by Frederick Delius. Back in Berkeley, I had listened to it hundreds of times.

If nothing else had happened, I think I could have replayed the whole piece in my head. Tears filled my eyes, and I stepped toward the door of the hut. Then I froze. A ragged Vietnamese boy of seven or eight was regarding me with great seriousness from the far corner of the hut. I knew he was not there—I knew he was a spirit. I had no belief in spirits, but that's what he was. Some part of my mind as detached as a crime reporter reminded me that "The Walk to the Paradise Garden" was about two children who were about to die, and that in a sense the music *was* their death. I wiped my eyes with my hand, and when I lowered my arm, the boy was still there. He was beautiful, beautiful in the ordinary way, as Vietnamese children nearly always seemed beautiful to me. Then he vanished all at once, like the flickering light of the Zippo. I nearly groaned aloud. That child had been murdered in the hut: he had not just died, he had been murdered.

I said something to the other two men and went through the door into the growing darkness. I was very dimly aware of the Lieutenant asking Poole to repeat his description of the uprights and the bloody chain. Hamnet and Burrage and Calvin Hill were sitting down and leaning against a tree. Victor Spitalny was wiping his hands on his filthy shirt. White smoke curled up from Hill's cigarette, and Tina Pumo exhaled a long white stream of vapor. The unhinged thought came to me with an absolute conviction that *this* was the Paradise Garden. The men lounging in the darkness; the pattern of the cigarette smoke, and the patterns they made, sitting or standing; the in-drawing darkness, as physical as a blanket; the frame of the trees and the flat gray-green background of the paddy.

My soul had come back to life.

Then I became aware that there was something wrong about the men arranged before me, and again it took a moment for my intelligence to catch up to my intuition. Every member of a combat unit makes unconscious adjustments as members of the unit go down in the field; survival sometimes depends on the number of people you know are with you, and you keep count without being quite aware of doing it. I had registered that two men too many were in front of me. Instead of seven, there were nine, and the two men that made up the nine of us left were still behind me in the hut. M.O. Dengler was looking at me with growing curiosity, and I thought he knew exactly what I was thinking. A sick chill went through me. I saw Tom Blevins and Tyrell Budd standing together at the far right of the platoon, a little muddier than the others but otherwise different from the rest only in that, like Dengler, they were looking directly at me.

Hill tossed his cigarette away in an arc of light. Poole and Lieutenant Joys came out of the hut behind me. Leonard Hamnet patted his pocket to reassure himself that he still had his letter. I looked back at the right of the group, and the two dead men were gone.

"Let's saddle up," the Lieutenant said. "We aren't doing any good around here."

"Tim?" Dengler asked. He had not taken his eyes off me since I had come out of the hut. I shook my head.

"Well, what was it?" asked Tina Pumo. "Was it juicy?"

Spanky and Calvin Hill laughed and slapped hands.

"Aren't we gonna torch this place?" asked Spitalny.

The Lieutenant ignored him. "Juicy enough, Pumo. Interrogation Post. Field Interrogation Post."

"No shit," said Pumo.

"These people are into torture, Pumo. It's just another indication."

"Gotcha." Pumo glanced at me and his eyes grew curious. Dengler moved closer.

"I was just remembering something," I said. "Something from the world."

"You better forget about the world while you're over here, Underhill," the Lieutenant told me. "I'm trying to keep you alive, in case you hadn't noticed, but you have to cooperate with me." His Adam's apple jumped like a begging puppy.

As soon as he went ahead to lead us out of the village, I gave twenty dollars to Spanky and said, "Two weeks from today."

"My man," Spanky said.

The rest of the patrol was uneventful.

The next night we had showers, real food, alcohol, cots to sleep in. Sheets and pillows. Two new guys replaced Tyrell Budd and Thomas Blevins, whose names were never mentioned again, at least by me, until long after the war was over and Poole, Linklater, Pumo, and I looked them up, along with the rest of our dead, on the Wall in Washington. I wanted to forget the patrol, especially what I had seen and experienced inside the hut. I wanted the oblivion that came in powdered form.

I remember that it was raining. I remember the steam lifting off the ground, and the condensation dripping down the metal poles in the tents. Moisture shone on the faces around me. I was sitting in the brothers' tent, listening to the music Spanky Burrage played on the big reel-to-reel recorder he had bought on R&R in Taipei. Spanky Burrage never played Delius, but what he played was paradisal great jazz from Armstrong to Coltrane, on reels recorded for him by his friends back in Little Rock and that he knew so well he could find individual tracks and performances without bothering to look at the counter. Spanky liked to play disc jockey during these long sessions, changing reels and speeding past thousands of feet of tape to play the same songs by different musicians, even the same song hiding under different names—"Cherokee" and "KoKo," "Indiana" and "Donna Lee"—or long series of songs connected by titles that used the same words—"I Thought About You" (Art Tatum), "You and the Night and the Music" (Sonny Rollins), "I Love You" (Bill Evans), "If I Could Be with You" (Ike Quebec), "You Leave Me Breathless" (Milt Jackson), even, for the sake of the joke, "Thou Swell," by Glenroy Breakstone. In his single-artist mode on this day, Spanky was ranging through the work of a great trumpet player named Clifford Brown.

On this sweltering, rainy day, Clifford Brown's music sounded regal and unearthly. Clifford Brown was walking to the Paradise Garden. Listening to him was like watching a smiling man shouldering open an enormous door to let in great dazzling rays of light. We were out of the war. The world we were in transcended pain and loss, and imagination had banished feat. Even SP4 Cotton and Calvin Hill, who preferred James Brown to Clifford Brown, lay on their bunks listening as Spanky followed his instincts from one track to another.

After he had played disc jockey for something like two hours, Spanky rewound the long tape and said, "Enough." The end of the tape slapped against the reel. I looked at Dengler, who seemed dazed, as if awakening from a long sleep. The memory of the music was still all around us: light still poured in through the crack in the great door.

"I'm gonna have a smoke *and* a drink," Hill announced, and pushed himself up off his cot. He walked to the door of the tent and pulled the flap aside to expose the green wet drizzle. That dazzling light, the light from another world, began to fade. Hill sighed, plopped a wide-brimmed hat on his head, and slipped outside. Before the stiff flap fell shut, I saw him jumping through the puddles on the way to Wilson Manly's shack. I felt as though I had returned from a long journey.

Spanky finished putting the Clifford Brown reel back into its cardboard box. Someone in the rear of the tent switched on Armed Forces' Radio. Spanky looked at me and shrugged. Leonard Hamnet took his letter out of his pocket, unfolded it, and read it through very slowly.

"Leonard," I said, and he swung his big buffalo's head toward me. "You still putting in for compassionate leave?"

He nodded. "You know what I gotta do."

"Yes," Dengler said, in a slow, quiet voice.

"They gonna let me take care of my people. They gonna send me back."

He spoke with a complete absence of nuance, like a man who had learned to get what he wanted by parroting words without knowing what they meant.

Dengler looked at me and smiled. For a second he seemed as alien as Hamnet. "What do you think is going to happen? To us, I mean. Do you think it'll just go on like this day after day until some of us get killed and the rest of us go home, or do you think it's going to get stranger and stranger?" He did not wait for me to answer. "I think it'll always sort of look the same, but it won't be—I think the edges are starting to melt. I think that's what happens when you're out here long enough. The edges melt."

"Your edges melted a long time ago, Dengler," Spanky said, and applauded his own joke.

Dengler was still staring at me. He always resembled a serious, dark-haired child, and never looked as though he belonged in uniform.

"Here's what I mean, kind of," he said. "When we were listening to that trumpet player—"

"*Brownie*, Clifford *Brown*," Spanky whispered.

"—I could see the notes in the air. Like they were written out on a long scroll. And after he played them, they stayed in the air for a long time."

"Sweetie pie," Spanky said softly. "You pretty hip, for a little ofay square."

"When we were back in that village, last week," Dengler said. "Tell me about that!"

I said that he had been there, too.

"But something happened to you. Something special."

"I put twenty bucks in the Elijah fund," I said.

"Only twenty?" Cotton asked.

"What was in that hut?" Dengler asked.

I shook my head.

"All right," Dengler said. "But it's happening, isn't it? Things are changing."

I could not speak. I could not tell Dengler in front of Cotton and Spanky Burrage that I had imagined seeing the ghosts of Blevins, Budd, and a murdered child. I smiled and shook my head.

"Fine," Dengler said.

"What the fuck you sayin' is *fine?*" Cotton said. "I don't mind listening to that music, but I do draw the line at this bullshit." He flipped himself off his bunk and pointed a finger at me. "What date you give Spanky?"

"Twentieth."

"He last longer than that." Cotton tilted his head as the song on the radio ended Armed Forces' Radio began playing a song by Moby Grape. Disgusted, he turned back to me. "Check it out. End of August. He be so tired, he be *sleepwalkin'*. Be halfway through his tour. The fool will go to pieces, and that's when he'll get it."

Cotton had put thirty dollars on August thirty-first, exactly the midpoint of Lieutenant Joys's tour of duty. He had a long time to adjust to the loss of the money, because he himself stayed alive until a sniper killed him at the beginning of February. Then he became a member of the ghost platoon that followed us wherever we went. I think this ghost platoon, filled with men I had loved and detested, whose names I could or could not remember, disbanded only when I went to the Wall in Washington, D.C., and by then I felt that I was a member of it myself.

2.

I left the tent with a vague notion of getting outside and enjoying the slight coolness that followed the rain. The packet of Si Van Vo's white powder rested at the bottom of my right front pocket, which was so deep that my fingers just brushed its top. I decided that what I needed was a beer.

Wilson Manly's shack was all the way on the other side of camp. I never liked going to the enlisted men's club, where they were rumored to serve cheap Vietnamese beer in American bottles. Certainly the bottles had often been stripped of their labels, and to a suspicious eye the caps looked dented; also, the beer there never quite tasted like the stuff Manly sold.

One other place remained, farther away than the enlisted men's club but closer than Manly's shack and somewhere between them in official status. About twenty minutes' walk from where I stood, just at the curve in the steeply descending road to the airfield and the motor pool, stood an isolated wooden structure called Billy's. Billy himself, supposedly a Green Beret captain who had installed a handful of bar girls in an old French command post, had gone home long ago, but his club had endured. There were no more girls, if there ever had been, and the brand-name liquor was about as reliable as the enlisted men's club's beer. When it was open, a succession of slender Montagnard boys who slept in the nearly empty upstairs rooms served drinks. I visited these rooms two or three times, but I never learned where the boys went when Billy's was closed. They spoke almost no English. Billy's did not look anything like a French command post, even one that had been transformed into a bordello: It looked like a roadhouse.

A long time ago, the building had been painted brown. The wood was soft with rot. Someone had once boarded up the two front windows on the lower floor, and someone else had torn off a narrow band of boards across each of the windows, so that light entered in two flat white bands that traveled across the floor during the day. Around six-thirty the light bounced off the long foxed mirror that stood behind the row of bottles. After five minutes of blinding light, the sun disappeared beneath the pine boards, and for ten or fifteen minutes a shadowy pink glow filled the barroom. There was no electricity and no ice. Fingerprints covered the glasses. When you needed a toilet, you went to a cubicle with inverted metal boot prints on either side of a hole in the floor.

The building stood in a little grove of trees in the curve of the descending road, and as I walked toward it in the diffused reddish light of the sunset, a mud-spattered jeep painted in the colors of camouflage gradually came into view to the right of the bar, emerging from invisibility like an optical illusion. The jeep seemed to have floated out of the trees behind it, to be a part of them.

I heard two male voices, which stopped when I stepped onto the soft boards of the front porch. I glanced at the jeep, looking for insignia or identification, but the mud covered the door panels. Something white gleamed dully from the backseat. When 1 looked more closely, I saw in a coil of rope an oval of bone that took me a moment to recognize as the top of a painstakingly cleaned and bleached human skull.

Before I could reach the handle, the door opened. A boy named Mike stood before me, in loose khaki shorts and a dirty white shirt much too large for him. Then he saw who I was. "Oh," he said. "Yes. Tim. Okay. You come in." His real name was not Mike, but Mike was what it sounded like. He carried himself with an odd defensive alertness, and he shot me a tight, uncomfortable smile. "Far table, right side."

"It's okay?" I asked, because everything about him told me that it wasn't.

"Yesss." He stepped back to let me in.

I smelled cordite before I saw the other men. The bar looked empty, and the band of light coming in through the opening over the windows had already reached the long mirror, creating a bright dazzle, a white fire. I took a couple of steps inside, and Mike moved around me to return to his post.

"Oh, hell," someone said from off to my left. "We have to put up with *this?*"

I turned my head to look into the murk of that side of the bar, and saw three men sitting against the wall at a round table. None of the kerosene lamps had been lighted yet, and the dazzle from the mirror made the far reaches of the bar even less distinct.

"Is okay, is okay," said Mike. "Old customer. Old friend."

"I bet he is," the voice said. "Just don't let any women in here."

"No women," Mike said. "No problem."

I went through the tables to the farthest one on the right.

"You want whiskey, Tim?" Mike asked.

"Tim?" the man said. *"Tim?"*

"Beer," I said, and sat down.

A nearly empty bottle of Johnnie Walker Black, three glasses, and about a dozen cans of beer covered the table before them. The soldier with his back against the wall shoved aside some of the beer cans so that I could see the .45 next to the Johnnie Walker bottle. He leaned forward with a drunk's guarded coordination. The sleeves had been ripped off his shirt, and dirt darkened his skin as if he had not bathed in years. His hair had been cut with a knife, and had once been blond.

"I just want to make sure about this," he said. "You're not a woman, right? You swear to that?"

"Anything you say," I said.

"No woman walks into this place." He put his hand on the gun. "No nurse. No wife. No *anything*. You got that?"

"Got it," I said. Mike hurried around the bar with my beer.

"Tim. Funny name. Tom, now—that's a name. Tim sounds like a little guy—like him." He pointed at Mike with his left hand, the whole hand and not merely the index finger, while his right still rested on the .45. "Little fucker ought to be wearing a dress. Hell, he practically *is* wearing a dress."

"Don't you like women?" I asked. Mike put a can of Budweiser on my table and shook his head rapidly, twice. He had wanted me in the club because he was afraid the drunken soldier was going to shoot him, and now I was just making things worse.

I looked at the two men with the drunken officer. They were dirty and exhausted—whatever had happened to the drunk had also happened to them. The difference was that they were not drunk yet.

"That is a complicated question," the drunk said. "There are questions of responsibility. You can be responsible for yourself. You can be responsible for your children and your tribe. You are responsible for anyone you want to protect. But can you be responsible for women? If so, how responsible?"

Mike quietly moved behind the bar and sat on a stool with his hands out of sight. I knew he had a shotgun under there.

"You don't have any idea what I'm talking about, do you, Tim, you rear-echelon dipshit?"

"You're afraid you'll shoot any women who come in here, so you told the bartender to keep them out."

"This wise-ass sergeant is personally interfering with my state of mind," the drunk said to the burly man on his right. "Tell him to get out of here, or a certain degree of unpleasantness will ensue."

"Leave him alone," the other man said. Stripes of dried mud lay across his lean, haggard face.

The drunken officer startled me by leaning toward the other man and speaking in clear, carrying Vietnamese. It was an old-fashioned, almost literary Vietnamese, and he must have thought and dreamed in it to speak it so well. He assumed that neither I nor the Montagnard boy would understand him.

This is serious, he said, *and I am serious. If you wish to see how serious, just sit in your chair and do nothing. Do you not know of what I am capable by now? Have you learned nothing? You know what I know. I know what you know. A great heaviness is between us. Of all the people in the world at this moment, the only ones I do not despise are already dead, or should be. At this moment, murder is weightless.*

There was more, and I cannot swear that this was exactly what he said, but it's pretty close. He may have said that murder was *empty*.

Then he said, in that same flowing Vietnamese that even to my ears sounded as stilted as the language of a third-rate Victorian novel: *Recall what is in our vehicle* [carriage]; *you should remember what we have brought with us, because I shall never forget it. Is it so easy for you to forget?*

It takes a long time and a lot of patience to clean and bleach bone. A skull would be more difficult than most of a skeleton.

Your leader requires more of this nectar, he said, and rolled back in his chair, looking at me with his hand on his gun.

"Whiskey," said the burly soldier. Mike was already pulling the bottle off the shelf. He understood that the officer was trying to knock himself out before he would find it necessary to shoot someone.

For a moment I thought that the burly soldier to his right looked familiar. His head had been shaved so close he looked bald, and his eyes were enormous above the streaks of dirt. A stainless-steel watch hung from a slot in his collar. He extended a muscular arm for the bottle Mike passed him while keeping as far from the table as he could. The soldier twisted off the cap and poured into all three glasses. The man in the center immediately drank all the whiskey in his glass and banged the glass down on the table for a refill.

The haggard soldier who had been silent until now said, "Something is gonna happen here." He looked straight at me. "Pal?"

"That man is nobody's pal," the drunk said. Before anyone could stop him, he snatched up the gun, pointed it across the room, and fired. There was a flash of fire, a huge explosion, and the reek of cordite. The bullet went straight through the soft wooden wall, about eight feet to my left. A stray bit of light slanted through the hole it made.

For a moment I was deaf. I swallowed the last of my beer and stood up. My head was ringing.

"Is it clear that I hate the necessity for this kind of shit?" said the drunk. "Is that much understood?"

The soldier who had called me *pal* laughed, and the burly soldier poured more whiskey into the drunk's glass. Then he stood up and started coming toward me. Beneath the exhaustion and the stripes of dirt, his face was taut with anxiety. He put himself between me and the man with the gun.

"I am not a rear-echelon dipshit," I said. "I don't want any trouble, but people like him do not own this war."

"Will you maybe let me save your ass, Sergeant?" he whispered. "Major Bachelor hasn't been anywhere near white men in three years, and he's having a little trouble readjusting. Compared to him, we're all rear-echelon dipshits."

I looked at his tattered shirt. "Am you his baby-sitter, Captain?"

He gave me an exasperated look and glanced over his shoulder at the major. "Major, put down your damn weapon. The sergeant is a combat soldier. He is on his way back to camp."

I don't care what he is, the major said in Vietnamese.

The captain began pulling me toward the door, keeping his body between me and the other table. I motioned for Mike to come out with me.

"Don't worry, the major won't shoot him. Major Bachelor loves the Yards," the captain said. He gave me an impatient glance because I had refused to move at his pace. Then I saw him notice my pupils. "God damn," he said, and then he stopped moving altogether and said "God damn" again, but in a different tone of voice.

I started laughing.

"Oh, this is—" He shook his head. "This is really—" "Where have you *been?*" I asked him.

John Ransom turned to the table. "Hey, I know this guy. He's an old football friend of mine."

Major Batchelor shrugged and put the .45 back on the table. His eyelids had nearly closed. "I don't care about football," he said, but he kept his hand off the weapon.

"Buy the sergeant a drink," said the haggard officer.

"Buy the fucking sergeant a drink," the major chimed in.

John Ransom quickly moved to the bar and reached for a glass, which the confused Mike put into his hand. Ransom went through the tables, filled his glass and mine, and carried both back to join me.

We watched the major's head slip down by notches toward his chest. When his chin finally reached the unbuttoned top of his ruined shirt, Ransom said, "All right, Bob," and the other man slid the .45 out from under the major's hand. He pushed it beneath his belt.

"The man is out," Bob said.

Ransom turned back to me. "He was up three days straight with us, God knows how long before that." Ransom did not have to specify who *he* was. "Bob and I got some sleep, trading off, but he just kept on talking." He fell into one of the chairs at my table and tilted his glass to his mouth. I sat down beside him.

For a moment no one in the bar spoke. The line of light from the open space across the windows had already left the mirror, and was now approaching the place on the wall that meant it would soon disappear. Mike lifted the cover from one of the lamps and began trimming the wick.

"How come you're always fucked up when I see you?"

"You have to ask?"

He smiled. He looked very different from when I had seen him preparing to give a sales pitch to Senator Burrman at Camp White Star.

His body had thickened and hardened, and his eyes had retreated far back into his head. He seemed to me to have moved a long step nearer the goal I had always seen in him than when he had given me the zealot's word about stopping the spread of communism. This man had taken in more of the war, and that much more of the war was inside him now.

"I got you off graves registration at White Star, didn't I?"

I agreed that he had.

"What did you call it, the body squad? It wasn't even a real graves registration unit, was it?" He smiled and shook his head. "I took care of your Captain McCue, too—he was using it as a kind of dumping ground. I don't know how he got away with it as long as he did. The only one with any training was that sergeant, what's-his-name. Italian."

"DiMaestro."

Ransom nodded. "The whole operation was going off the rails." Mike lit a big kitchen match and touched it to the wick of the kerosene lamp. "I heard some things—" He slumped against the wall and swallowed whiskey. He closed his eyes. "Some crazy stuff went on back there."

I asked if he was still stationed in the highlands up around the Laotian border. He almost sighed when he shook his head.

"You're not with the tribesmen anymore? What were they, Khatu?"

He opened his eyes. "You have a good memory. No, I'm not there anymore." He considered saying more, but decided not to. He had failed himself. "I'm kind of on hold until they send me up around Khe Sahn. It'll be better up there—the Bru are tremendous. But right now, all I want to do is take a bath and get into bed. Any bed. Actually, I'd settle for a dry level place on the ground."

"Where did you come from now?"

"In-country." His face creased and he showed his teeth. The effect was so unsettling that I did not immediately realize that he was smiling. "Way in-country. We had to get the major out."

"Looks more like you had to pull him out, like a tooth."

My ignorance made him sit up straight. "You mean you never heard of him? Franklin Bachelor?"

And then I thought I had, that someone had mentioned him to me a long time ago.

"In the bush for years. Bachelor did stuff that ordinary people don't even *dream of*—he's a legend."

A legend, I thought. Like the Green Berets Ransom had mentioned a lifetime ago at White Star.

"Ran what amounted to a private army, did a lot of good work in Darlac Province. He was out there on his own. The man was a hero.

That's straight. Bachelor got to places we couldn't even get close to——he got *inside* an NVA encampment, you hear me, *inside* the encampment and *silently* killed about an entire division."

Of all the people in the world at this minute, I remembered, the only ones he did not detest were already dead. I thought I must have heard it wrong.

"He was absorbed right into Rhade life," Ransom said. I could hear the awe in his voice. "The man even got married. Rhade ceremony. His wife went with him on missions. I hear she was beautiful."

Then I knew where I had heard of Franklin Bachelor before. He had been a captain when Ratman and his platoon had run into him after a private named Bobby Swett had been blown to pieces on a trail in Darlac Province. Ratman had thought his wife was a black-haired angel.

And then I knew whose skull lay wound in rope in the back-seat of the jeep.

"I did hear of him," I said. "I knew someone who met him. The Rhade woman, too."

"His *wife*," Ransom said.

I asked him where they were taking Bachelor.

"We're stopping overnight at Crandall for some rest. Then we hop to Tan Son Nhut and bring him back to the States——Langley. I thought we might have to strap him down, but I guess we'll just keep pouring whiskey into him."

"He's going to want his gun back."

"Maybe I'll give it to him." His look told me what he thought Major Bachelor would do with his .45, if he was left alone with it long enough. "He's in for a rough time at Langley, There'll be some heat."

"Why Langley?"

"Don't ask. But don't be naive, either. Don't you think they're…" He would not finish that sentence. "Why do you think we had to bring him out in the first place?"

"Because something went wrong."

"Oh, everything went wrong. Bachelor went totally out of control. He had his own war. Ran a lot of sidelines, some of which were supposed to be under, shall we say, tighter controls?"

He had lost me.

"Ventures into Laos. Business trips to Cambodia. Sometimes he wound up in control of airfields Air America was using, and that meant he was in control of the cargo."

When I shook my head, he said, "Don't you have a little something in your pocket? A little package?"

A secret world—inside this world, another, secret world.

"You understand, I don't care what he did any more than care about what *you* do. I think Langley can go fuck itself. Bachelor wrote the book. In spite of his sidelines. In spite of whatever *trouble* he got into. The man was effective. He stepped over a boundary, maybe a lot of boundaries—but tell me that you can do what we're supposed to do without stepping over boundaries."

I wondered why he seemed to be defending himself, and asked if he would have to testify at Langley.

"It's not a trial."

"A debriefing."

"Sure, a debriefing. They can ask me anything they want. All I can tell them is what I saw. That's *my* evidence, right? What I saw? They don't have any evidence, except maybe this, uh, these human remains the major insisted on bringing out."

For a second, I wished that I could see the sober shadowy gentlemen of Langley, Virginia, the gentlemen with slicked-back hair and pin-striped suits, question Major Bachelor. They thought *they* were serious men.

"It was like Bong To, in a funny way." Ransom waited for me to ask. When I did not, he said, "A ghost town, I mean. I don't suppose you've ever heard of Bong To."

"My unit was just there." His head jerked up. "A mortar round scared us into the village."

"You saw the place?"

I nodded.

"Funny story." Now he was sorry he had ever mentioned it. Well, think about Bachelor, now. I think he must have been in Cambodia or someplace, doing what he does, when his village was overrun. He comes back and finds everybody dead, his wife included. I mean, I don't think *Bachelor* killed those people——they weren't just dead, they'd been made to beg for it. So Bachelor wasn't there, and his assistant, a Captain Bennington, must have just run off—we never did find him. Officially, Bennington's MIA. It's simple. You can't find the main guy, so you make sure he can see how mad you are when he gets back. You do a little grievous bodily harm on his people. They were not nice to his wife, Tim, to her they were especially not nice. What does he do? He buries all the bodies in the village graveyard, because that's a sacred responsibility. Don't ask me what else he does, because you don't have to know this, okay? But the bodies are buried. Generally speaking. Captain Bennington never does show up. We arrive and take Bachelor away. But sooner or later, some of the people who escaped are going to come back to that village. They're going to go on living there. The worst thing in the world happened to them in that place, but they won't leave. Eventually, other people in their family will join them, if they're still alive, and the terrible thing will be a part of their lives. Because it is not thinkable to leave your dead."

"But they did in Bong To," I said.

"In Bong To, they did."

I saw the look of regret on his face again, and said that I wasn't asking him to tell me any secrets.

"It's not a secret. It's not even military."

"It's just a ghost town."

Ransom was still uncomfortable. He turned his glass around and around in his hands before he drank. "I have to get the major into camp."

"A real ghost town," I said. "Complete with ghosts."

"I honestly wouldn't be surprised." He drank what was left in his glass and stood up. He had decided not to say any more about it. "Let's take care of Major Bachelor, Bob," he said. "Right."

Ransom carried our bottle to the bar and paid Mike. I stepped toward him to do the same, and Ransom said, "Taken care of."

There was that phrase again——it seemed I had been hearing it all day, and that its meaning would not stay still.

Ransom and Bob picked up the major between them. They were strong enough to lift him easily. Bachelor's greasy head rolled forward. Bob put the .45 into his pocket, and Ransom put the bottle into his own pocket. Together they carried the major to the door.

I followed them outside. Artillery pounded hills a long way off. It was dark now, and light from the lanterns spilled out through the gaps in the windows.

All of us went down the rotting steps, the major bobbing between the other two.

Ransom opened the jeep, and they took a while to maneuver the major into the backseat. Bob squeezed in beside him and pulled him upright.

John Ransom got in behind the wheel and sighed. He had no taste for the next part of his job.

"I'll give you a ride back to camp," he said. "We don't want an M.P. to get a close look at you."

I took the seat beside him. Ransom started the engine and turned on the lights. He jerked the gearshift into reverse and rolled backward. "You know why that mortar round came in, don't you?" he asked me. He grinned at me, and we bounced onto the road back to the main part of camp. "He was trying to chase you away from Bong To, and your fool of a lieutenant went straight for the place instead." He was still grinning. "It must have steamed him, seeing a bunch of round-eyes going in there."

"He didn't send in any more fire."

"No. He didn't want to damage the place. It's supposed to stay the way it is. I don't think they'd use the word, but that village is supposed to be like a kind of monument." He glanced at me again. "To shame."

For some reason, all I could think of was the drunken major in the seat behind me, who had said that you were responsible for the people you wanted to protect. Ransom said, "Did you go into any of the huts? Did you see anything unusual there?"

"I went into a hut. I saw something unusual."

"A list of names?"

"I thought that's what they were."

"Okay," Ransom said. "You know a little Vietnamese?"

"A little."

"You notice anything about those names?"

I could not remember. My Vietnamese had been picked up in bars and markets, and was almost completely oral.

"Four of them were from a family named Trang. Trang was the village chief, like his father before him, and his grandfather before him. Trang had four daughters. As each one got to the age of six or seven, he took them down into that underground room and chained them to the posts and raped them. A lot of those huts have hidden storage areas, but Trang must have modified his after his first daughter was born. The funny thing is, I think everybody in the village knew what he was doing. I'm not saying they thought it was okay, but they let it happen. They could pretend they didn't know: the girls never complained, and nobody ever heard any screams. I guess Trang was a good enough chief. When the daughters got to sixteen, they left for the cities. Sent back money, too. So maybe they thought it was okay, but I don't think they did, myself, do you?"

"How would I know? But there's a man in my platoon, a guy from—"

"I think there's a difference between private and public shame. Between what's acknowledged and what is not acknowledged. That's what Bachelor has to cope with, when he gets to Langley. Some things are acceptable, as long as you don't talk about them." He looked sideways at me as we began to approach the northern end of the camp proper. He wiped his face, and flakes of dried mud fell off his cheek. The exposed skin looked red, and so did his eyes. "Because the way I see it, this is a whole general issue. The issue is: what is *expressible?* This goes way beyond the tendency of people to tolerate thoughts, actions, or behavior they would otherwise find unacceptable."

I had never heard a soldier speak this way before. It was a little bit like being back in Berkeley.

"I'm talking about the difference between what is expressed and what is described," Ransom said. "A lot of experience is unacknowledged. Religion lets us handle some of the unacknowledged stuff in an acceptable way. But suppose—just suppose—that you were forced to confront extreme experience directly, without any mediation?"

"I have," I said. "You have, too."

"More extreme than combat, more extreme than terror. Something like what happened to the major: He *encountered* God. Demands were made upon him. He had to move out of the ordinary, even as *he* defined it."

Ransom was telling me how Major Bachelor had wound up being brought to Camp Crandall with his wife's skull, but none of it was clear to me.

"I've been learning things," Ransom told me. He was almost whispering. "Think about what would make all the people of a village pick up and leave, when sacred obligation ties them to that village."

"I don't know the answer," I said.

"An even more sacred obligation, created by a really spectacular sense of shame. When a crime is too great to live with, the memory of it becomes sacred. Becomes the crime itself—"

I remembered thinking that the arrangement in the hut's basement had been a shrine to an obscene deity.

"Here we have this village and its chief. The village knows I but does not know what the chief has been doing. They are used to consulting and obeying him. Then—one day, a little boy disappears."

My heart gave a thud.

"A little boy. Say: three. Old enough to talk and get into trouble, but too young to take care of himself. He's just gone—*poof.* Well, this is Vietnam, right? You turn your back, your kid wanders away, some animal gets him. He could get lost in the jungle and wander into a claymore. Someone like you might even shoot him. He could fall into a booby trap and never be seen again. It could happen.

"A couple of months later, it happens again. Mom turns her back, where the hell did Junior go? This time they really look, not just Mom and Grandma, all their friends. They scour the village. The *villagers* scour the village, every square foot of that place, and then they do the same to the rice paddy, and then they took through the forest.

"And guess what happens next. This is the interesting part. An old woman goes out one morning to fetch water from the well, and she sees a ghost. This old lady is part of the extended family of the first lost kid, but the ghost she sees isn't the kid's—it's the ghost of a disreputable old man from another village, a drunkard, in fact. A local no-good, in fact. He's just standing near the well with his hands together, he's hungry——that's what these people know about ghosts. The skinny old bastard wants *more*. *He* wants to be *fed*. The old lady gives a squawk and passes out. When she comes to again, the ghost is gone.

"Well, the old lady tells everybody what she saw, and the whole village gets in a panic. Evil forces have been set loose. Next thing you know, two thirteen-year-old girls are working in the paddy, they look up and see an old woman who died when they were ten—she's about six feet away from them. Her hair is stringy and gray and her fingernails are about a foot long. She used to be a friendly old lady, but she doesn't look too friendly, now. She's hungry, too, like all ghosts. They start screaming and crying, but no one else can see her, and she comes closer and closer, and they try to get away but one of them falls down, and the old woman is on her like a cat. And do you know what she does? She rubs her filthy hands over the screaming girl's face, and licks the tears and slobber off her fingers.

"The next night, another little boy disappears. Two men go looking around the village latrine behind the houses, and they see two ghosts down in the pit, shoving excrement into their mouths. They rush back into the village, and then they both see half a dozen ghosts around the chief's hut. Among them are a sister who died during the war with the French and a twenty-year-old first wife who died of dengue fever. They want to eat. One of the men screeches, because not only did he see his dead wife, who looks something like what we could call a vampire, he saw her pass into the chief's hut without the benefit of the door.

"These people believe in ghosts, Underhill, they know ghosts exist, but it is extremely rare for them to see these ghosts. And these people are like psychoanalysts, because they do not believe in accidents. Every event contains meaning.

"The dead twenty-year-old wife comes back out through the wall of the chief's hut. Her hands are empty but dripping with red, and she is licking them like a starving cat.

"The former husband stands there pointing and jabbering, and the mothers and grandmothers of the missing boys come out of their huts. They are as afraid of what they're thinking as they are of all the ghosts moving around them. The ghosts are part of what they know they know, even though most of them have never seen one until now. What is going through their minds is something new: new because it was hidden.

"The mothers and grandmothers go to the chief's door and begin howling like dogs. When the chief comes out, they push past him and they take the hut apart. And you know what they find. They find the end of Bong To."

Ransom had parked the jeep near my battalion headquarters five minutes before, and now he smiled as if he had explained everything.

"But what *happened?*" I asked. "How did you hear about it?"

He shrugged. "We learned all this in interrogation. When the women found the underground room, they knew the chief had forced the boys into sex, and then killed them. They didn't know what he had done with the bodies, but they knew he had killed the boys. The next time the V.C. paid one of their courtesy calls, they told the cadre leader what they knew. The V.C. did the rest. They were disgusted—Trang had betrayed *them*, too— betrayed everything he was supposed to represent. One of the V.C. we captured took the chief downstairs into his underground room and chained the man to the posts, wrote the names of the dead boys and Trang's daughters on the padding that covered the walls, and then...then they did what they did to him. They probably carried out the pieces and threw them into the excrement pit. And over months, bit by bit, not all at once but slowly, everybody in the village moved out. By that time, they were seeing ghosts all the time. They had crossed a kind of border."

"Do you think they really saw ghosts?" I asked him. "I mean, do you think they were real ghosts?"

"If you want an expert opinion, you'd have to ask Major Bachelor. He has a lot to say about ghosts." He hesitated for a moment, and then leaned over to open my door. "But if you ask me, sure they did."

I got out of the jeep and closed the door.

Ransom peered at me. "Take better care of yourself."

"Good luck with your Bru."

"The Bru are fantastic." He slammed the jeep into gear and shot away, cranking the wheel to turn the jeep around in a giant circle in front of the battalion headquarters before he jammed it into second and took off to wherever he was going.

Two weeks later Leonard Hamnet managed to get the Lutheran chaplain at Crandall to write a letter to the Tin Man for him, and two days after that he was in a clean uniform, packing up his kit for an overnight flight to an air force base in California. From there he was connecting to a Memphis flight, and from there the army had booked him onto a six-passenger puddle jumper to Lookout Mountain.

When I came into Hamnet's tent he was zipping his bag shut in a zone of quiet afforded him by the other men. He did not want to talk about where he was going or the reason he was going there, and instead of answering my questions about his flights, he unzipped a pocket on the side of his bag and handed me a thick folder of airline tickets.

I looked through them and gave them back. "Hard travel," I said.

"From now on, everything is easy," Hamnet said. He seemed rigid and constrained as he zipped the precious tickets back into the bag. By this time his wife's letter was a rag held together with Scotch tape. I could picture him reading and rereading it, for the thousandth or two thousandth time, on the long flight over the Pacific.

"They need your help," I said. "I'm glad they're going to get it."

"That's right." Hamnet waited for me to leave him alone.

Because his bag seemed heavy, I asked about the length of his leave. He wanted to get the tickets back out of the bag rather than answer me directly, but he forced himself to speak. "They gave me seven days. Plus travel time."

"Good," I said, meaninglessly, and then there was nothing left to say, and we both knew it. Hamnet hoisted his bag off his bunk and turned to the door without any of the usual farewells and embraces. Some of the other men called to him, but he seemed to hear nothing but his own thoughts. I followed him outside and stood beside him in the heat. Hamnet was wearing a tie and his boots had a high polish. He was already sweating through his stiff khaki shirt. He would not meet my eyes. In a minute a jeep pulled up before us. The Lutheran chaplain had surpassed himself.

"Good-bye, Leonard," I said, and Hamnet tossed his bag in back and got into the jeep. He sat up straight as a statue. The private driving the jeep said something to him as they drove off, but Hamnet did not reply. I bet he did not say a word to the stewardesses, either, or to the cabdrivers or baggage handlers or anyone else who witnessed his long journey home.

3

On the day after Leonard Hamnet was scheduled to return, Lieutenant Joys called Michael Poole and myself into his quarters to tell us what had happened back in Tennessee. He held a sheaf of papers in his hand, and he seemed both angry and embarrassed. Hamnet would not be returning to the platoon. It was a little funny. Well, of course it wasn't funny at all. The whole thing was terrible—that was what it was. Someone was to blame, too. Irresponsible decisions had been made, and we'd all be lucky if there wasn't an investigation. We were closest to the man, hadn't we seen what was likely to happen? If not, what the hell was our excuse?

Didn't we have any inkling of what the man was planning to do?

Well, yes, at the beginning, Poole and I said. But he seemed to have adjusted.

We have stupidity and incompetence all the way down the line here, said Lieutenant Elijah Joys. Here is a man who manages to carry a semiautomatic weapon through security at three different airports, bring it into a courthouse, and carry out threats he made months before, without anybody stopping him.

I remembered the bag Hamnet had tossed into the back of the jeep; I remembered the reluctance with which he had zipped it open to show me his tickets. Hamnet had not carried his weapon through airport security. He had just shipped it home in his bag and walked straight through customs in his clean uniform and shiny boots.

As soon as the foreman had announced the guilty verdict, Leonard Hamnet had gotten to his feet, pulled the semiautomatic pistol from inside his jacket, and executed Mr. Brewster where he was sitting at the defense table. While people shouted and screamed and dove for cover, while the courthouse officer tried to unsnap his gun, Hamnet killed his wife and his son. By the time he raised the pistol to his own head, the security officer had shot him twice in the chest. He died on the operating table at Lookout Mountain Lutheran Hospital, and his mother had requested that his remains receive burial at Arlington National Cemetery.

His mother. Arlington. I ask you.

That was what the Lieutenant said. H*is mother. Arlington. I ask you.*

A private from Indianapolis named E.W. Burroughs won the six hundred and twenty dollars in the Elijah fund when Lieutenant Joys was killed by a fragmentation bomb thirty-two days before the end of his tour. After that we were delivered unsuspecting into the hands of Harry Beevers, the Lost Boss, the worst lieutenant in the world. Private Burroughs died a week later, down in Dragon Valley along with Tiano and Calvin Hill and lots of others, when Lieutenant Beevers walked us into a mined field, where we spent forty-eight hours under fire between two companies of NVA. I suppose Burroughs's mother back in Indianapolis got the six hundred and twenty dollars.

Peter Straub is the author of seventeen novels, which have been translated into more than twenty languages. They include *Ghost Story, Koko, Mr. X, In the Night Room,* and two collaborations with Stephen King, *The Talisman* and *Black House.* He has written two volumes of poetry and two collections of short fiction, and he edited the Library of America's edition of H. P. Lovecraft's *Tales* and the Library of America's 2-volume anthology, *American Fantastic Tales.* He has won the British Fantasy Award, eight Bram Stoker Awards, two International Horror Guild Awards, and three World Fantasy Awards. In 1998, he was named Grand Master at the World Horror Convention. In 2006, he was given the HWA's Life Achievement Award. In 2008, he was given the Barnes & Noble Writers for Writers Award by Poets & Writers. At the World Fantasy Convention in 2010, he was given the WFC's Life Achievement Award.

The Serpent
Wayne Karlin

The Rondezvous Bar and Lounge sits off one of the main side roads in the County. If not for the misspelled sign in front of the gravel parking lot, the permanently sputtering and fly speckled neon Budweiser advertisement, and the Happy Hour sign behind the dirt-filmed glass of the window, it could be taken for the house of a heart-broken widower who no longer gave a damn: loose boards, green paint peeling off loose boards, a porch shaded by a sagging tin overhang, the roof shingles winged up here and there or missing in patches, with the underlying creosote sheets showing through like wounds. The sign always bothered me when I drove by the place, as if the misspelled French would confirm some redneck stereotype of the County to visitors. Once I pulled in, had a beer, and mentioned the mistake in the spelling to the owner, Tom Delaney. Delaney, a three hundred pound man with a shaved head, Fu Manchu moustache, prison tattoos and cigarette burn scars on hairy arms, had lowered his head, looked at me and growled, "What are you, a Democrat?"

He gave me the same look as I came in now. He was wearing black Harley-Davidson t-shirt, sagging black jeans, and scuffed engineer boots. He wiped the bar counter with a rag that looked like it could have been used to wipe grease from his motorcycle, if he had had one. He didn't. Some of the tattoos that had been on his arms were gone also, replaced by the red burn and pucker of laser scars, defoliated patches in the pelt that covered his arms. The tattoos had included the shamrock symbols of the Aryan Brotherhood, but as it turned out, he'd never been in prison or owned a motorcycle, in fact, drove a Subaru wagon and had bought the bar, apparently fulfilling the shape of some life-long dream, after he'd sold an arts and crafts supply store his family had owned in PG County. When I'd gotten his background information from our sheriff, Russell Hallam, I'd felt disappointed: it turned both he and the bar were concepts themselves, like the 50's-style diners I'd see in Bethesda or Tyson's Corners or Annapolis, as if nothing of my time could be anything but shadows on the cave wall, as if it all had to legitimize itself through older models. Delaney's tattoos had gone after some actual Aryan brothers had seen them and had given him a choice between erasure and amputation.

As far as I knew, though, none of the other clientele saw the bar or Delaney as anything more than they purported to be. I'd never told anyone what Hallam had told me about Delaney, and as long as the Brotherhood didn't come around, he was a man content in his reinvention, at it for so long that he'd become it.

As soon as my eyes adjusted to the darkness, I spotted Joleen Baird, sitting in a booth near the toilet, a glass and a nearly empty pitcher of draft beer in front of her, her finger pushing thin wakes out of the net of foam on the scarred table top. She was the only customer, which, it being ten in the morning, was not surprising, though not always the case. She turned to me and I saw her in the light of the Coors neon waterfall near the mirror. She looked lacquered. I don't mean drunk. It was the word that came into my mind as I stared at her. As if someone had poured a gallon of lacquer over her head that had stiffened and sheened her. Her blond hair sat like a helmet on her head, and her face, bright red lipstick, penciled eyebrows, artificial lashes, looked as if a wax death mask had been fastened to it. Like the bar and Delaney, she'd become a painting of herself. Thinking that, I remembered how in middle school I'd tried to earnestly explain to her the correct the spelling of her name, some early marker, I suppose, of my journalistic predisposition. It should be J-o-l-e-n-e, I told her. Later, I found out that the spelling she used came from her mother, Lurleen, who either didn't know the right spelling, didn't care, or wanted to tag their names together. At the time though—we were on a school field trip—she didn't explain, just threw me off the dock where we were sitting, into Milburn Creek.

I ordered another pitcher from Delaney. As I reached for it, he seized my wrist.

"You all be gentle now," he growled.

I twisted away, and then we both looked down at the bar, as if the beer spills and beaded scrawls of liquid on it were runic puzzles.

"No problem, Tom," I said.

I took the pitcher and a glass and went over to the booth.

"Have a seat, hon," she said. She wasn't slurring her words. Her eyes looked as dead as the rest of her face. Her lips barely moved as she spoke. It was like I was interviewing an oracle. In high school Joleen had always seemed older than her age, one of those girls wise with some sardonic knowledge she'd inherited from a long line of women who were never disappointed because they never had any expectations. One day her mother had burst into our classroom to cuss out her teacher and drag Joleen out of school: a foul-mouthed, obese woman with blotched skin, dressed in a halter top that lifted cleavage that looked like flabby buttocks, too-tight jean shorts bulged with her actual behind, her pasty and stubbled legs bruised with needle scars. Lurleen had brought along her then-boyfriend, a black man half her size and wearing a lime green suit, yellow shirt with flared collar, and pointed, patent-leather shoes. Such couples weren't unusual in the County, and I'd never thought much about it before. But unable to bear looking at Joleen, who'd sat two rows across from me, wearing an expression of the most abject humiliation I'd ever seen on a human face, I'd concentrated on him instead. He was silent, just nodding now and then at his woman's string of obscenities at Mrs. Colby, who, apparently, had questioned some bruises she had seen on Joleen's face. In spite of his clothes, he'd not been a bad looking guy, and it made me wonder for the first time, about the depth of racial wounds and insecurity that would make Lurleen Elliott seem a trophy to him.

Joleen didn't go back to school after that day, and I hadn't seen her again until I saw copy and a photo for her wedding announcement in my paper, the *Reporter*. She had not taken on her mother's obesity; in fact looked too thin, meth or crack thin, I'd thought, but her eyes were shining in the photo. Her fiancée, Jonathan Baird, was a black man also, and when I'd first heard that, I thought of her mother and wondered if Joleen had inherited her racism, for I'd come to think that was the other side of her mother's string of relationships with certain kinds of black men; either cashing in on the over-drawn account of her skin and its privileges, or punishing herself for being herself by becoming a punch-board pay back for 400 years of bad times. But Baird was not a dealer or thief; he was the pastor of The Holy Church of the Redeeming Christ, a Baptist, store-front operation. To my surprise, Joleen invited me to the wedding—one of a group of people she had known in high school from social circles that tended to look down at her own as trailer trash, and who, I figured out later, had all been in the classroom that day. She'd needed, I realized, to show us this, as if to replace the scene she assumed burned in our memories as it must have in hers. I came—I was only one of three who did—and I'd found I liked Baird; a tall, slender man with bright, intelligent eyes and a small, arrow-shaped head that seemed incongruous with his deep, Baptist preacher voice. He owned a kind of trembly gentleness with Joleen, as if she was a blessing to his life he was afraid to dissolve with a harsh word or action. She had been the same way with him, at one point in the ceremony, presided over by his sister—also a minister—reaching over and touching his lips with a kind of grateful wonder that wrenched my heart.

"He saved me," she said to me now. She raised her eyes, the mask of her face, and I understood that what she meant was that she was now lost. Whatever she had been was scraped out to her shell.

"Can you tell me about him?"

"Sure I can, honey. But not so's you all will know him. That's the bitch, ain't it, Hunter. You get people looking at you like you're shit, telling you you're shit every day your life; you get a fat bag of hate and spite for a mama, look at you like you something she meant to flush down the toilet, and then you get a miracle. This sweet-touching man who tells you he sees what's shining in you and from you. Shakes when he touches you, each time, like you're a gift he's unwrapping, and every time it's a surprise and a delight to him. Yeah, I know," she reached out and patted my forearm, "you want me to tell you the war. Tell you how it went into his veins like poison. But I gotta tell you, you all got to understand about the sweetness of this man. He talked Jesus and I didn't give a shit about no Jesus, but when I saw my Jonathan, I believed, because I could see Jesus in him, like a shining gentleness. I believed."

"Did you talk to him, when he was over there."

She nodded, pantomimed putting a phone to her ear. "Yeah, sure. Telephone, sometimes. Computer more often. It's so weird, honey, you know he's seeing Lord knows what and you're talking about the broken hot water heater, and the church supper and then he starts talking like I'm not even there, like he's talking to Jesus himself and I'm not more than that telephone, that modem, and he's saying that he's supped with horror. That's the words he uses, that he's supped with horror. What you say to someone, they tell you that? Hey, darlin', I had to have the septic drained and I maxed out the Visa? I mean, they don't make him no chaplain, like he should be, right. But the others, they all pour it into his ears, all their shit and meanness and being scared, cause it don't matter, he's a minister a God and they know it. So they pour it all in."

"Was there any particular stories you remember?"

She laughed. It was a terrible laugh and there was no light in her eyes when she looked at me.

"You want to sup with horror, Hunter?" She picked up her glass, turned it, so the dull red light of the bar gleamed in it. "You want to have a beer with horror? That why you're here?"

"I want to tell his story, Joleen."

"Well, ain't you something. Ain't you something that likes sits on the barn roof waiting to see what some dead meat it can pluck and chew. Some road kill on the asphalt."

"Is that what you think?"

She looked away, and then looked back at me and sighed. "No, man. No, you got a good heart, I know that. Know that since you was this gawky thing looked at me like it was your heart breaking stead of mine, my fat bitch of a mother comes to class. I could of killed you that day." A slight smile twitched her lips. "You all want his story, tell the world, all that? Thing is, Hunter, was he didn't have no story. He was what he was here. He listened, Hunter. That's what he did. That's what he did as a preacher. He could shout out with the best, but he could be still and safe too, Hunter. He didn't have no story. He took in everybody else's story. Kid who saw his friends all in pieces around him and tried to stick them back together. Guy who ran over a little girl cause she stood in the road. Guy who saw his own mother and fathers' faces in the faces of the Iraq family they lined up against the wall, man pissing himself. You heard the stories, honey. He was what he called a receptacle. Know what that means? It's a garbage can. They kept throwing the stories in and he kept trying to bring Jesus out for them, but after a while, he couldn't find him. After a while, he knew he had to sup with horror himself."

"What does that mean?"

"You tell me. You think those words mine?"

"He did something," I said. Not a question.

She filled her glass from the pitcher, drank it down. Laughed.

"Went down to the crossroads, you know those words? Needed to be inside their stories, him, place they lost a Humvee or Bradley, or whatever they call them, and then another, same place, six guys, and he went down there, helped plant a surprise for the hajis or gooks or whatever they call them. So it happened, just like you would figure it would happen you're in a place the worst is always going to happen. Command detonated. Not whatever they call them. Command detonated, his exact words, his finger on the button. Finger of God. Presses the button, smokes the hajigooks who a course turn out to be ma and pa and two little kid gookhajis, coming back from their memaw's or something. Something like that."

She closed her eyes. Her face, which had seemed so stiff, now seemed ready to shatter like the surface of a mirror. "See, Hunter. See, the thing is, Hunter, I did it. I did it to him. Took what I loved most, only gold I found on the surface of the earth, and I turned it into shit."

"I'm sure that's not true, Joleen."

Her eyes blazed. "What the fuck you know about it, you? Don't give me that weak, watery not your fault shit. Who you think you are? My Jonathan, he was the preacher. Not you, asshole."

"I'm sorry."

"That's for sure. I tell you, it's my fault, you fucking listen. I thought that's what you here for."

"I'm listening."

"It was such a damnation stupid thing. Like I thought it would make him feel, maybe not better, but, I don't know, connected, maybe. So we on the computer link, right, and I can like see him, some tan canvas behind him, him blocking out everything else over there, like he's doing it deliberately. You know, shielding me with his body. Those guys take a grenade for their friends? He'd a done that, he was a noble man."

"I know he was."

"You don't know shit. So we're talking, right, and I give him this little bit of information I got from some on-line article or some shit, says that Iraq is where the original Garden of Eden was. And for a long time, he says nothing. Just stares, outta my screen. Then he laughs. It's an awful laugh, Hunter, I can't tell you. Says, 'I am the serpent, baby.' I say, 'my sweet darling, you ain't no such a thing.'" He just looks at me, says, 'Don't make no difference. Once you hear it, once you see it, you know it's there.' Laughing again, shaking his head like it's all clear to him now. Then he cuts the connection."

She put her hand on my forearm again.

"Maybe that's it. Maybe he couldn't shake the devil out. But the thing I keep thinking, maybe it's wrong. I still don't believe he took his own life."

"Why's that?"

"You ever knew a black man who hung himself?"

***

I played the recording to Ashley that evening. Joleen's voice said: "They got too many others willing to do the work." I shut the Marantz. There was more on the tape, but I wasn't sure how I would deal with it, if I would use it in the article at all. What Joleen had described to me went beyond the kind of psychosis I could describe in a newspaper story, and I didn't know if it had too. I kept thinking of Joleen's face when her mother had come into her classroom, the humiliations and wounds of a childhood soothed by the hope that Jonathan Baird had brought into her life.

Ashley held up her hand, as if to say physically block Joleen's words. "There's so much God damn pain," she said. "I wish you would just stop now. Turn in this story, and then stop, Hunter."

In bed, we watched a netflix DVD about a Korean ex-convict who falls in love with a girl whose body was twisted with muscular dystrophy; she could only speak in cryptic, bubbly mumbles. It ended sweetly, but was probably not the best film for me to see that night, though later I wished I could have seen its tendrils in the images that nailed into my brain instead. Later, sleepless, I got quietly out of bed. Ashley stirred, murmured, a bubble of saliva forming on her lips. I went into the kitchen. There was a patter of rain against the window above the sink, the first after a three week drought though too weak to break it. I opened the window and let the cooling breeze and a mist diffused by the screen wet my face. The whine of the heat pump motor started. I went out to the living room thermostat and turned it off and the noise of the fan shuddered and stopped. I opened the living room windows, heard the rain beating against the surface of the creek, raising and bringing that fecund smell of silt and estuarine salt water, the blood of the earth, to my nostrils. The Marantz recorder lay on the kitchen table like a bomb. I thought of how Joleen described finding her husband; he'd hung himself in their closet when she went out; his tongue had been blackened, its tip protruding from between his lips. I went to the cabinet, took out a bottle of Jameson's and poured a drink, and then sat in front of the window, the lights off, the occasional flash of lightening illuminating the room, scrambling the shadows into shapes I didn't want to look at. The whiskey burned my mouth, warmed my throat, and I let myself think about the rest of Joleen's interview. For reasons I wasn't certain of myself, I hadn't played it for Ashley.

Joleen had sensed her husband's distance and difference from the beginning. But she hadn't expected him to be untouched. The whole National Guard unit came back together, and all around her families were waving silly signs, and then were embracing and kissing their soldiers, laughing. Baird had seen her, and she was grinning enough to split her cheeks, running to him, throwing her arms around him. He embraced her, but his back felt stiff under her hands, a coldness coming off him, as if he'd been sitting next to an air conditioning outlet on the bus, and his lips, when she kissed him were clenched tight and felt thin and dry under her own, the little lick he darted between her lips more tentative than passionate. She noticed that the other men were hugging each other, giving high fives, shaking hands, saying their farewells, but no one came near her husband. They parted on each side of him, as if he was in a bubble. She thought it strange, since he'd told her how the others would come to him, tell him their stories, and she knew that was true from letters and emails soldiers and their families had sent her, telling her how her Jonathan had been there for them, held their minds in place with the compassion of his eyes and the rock hard grip of his faith, giving them meaning amid the terrible erasures all around them.

They barely spoke on the ride home. He pressed his forehead against the window and looked outside at the passing, familiar scenery, and she thought, good, let it fill him up with green, drive out the terrible tan emptiness which is how she pictured Iraq. In the house, she'd set the table and had prepared his favorite meal, the County dish of ham scored and stuffed with kale and spices, wrapped in cotton and steamed; hot biscuits, collard greens, mashed potatoes and gravy, sun tea in a glass pitcher beaded with condensation. He'd sat rigidly in the chair, his body stretched with tension and swaying slightly, his eyes darting here and there. He took a fork-full of the potatoes, brought it up to his mouth, and licked it slightly, his tongue darting in and out, before putting it in his mouth. Seeing this, Joleen shuddered, and he noticed and looked at her with half-lidded eyes. She felt ashamed. She stood up, took his hand and led him to the bedroom. She had anticipated their sexual reunion for months, sustained herself with fantasies. But what she felt now wasn't erotic; it was utilitarian: she would use her body to join him back into their lives. He let himself be led, silently. As she undressed, he sat rigidly on the bed, staring straight-ahead without blinking, his body swaying slightly, to and fro. It unnerved her. He let her undress him. Then he began touching her with the tip of his tongue, all over her body. He was not kissing or licking her flesh; all she could think of was the way his tongue had darted out to touch his food. Before, when they'd made love, his skin would always be covered with a thin layer of sweat, and she loved the sharp, salty smell of him, but now his skin was cold and dry. She told herself that it was because his body had become accustomed to the aridity of the desert and had taken it into itself, but when he embraced her and twined himself around her, she couldn't help it, she screamed. He immediately loosened himself from her, and when he looked at her, she saw his eyes were filled with tears, his head swaying. I'm sorry, she started to say, but he slid out of bed, and before she could say anything else, he went to the closet, opened the door and went in, and then closed the door. She lay for a long time, her heart hammering in her chest, trying to block out the sound noise she heard or thought she heard from behind that white door, air escaping from between pressed lips. She shook her head, got out of bed, crossed the room, and opened the door. He was on the floor, against the back wall and the skin of his flank, as it caught the light, looked to her like the curve of a coil.

She thought: *what have I brought into my home?*

Wayne Karlin has published seven novels: *Marble Mountain, The Wished-For Country, Prisoners, Lost Armies, The Extras, Us,* and *Crossover* and three works of creative non-fiction: *Rumors and Stones: A Journey,* and *War Movies,* and *Wandering Souls: Journeys with the Dead and the Living in Vietnam.* A Vietnam veteran, as American editor for Curbstone Press' *Voices from Vietnam* series, he edited and adapted translations of writers from Vietnam, including the anthologies (with Le Minh Khue and Truong Vu), *The Other Side of Heaven: Postwar Fiction by Vietnamese and American Writers,* which received a Critics' Choice Award for 1995-1996, and (with Ho Anh Thai) *Love After War: Contemporary Fiction from Vietnam,* an anthology chosen by *The San Francisco Chronicle* as one of the 100 best books of 2003. A script writer, technical advisor and actor in the Vietnamese film *Song of the Stork,* a Vietnamese-Singaporean co-production which won the Best Feature Film title at the Milano Film Festival, and was the first Asian film chosen in the Official Selection of the Taormina Film Festival in Italy. He is a professor of languages and literature at the College of Southern Maryland.

You're Worth It
Nick Russell

She got on the bus at a small town stop between Hollywood's hills and New York's skyscrapers, soft summer blouse and blue jeans slow-walked her way down the narrow metal path that stank of sweat & fast food grease, plopped onto the aisle seat beside the man wearing a landmine strapped to his chest, said: "This is me—*sorry*."

The vehicle's pneumatic door hissed/clunked/closed.

The bus lurched back onto the highway.

Out the windows, sunlight trapped America's empty tan and gold fields.

A man or a woman or honeymooners could walk across them.

Probably not die.

Not leave something for the wolves, the coyotes, the birds and the earth.

The landmine strapped to his chest under the zipped-up black leather jacket didn't explode as Cal shifted in his bus seat to give her more room. He told her: "You got no reason to be sorry."

She put Cal in her blue eyes.

"All the other seats are full or funky," she said to the man about her age who in the warmth of the bus didn't need to be wearing his black leather jacket zipped closed. "I had to sit beside you. What I'm sorry for is if that brings you trouble."

"Trouble's on every ride," said the man wearing a landmine.

"Yeah." She stared at the bus's rearview mirrors.

She looked like she stood in front of a bathroom sink mirror and used scissors to close crop her dirty blonde hair. She also could have just gone to her 10-year high school reunion where nobody would have been lying if they said she looked terrific.

Except the smile lines by her blue eyes and wide lips seemed like fading scars.

Cal didn't care. Couldn't. Wouldn't.

Reality rules.

His chest held a landmine.

"So far, so good," she whispered.

To herself.

And *yes*, Cal knew that, but ripping out of him came: "*Good?*"

She shrugged. "Now. So far."

"We're stuck on a bus in the middle of the great American nowhere."

"But we're moving. At least we got that choice. And took it. Said *yes* to something instead of just screaming *no*."

Cal stared at her: "What are you running from?"

She looked out the bus's side window: "Everything about me that I hated."

Her reflection on the window was superimposed over the empty land flowing back to where they'd been.

She asked him: "What are you running from?"

The window reflected Cal's face beside hers as he said: "Everything I loved."

Couldn't help her smile, *never could*, as she whispered: "Ain't we a pair."

"Aren't," he said.

"Oh," she said. "You're one of those."

"Not anymore," he said. "But old habits can trip you up."

"Who was she?" asked the woman sitting beside him on the aisle of the bus.

"Never got to have a *she*." Why couldn't he straighten the corners of his lips? "I mean, 'never had a *she* she."

"So it's some *them*," she said. "Why are you running from them?"

"I wasn't smart enough to save them," he said and then she knew. "I ordered them to patrol there. An old field. Not our war.

"Landmines," he shook his head. "Buried things go boom and everybody dies."

"How long' you been carrying that?" she said.

He shifted *oh so slightly* with the weight of the landmine strapped to his chest.

She can't see inside my black leather jacket, thought Cal. She can't see there.

"Seven years, six months," he shrugged. "Nine days."

"That's a lot of yesterdays." She shrugged, too. "Maybe after a certain point, all our bad times are just like yesterday's landmines. It's smart to know they're buried there. Smarter to stay clear of them. Smartest to get rid of them 'best you can. Move on."

They turned from their window reflections to see each other.

He told her: "Wherever you're going, I hope you get there."

The bus rumbled over a highway bump.

Everybody blinked.

"Now I'm sorry," he said.

"You've got nothing to be sorry for."

They both knew in their bones that she *meant it*.

Still, he said: "I put you in an awkward place."

"I sat here," she said.

Cal tried to make a joke. He used to be able to make a million jokes, and now riding in this bus with the landmine strapped to his chest, he tried to joke to the woman beside him: "Didn't your mother tell you not to talk to strangers?"

Her smile cupped the man in the black leather jacket.

"Did you always do everything your mother told you to?" she said.

"Besides," she added, "if strangers nail you, it's at least...random savages. Not personal. It's the ones who you love, or think you love, or wish they were who you love, those are the ones who make you bleed."

The blue stones her eyes softened like sky as she said: "Strangers I can handle. We're on equal terms."

They looked away from each other.

Toward the front of their rumbling silver vehicle.

To the rearview mirror mounted up above the skeletal driver.

Saw reflections of spinning red cop lights coming up behind the bus.

She said: "That's for me."

He said: "That's for me."

A cop siren vibrated the metal bus.

The old man who smelled funny, the woman who moved her lips while she cradled her baby, the man who hadn't gotten the job, the college kid who was realizing he'd never make enough to pay back all the loans he owed, everyone crowded onto that bus stirred except for Cal and the woman who sat beside him and a drunk 20-Something snoring three aisles back and to the left amidst a fog of summer beer fumes.

The driver used the announcements' loudspeaker: "Everybody sit tight."

"That's for damn sure," said the woman sitting beside the landmine-strapped man.

As Cal said: "Damn right."

The silvery cylinder they rode shuddered and braked and pulled off to the side of the road. Brakes hissed, tossed Cal forward...

He absorbed the de-acceleration's inertia with his hands on the seat in front of him so his chest didn't bump it with the landmine's push/cock/release/BOOM trigger.

The shudder of *full stop* settled him into his seat beside her.

"Pretend you don't know me or care," she said.

"Just step aside and let me go," he said.

The bus door hissed/clunked/folded open.

He stomped onto the bus all mirror sunglasses and brown state trooper's uniform and black leather gloves with a badge of gold and a Marty Robbins big iron on his hip.

The bus driver said: "Officer, I wasn't—"

"Shut the fuck up and watch your windshield," said the cop.

Then he stalked into the aisle.

Saw the cropped blonde woman sitting next to a black leather jacketed guy.

Stopped with one of them reflected in each lens of his sunglasses.

Said: "Get up and let's go."

She got to her feet.

So did Cal, bent a bit because of the overhead luggage rack for his window seat.

The cop growled: "What the fuck are you doing, mister?"

The woman reflected in the cop's sunglasses said: "Leave him out of it, Josh, and get off our bus and get gone, 'cause it's all over."

"Don't make me put the cuffs on you, Rene." The cop reared up with the altitude of authority from his gun to his badge to his mirrors-hidden eyes. "This woman's already got the law on her, folks. She's a fugitive."

"The only law on me will be when I don't show up for disposition in divorce court. I can get fined and the court might automatically find against me, but I don't give a shit about that or what it costs and it's not a *go-to-jail* offense. Even it was, time behind bars would be worth it because I'd be gone from you."

"One way or the other, I'm taking you off this bus."

Hunched-over but standing Cal said: "You're only accounting for one fugitive."

"Mister, I'm not going to tell you to sit down again."

"Who cares."

Everyone on the bus held their breath.

Everyone felt the cop blink behind his mirror sunglasses.

"You know why I don't care?" said the black leather jacketed man standing beside the chopped-blonde woman. "Your cruiser parked out front of the bus alongside the road: you should have been listening to your police radio."

Cal and the woman beside him saw Josh's black gloved right hand ease toward his holstered 9mm as that state trooper said: "What are you talking about?"

"Odds are there was an APB for a white male, black leather jacket, AWOL from a locked mental ward at the Vet's hospital outside of Chicago. Or it could have been report of a theft from a military museum in Indiana."

"Theft of what?" said the cop.

"Watch our hands," said Cal. "That's what the Academy should have taught you. That's what you should know. That's what's key for us."

"What '*us*'?"

"Her—*Rene*. She might be an outlaw, but she's no criminal. But more importantly, there's your hands."

"What about them?"

"You're wearing black leather gloves. Like my black jacket. But it's summer."

"Driving gloves."

"Driving where? Everybody here on the bus would only I.D. you as *cop* and would be scattered hundreds of miles from here if, days from now, somebody found some tragedy alongside some back road, some other American woman who got dead for no more reason than being who she was. You're wearing black leather gloves and no fingerprints and even if you weren't, odds are, you already crafted your alibi but don't you think you better pay more attention to my hands—*Josh*?"

"Show me your—"

"See? They're right out in front of you.

"Now," said Cal. "Nice and slow—*like you want*—watch my empty hands as barely touching anything—*barely touching*—I unzip my leather jacket and pull it open."

This man who bought a ticket for that bus did just that.

"What..." said trooper Josh.

"What's strapped to your chest?" said Rene to the man standing hunched beside her in the row of bus seats.

"A custom-rigged Klaymore 9-Z pressure release activated landmine."

"Oh my God!" yelled somebody on the bus.

A young girl screamed.

Josh's black gloved right hand grabbed his service 9mm as he dropped into the combat firing stance on the metal floor of the bus aisle to zero the—

"I'll explode if you shoot!"

Nobody moved.

"If you hit the mine—BOOM! If you drop me third-eye-dead, then I'll fall—BOOM! Kill radius for the Klaymore 9-Z is approximately 40 meters including through metal skin of non-armored vehicles.

"Like a bus," added Cal. "Whether you're on it or dived off."

Rene whispered: "Why do you have a bomb strapped to your chest?"

"A landmine," corrected Cal.

"I thought you said you weren't one of those stickler for details guys anymore."

"Don't make me laugh—*I mean it*. I jiggle..."

"Shake, rattle and roll," she whispered. "And *boom*."

"Close enough."

"Here I thought I'd finally picked the right seat."

"You would have been OK. I'd have gotten off in a few stops. Waited until the bus drove away. Walked out into the prairie. Spread my arms wide like I was going to make a snow angel. Fall forward...Never hear the sound of my own going. Or make a mess for somebody to see or witness or carry. Just leave something for the wolves, the coyotes, the birds and the earth."

"There are easier ways to suicide."

"Easy has never been enough for me." Cal took a risk. Shrugged. "Call it poetry."

"I'm OK with poetry," she said, "but I try to be a great song."

Trooper Josh yelled: *"Put your hands—"*

"Really?" said Cal. "We're still supposed to pretend that you're in charge here?

"And *that*, ladies and gentlemen," continued Cal, "is part of our new problem."

"What do you mean?" said Rene.

"What the fuck are you guys doing he's got a bomb!" yelled the bus driver.

"Shut the fuck up!" yelled trooper Josh and Rene and Cal.

Everyone else was or had or did.

"Whatever happens now," said Cal, "trooper Josh has got himself a bus full of witnesses—or if the mine goes off and they're dead, he will be, too."

Cal sighed. "Was it too much to ask to let a guy go off and suicide in peace?"

"Suicide is never about peace," argued Rene. "You kill somebody, you kill something beyond that body. You kill a home for hope. You do violence to everybody who knows you—hell, who just met you on a bus. And even if you get away with it, even if we don't know you blew yourself up, you giving up means we can't count on you and everybody needs everybody else in this fucked up world, but..."

Rene frowned.

"Why the black gloves, Josh? This landmine guy—"

"My name is Cal."

"Cal," she said. *"Really?"*

"I never liked my name either: *Cal*-vin. I shortened it, Cal, but it's Calvin, like—"

"Like the President Calvin Coolidge," she said.

"Like the Calvin in the Sunday color comic strips when we were kids."

How the hell can I grin now? thought Rene.

"His black gloves signaled our problem," Cal told her.

"Why, Josh?" she said. "Why would you want to—"

The trooper's wife of five years blinked.

Whispered: "I wasn't crazy.

"You," she told the man wearing mirror sunglasses who swung his aim off landmined Cal to her. "When we started out, I thought you were the ultimate good guy. That you were a cop 'same reason I'm a nurse, stop the pain and the hurting, the...

"Who was it?" seethed the scheduled to be legally divorced woman.

"Shut up, Rene!"

"Some meth crew? Some stick up guys or corporate polluters dumping toxic waste out drag hoses as their tanker trucks roll over public roads at night? Or was it the worse of the worst, some pedophile ring slavery monsters who you took money from to let run the highways—to protect them on our highways? That's what I felt under all the other lies I bought for so long, but silly me, I still worried it might be my fault.

"The divorce," she said. "You never really loved me—Hell, because you were lying at your core, you never even *knew* me just like I only thought I knew you. You've got bimbos, so I couldn't figure out why you were fighting the divorce. Even now, I can't figure...Your dirty money would stay hidden, my lawyers, me, we weren't..."

Cal said: "It wasn't about any money your divorce would reveal. It was you leaving him meant he wasn't in control. Not as long as you were walking around without his say-so. How can you trust a man who's not in control to be controlled by your deal? Plus, who knows what you know."

"You're killing me so your *they* won't kill you," whispered Rene.

"And now we've all got a problem," said Cal. "Saw it after I saw your black gloves, Josh. Your hands, your face, the way you stand: You've got the killing look.

"I know it," said Cal. "You know the killing look, too."

Don't call it a smile Cal made as he told trooper: "Describe me."

"Don't hurt anybody, Cal," said the woman beside him. "I can go with him."

"Too late," said Cal. "If I do or allow one of those, the other can't happen."

"I got a fucking gun!"

"And what, 18 bullets? Two spare ammo mags? Enough for a slaughter. Can't let you do that."

Somewhere in the bus a voice whispered: *Jesus! Jesus! Jesus!"*

"No way I'm not walking out of this!" The trooper's gun never waivered. "And if I don't walk away free, then no way she does."

"You blame her for what you did?"

"What I did was never enough for her."

"You're right. She's worth more than I got, too." Cal shrugged. "So you and I, we're...We're on the same bus."

They all heard the sound of another siren, wailing closer.

They all remembered cell phones on terrified citizens.

Cal told Rene: "Step into the aisle. Let me past you."

"I'll shoot!"

"Who?" said Cal. "And then what?"

And then—*oh then*—Cal let the back of his right hand held low, held far from the palm-sized push trigger plate of the landmine strapped to his chest, held out of sight of the mirror sunglasses, Cal let his right fingers brush *oh so softly* against the warm electric flesh of Rene's heartside hand.

And *sure*, it was just a touch, a brush to prompt Rene to step into the bus aisle, but Cal felt it, even if it was only one more *doesn't matter* in our cosmic nevermore.

Rene moved out of the way.

Their touch...vanished.

"Step back," Cal told her.

"Let me be in front," she argued.

"Wouldn't do any good," said Cal. "And wouldn't be the smart move."

Cal stepped into the narrow aisle, finally able to stand tall, landmine chest aimed toward the front of the bus, toward Josh and his gun, toward the windshield beyond.

Josh locked his aim on the landmined man: "What are you doing?"

"What you want," said Cal. "Getting you and me off this bus."

From behind Cal, Rene said: "Me, too."

Cal said: "No you're not!"

Josh said: "Damn right!"

"My choice," said Rene. "I'm not one for hiding or pretending it's safe."

Outside the bus, a siren screamed to a halt. A car door slammed.

"Eyes on me, Josh!" called Cal with his command voice of yore. "You take one step back, I take one step forward. *Good! Now another.* You gotta make the turn, back down the stairs...*easy!* You don't want to fall. And you sure don't want me to fall."

One step at a time.

That's how the county deputy who was the nearest available officer to respond to a dozen 911 cell phone calls saw them come off the silver metal bus: *one step at a time.*

The state trooper, weapon aimed, backing down into the sunlight on the highway.

A black leather jacket guy stepping out forward—*What the heck is on his chest?*

A woman, pretty, older than the deputy who didn't want anyone to know that this was his first day solo "on the job," she climbs off the bus behind the other two, hands out like she's worried about catching the black leather jacket guy the trooper is aiming at.

The deputy drew his sidearm: "Sherriff's department! Nobody move!"

They all froze: three people who got off the bus, their eyes on each other as they stood in a line on the highway in the gunsights of the rookie deputy.

"Hear that, Josh?" called black leather jacketed guy. "Back-up is on the scene. Only who is that young guy, weapon drawn? Who's he backing up? You? Or the law?"

"Trooper!" called the deputy. "I'm on the two suspects!"

Obviously.

Josh's black mirror sunglasses and V-gunsight whirled/locked on the deputy.

"*No!*" yelled Cal and Rene.

"What the heck?" yelled the deputy—who suddenly knew enough to take his own advice and Not Fucking Move.

Black leather jacket yelled: "You shoot him, I go down, too! We all go BOOM!"

"What...what do you mean, '*shoot me*'?" yelled the deputy. "And all...*go boom*?"

"He's got a landmine strapped to his chest!" yelled the woman.

"A...*a landmine*?"

And that guy told the trooper: "What's it going to be, Josh?"

The black mirror sunglasses slid down a sweaty nose as Josh struggled for breath and words. "You...you people made me...you..."

"We were on the bus," said Cal. "We were on our way gone."

Rene said: "This is all on you, Josh. You always want control. Look where that got you. We're all standing on the side of the road and your gun and your badge and your hard heart, soft eyes lies aren't any good against a landmine."

Cal said: "*Go.*"

"WHAT?" said Josh and Rene and the *where should I aim* & *dying to pee* deputy.

"The blast radius of the Klaymore 9-Z is 40 meters. That's all of us. That's the whole bus. That's your parked cruiser and the sheriff's car, too."

"Deputy," corrected the young man who could barely hold his gun.

"Sorry," said Cal, "I try to be precise, but I'm making this up as I go along."

"That's OK," whispered the deputy.

"Get in your cruiser," the black leather jacketed man told the state trooper with the cockeyed mirror sunglasses and the gun in black gloved hands. "You got a head start, I'll be sure of that, cover you here. You'll be able to hear the radio calls when they come after you. You got a better shot of running from everybody *now* if you run *now* and you run with no more blood on you than you got *now*."

The woman stepped—*slowly, oh so slowly*—stepped around the guy with landmine or bomb or *whatever* death was strapped to his chest, stood beside him and told the state trooper: "You've got this one last chance, Josh. Don't blow it."

"Don't blow it!" yelled the deputy, thinking of only one thing.

The state trooper trembled like he would explode.

Yelled: "I could have had it all!"

"*Yeah*," said the man in the black leather jacket and landmine.

"*Yeah*," said the woman with chopped blonde hair and a white lined ring finger.

The trooper ran to his cruiser, climbed in and tore off down the highway, red lights whirling and siren blaring.

The wind stirred the prairie alongside a lonesome American highway where a bus and a sheriff's cruiser were parked and a man and a woman and a deputy stood.

The deputy whispered: "What now?"

"There's a fugitive from a whole lot of what's wrong fleeing this scene in a state trooper's car," said the man in the black leather jacket. "Pursue, call for back up, especially if it looks like you're going to catch him. I'll stay here, and...take care of the explosive ordinance device. Down the road, that's a notion you and her and all the witnesses on the bus can convince your boss was reasonable."

"I don't think I'll be a deputy down the road," said the rookie on his first solo day.

"Maybe you will, maybe you won't," said the black leather jacketed man. "What are you going to do now?"

The young deputy looked at the man who'd once been like him, said: "My duty."

The deputy ran fast but ran tall to the sheriff's cruiser, climbed in, hit the gas and the lights and siren, filled one hand with his radio mike as he tore off down the highway in pursuit of spinning red lights he could no longer see.

The wind blew across the prairie in the great American nowhere.

Past a bus parked alongside the highway.

Past a man and a woman standing side by side.

"Get back on the bus," he told her. "Get it and all of them out of here. I'll wait for...I'll wait. You go now."

"If I go, there'll be no reason left here to come back."

"Go. You earned it. You deserve it."

"You know one thing you deserve?" she said.

He had to ask *what*.

"A better name. Cal is so..."

"It's short. Gets the job done."

"Yeah, but it's *whiney*. And not you. Go short, but go..."

Then she smiled.

Stepped in front of him.

Almost close enough to touch the landmine over his heart.

"*Vin*," she said. "Cal-*Vin*. Short. Strong. New. Not the start, the *what's next*."

The wind whispered around them.

Then he said: "What's next is you go."

"That landmine on your chest. You built that yourself, right? I mean, not the landmine. That got given you or you got crazy and claimed it. But the rig, the setup with you wearing it all primed. You did that yourself."

He shrugged.

"So you're usually precise. Got smarts. Skills. Conscience and consciousness. Guts—oh, and don't forget: *poetry*."

"And a landmine on my chest."

"DRIVER!" she yelled. "Get your damn bus out of here!"

That machine's pneumatic door hissed/clunked/closed.

The bus lurched back onto the highway, lumbered *roared* past the man and woman standing on the side of the highway. A silver streak going, *gone*.

"What did you do that for?" yelled the man, yelled Cal, yelled *oh if only he could be* Vin. "I gotta do what I gotta do!"

"Me, too," she said.

Wrapped her arms around him and pulled herself tight against him and—

SNUNK!

They heard the metal pressure plate arm the landmine strapped between them.

He threw his arms around her, pulled her tight, held her like he'd never held any woman before: as soon as pressure 'stepped' or eased off the landmine...

"What have you done?"

"Figured that a precise, smart, skilled, gutsy, conscience, conscious, poetic guy like you would have built his rig with some kind of safety deactivate switch you could reach to prevent an explosion from wrecking a greater good than you being gone."

"What if you're wrong? What if I can't do it? What if we both blow up?"

He felt her smile reshape his whole world.

As she said: "You're worth it."

Nick Russell is an American author who's lived in Los Angeles, Oregon, several East Coast and heartland cities. He's worked on a road crew, been a gravedigger, a bureaucrat, and a roadie. This is his first published piece of fiction.

The Leper Colony
Amy Wallace

When I was a precocious boy of six, I found a book in my father's voluminous collection—*Father Damien: A Life Among the Poor and Helpless.*

I was permitted to read anything I was tall enough to reach, stepladders included.

I opened the book at random, read:

"And Father Damien knelt to the leper, and the leper's virulent limb. The holy man sucked the pus from the suffering one's open wound, and did not taste the bitterness."

This was something new. Something...disgusting.

The book slammed shut with my horror.

The closed book of Father Damien nested on its shelf for 40 more years. I scrupulously avoided it. But it had taken dark root in my mind. The image of a pus-filled mouth never left me.

In this life of bitterness, maybe that somehow affected my early ambition to help people. Perhaps a kibbutz. Would they accept this Catholic boy if I converted to Judaism? This notion gave way to a plan to join the Peace Corps.

My draft number was high, so I luckily missed serving in the Vietnam War. Like everyone of my generation, I carried iconic images of that holocaust: A Vietcong getting his head blown off at shockingly close range. Ho Chi Minh in his garden taking tea. One image haunted me more than others: the burning Buddhists.

For nothing else had given me that Father Damien feeling again, the feeling that drove my life, until I flipped on the TV one Friday night and saw them.

A group of shaved-headed acolytes, sitting in the lotus position, being doused with oil by their fellows. And then . . . *blam!* They burned.

Human torches.

They never lost the lotus position.

If at six, I knew that a mouthful of pus was terrible, too terrible to stop thinking about, then as an adult what was I to make of this? Where, on the scale of human suffering, did the decision to burn and die, and never to scream, enter into things?

I finally did my service in the Peace Corps in Chad. I saw things too horrible to write about, was a part of helping and healing them when help was possible.

While my co-workers often vomited up their horror, I was known for my cool. I compared every sensation to what Father Damien must have felt, sucking up pus, and somehow what I saw in the Peace Corps did not supersede what I'd found in that book. If I'd written a memoir of my inner fears and dreams, I could have called it A Mouthful of Pus. As for the monks and nuns who burned alive, that I avoided considering.

The standards we set, set us.

You know that. You have your own.

My Peace Corps transition left me watching animals live and die as a vet's assistant. If that sounds small to you after the Peace Corps, try telling a five-year-old girl her cat has to die as she clutches her doomed animal tight in her arms.

I didn't take Catholic orders, that didn't seem difficult enough.

I became a Buddhist.

Found my way into a business to package tours of Southeast Asia with my father after we lost mom. Something to take our mind off her, we told ourselves. We didn't like to say much about her, except: "Mom would have loved this." That "this" meant washing elephants and giving rice to the priests. When we went to the arcades in Cambodia and shot AK-47's, such a cliched American bonding for father and son, we said: "Mom would have hated this."

Dad never told me how sick he was. When we finally got home and threw him in the car to drag him to the doctor, he was dying of cancer.

"Don't hover," he said grumpily when I spent those 'Quality Weeks' with him.

I miss him more that I can say.

After he passed, I dismantled the house. And there, among his books I was boxing for the estate, I found *Father Damien: A Life Among the Poor and Helpless*.

Awash in dust motes, I brushed its' cover, daring it to fall open to that first kaleidoscopic pus-sucking moment in my life. Nothing happened.

I shoved the book away as a breeze ruffled it's pages, placed it in between huge, un-scary tomes that it might stay closed forever. In between Hegel and Napoleon lay this fuel for my nightmares. And inspirations.

That night I couldn't sleep, sick with missing Dad. And in that longing for my father, I realized something else—my restless calling was back.

I had to do something really difficult. I had to do something good.

I had kept my personal effects to a minimum, sold mom and dad's house with it's furniture and contents, and within a year was installed in an ashram in Vietnam. It wasn't a kibbutz, or The Peace Corps, by a long shot. But I was prepared in a practical way, at least, though emotionally I was at sea.

My head was shaved. I received my robes and begging bowl.

Of course, I chose a monastery that served as a leper colony.

There was a lot of incense burning at our meals, all around the temple, as if the smell of incense was supposed to cover other odors of this world. It took a long time before the sickly sweet smell stopped making me gag. I grew thin.

The shaved-headed nuns were kept entirely separate, and while I had never been much of a romantic, I found it strange to be apart from the society of women.

And then there was the frankly dull routine of the devotions with my brothers. The only service that made me feel truly alive was treating the lepers, some of whom were oddly sensitive about the areas where their limbs had fallen off. I don't mean mentally, I mean physically. They often shirked when I dressed their stumps, but lepers aren't supposed to feel pain. I guess it was their horror.

The fields of Vietnam and Cambodia were riddled with land mines. Any moment a farmer, tilling his rice field, could lose everything, or maybe worse, a hand, a leg, a face. A day didn't pass when I didn't obsess on the horror of these farmers. Every step over their earth was a game of Russian Roulette.

Then I met Mikey. His real name was Hieu, Hieu Hong, but he wanted an American name so I dubbed him Mikey, much to his satisfaction. He was 14, and he wanted to grow up to be a doctor, to help.

He volunteered at the monastery, cooking rice, sneaking the odd onion or carrot into the big pot. Serving us. Praying with us.

Until one day when Mikey helped his dad farm their fields.

We heard the mine explode.

By the time I saw Mikey, he had no hands, and only one arm and few toes.

His sad eyes searched face for answers: "How does this help?"

"I don't know yet, Mikey. Maybe by showing people another way."

"Well," he said, "someone has to learn."

He frowned. "I guess, if more people in the world knew how bad it was here with the mines, they'd come and help."

Mikey asked why I was in the ashram.

"To help people."

"Then be a do-er!" he said. "You're not a a leper, you can do stuff!"

He left in pain with his toeless shuffle.

There were subterranean mutterings that one could barely hear on the ground floor of the ashram. Although I spoke French, Vietnamese and Cambodian, I couldn't make out what was being said in those basement vaults. There was a rumor that the worst cases of leprosy lived down there. Sometimes the noises I heard coming from down below seemed like the faint echoes of screams.

And there were other rooms in the temple that were definitely sacrosanct. We lesser acolytes could not penetrate below. The cases of leprosy I treated were pretty damn bad, but for the record, I never sucked pus, though I thought about it a lot.

Then one bright Sunday came real screaming. A monk had gone mad, emerging in a violent panic from the vaults. Sometimes monks go crazy just meditating. We were told it was "the grief of the dharma" and that we would recover. This man never stopped gibbering, and he took his meals alone, when he ate at all. Apart from his babbling, he never spoke another word.

Most curious were his burns. He had 2nd degree burn on his left forefinger and thumb, as if he had picked up something unspeakably hot. Perhaps cooking tongs. This would have been a logical explanation, except for the fact that he had a 3rd degree burn on his foot—one toe was gone—and the left side of his face was grotesquely burnt, leaving only part of his nose. He could offer us no explanation, and if any of his senior monks knew what had happened, they weren't talking.

It's a truism that my Western mind was a noisy one, more active and less at peace than those of my fellows. Even the lepers seemed quieter at heart than I did.

I didn't want women, a head of long hair, or a steak. I wanted to know what happened to that monk—somehow I didn't think it was a cooking burn—and I longed to know what was way downstairs in the vaults.

There was no hurry. Years of rigorous study and service had trained me to wait. When you work in a leper colony—or an ashram, and you come from the West, sometimes you have a sort of patron saint. Usually it's the Buddha. Mine was Father Damien.

My mentor in the temple was a severe acolyte and he watched me closely. Though we spoke rarely, I suspected he was a brilliant man

One day, after five years of my impeccable devotions—I know conceit means I'm not "there" yet—my mentor asked if I would like to come below.

Solemnly, I nodded.

First, there were the vaults—rooms upon rooms, intensely clogged, though orderly—housing giant sculptures of the Buddha and countless scrolls. A lengthy walk took us through numerous holy rooms, we descended yet another staircase (had there been five? six?) and reached a steel door.

Beyond the steel door, I guessed, probably were crumbling holy scrolls and maybe some astoundingly antiquated paintings of the Buddha sitting beneath his tree.

And yes, there were several hundred such items. But what I was not prepared for was the sight of at least 500 of my fellow acolytes—monks *and* nuns—sitting in the deepest meditation.

If they saw us they gave no sign. Each sat with a brazier by his right hand side, which exuded such heat that even in the stillness of meditation, the Buddhists all dripped profuse sweat.

I was truly flustered, afraid. I had grown used to the heat of Vietnam, but now I too began to sweat.

My guide tapped me on the shoulder. He sounded like a Maharishi or a Mafioso. Where would I go if I followed him? To Jimmy Hoffa's boots? But follow him I did, into another, smaller sanctum, far less populous.

Here, the very holy were deep in practice.

Putting first their fingers, then whole hands, into white-hot braziers.

Some flinched, yanked their hands away. One even screamed.

But the others held their hands steady. Horrified, riveted like a deer in headlights. I watched as one by one, they removed their hands. Some were blistered and surely would be scarred; others appeared to be unburnt, just tender. Buckets of cold water were brought. One student fainted.

My mentor addressed me.

"And this is what you want, round-eyes?"

I swallowed, I nodded.

For what was beginning to happen, really happen, after so many years, was my knowing that Father Damien feeling.

My guide appeared to sense that. With a few muttered words to a nearby monk, and without a goodbye, he left me in The School For Burning.

I told myself I was tough. But really, I wanted to throw up. Most of all I wanted to cry. Half the acolytes I'd seen I'd mistaken for lepers. But no. They were students in progress, they had burned off legs, noses, fingers, genitals., then come upstairs to heal—give up, or simply take a moment's peace.

And I did it.

With them.

We submitted our limbs to burning, trying to remain unflinching, as an offering, as what we could do, how we could be doers. I thought of Mikey a lot, and the landmine victims, all the victims of wars, everywhere.

Until the day when we burned from within. Pain is the great denominator, and burning one of the greatest pains of all. To burn alive. To transcend life and pain. To meditate, and never to lose the lotus position. Simply to topple over. And maybe in your fall to help awaken a sleeping world to the truths of pain and leprosy, cancer and landmines, and maybe, just maybe, then awakened minds become different "do-ers."

Finally, I tasted a mouthful of pus. It was sweet.

Thank you, Father Damien.

New York Times bestselling writer **Amy Wallace** created, with her father, novelist Irving Wallace, and her brother, author and Olympics historian David Wallechinsky, the internationally successful *Book of Lists* series. She also authored the biography *The Prodigy*, the memoir *Sorcerer's Apprentice: My Life with Carlos Castaneda*, and the novel *Desire*, among many other books. Her short fiction appeared in the anthologies *Help! Wanted* and *Evil Jester Digest Volume 2*. "The Leper Colony" was the final piece of fiction she completed before her untimely death in August, 2013. She is forever missed.

NOTE: Thanks to James Grady and David Wallechinsky for their assistance in editing Amy's original manuscript of this story.

Mr. Ho & The Silence
Eric Shapiro

I almost didn't want to go to Danny's house, but he has the Ping-Pong table in the backroom, and we always have such good afternoons there, thwacking the ball back and forth 'til we feel like we can't breathe.

And I like Danny, too. He's not my best friend—that's Alex—but he's still a good buddy. He's easy to be around and isn't a jerk, or mean.

The problem with going to Danny's house, especially on a Saturday, is his father, Mr. Ho.

Mr. Ho's not a jerk, either, or mean. In fact, he's a nice man. He smiles when he sees me and says, "Hello, Jared." And sometimes when me and Danny are laughing around the Ping-Pong table, I overhear Mr. Ho laughing, too, even though he probably doesn't know what we think is funny.

No, the problem with Mr. Ho goes back to one Saturday in September, at the beginning of the school year. Since me and Danny went to separate grade schools, we didn't ever meet each other 'til junior high. That September gave me headaches. I was always nervous about making my way around the hallways of my new school, and seeing so many new faces that I hadn't known in grade school. Danny and me got along quick, though. First period, we were in Math together. Then again in fourth period for Study Hall.

And we shared the same lunch period.

So it kind of seemed like we were meant to hang together.

The first time I went to his house that September was a Tuesday, so Mr. Ho wasn't home. Danny told me he was retired (and he must have had a good-paying job, 'cause their house is really big), but that he spent time at the library on weekdays, usually going in during the late morning with a coffee and reading newspapers and books on history 'til it was late in the afternoon.

He knew how to use the computer, Danny said, but he preferred the library because he worried the computer would strain his eyes.

But the more I think about that explanation, the more I think the library has less to do with having stuff to read on paper and more to do with having so much silence.

***

Because the second time I went to Danny's house was a Saturday, and Mr. Ho was there. From the second I met him, I thought he was okay. Harmless man with some white hair. His smile went all the way up to his eyes. And there was, at points, that laughter from the kitchen as he heard us two laughing in the backroom.

But on that Saturday I won a game, and I didn't just win it, but I did really good. I kicked Danny's ass, actually, and he's far from a bad player. And after I won, I got kind of wild. I said, "*OH!*" and then screamed, "I just TOTALLY DESTROYED YOU!"

And Danny, blushing, kind of laughed.

But Mr. Ho came over to the backroom door and closed it.

Not slammed. But he wasn't gentle, either.

Then Danny kind of looked at me, guilty, and said, "You should be more quiet around my dad."

***

It was awkward kind of for like a minute—or not even. We just went back to playing, and a couple times I got a little loud, but either Danny reminded me or I reminded myself.

And I went back there mostly on weekdays, but Saturdays, too, and it was always fine.

But then there was this one Saturday in November when we were in Danny's bedroom and he'd downloaded this awesome song by Cage the Elephant, and while we played it (over and over, like 35 times) I turned it up. Then Danny (not wanting to make a big thing out of it) turned it back down.

But later I forgot and turned it up again.

And soon Mr. Ho was in the doorway, even though the door had been closed, and there was no smile anywhere near his face, and not his eyes, and he acted like I wasn't there but said to Danny, "Go play Ping-Pong!"

Then that time he slammed the door.

My shoulders jumped.

I apologized to Danny, and he shook his head, like: *no worries.* I asked, "How come he gets so mad about noise?"

Then Danny's shoulders rose, not jumped. He shrugged, said, "He used to live in Vietnam."

I nodded like I understood, but I still don't even know what that means. I mean, I know they had a war there, so maybe Mr. Ho fought in the war and didn't like the loud bomb sounds?

Probably.

Danny wouldn't explain it.

We played Ping-Pong.

***

But today it's a Saturday and there's no one else to hang with. Alex is away with his dad, and Neal says he has to study 'til at least lunch, and besides I think Danny might even be my best friend. I haven't known him the longest, but time always goes by fast with him.

And he's got the Ping-Pong table.

So I walk up the porch steps, take a breath, and ring the bell. I figure as long as I'm quiet there won't be a problem. Mr. Ho's no doubt a nice guy even though he gets uptight.

I gotta admit, though, that I almost get scared when the old man opens the door.

I've never had to talk to him one-on-one, or alone.

But here he is, and his face is harder than I thought it was, with the sunlight on his skin. He smiles a little, though. And seems happy to see me.

I say, "Can Danny play?"

I know that "play" isn't what a kid my age should call it anymore, but that seems to be the word Mr. Ho would like.

"Danny's at swimming," Mr. Ho says.

Oh, yeah. I forgot he was on the swim team now. December's no excuse not to swim in Orange County.

Suddenly I feel alone. What am I gonna do today?

"Okay," I say. "Maybe I'll see him tomorrow."

"That would be fine," Mr. Ho says, nodding.

And as I walk away, he watches me. And I wonder why he can't take noise. And I'd like so much to ask him why.

If I did, maybe he'd say to me:

When I was exactly your age, son, I was walking with my cousin, Han, along a lengthy dirt road to go find water and bring it to our parents. We were laughing and joking in the midday sun, when Han skipped ahead of me and a landmine exploded, shredding her into a great black mist, some of which I tasted in my mouth.

But it's not the taste that I remember, son.

It is the sound.

But I can't know what's in the man's head. And maybe I'm better off not ever knowing. I'd definitely never really ask. So I move on.

Think about my day.

Keep quiet.

Eric Shapiro is a filmmaker, screenwriter, author, and ghostwriter. His first feature film, *Rule Of Three* (2010), was released to iTunes and Netflix after winning Best Actor at the Fantasia International Film Festival and Best Acting Performance at Shriekfest. His recently completed feature film, *Living Things*, has been endorsed by PETA (People For The Ethical Treatment Of Animals) and is due for release by Cinema Libre Studio in April, 2014. He wrote the books *Love & Zombies* (2013), *The Devoted* (2012), *Stories For The End Of The World* (2010), and *Short Of A Picnic* (2002). His novella *It's Only Temporary* (2005) was on the Preliminary Nominee Ballot for the Bram Stoker Award in Long Fiction. He has had short stories published in fiction anthologies alongside work by Ray Bradbury, Stephen King, Neil Gaiman, Chuck Palahniuk, and many others. Eric lives in Los Angeles with his wife, Rhoda Jordan, and their son, Benjamin Shapiro.

The Fifteen Minute Room
C. Courtney Joyner

The room was at the top of twenty steps leading from Soi Summitt to the first landing where customers gave their money to Solo for the fifteen minutes. There was a bed, Brittney Spears sheets lying in the corner in a heap, a nightstand with a lamp, an open drawer with condoms and lube, and all around the thick smell of the body that had been lying there for the four hours in the Bangkok night.

Connie tasted the smell in the back of his mouth. He was used to it, but the heat made it feel like all the air had been sucked out of the room. He had to step in the hallway for a breather and a cigarette.

He leaned against the door jam, lighting and drawing deep. He'd opened the pack almost two weeks before, but they still tasted better than the room's air.

A few girls walked by the open door, peeking inside at the body lying across the mattress, the blood pooled around it turning black and soaking in. A few snickered. None had anything real to say. They just wanted to get back to the streets for the eleven o'clock push.

Solo opened his palm, silently bumming a smoke. Connie gave it to him, tossed him his lighter, said, "I'll want that back."

Solo nodded, "I ain't no thief."

"How many times have I busted you?"

"Three times."

"You remember what for?"

"Stealing copper wire. Always makes you feel big, Khai-Khao."

The heel of Connie's hand hit Solo's head just hard enough to buckle his knees so Connie could take the .32 automatic that was trapped between Solo's gut and his belt.

Connie said, "That makes me feel big."

He picked up his lighter, lit the smoke still dangling from Solo's mouth, moved back into the room just as the last pictures were flashed of the victim.

Connie nodded, and two other cops wearing rubber gloves turned the nude body over and freed another burst of wincing-smell. One cop choked.

From the hallway Solo said, "Jesus God, get him out!"

Putrefaction was starting its crawl around the victim's belly and genitals where most of the stab wounds were. There were deep cuts on the palms of his hands, as if he'd shielded his eyes during the attack.

His mouth was horrific. Slicing away his top and bottom lip let rigor freeze him in a permanent, swelling kiss that revealed mismatched teeth. His eyes were open, shocked.

His clothes hung in a small closet, behind an old shower curtain, on a single hanger. Connie let the others do what they had to with the body while he looked through the victim's pants. They were neatly creased, hanging properly, with a set of keys, Baht in the right front pocket, a plastic comb buttoned in the hip.

The jacket matched the pants. Connie flipped back the lapels to check the stitching. Good quality. The lining sported a label: "Maison de Bonneterie, Amsterdam."

He used a handkerchief to pull the victim's wallet from an inside pocket, drop it into an evidence bag. One of the other cops zipped the seal, made a note on the side.

Connie stuffed the handkerchief back into his coat; it had all been for show anyway. This would be no different than the last three, with no fingerprints other than the victim's on anything, least of all his wallet, which would be empty except for personal pictures.

Connie held his nose and kept his mouth open, gasped for air as they moved the body on a sling stretcher out of the room.

Connie said to Solo, "He's gone."

Solo was holding his head, weaving for effect. "You want to ask me here, or do I go with you? If I go with, you got to let me call Auntie Rose to cover for me."

"I always liked your Aunt Rose."

Solo flicked away the cigarette Connie had given him. "Old lady does better with the customers than I do. They never give her no shit. I call her, then I call my lawyer."

"Sorry I hit you."

Solo said, "You're a fucking cop, you shouldn't be so sensitive."

***

"How many colors?"

Tak looked at Connie with a blank expression that wasn't truly empty, just a cue for him to keep talking, tell her what it was he really wanted.

Connie said, "How do you get all those colors, that rainbow around your eyes?"

Tak was lying on the patched leather couch, staring at the stained ceiling. She drank some of her Diet Coke with lemon. "You've seen me do it a hundred times. First the blue, then the green, then the last bit of purple."

"With the sparkles."

"That's what you like."

Connie said, "It's the way you always do it."

She sat up, "Why do cops always talk in circles? When it's in the back, you know what to say. Out here, you never get to it. Waste my time."

"I'm paying for it."

Tak leaned back on the couch. "Then you'll let me take a nap."

"If that's what you want. How's your mother?"

"Alive."

"Did your little cousins like their birthday present?"

Tak said, "They fight over who gets to be the troll."

"Bilbo Baggins."

"Whatever. They fight over that. I like Call of Duty Five, but it was a good present, good game for them."

Connie said, "They have imagination."

"And you have too much, *Khai*."

He didn't anger. "What do you mean?"

Tak sipped her Coke again, kept her eyes closed, like she could talk her way to sleep. "You're thinking about the girl."

"She's the one I'm trying to find."

"It's the men. You don't know why they want her. You know less than anybody. A few guys come in here, talk about what they read in *The Post*, worry they'll get stabbed."

Connie said, "There wasn't supposed to be anything, but you can't avoid rumors. The world runs on them."

"You talking in circles again." Tak sat up. "Maybe they heard something on the block. Or maybe somebody confessed during a blowjob. Take your pick. It's the man, not the girl. You get too hung-up on us."

Connie looked around The Eve Club at the small frames, long black hair, tiny noses and slices of eyes. Some were too girlish. Others stalked the place with sure moves. A group sat by the door, singing along with Miley, waving to passing customers. Lots of giggles about fat ones, whispering to each other, flirting with passers-by to get them to come in.

Tak said, "It's so easy. You don't think I never wanted to kill somebody?"

"Me?"

She stood, sucked ice and air through her drink straw. "No, you like me. And you tip good. But you talk too much."

Connie said, "Because you help me get things clear in my mind."

Tak held out her hand, and he pressed 750 baht into it. She shrugged.

He said, "Not bad for not doing anything."

"But I really wanted to sleep."

A guy at the bar wearing a Steven Segal t-shirt raised his hand, and the *Mamasan* gave Tak a nod.

"See, that's the kind of customer *I* like. Don't forget the Raybans, you always do."

Tak laughed as she panther-walked to the guy. Connie stood, absently checked the gun in his shoulder holster, and kept his eyes on the carpet, heading for the front door, not wanting to see Tak at this moment.

The glare from the walls of neon along Soi Cowboy were cut by the wrap-arounds, but just barely, as Connie adjusted them on his nose. The lack of pigmentation in his eyes brought every needle of light to them, and he often had to squint, even at night, even wearing the dark glasses.

Starting down the alley between Soi 21 and 23, Connie acknowledged the souvenir vendors who waved, the go-go bar girls who knew him. The music blaring from a hundred different doorways sounded like a continuous argument that was somehow in rhythm with the movement of the night crowd.

A Marine in cammo greens took a picture of Connie with his phone; how many Albinos were they going to see that night, and what a story if they knew he was a detective.

An old lady spit tobacco, calling out *"Khai Khao"* from her place behind the fruit stand. Connie nodded to her. She'd known him since he was a kid, when they started calling him "Egg White," instead of Conrad. He hated it, but less so from the old ones or Tak, who just thought it cute. Still, Connie secretly liked that he was so well known around the blocks that he had a nickname. As a cop, sometimes that helped.

He bought satay from a griller, grabbed a folding table to eat the skewers under the blinking sign for The Dollhouse. Watched the girls in their shorts with racing stripes across their butts urging the tourists with a little dance and snaking arms.

If they were around long enough, he knew them by name. He could tell if they were from Isaan to the west or from the mountains. He figured one to be Filipino. She changed places on the sidewalk with a Thai girl. Some other painted face took her place.

Tak always laughed at his sentimentality, but Connie couldn't think of the girls as invisible, without a past or family. He couldn't follow the line of the department, cab drivers, tourists, the mama sans.

Connie stood, walked toward the street, turning on his heel to see the Dollhouse girls. One of them blew him a kiss. He saw the girls by Déjà Vu and Midnight Club flashing the same smile, doing the same dance, offering everything.

***

Traffic officers lounging in the officer's lounge of the Metropolitan Department watched the Assistant Director General, in full uniform, stand before a bank of microphones and reporters, assuring the world of the security of the upcoming elections.

Connie eyed the TV, but couldn't listen to the Assistant's flat, measured voice for long, walked out. An hour later, he was in his office, having to read a letter out loud like a kid in math class who was being punished for shooting spitballs.

Connie also kept his voice flat as he read: "Events of this kind are a great distress to the consulate, and we trust the Metropolitan Police Department to marshal all of its capabilities to bring this case to a swift close, with the guilty parties in custody."

He studied the last paragraph over the seal of the Secretary to the Dutch Ambassador, when the Assistant Director punched, "And what do you make of that?"

Connie waited for the Assistant Director to answer his own question.

"And what do you make of that? I'll tell you detective, I see many problems ahead, unless you start doing your job more effectively." The Assistant Director brushed his the sleeves of his uniform. "And I have severe doubts. We have been gifted with four men dead, all foreign nationals. We've seen few results from you."

Connie was going to say something, waiting for the Assistant Director to take a breath, or leave an opening. But he didn't. Connie rubbed the sun's sting from his eyes.

"I wonder if the case would be further along if it was four dead massage girls. Then would it have your full attention? I will have to answer this letter, and I won't be embarrassed when I do it. You will have someone in custody."

The Assistant Director snapped a cloth across his boots, put on his cap and gloves. "Your background excuses your propensity to wallow in filth. That's been useful in the past. Use it now, or the consequences will be grave, I assure you."

***

Solo said, "Grave consequences, he said that? Those words? Jesus."

Connie sat across from him at the scarred table in interview room three. The walls were mirrored and stained. Solo played to his own reflection more than to the other cops listening in. Someone had gotten him a DeDe coconut juice, and he drank from the bottle as he watched Connie flip through a large file folder.

"Is that this case, all those papers?"

"Yeah."

"For one man?"

Connie said, "Just tell me what happened again."

"All that shit stacked up, and what I got to say won't cover a page. Come on, Khai, I made my statement."

"You made *a* statement."

"Typical *Ma* cop. Take orders from guys who think they're better than you, and he's a customer, who never pays. At least you're honest, Khai. Always been that."

"Because I never took a pay out from you?"

"I never offered."

Connie said, "So give me something else. Again, what about her?"

"Nothing. A ghost. Look, I'm collecting five buildings, running around like crazy. A Nana boy got sick, so it was stupid luck that I was there when this Dutchman got killed. Why didn't they go to the Ambassador?"

"That's where he was staying?"

Solo finished his coconut. "Maybe. He had some partner with him, I think that's what he said, but I was counting the money."

"Hard work, is it?"

"You should know, you used to do it in a previous life."

***

Connie liked the Bureau du Coroner: when you walked down the stairs to the basement, the temperature dropped twenty degrees. The air still felt thick against your skin, but it was cool, and the lighting poor, so he could take off his sunglasses as he walked toward the room where Grace was singing:

"*Delta Dawn, what's that flower you have on?*"

She asked the question as she drew the scalpel from the belly up to the sternum of the Dutchman's body, the skin separating easily. Her voice rose an octave.

"*Could it be a faded rose from days gone by?*"

Grace looked up, smiled as she inserted q-tips into the edges of the stab wounds, widening them, and then she took a picture of each.

"*And did I hear you say he was a-meeting you here today—*"

Grace took off her ear buds, snapped the last picture.

"The knife is a long blade, like a machete, but with teeth on the edge."

"You can't tell me anything different?"

"What would you like to hear?"

Connie said, "That you know her name and phone number. You can even sing it."

Grace wrinkled her nose, embarrassed but proud. "This place has great acoustics. Your number four was killed the same way as numbers one, two, and three. But different ages, from different countries. I'm still waiting on all that paperwork, thank you."

Connie stood at the foot of the steel examining table as if laying out what he knew would get a reaction from the corpse: "Two of them lied on their visas and one had a record with Interpol for trafficking in stolen fire arms. Interpol said they had an on-going case, which means—"

"That you're screwed, blued, and tattooed."

"Now you sound like Tanya Tucker. My CI thought there was a partner. His phone was gone. Please tell me there was something else in the personals."

"Other than liking pretty little girls, with great, big knives?" Grace held up an evidence bag, with a single business card in it. "Probably fell out of his pants. They found it under the bed, but only his fingerprints on it."

Connie took the card. It had a gilt edge, and was embossed: "Claude Vernous/Leon Steiner. Import/Exports. Amsterdam, London, Bangkok."

Grace put her ear buds back on, brushing her red hair out of the way first. "Well, at least it isn't the Russian mob."

***

Connie carried a photocopy of Vernoux's visa and passport as he walked around the side of Club Isis, up the steps washed in golden light to the large, double-doors beside the waterfall. The massage parlor's manager greeted him by name. A beautiful girl in a yellow silk dress took Connie's hand, led him to the second floor where Steiner had agreed to meet him.

The marble stairs led directly to the "fish bowl," the glass-enclosed area where about forty girls sat on small couches, reading, chatting, and all looking up as the hostess brought a new customer onto the floor. Outside the bowl, the "sideline" girls stood by their lounges, all with welcoming smiles.

One or two frowned when they saw Connie, flopped back down in their seats.

"You're known here, Officer Pierce. Actually, with your looks, I'd think you're known everywhere. My humor, please."

Steiner was a short man in his fifties, fit, with a shaved head and a practiced ease of manner. He wore too much cologne, and like his dead partner, fine clothes. Connie took a place opposite him. The young lady in the yellow dress handed him a flute of champagne, plus a menu of the "model girls" waiting on the third floor with a list of the bar fine next to each and rental prices of the private rooms on the fourth floor.

Connie took off his glasses, flipped through the pages for any familiar faces, said, "She doesn't know me."

Steiner laughed, "Go up a floor, and the price goes up too. Every level, an improvement, right? But I like it here in the afternoon. Second floor, lots to choose from, then after dinner, the third floor. You never partake? Not once? Your friends are expensive, but worth it."

Connie looked up, "Too expensive for your partner?"

"They haven't told me when I can claim Claude's body. I have to get him home. God knows what this heat is doing to him."

"You seem to be handling your grief pretty well."

Steiner poured himself his own glass, "You said *partner*. Correct. Not friends, not really. We did business together and I knew him."

"What business? This?"

Steiner laughed. "Hardly. Here, a different kind of menu."

The front of the folder was the image of a tank in flames, and inside a catalog of anti-tank and anti-personnel mines, and small cluster bombs. The text was in French.

"You make landmines?"

"We supply the raw materials to factories in Singapore and specialty companies in Africa. They do the manufacturing and distribution. We have no control over the final product. All perfectly legal, if that's what you're thinking."

Connie said, "I wasn't thinking that."

Steiner said, "Good. It would be hypocritical to be judged by a policeman from Bangkok. Or New York."

"Why are you here? Making a deal?"

"We had meetings in the area, decided on a little vacation. What better place?"

Connie fixed his red eyes on Steiner. "What was he doing on Soi Cowboy? Why not here?"

"Because Claude was a cheap prick. And, he couldn't find what he wanted here. Your staring is disconcerting."

"What did he want?"

Steiner broke from Connie, took in the girls around him, said, "Nothing here. These girls are...complete. He wanted someone with injuries, a missing limb. Considering some of our business partners, an ironic fetish. My intention is to keep this from his wife and children."

"That's a friendly gesture," Connie stood. "They won't hear it from me. Other than you, who knew?"

Steiner said, "The one who set it up. Claude's phone wasn't working, so they sent me the text."

Steiner handed Connie a cell phone, gestured for more champagne and a sideline girl to join him. Connie read the text, saw the hash-tag, left without another word.

***

"We're supposed to be cousins!"

Connie hit Solo again, not with his hand, but the side of the .32 caliber pistol from his shoulder holster. Solo tumbled to the ground, holding his face, wiping away the blood, then tried to get up, but always with another lie.

So Connie hit him again, but not too hard. "We're third cousins."

"That don't mean nothing? God, what an asshole!"

"It means you weren't straight with me."

Solo got up again, his hands raised to deflect the pistol, but Connie handed him a blue ice pack. Solo pressed it against his face, said, "I'm not you. I care about how I look."

"Now are you going to tell me about her?"

"It's what I said. This guy was looking, and I knew this girl had some special qualities."

"How did you know?"

Solo moved the pack from his jaw to his cheek, "She told me. I was never with her! I never even saw her in person. You know how it works, they send you a message, let you do the broking. That's all I was, the broker."

Connie used a paper napkin to wipe the blood from his pistol. "So this girl, she's missing an arm, or what?"

"I don't know! I saw her from far away, and she had on a big coat, and some kind of floppy hat."

"Is she still in touch? Think hard about this answer."

Solo said, "You want me to reach her?"

"What do you think?"

***

The neon along the Cowboy chased the sun, never going off, always flashing, waiting for the night to show itself off. The Soi was just coming to life as Connie and Solo made their way through the small alley to the two buildings at the end of the block.

Connie was wearing a clean shirt, a knotted tie, with his gun and handcuffs on his belt. His pure white hair was combed straight back, the Raybans over his eyes.

Solo borrowed a pair of old sunglasses from his cousin to hide some bruises. They stopped at the steps of the last building, the music from the clubs building behind them, fighting for space in the night air.

Connie said, "You're going up with me."

"This ain't a set-up, I know better than that."

"You're going."

Twin girls with belly tats came down the steps, said, "Hi, *Khai*!" and were instantly lost in the moving street crowd as Connie and Solo walked up to the first landing.

Solo said, "What I don't get is why here, why you doing this this way?"

Connie looked at his cousin. "Know anything about shame? These little rooms are for hiders, anything can happen. That's what she's counting on."

"You think too much, man."

They reached the door to the last room on the floor. Connie checked his gun. Solo shook his head. "That cannon'll be enough."

"When?"

"Told you, I set it for eight. I don't know if she'll be here or not, so don't come after me if this don't work out."

"Just wanted to see if you kept your story straight," said Connie. "You did your part."

The room was dark when Connie entered, but he could see it all: the small bed, a table with a few magazines, a lamp, an enormous teddy bear resting in the corner. He moved toward the bear.

A blade slashed the back of his neck. Connie whirled, drew his gun and fired.

The flash showed the girl as she slammed backwards against the bathroom door and dropped. Connie took two steps toward her, the pistol steady even as the red spread across the shoulders and back of his jacket.

From the hall, Solo said: "Cousin, you all right?"

Connie closed that door with his foot. "Stay out! I'm fine, but stay out!"

The girl looked up at him, her arms by her side, her legs tucked under her.

She said, "You didn't kill me."

"No."

"But I tried to kill you."

Connie kept the gun steady, sat on the floor opposite her, rested against the edge of the bed. "Was that the plan? To have me kill you?"

"I don't know. Maybe."

"You're not Thai. Cambodia?"

She looked at Connie, the palm of her hand pressing over the bullet hole in her shoulder. "How did you know?"

"I can tell. That's something I can do."

"You got X-Ray vision? Take off your glasses so I can see your eyes."

Connie hooked the shades on his thumb, pulled them off. The girl shook her head as he said: "Never seen anything like me?"

"Those rabbit eyes, what are you?"

"They used to call it 'halfie' for half-breed. My father was in the Merchant Marine, and my mother worked the Cowboy, so I know it. Know everything here, until you. What about the men? All four?"

The girl regarded Connie for a moment, then decided. "All devils, they all deserved to die."

"Because of their jobs?"

"Their lives."

Connie lowered the gun. "I thought you were missing a limb. That's what I asked for."

"No, I'm whole, it's just a trick for the perverts. But my baby sister, her body is just bits and pieces. And my brother, riding his bike? Is it better that he died instead of living without arms and half a leg?"

"The landmines."

"They're supposed to be marked. They're not. They're supposed to be gone. They're not. Cambodia is still a war zone, and what did we do? Forty years later, and it's still not safe to walk to school, or play. What did my brother or sister ever do?"

Connie said, "Those men took a lot from you."

"You think I'm wrong?"

"I want to understand."

"The cop's brain." The girl managed a smile. "And that those men who want to be with a woman who's suffered? What do you think of that?"

Connie said, "Very damn little."

"But you shoot me, not them."

"I think you wanted me to. I think you want to end it this way."

The girl looked at the blood covering her palm, sticky between her fingers. "You know a lot of people who've killed somebody? What are their reasons?"

"Money, sex, accident. Not as good as yours."

"Then do me a favor and shoot again."

"I can't."

"I knew what I was doing, found the bastards online, chatted them up."

"You did better than our own investigators."

"Because they wanted a girl. I went to the cafes for months, then offered myself. I had a gun, but threw it away, because I wanted to use that." She nodded to the serrated combat Bowie knife on the floor beside her. "I'm not crazy, and isn't that worse? To know everything?"

Connie said, "Actually, it is."

He stood up.

"I knew I was walking into something," she said, "and thought you'd end it for me. I did what I wanted to do and you're supposed to be a cop."

Connie put a hand under her arm, lifted her up. "I am, that's why I'm getting you an ambulance."

The mace came out of her pocket, dousing Connie's eyes and twisting him back onto the bed as grabbed her knife and ran for the door. His scream was choked as he stumbled for the bathroom, doused his eyes, stumbled to the hallway.

Solo was on his knees, holding his arm, which had a deep cut. "She's gone."

Connie started down the stairs.

Solo said, "Not the street. Up top."

The door to the roof was a sheet of plywood, nailed in place. It had been kicked down from the inside. Connie stepped around it, gun-ready.

But there was only a light breeze, the sound from the Cowboy, and the wash of neon. He moved to the edge of the roof, looked down at the Soi: people, girls, traffic. No one lying in the street, no one charging through the alley.

Connie wiped his eyes on his sleeve, and knelt down, to find a woman's shoe, spotted with fresh blood. He didn't know if it was his blood, or hers.

He stood and the wave hit him. His legs gave way, and he hit the tarpaper roof, the pistol scuttling away.

***

Tak said, "Let me look."

Connie stayed on the couch, let her crawl around him.

He said, "More than twenty stitches back there, and a pint of blood."

"I can't picture you fainting."

"She cut deep."

Tak said, "Because you let her. That's always your problem, Kai."

Mamasan raised her hand, but Tak let one of the other girls go to the bar.

"You're not working today?"

"No. I thought you might come in and you don't know where I live."

Connie rubbed his rabbit eyes. "No, I don't."

C. Courtney Joyner is an award-winning writer who has scripted movies and television for more than 30 years, including *The Offspring* starring Vincent Price, and *Prison*, starring Viggo Mortensen. As a novelist, he created the western series *Shotgun* for Pinnacle Books, and is currently writing a new adventure series for Tor.

In the Waiting Room,
Trading Death Stories
John Skipp

Okay. Funny story. So I'm walking my dog, Princess Balsac, so named because her face had more wrinkles than my scrotum. I don't know. Some kind of weird mutt mix. Like part boxer, part Shih Tzu, part gorilla? We never quite figured it out.

Anyway, it's our morning constitutional, about 5:40 ayem. My favorite part of the day, just walking and thinking, clearing my head for the chaos to come. Beating the crowd, as the fiery sun rises up over my beloved, embattled Los Angeles.

The Princess is sniffing around like crazy to either side of the road, ardently checking her pee mail. Yeah, exactly. My dad used it to call it "reading the morning paper", back when that was a thing. Lot of dogs in our neighborhood, leaving messages for each other, like graffiti for the underground railroad in the slavery days. This piss spritz means Rosco, or Pistol, or Dexter, or one of the local coyotes was here. And they went thataway.

At a certain point, I have to drag her forward or we'll never get done. If she needs to leave a message, that's one thing—on a practical level, pee and poop is what this journey's all about—but I've got shit to do myself, and you don't get much exercise from standing around.

So we go gallivanting down the street, serving as the neighborhood's snooze alarm, as house after house erupts with barking, groaning, and shouting, "Shut the fuck up, Clancy! JESUS!"

Just another morning in America.

There's a long sharp slope on Cazador, with houses on the left and a sheer drop on the right with a little island of grass and tree. This is one of Miss Balsac's favorite crapping zones, and she strains the leash to get up off the pavement and onto that favored ground. I laugh and run with her, hopping the double curb and trundling downward.

Halfway down the hill, there's a plastic Arrowhead water bottle one-quarter filled with something brown and hideous. Like a trucker bomb loaded down the driver's wrong flume, then carelessly lobbed out the window. It's been there for three months, and *nobody* wants to touch it. Except my Princess, who—like all dogs—is helplessly drawn to all things rancid.

"No, baby!" I say for the ninetieth time, yanking her close and away and just past, where she squats and disgorges. "Good girl!" I say, pulling the plastic bag from my back pocket.

And as I do this, I'm thinking about all the things we don't wanna touch. Are afraid to touch, anymore, since the war came home.

I'm thinking about the Dairy Queen tragedy, just the week before, half a mile down the hill. A girl's softball team, loaded into one of their mom's SUVs, rolling over a paper bag stuffed with C4 and left in a pothole in the parking lot out back. They had come to celebrate their varsity triumph—Yankees vs. Patriots in a squeaker, 4-3—when their tire, then their engine, then their bodies exploded.

All dead. And for what? Some people said it was obviously random and psychotic. Anybody could have parked in that spot. Others thought it was anti-Dairy Queen or something, making a forceful and ugly statement about sugary treats, or the minimum wage. Still others maintained it was specifically targeted at female athletics: the new American version of Muslim extremists burning schools where little girls went to learn.

I'm thinking all this as I lean down to scoop up Princess Balsac's steaming softserve heap, mindfully doing my part to help keep the streets clean. It's like the least I can do.

We round the bend onto Falstaff, continuing down. There's a nice white elderly lady walking a nice white elderly poodle that yaps and strains at its leash, pointlessly wanting a piece of my pooch, even though my girl could snap its neck in a second. We humans steer our dogs to opposite sides of the street, exchange friendly good mornings, keeping pointless conflict at bay like the civilized people we are.

Barky and Jumpy are alerted by our approach, as usual, behind the fence that constrains them from the world: Barky barking by the gate in his coal-black coat, Jumpy running circles and leaping three feet in the air at every turn, like a Little Rascals mascot with a circle around one eye.

Princess Balsac is likewise whipped into a frenzy, and I wonder what they'd do if that fence ever came down. Would they tear each other open and apart, in brute savagery? Would they tussle and sniff each other out, assess some pecking order, show each other what's what? Would they relax, become friends? Odds are good we'll never know.

I yank her back from the fence, as Barky barks and Jumpy jumps. We continue on.

And then I see the envelope.

It's just laying there, in the middle of the street. Padded. Gray. Its backside up. Whatever address it's aimed at is flush against the pavement, unreadable.

Princess Balsac and I approach, one step at a time. And with every step, I wonder more. It's way too early for UPS or FedEx, not to mention US mail. Best I can figure is that it got accidentally dropped, or maybe fell off the roof of a car driven by someone who forgot they put it there, got distracted, then got in and motored. Something I've done more than once.

There's a squirrel in a tree, and Princess charges toward it, off to the left. I'm pulled forward, forcibly yanking her back. We're less than three feet from the envelope, but she couldn't care less. "Fucking SQUIRREL!" is the whole of her universe.

I look at the envelope, now directly before me. Someone's message to someone. Thwarted pee mail. And I could help. Pick it up. Put it in the right person's mailbox.

I crouch, reaching down.

And suddenly, a terrible fear grips me: so hard, so strong, that I freeze in my tracks. Fingers inches away. It's so stupid, yet so clear. An instinctual feeling. Saying *no no no*.

A car is coming up the road. Princess Scrotum and I are in the way. Odds are good that this envelope will be run over. Probably something someone wanted.

I pick it up.

My arm explodes.

In the second that my hand vaporizes, my face catches fire and implodes, pushing my brain out the back of my head in a flaming spray: red, then black, then gone.

And here I am, with you.

So how is this a funny story? Well, it's fucking pointless, just for starters! I'll never even know whose side I died for. Could have been your side. Could have been mine.

So tell me: how and why did *you* die?

John Skipp is the only *New York Times* bestselling novelist to win a pornographic Oscar for a scene with a singing penis. His splatterpunk novel *The Light at the End* inspired the character of Spike from *Buffy the Vampire Slayer*. His 1989 anthology *Book of the Dead* was the beginning of modern post-Romero zombie fiction. His short fiction with Cody Goodfellow has graced *Hellboy: Oddest Jobs* and the latest *Zombies vs. Robots* collection. Their latest book is *The Last Goddam Hollywood Movie*. He is also the editor of four massive, encyclopedic anthologies (*Zombies, Demons, Psychos, Werewolves & Shapeshifters*), and editor-in-chief of mainstream-meets-Bizarro publishing imprint Fungasm Press. And as filmmaker, he and Andrew Kasch have co-directed the award-winning lactating manboob horror comedy *Stay at Home Dad* and the Slow Poisoner music video "Hot Rod Worm", with *Robot Chicken* stop motion animator Michael Granberry, in which Skipp also plays the bongos. He lives in L.A.

www.ingramcontent.com/pod-product-compliance
Lightning Source LLC
Chambersburg PA
CBHW020049180626
46812CB00006B/2245